HESTIA STRIKES A MATCH

HESTIA
STRIKES
A
MATCH

CHRISTINE GRILLO

 FARRAR, STRAUS AND GIROUX   NEW YORK

Farrar, Straus and Giroux
120 Broadway, New York 10271

Copyright © 2023 by Christine Grillo
All rights reserved
Printed in the United States of America
First edition, 2023

Title-page hand-lettering and illustrations by Na Kim.

Library of Congress Cataloging-in-Publication Data
Names: Grillo, Christine, 1969– author.
Title: Hestia strikes a match / Christine Grillo.
Description: First edition. | New York : Farrar, Straus and Giroux, 2023. |
Identifiers: LCCN 2022055061 | ISBN 9780374609979 (hardcover)
Subjects: LCGFT: Novels.
Classification: LCC PS3607.R5544 H45 2023 | DDC 813/.6—
dc23/eng/20221130
LC record available at https://lccn.loc.gov/2022055061

Designed by Abby Kagan

Our books may be purchased in bulk for promotional, educational, or business
use. Please contact your local bookseller or the Macmillan Corporate and
Premium Sales Department at 1-800-221-7945, extension 5442, or by email at
MacmillanSpecialMarkets@macmillan.com.

www.fsgbooks.com
www.twitter.com/fsgbooks • www.facebook.com/fsgbooks

1   3   5   7   9   10   8   6   4   2

HESTIA STRIKES A MATCH

1

IT'S ALL GOOD

Two months after the war began, I found myself single—abandoned. I was shaken, a little manic, already lonely. I dipped into the new-to-me online dating world, and before I could really figure out how the apps worked, I unwittingly flirted with guys from the other side. I even went on a date with one. The fact that his profile mentioned the word "freedom" so many times should have tipped me off, but he was nice-looking, and let's be honest, loneliness is its own form of brain damage.

Some apps screened out the confederates, so I started to use those exclusively. Within a few months, I had a short list of men who'd hearted me back, whose grammar was good enough, and who seemed like solid unionists—but not too fanatical.

I wasn't exactly looking for the love of my life. Or maybe I was. Per usual, I didn't really know what I wanted.

I knew that I didn't want to fall hard for anyone, because I could still remember that when you fall hard for someone, everything is awful. You don't sleep. You ask yourself too often, Does he love me as much as I love him? Am I sexy? Am I interesting? It's nice to have new-relationship energy, but it's a lot to manage. I was neither sick enough nor well enough for that kind of nonsense.

✳

Then I saw Ethan's profile, and I thought, This could work.

In his pictures, he looked fit and handsome, with wavy hair, but I knew I wouldn't be in danger of falling too hard, because he'd written, "I'm doing my up-most to live life to the fullest."

"Live life to the fullest" isn't the *worst* thing a person could write, and it's less grating than, say, "Work hard, play hard," which, for some reason, is something men brag about. It was "up-most" that reassured me. In my thirties, "up-most" would have been a hard pass, but at forty-two, it was a point in his favor. "Up-most" nearly guaranteed that I wouldn't do myself the disservice of falling head over heels, as they say, which might be fine for people who are less clumsy than I am.

✳

The war had begun in earnest in February. Or rather, that's when it began *officially*. The warfare had been quite earnest for years, but we were in the habit of giving it names like "arson," or "shootings."

This wasn't like the first civil war: there was no epic warfare, no impassioned "My very dear wife" letters home from the front, no battlefields soaked in sorrow. A dozen states had seceded, but there weren't official battles, army against army. When there *was* fighting, it was usually over resources, like oil or natural gas, inconveniently located in Louisiana or Arkansas. The confederate army was armed to the teeth, composed of local police forces, ICE agents, Border Patrol, and private militia volunteers who were itching to use their guns. Day to day, though, the war felt less like an organized conflict and more like a free-for-all, with random confederate desperadoes using guns and pipe bombs to terrorize ordinary Americans. To create chaos, to make us afraid, they went after us in movie theaters and grocery stores, and our military approached them as foreign terrorists, trying to root them out in their militia dens. It was particularly bad in the border states, like here in Maryland.

We called ourselves Americans, unionists, and patriots, and we called our country the United States of America. Annoyingly, supporters of the New Confederated States of America thought of themselves as patriots, too, and they painted themselves as romantic rebels trying to save what was still worth saving of the "real" America they loved. "Spare me," my husband would say whenever he heard their speeches.

He was among the traumatized idealists who felt America wasn't retaliating hard enough. He wanted us to crush the traitors. In February, he took a course on hand-to-hand combat. March, he learned how to use a dazzling array of weapons. Come April, he left me to join a pro-Union paramilitary group that wanted to take back, by any means necessary, the states that had seceded. "There are good people trapped in those states," he said, "and they're not able to leave." Our marriage had been troubled for some time—the war gave him an out.

*

By summer I realized that my assorted freelance assignments weren't paying the bills. I'd carved out a beat for myself with articles that showed Baltimore as urban and urbane. My editors had wanted stories that made us look well-gardened and vibrant, with lush parks, quirky people, artisanal shops, quaint architecture, and socially responsible businesses—and I obliged. But the civil war required everyone to take a new tack. I didn't have the skills or the stomach to pivot toward war stories, so I looked for another line of work.

In June, I took a job at a retirement village near the Inner Harbor. I told myself it would be a safe workplace, because not even a confederate would bomb a facility full of the elderly, right? And I liked the tagline: "We're on the left side of history."

I was hired by Ed, a former journalist himself, who had gone the "straight job" route and become a director of communications. Three times in that interview he mentioned that he'd been intending to retire, but then the war came along and muffed everything. He and his wife had been planning a move to their place in Boynton Beach.

"But who the hell wants to move to Florida now?" he asked.

As far as the job was concerned, he wanted me to help him build a more close-knit community of residents at Harbour Pointe, and their extended families. I was going to grow and amplify their online presence. Every time he said the words "grow" or "amplify," he scowled.

"You're not a dinosaur like me," he said. "I'm sure you know how to grow and amplify."

I told him I had ideas about both.

In one of our early team meetings we were starbursting, or maybe that day it was mind mapping, and I said the words "oral history project." Ed wrote it on the whiteboard, and I immediately regretted what I'd said.

"Erase it," I said. "Bad idea."

"No take-backs," said Ed.

Once it's written on the whiteboard, it's too late.

"We can give it the Tuesday- and Thursday-morning time slots in the Treehouse Studio," he said.

Then he wrote "Scribbles," in quotation marks.

"Can we make it more of a *'written* history' class?" he asked.

Sarah, the direct-report who predated my arrival, grimaced. She was young and poised, a genuine professional, but occasionally she made faces.

"Oral histories are oral for a reason. People like to talk, and they don't like to write," she said. "Why can't we keep them oral?"

"I'm thinking about the results, the 'product,' as they say," said Ed. "The families will like a beautiful, printed, bound book more than they'd like, what—A *sound file*? An *MP3*? We can't give these families a *WAV* file."

"We could get them transcribed," she said.

"If I had a budget for that . . ." he said, trailing off.

Sarah relented, then told me, because I was new, that very few of the villagers would have much of an estate to pass down. "At least this way they'll leave a book."

"I'm not qualified to teach an oral history class," I said. "Or a written history class. Or any class."

"You're a fantastic writer," said Ed. "I read your clips."

During several months of working at the village, I'd learned that Ed had a bad habit of overstating everything. He had kids—"grown-up rug rats," he called them—and I wondered if maybe this kind of cheerleading was what some fathers did.

"It'll be a great use of your talents," he said.

Sarah rolled her eyes so hard it was almost audible, but she said no more.

And just like that, against my better judgment, I was leading Scribbles, a writing class focusing on lived history. But it got me out of the office section and into the residential wing. It took me away from marketing platforms, mailing lists, and content management systems. It forced me to interact with people.

And Scribbles is how I met Mildred, for which I'm so, so grateful.

$$*$$

Every day I woke up and steeled myself to look at my phone, which almost always had bad news. The Conflicted app that everybody used curated all the terrible updates of the civil war and delivered it via a flashing red rhombus alert. Was the rhombus supposed to evoke an emergency vehicle? That was one theory.

You could set up your preferences, of course. In the beginning, I had all the news, local and national, delivered to me in real time like a nonstop fire hose. Over time, I refined my settings and opted for a curated daily digest of top national stories, with local events delivered more immediately. When the twelve states drafted their "Declaration of Immediate Causes that Impel Secession," I saw it in the next morning's digest. Ditto when the governor of Florida was appointed the provisional president of the New Confederated States of America.

In September, when the confederates poisoned Baltimore's reservoirs, I received that alert right away. I hated spending money on bottled water, hated even more to put so much plastic waste into a bogus recycling stream, but drinking from the tap wasn't an option.

The alerts came quickly in October, too, when the confederates bombed the grids running the sewage-processing plants. "Day three of Baltimore smelling like sewage—city asks residents not to flush" the headlines ran. I'll give the confederates this: they knew how to chip away at an already fragile infrastructure. It didn't take much. Blow up a server farm or bomb a cell tower, and we were hobbled. Also, they had us on tobacco, and I was surprised to see how demoralizing it was for smokers, who were getting screwed by ever-rising cigarette prices. For years, Baltimore promoted itself as the city that reads, but apparently, we were also the city that smokes.

＊

Online dating turned out to be a great distraction from all of it. Consulting with Mildred about dating was another. In November, Ethan and I volleyed a few messages to each other, and I asked Mildred for her hot take on Ethan's profile. As usual, she was at the front desk, watching over the lobby, leaning on her fancy cane with the silver owl's head, a gift from her stepsons. She liked to flirt with the young French peacekeeper who patrolled our corner. (She thought he might be Belgian, not French, but we didn't want to ask and risk insulting him.) He was in the habit of coming into the retirement village to use the bathroom, and since you can't have too many peacekeepers keeping an eye out for you during a civil war, we staff members and residents alike fawned over him. But when

Mildred saw me coming, she blew him a kiss and turned her attention to me.

"Did you remember my ashtray?" she asked.

"Mildred," I said, "do I ever forget your ashtray?"

She leaned on the silver owl's head, watching the peace-keeper walk out of the lobby, her eyes on his ass, his hand on the weapon clipped to his hip.

"He's keeping it tight, wouldn't you say, Hestia?" she asked.

Because one of Mildred's stepsons was a major general in the U.S. Marine Corps, the retirement village made an exception for her: she was the only resident allowed to smoke in shared spaces, but she had to do it discreetly, in the therapy garden. In exchange for this favor, the major general reassigned a platoon of Marines that had been scheduled to quarter in the poolside independent living units. Their new home was a community college a few blocks away. We saw them all the time, jogging along the harbor in the workout clothes that Mildred complained were too modest.

We walked to the therapy garden and seated ourselves on two chairs with dry cushions. It wasn't too cold for November, just cold enough for Mildred to wear her smokers' gloves with the fingertips cut off, of which she was inordinately proud. I handed her the ashtray and her menthol 100s (imported, of course, no traitor tobacco for Mildred), and lit her cigarette. Then I showed her Ethan's pictures. She swiped gleefully and repeated her favorite phrase, "Keeping it tight."

At eighty-four, she'd buried three husbands, and she liked to say, "I was very lucky in my life, I married two wonderful men."

I've only buried the one husband, and that was only in my mind, so she's the authority.

"Handsome boy," she said. "His hair looks real."

She lingered over the one where he was rigged up in a tall, piebald tree, and reminisced about a similar tree from her childhood. In the photo, he was tied to the tree with ropes attached to belts, one around his waist, and two around his thighs, snug against his ass.

"I'd tap that like Morse code," she said.

"Mildred," I said. "The mouth on you."

"I'm eighty-four, I can say whatever I want," she said.

"Your brain is a marvel," I said.

"'My brain? It's my second favorite organ,'" she said.

She was forever quoting Woody Allen, whose films were a secret pleasure for her. When she was younger, her friends disapproved because he was Jewish, and now her friends disapproved for other reasons, but she refused to give up the movies. I'd been icked out by him decades earlier, when I watched *Manhattan*, but I didn't judge Mildred.

Her first husband, a man she called Yitzy, although I don't think that was his real name, had introduced her to Allen's films. She was a Maryland High WASP, one of those girls who grew up riding horses and drinking iced tea. As an adult she transitioned from riding breeches to tennis whites. She had pearls, several sets. She spent most of her life after age ten starving herself "just a little bit," to avoid becoming stout, as "stout" was the worst adjective that anyone could use to describe a woman. She told me she faked orgasms, even after she learned how to have real ones, because sometimes she was just too undernourished to go for the brass ring. She married rich men, and she always had a housekeeper, and some days—and this she kept a secret from most people—she sent the nanny home and sat on the floor with her daughters, finger-painting or doing Play-Doh. Those were some of her favorite days, she said, the Play-Doh days.

She paused on a particularly handsome photo of Ethan.

"I'm not saying you should love him and leave him," she said, "but you should definitely love him."

Her smoky exhale scooted past my cheek.

"And then you should leave him," she said.

I knew she had a good reason. "Why?" I asked.

"He's too handsome. No one wants to be married to a man that handsome. You'll always worry about him being lured away."

She suggested that for our first date we meet somewhere public, so I could see if a lot of women flirted with him and how he handled it. It would be good for me to have that kind of information, she said.

I was still uncomfortable meeting people in public, because you never knew if your restaurant, or your bar, would be the one where the next pipe bomb would explode in a parked van. Every date, every drink with a friend—it was a risk. But what else could you do? Civil war or no, you still need to meet friends, and you still want the thrill of a first kiss. Pipe bombs can kill you quickly, but loneliness will kill you slowly. Life is a near-constant calculation of risks.

✳

As for Scribbles, five people signed up, and their attendance was spotty. The Treehouse Studio was a room with a skylight and a few potted lemon and kumquat trees. There were cozy chairs and small tables. In those first sessions, I offered a combination of in-class writing exercises and at-home assignments, but I learned quickly that my students were not willing to do homework. Mildred reminded me, "Life is short, my dear."

I completed every assignment along with my students, which seemed only fair. At the end of each class, I invited them to share some of what they'd written, if they wanted to, but I never took up precious time sharing my own. Mildred rarely shared, but that was fine. I probably enjoyed the class more than any of the villagers: I had no children, no husband, no siblings, and the rift between me and my parents was becoming a chasm. I figured that someday my Scribbles might be all that was left of me.

What fascinating lives the villagers had led, what history they'd seen. I was hoping they'd write about their experiences with pogroms and famines, wars and revolutions. But instead of writing about crossroads in modern history, they wrote about the best friends who had betrayed them, the fathers and mothers who drank too much, the abandonments. And always, love. The love that got away. The love they didn't get. The love that changed their lives.

I learned that Mildred's second wedding took place in Memphis at the very hour when Martin Luther King Jr. was shot on his hotel room balcony.

But she didn't write about Dr. King. Instead, she wrote about her daughters, Ruth and Annie, how she loved them both so much, and how, inexplicably, they couldn't stand each other. Their rift had been expanding for decades, a little wider each time Ruth posted on social media in support of women, people of color, trans people, and the environment, or Annie posted about how her country was just fine the way it was, love it or leave it. Mildred begged them to stop, but neither could refrain, and neither would unfollow the other. The fact that her daughters hated each other was the Great Heartache of Mildred's life.

I researched oral history projects and pulled together a

collection of prompts and best practices. Good prompts, I gathered, were the heart of oral history. You can't do questions with yes or no answers. Ask a question that allows the mind to wander. Encourage your respondents to share their opinions.

"Make sure you write your own responses to the questions, Hestia," Ed reminded me. "You'll want them someday."

I doubted that very much, but I did what Ed asked, in part because he'd become a sort of father figure, and in part because I was so grateful that he had hired me. Every day I went to work and felt thankful for a job where there were guards, and metal detectors, and a state-of-the-art surveillance system minded by someone in a small room.

∗

Question 1: In your own words, what is this war about?

DOROTHY: *People say this is America's second civil war, but come on. It's the same civil war from more than one hundred fifty years ago. We're in season 2, episode 1. For chrissake, in February, when they named themselves the New Confederated States of America, that's when they showed us who they are. It's so simple that it's boring. It's always racism. And misogyny—of course. The perfect cocktail. A Black Madame President was a bridge too far. People are as common as pig tracks.*

CHARLES: *The confederates think of themselves as freedom fighters. Some of my nieces and nephews are Black, and some are white, but all of them call confederates "zombies," because zombies are beyond reason. You can't save zombies. My niece told me you have to shoot zombies in the head.*

JEFFREY: *I knew for years before it was official that we were in a civil war. Years! Everyone else had their heads up their asses. The warning signs were right in front of us. Mass shootings. Wing nuts all over the country shouting, "What about my rights?" For crying out loud, there were nooses on tree limbs. It's the Cracker Rebellion.*

CLARA: *It's a war of goddamned grievances. They want states to make their own laws. We want the federal government to make the laws. They think it's the War of Northern Aggression, and we think it's the War of Southern Aggression. We're operating on two entirely different vibrations in this country. We union- ists want to make things better for everyone. But only half of America is on that frequency. The other half? I don't like to use the word "hate," but that half of America hates us.*

✳

The first Wednesday of every month, the retirement village hosted an ice cream social for the villagers, and in December, Mildred invited me. When I was shy about the toppings, she badgered me to heap more chocolate jimmies onto my scoop.

"The toppings are the best part, dear," said Mildred.

She put several spoonfuls of crushed cookies onto her ice cream and grilled me.

"What are you waiting for? Get off the dime," she said. "Tell Ethan you want to meet."

"He's too handsome," I said. "I'm not as good-looking as he is."

"Men only care about looks in the abstract," she said. "If you're willing, he'll have you."

"That's gross," I said.

"I know, dear," she said.

Jeffrey, one of the villagers in Scribbles, bustled his way next to us at the toppings table. He was old and stooped, but spry. Mildred had once called him a "pip." Apparently, his hearing was still good.

"What *she* forgot to say," he said, pointing to Mildred, "is that you're good-looking *enough*. And she's right: men aren't picky. Not like women, anyway."

This was a topic I would have loved to explore with Jeffrey, thinking that a bent-over old man might tell me the truth about what really matters to men. But he moved on. He searched the toppings table and found a jar of walnuts in syrup. He held it up and turned around to show the villagers in line behind us.

"Wet nuts," he said, ecstatic. "I have wet nuts!"

"That man is eighty-seven years old," said Mildred.

✳

Ten months into the official start of the shit show, we were all getting used to life in the new, smaller United States. The war was tragic, but when those twelve states seceded, they took their Congress members with them, and it was as if America unloaded a ton of dead weight. It reminded me of that joke: What's the best way to lose 150 pounds fast? Break up with your bad boyfriend. Of course, the Union still had states that sent right-wing nutjobs to Congress, but we lost most of them, enough to make some changes.

Ethan and I had our first date at a restaurant that I chose. For outings, I relied on the Safe Zones app, which was different from the Conflicted app. Safe Zones tracked disruptions and violence, like traffic light outages and skirmishes, and suggested the locations most likely to be secure. It was like Waze, but for civil unrest.

I chose a low-key burger place with a bar. The bar was set up in such a way that from any barstool, you could see the front entrance *and* the back entrance, which was important. I arrived early.

He'd arrived even earlier than I did, because when I walked in, I found him deep in conversation with an older, beautiful woman at the bar. She was holding one of her hands over her heart while she listened to him. I couldn't make out what he was saying, or why she was so rapt. I sucked in my stomach and approached them as any confident, self-assured woman would.

"Are you Ethan?" I blurted.

The woman at the bar took her hand off her heart and resigned herself to her drink.

"Are you Hestia?" he asked.

"It is I."

"Is that your real name?"

It was, yes, my real name.

"I thought it was a dating site name," he said.

I gave him the micro-story about how my parents had been professors of ancient Greek and Roman history, back when there were departments of Classics.

"So, Hestia's a Latin thing?"

"Greek," I said. "She's a goddess."

"Cool," he said.

"Oh yeah, very cool," I said. "My flame is never allowed to burn out."

He was almost as handsome as his profile pictures. His hair was that nice in-between, on its way to silver but not there yet, and had an exciting life of its own. He had the right amount of beard and mustache, more than "I'm giving this a try," but less than "The civil war has messed up the trade routes so bad I can't get a razor." Someday he'd be a silver fox, but not today. He wore his tallness well, no slouching, and his shoulders were broad but not so broad that I felt bad for his mother giving birth to him. His stomach was concave, which had become more and more of a turn-on as the years passed and convex became the norm.

Of course, I'd *always* had a convex stomach. I wasn't trying to starve myself.

He turned in the opposite direction of the woman he'd been talking to and offered me the empty stool next to him.

"I saved you a seat," he said.

In my mind, I ran through the pictures of him on his dating profile. In at least two of them, maybe more, he was holding or playing a guitar. (About 70 percent of straight men's profiles had a photo with a guitar. Men and their guitars—they love each other very much.)

"I almost didn't recognize you without the guitar!" I said.

"Really?" he asked.

"No, it was a joke," I said. "I recognized you."

He said, "You look just like yourself in that picture with the white oak, where you're hiking."

"Is that a white oak?" I asked.

"Yeppers," he said.

"So, you're one of those people who knows about trees," I said.

He told me that he was a certified arborist, which, he made clear, is way more than just a guy who does tree service.

"I have training in tree health and tree biology," he said.

"That's lovely," I said. "I like trees."

"Me too," he said.

At the very least, we had that in common! I was embarrassed about how little I knew about trees.

Despite being a certified arborist, his day-to-day work life was more tree service than tree biology. Apparently, people will pay to have trees pruned and removed, but they're not as keen to pay someone to nurse a tree to health. Blights, for example, will be ignored for years.

This had been a bad year for Japanese maples, he told me.

"The bark's just falling right off 'em," he said.

He then showed me a picture of his truck, which had the words ROPE 'EM AND RIG 'EM in large letters across the side.

"It's a gas guzzler," he said, "but it's what I've got."

Baltimore did pretty well on gasoline, most days. Almost all of the oil refineries were in confederate states, which was a problem, but California had a couple, and when it came to the war, they did not play. They stationed soldiers along the pipelines that carried oil to the East Coast. Also, there were a few refineries outside of New Orleans, which we controlled most of the time. Poor New Orleans, stranded in Louisiana, like West Berlin in East Germany.

He had a copy of Conflicted on his phone, too, and I could see that he had unread alerts. What kind of person can resist reading the alerts? He saw me looking at the phone and picked it up and read one of the headlines out loud.

"'Florida and Texas printing their own currencies—other ten states want united currency,'" he said. "What a bunch of bozos."

I didn't want to talk about the war. I asked him to tell me about his job.

"I just did my first solo crane removal," he said.

"What does that mean?" I asked.

"It means I get to keep my man card," he said.

"Thank goddess," I said.

"I do a lot of storm cleanup, too," he said. "Hurricanes are good for business."

"Hurray, climate change," I said, and he smiled, as if he got the irony.

He told me funny stories about getting stranded in the treetops, about limbs clumsily felled, and about public urination.

"When I'm a hundred feet aloft in a tulip poplar, I will most certainly pee on its trunk," he said. "I won't pee off the side, though. That's rude."

There was a lull in conversation, and I took a moment to look out the window and scan the street, checking all four street corners. It was about five in the evening and getting dark. We were an hour from curfew.

Ethan tapped his fingertips on the wood.

"They probably used a water-based poly to finish this," he said.

Then he added, "Poly is polyurethane."

Did I look like the kind of woman who didn't know what "poly" is?

"Oh," I joked, "so you weren't talking about polyamory?"

"I don't know what that is," he said.

That earned points in his favor, because while I know that polyamory is pragmatic and favored by the levelheaded people of the world, I also know that I'm not nearly evolved enough to practice it. There's just some programming that some of us can never rescue ourselves from.

I decided to be interested in the bar's varnish.

"Water-based?" I asked in a possibly sexy voice.

"I'd say so," he said. "It isn't as durable as oil-based, but it doesn't yellow the way the oil-based does, if you know what I mean."

"I do know what you mean," I said.

"I'm going to say semigloss, too," he said. "It's shiny, but not, like, supershiny, if you know what I mean."

"I do know what 'supershiny' means," I said, again trying the sexy voice.

He didn't seem to think I was funny, but he didn't get offended, either, so it was a wash. Of course, it's better when they think you're hilarious, but that doesn't happen often. That's girlfriend territory; Mildred gets me. It's fine.

After more pleasantries about varnish, I steered the conversation back to the woman he'd been talking to when I walked in.

"What were you and that lady talking about?" I asked.

"She was telling me about her brother," he said. "He was one of the unionists who got killed in the February Third Sedition, when Madame President was sworn in."

"That's awful," I said, feeling like I'd been punched. "But why was she looking at you like she wanted to give you a hug?"

"Well," he said, "I was telling her about the shooting in my hometown."

"Oh, your hometown," I said. "That's terrible. That's sad."

I didn't ask any more about the shooting in his hometown.

"It wasn't a big thing," he said. "We were just chatting."

"She put her hand on her heart," I said.

"She probably always does that," he said.

That statement endeared him to me.

He seemed like one of those people who gets a charge out of being around other humans, the more the merrier. Life must be so much easier for extroverts. Sometimes I envy them. What would evolutionary biologists say is the advantage of being an introvert, anyway? Maybe the civil war will show us. If I ever have to sequester myself away for years, or hide under floorboards, being an introvert may be helpful.

"Tell me what it's like to be such an extrovert," I said. "Regale me with your tales."

He laughed and smiled and told me I was cute.

He ordered a cheeseburger with bacon, and I ordered the same thing.

"That's not weird, is it?" I asked.

"Is *what* weird?" he asked.

"Me ordering the same thing," I said.

"Did you order the same thing?" he asked.

I once dated a man who, after a year, was surprised to notice a pretty big scar on my stomach. It had been right there the whole time. About half of the men I'd dated were like that, and I would have given just about *anything* to spend a day in that kind of brain, finally able to understand what life feels like when you don't notice every single thing that happens around you. Do they just think about stuff they *care about* all the time? Is it wonderful to spend your time only thinking about the stuff you *want* to think about? Or, maybe they just turn off their thinking. Is that possible?

We ate our burgers and talked—about nothing, really, but in a nice way—and I even ordered one of those cocktail-milkshakes with a silly name.

He drank peppermint schnapps on ice, which I could have been embarrassed for him about, but peppermint schnapps is its own punishment. Live and let live. Actually, we laughed a lot, which was partly because of my milkshake and partly because he was just easy that way. I told him about my job as a communications associate in the retirement village, which was, essentially, to market upscale dorm rooms to the elderly.

"What was your college degree in?" he asked.

"You mean my ivory-tower brainwashing?"

He looked confused.

"Sorry," I said. "That was bitter of me. I'm working on being less bitter."

"That's all right," he said. "I mean, we're in a civil war."

"My major was comparative literature," I said.

"I don't know anything about it," he said, "but it doesn't sound like brainwashing."

"My parents think it's funny to say that I majored in sheeple."

"That doesn't sound very nice," he said.

"They're not always nice," I said.

We talked for a few minutes about my parents, and how they seemed to be flirting with embracing the New Confederacy. Their latest outrage had been about compulsory anti-racism training at the college where they worked; they were deeply offended. "We're *not* white supremacists, Hestia, and neither are you!" they'd told me recently. "We raised you better than that," they'd said.

"Sounds like they're looking out for you," Ethan said.

"They look out for me, but they really want to yell at someone about their hurt feelings," I said.

I changed the subject back to work. As I ran out of questions to ask about arborist things, the bartender was giving the ten-minute warning.

"You *do* have to go home, and you *cannot* stay here," she said.

The UN peacekeeper on the sidewalk rapped on our windows with his club and gave the curfew signal. It wasn't official, but a lot of the keepers did it: they motioned "bottoms up" and then made the "kill it" gesture, cutting their throats with their hands.

You can always hear the whole restaurant sigh when that happens.

It was the make-or-break moment for the date, and I could tell by the way Ethan looked at me that he would like to try a second date.

"I hope we can do this again," he said.

✳

Question 2: Do you remember where you were on February 3, when you found out President 46 had died?

CLARA: *It was so cold that day, the day after Imbolc, which is halfway between the winter solstice and the spring equinox. The sap in the trees is supposed to start flowing and the ewes start lactating. I still had my prayer candles out, and when I heard the president had left the planet, I released healing energy into the world.*

CHARLES: *I was in Tai Chi class, and the director rushed in and canceled class. We watched the news in the Café des Artistes. The right-wing TV news anchors didn't even stop for a second to acknowledge that a decent man had died. They were furious about Madame President getting sworn in so quickly. But what did they want us to do? Hit pause?*

JEFFREY: *I was visiting my daughter at her house, and her kids came running downstairs with the news. My granddaughter said the right-wingers were having "mantrums" about the new Madame President. "Mantrums." You gotta love that.*

DOROTHY: *My friend was making me take a walk along the Inner Harbor, and it was frigid. She has that awful news alert thing on her phone, and tears rolled out of her eyes and actually froze on her cheeks. They were so beautiful, her frozen tears, but I knew that the poet was right: the world is ugly, and the people are sad.*

✳

For our second date, Ethan and I drove out to the county in ROPE 'EM AND RIG 'EM, and we took a long walk through a nature reserve known as Soldiers Delight. A designated wildland, it was a barren, serpentine grassland, and Ethan said it was a unique ecosystem with endangered plants. Before the war, the state of Maryland had done controlled burns of the invasive Virginia pines, but the state's money for parks had been diverted.

Once we picked a trail, it was obvious that Ethan knew his way around. As we walked, he pointed out abandoned burn sites and the occasional gnarled oak. It was mostly grass, with only a few stunted trees, and he commented on each tree, greeting some of them as if they were old friends.

He had a way of standing in front of a tree and assessing its happiness. "This pine is not happy," he said several times—he explained that there was a blight on it. He ran his fingers along the limbs and said, "This fella's nearing the end of his life.

"But this oak is very happy!" he said.

One of the trails led to a tiny stream, and we took one of them down to the water. There was a downed tree limb that had fallen from an earlier storm, and Ethan held my hand to help me balance up and over. That happened again, and he put his hand on my waist to hold me steady. Once, we encountered a puddle, and he put his hands on my waist and lifted me over it. It seemed so old-fashioned, presumptuous even, but I liked it. I loved it, actually.

While we walked, I noticed that he was often humming tunes from old rock-and-roll songs. He'd turn to me and ask if I knew the song. I'd shake my head, and he'd sing a few lines, and ask if I knew it yet. I could guess the song about 50 percent of the time, and it made him happy when I did.

"I could probably learn that on the guitar," he'd say, an offering.

Sometimes on a date with a new guy, I'll invite him to tell me about his last weird dream, because you can tell a lot about a person that way. It's not so much the dream itself that's revealing, but more how they tell you about it. It's also a good opportunity to listen to how their voice sounds, see how they move their hands when they talk.

Ethan's voice was authentically masculine.

"So, I was just floating above the city," he said. "I flew over my parents' house and my apartment building, and the playground where there was that massacre, but this was before the massacre, and all the kids were alive and playing," he said.

He didn't move his hands much when he talked.

"It was great to fly like that, you know?" he asked.

"I never have flying dreams," I said.

"That's sad," he said.

I agreed.

I wanted to ask him more about the massacre he'd mentioned, but I also didn't want to ruin the date. I thought it might be too soon to share our battle stories, and I had a feeling he'd lost someone important, but it's so hard to know what is the right time to talk about these things.

My dreams are almost always about being late, or lost, but I told Ethan about my best dream, where my house was burning down (I've never owned a house) and I stood outside and watched it. In the dream, I had my phone and my passport, and was surrounded by animals who'd come to watch it burn, too. I watched the licking flames in the company of opossums, crows, and a fox.

"It was the most peaceful dream I've ever had," I said.

He took my hand to lead me across a mucky patch by the stream.

"Have you ever had the dream where you're naked in front of people?" he asked.

"No," I said, "sorry."

"I've had that dream," he said. "A lot, actually."

"That seems like a pretty normal dream to have," I said.

"I guess lots of people are afraid of being naked in front of other people."

"I guess so," I said.

We kissed on that date, under what he said was a black-jack oak, my feet sinking a little into the mud by the stream. I wasn't sure he was going to do it at all. I hadn't been able to figure out whether he liked me or not. But he kissed me, so it seemed like he must have had some feelings for me. He didn't ask, he just did it, just put his hand on my face and gently pulled me to him, which I appreciated, because sometimes it's nice to feel swept up a little. It was December, so I'd been chilly the whole time, but this made me warm. We kissed for quite a while, and then he suggested we head back to the truck to warm up.

When he dropped me off at my apartment, I was trying to figure out how to invite him in, and how much we should do when we were inside. Forty-two years old, and I still hadn't figured out how to do this right. Do you sleep together early so as to answer the critical question about chemistry and not waste time, or do you wait for a while, for all the reasons that people wait? But he relieved me of my calculations. "I'm going to walk you to the door and say goodbye," he said.

"You are?" I asked.

"I am," he said. "But I'll kiss you again for a good long time."

✳

Question 3: What do you remember of the February 3rd Sedition, when Madame President was sworn in?

CLARA: *Mars and Jupiter were squared that day, which made it a bad day for energy and violence. But Mars was also conjunct with Venus, which should have meant good things for love. I didn't see the love.*

CHARLES: *I was doing my afternoon stretches, watching on TV, and I could see the grief written on Madame President's face. She was in mourning, after all, her friend had died. She was dressed all in black. The confederate militias had converged on the Capitol and looked ridiculous in their little camo outfits. Washington was lousy with them, and they were looking for a fight. But Madame President made sure the military was there, and the Guard, also. I think she knew a lot of guys were going to have a conniption when she was sworn in.*

JEFFREY: *My grandson was driving me back to the village, and we were listening on the radio when the confederate militias fired the first shot. Who or what were they trying to hit? I haven't the foggiest idea. But they killed someone, maybe it* *was an accident, who knows, and that's when all hell broke loose. The military does not like being fired on, by their own countrymen, no less. There were anti-fascist militias there, too, and they jumped into the action. My grandson said, "Holy shit, melee fighting," which is what they call it in all those wargaming programs.*

DOROTHY: *It was pure chaos. So gross. That was the day the confederates showed us that they were capable of much worse than we'd thought. We realized that garbage-people do exist. Suddenly, all of us lefties and liberals* loved *the military, prayed for the military. Life is such satire. Love the one you're with, that's how it works.*

✳

After my walk in the woods with Ethan, my brother-in-law Jamie called and asked if I'd come over for dinner. He was my husband's sister's husband, which made me Aunt Hestia (by marriage), and it had been ten months since his wife had died. She'd been killed right after the February 3rd Sedition, in a ShopRite, by confederates gone wild.

I'd done only a mediocre job of being there for them as they mourned, but in my defense, it was awkward with my husband gone. I sent cards or little packages every few months, nothing big. Over the summer, I went to the twins' graduation from fifth grade, and I went to one of the little boy's soccer games.

But Jamie wanted to know if I'd come over for dinner. It would be nice, he said, for all of us who were "still around," his words, to stay connected, even if we weren't related by blood.

"The kids are crazy about you," he said on the phone, which was news to me.

The girls were almost eleven, and the boy was eight, and as an only child I found myself overstimulated by the whole thing, the rapid-fire shifts in conversation, the way everyone talked over each other, and teased each other, and the way Jamie did backflips to keep everything moving along. He supported and encouraged them endlessly. Struggling with math? You're so smart, I know you'll figure it out, and let's get you a tutor. Trouble with friends? You're such a great kid, this is just a blip, you're going to have so many friends in your life. And running through all of his enthusiasm, just below this frenetic energy, was a river of grief. No one said it, but I felt like it was implied in everything they said. The way they supported each other, you could hear it: I miss my mother; I miss my wife.

Watching Jamie made me feel useless and fatigued, but it was comforting to connect with them again, especially because I didn't have plans for the holidays. I offered to help clean up from dinner, but Jamie declined.

"Thank you," he said, "but I have to help them with homework, then walk the dog, and then I'll change into my pajamas and do the dishes and fall into bed. I couldn't leave you to clean up this mess all by yourself."

"But you'll be by yourself when you do it later," I said. "You do that every night, don't you?"

"Hestia, I'd feel bad," he said. "I don't want to be a bad host."

I told him that was pretty silly.

"Maybe next time," he said. "Will you come again next month?"

We agreed we'd try to do this every month. It felt like a good idea.

✳

Meanwhile, Ed urged me to "shake things up" in Scribbles. He kept pushing me to write and share my own entries, but I didn't want to, because I knew that Jeffrey, Clara, Dorothy, Charles, and Mildred were way more interesting.

"At least ask some provocative questions," he said. "You're a writer."

"Stalled writer," I corrected him. "Maybe a failed writer."

"Not-yet-wildly-successful writer," he corrected me.

I have no idea why Ed believed in me, but I knew it wasn't anything creepy. Maybe it was a paternal reflex on his part.

When he hired me in June, I was still prone to random crying fits over my husband leaving me, and I decided to confide in him so he wouldn't think I was a freak.

"I'm on my third marriage with two divorces under my belt," he said, "so I think I qualify to give you some advice."

I waited for it, and he said, "It gets easier. Every day, a little easier, so just hang in there. Couple years from now, you're going to wake up and feel normal."

He was twenty-five years my senior and a borderline Marxist, with a great interest in people and a passing interest in his career. It was a safe relationship, because there were no romantic feelings between us. What I felt for him was much more dignified than what I felt with boyfriends.

Sometimes I tried to get him to go to the ice cream socials, but he always declined by saying, "I'm from Texas," as if that were all the explanation I needed. As if Texans wouldn't be caught dead near marshmallow fluff.

In a turn of the tables, he'd confided in me that his current marriage was circling the drain.

"I think we're at the beginning of the end stage," he said.

His first wife was an oncologist, and he still had the habit of speaking about things in medical terms, which he'd picked up from her.

"My prognosis is three years," he said.

∗

Question 4: What do you think has been the lowest point so far of the Second Civil War?

CLARA: *Those three or four days after Madame President was sworn in, when confederate militias assembled in major cities and opened fire inside museums, libraries, universities, even YMCAs, when they bombed Black churches, synagogues, and mosques—those were the worst days of my life, except for some other days that you're too young to hear about. And those dipshits calling it the Purge.*

CHARLES: *That massacre the confederates called the Purge was the worst. Members of Congress flew to their home states to see it with their own eyes, but they couldn't do anything about it. Madame President was a smart cookie, though. Within the first day, she was relocating all the U.S. troops from Southern bases to bases in the Union.*

JEFFREY: *Thank goodness the military was able to stop the Purge, at least in the Northeast. The rest of the country, it was too far gone already, the police were all confederates, ICE was confederate, Border Patrol was confederate.*

DOROTHY: *I'm so tired of people being ugly. It's exhausting.*

＊

On my third date with Ethan, as we were kissing, I thought about that photo of him in his work clothes, roped into a tree. I pictured the belts wrapped around his thighs, right under his ass, and the metal hitch that held him aloft.

"Maybe you should trim my tree," I said, and he did.

One of the nice things about sex with Ethan was that he was as vanilla as I was. We settled quickly on the three classic hetero positions, and he didn't seem to need anything more than that. He just liked to have sex, nothing fancy. No toys, no props, no gels or required reading. It was perfect.

I remember dating before the days of free online porn. Men didn't come at you with so many *ideas*. I'd gotten good at screening out the lifestyle that didn't appeal to me on the dating app: "nesting triad," "anchor partner," and "kitchen table poly" were not going to work. I'm more of a jealous type than a not-jealous type. Give me one mundane detail about a lover from your past, and I'll imagine the whole story of your love affair, every sex scene, every kiss in the rain, every adoring gaze from across the room, because I need to understand what happened. It's a quest for knowledge, and it's torture. All of this to say—ethically nonmonogamous is not my bag, and Ethan, goddess love him, didn't even seem to know that ethically nonmonogamous was a thing.

I also have a sixth sense about cruelty: I've never fallen for a cruel man, although there are plenty. I'm good at self-preservation.

One of the best things about dating Ethan was that somehow, with him, I felt safe going on bona fide dates, real outings. We went to taverns and restaurants. Maybe it's weird how, during a civil war, you can still go to the raw bar or the gelato shop. But people have to make a living, and the violence isn't *everywhere*, just *somewhere*. At first, when you see a guard with a massive firearm standing outside the shop door, it's unsettling. But you adjust. Soon it seems normal enough.

There were a few bars we frequented, and he always knew somebody there. More often than not, when we entered a bar, someone would call out, "Ethan, my man!" He had the nicest friends, people I wanted for my own friends, and they were always cheerful and warm, or at the very least, entertaining.

When we went somewhere that was new to him, he struck up conversations with strangers. He was somewhere between cordial and jolly. He had good gut feelings about who was all right to talk to, so we never found ourselves in accidental conversation with a confederate. I always went home slightly drunk and in good cheer.

∗

In January, we drove to the Eastern Shore to visit his mom and sister and go to the annual watermen's festival. We'd only been dating about six weeks, so I was flattered that he asked, but I was also nervous about being out there, east of the Choptank River. "Transchoptankia," is how H. L. Mencken referred to it when he wrote about the racism, the lynchings, and the all-around despicable behavior of white people who lived there. I'd like to say that in nearly one hundred years, the Eastern Shore has progressed, but I'll reserve judgment on that.

I changed the settings on Conflicted to show me news from the Eastern Shore, and I have to say, the marshes were crawling with confederates.

When I was young, my parents and I spent the summers camping in our RV on the Eastern Shore, exploring coastal, sun-washed Virginia towns. Cape Charles and Chincoteague were two of my favorites, and they had decent RV parks. Back then, the Shore felt like a foreign country. We were "educated" Northern Virginians poking around in a vast stretch of tidewater that some people called "the real Virginia." The store owners and park managers proudly displayed on their walls relics from the first civil war: confederate muskets, confederate flags, framed letters, and even photos of the great-great-great-granddaddies who gave their lives for the epic, romantic Lost Cause.

Inevitably, every summer, there was some boy my age in some RV park who tried to chat me up about an ancestor who fought under General Lee. It took me a few years, but eventually I realized the boys were bragging—it was supposed to impress me. One evening, watching the sun go down on Tangier Island, a boy joined me and my parents while we played cards outside our RV. He asked me if I'd like to hold his musket, which had belonged to an ancestor.

I was about twelve, and I shrugged it off. I didn't want to hold that musket.

"No, thank you," I said.

"You sure?" he asked.

"General Lee was a traitor," I said.

"Don't be rude," said my father, who hated it when I blurted, because blurting is the opposite of self-control.

"Think before you speak," said my father.

"I did," I said.

"Clearly, you didn't," he said.

My mother redirected. She leaned over and whispered in my ear.

"That boy's flirting with you, Hestia," she said.

"So I have to fondle the traitor's musket?" I whispered back.

"Do the right thing," she said. "Don't be rude to that little boy."

When I told Ethan about these trips and my apprehension about the Shore, he told me not to worry. We'll be in the Maryland part, he said, not Virginia. Maryland was still part of America, he said, with a governor who was using everything in his power to keep it from going to the confederates, including the National Guard, the UN, and the Annapolis cadets. I didn't say it out loud, but I thought it was only a matter of time before America lost the Eastern Shore.

"It feels really confederate here," I said, as we headed south from the Bay Bridge.

"My family isn't," he said.

It was oyster season, time for the big festival, which Ethan attended every year. He knew many of the watermen, and most of them were nice-enough guys, some of them funny, even. Their shucking impressed me, and some of them really showed off. One of the more kindly watermen slowed down, gave me a knife, and patiently taught me how to shuck my own oyster. It took a minute, but eventually I got the knack. The hinge was the key! It was such an unexpected relief to learn something that could qualify as a survival skill.

I hadn't known there were so many ways to eat a raw oyster. You can do it with hot sauce, with horseradish, with lemon juice, even with a piquant drizzle of chimichurri-like flavors. I was there for all of it. Ethan made it even more fun.

One of the oystermen cooked his oysters on a barbecue and handed them to me one at a time. After the third one, he started grousing about Harriet Tubman.

"They put up that big museum about her over there, and it's all just made-up," he said, pointing down the road. "If you think about it, there's no way any one person could've done all the things they said she did."

"I like her," I said.

"Ms. Tubman might've been a nice lady," he said, "but she ain't all they say she is, no ma'am. They're making up history."

"Who's making up history?" I asked.

"All those Tubman people," he said.

"Tubman people?" I asked.

"You know who I mean," he said.

"I think I do know who you mean," I said. "You're talking about historians, right?"

He became exasperated and shook his head, closed his eyes. He gave me what I knew was the last oyster he'd cook for me, and I barely tasted it. The museum was only about ten miles from where we were, and it occurred to me that the only reason it hadn't been blown up was because the Guard was stationed there twenty-four seven. Real quick, I checked my Safe Zones app to make sure we weren't in danger.

I found Ethan and told him about the exchange.

"Who, Leroy?" he said. "I've known him all my life."

"He's a Tubman Truther," I said.

"Nah, he's all right."

"He was kind of showing his ass," I said.

"Nah, he's fine."

He insisted that Leroy meant no harm. These were Ethan's people, not mine, and I decided to believe him.

His mother was nice to me. I wouldn't go so far as to say *warm*, but she and Ethan's sister were welcoming enough. I supposed they'd met a lot of girlfriends over the years, and they'd probably learned the hard way not to invest too quickly in new ones. She was a widow, Ethan had mentioned that, so when she was territorial about Ethan, I gave her a pass.

"He's the youngest," she told me. "He'll always be my baby. He was such a sweetheart."

The day was way more fun than I would ever have predicted a winter day filled with oysters and oystermen could be, and I realized I liked Ethan more than I had intended. In hindsight, I probably should have pumped the brakes, but did I? The answer to that question would be "No, I did not."

After the festival, as we headed toward the mainland, he pulled off the road onto a narrow path.

"Here we are," he said, putting the car into park. "The corner of Corn and Soy."

He'd found the one cornfield that still had tall stalks, shielding us from the road. I decided to be coy.

"Are you going to teach me something about maize now?" I asked.

He kissed me on my neck and ran his hand down the side of my body.

"Oh, so, we're doing *that*?" I asked.

He moved his hand onto my waist and pulled me toward him.

"People swear that oysters are aphrodisiacs," he said.

He kissed my ear.

"Maybe you just like having sex in fields," I said.

"Could be," he said.

It was so cold, and we stayed in his pickup, which didn't have a back seat but did have heat. Somehow, we maneuvered around the steering wheel, and it felt especially amorous. It could have been the oysters, or it could have been a thousand other things. Who can say for sure?

✳

There *was* the issue of the guitar. Mostly, it was manageable. He seemed to think he was pretty good, and he sounded perfectly fine to me, but I'm no connoisseur. I enjoyed it, and I told him so. Men have this incredible skill: they're able to have high opinions of themselves. Try finding an intelligent woman with that skill. I think what Ethan loved most in the world was music, in particular the music he participated in making. Get him started, and he'd talk for a long time about where and when he last performed, how many people were in the audience, and how they responded to the music.

"And then this older woman at the front of the room stood up and started dancing, and then this other lady stood up and started dancing, so that was two people dancing," was the climax of one of his stories.

"And then me and the bassist found this great groove," was another climax.

I wished that I could love something as much as he loved playing guitar. If we're being honest, his pure joy over making music made me feel even more impaired. Dating a happy, balanced person is not easy, because when you don't have to think about their brokenness, you have more time to focus on your own.

As I learned more about his ex-girlfriends over the months, I realized that he wasn't particular, and I wondered if his lack of particularness was why he was so well-adjusted in general. If he wasn't choosy about girlfriends, he probably wasn't choosy about anything, and if you're not choosy, then you probably don't suffer.

"Hey now, Hestia Harris, you weren't looking to fall in love," I reminded myself.

I couldn't figure out why I was beginning to feel so uncertain about being with Ethan. When I'd hearted him on the app, I'd been thinking it would be nice to have one person to text with and watch television with and have sex with and maybe even eat dinner with. It was supposed to be no big deal. To my chagrin, though, I realized I wanted a little more. I petitioned the goddess: Please, don't make me seek love, not yet, it's too soon and I'm too much of a mess. But, maddeningly, I also seemed to want a passionate romance, and instead he seemed merely content. I was the perfectly acceptable person he was with at the moment. I was not the person he stayed up late at night thinking about. I checked the boxes, but I wasn't a whole new checklist or anything. And apparently, I wanted to be a whole new checklist.

✳

"But why do you want him to be swept away, dear?" Mildred asked.

We were in the Serenity Room, a space intended for "visiting." Sometimes Mildred and I hung out there, when she wasn't insisting on cigarettes.

"I'm sure it's my stupid ego," I said.

"He doesn't sound like that type of person," she said.

"Or maybe it's me," I said. "Maybe I'm not the sort of girl who sweeps men away."

She looked genuinely sorry for me.

"You can never know another person's mind," she said. "I'm sorry to tell you this, but you'll never get the answers you're looking for. That's the tragedy."

"But I don't like feeling this way," I said.

"Nobody does," she said.

"But sometimes people sweep each other off their feet," I said.

"Oh, Hestia, when people get swept off their feet, it's usually because they're lonely," she said. "The lonelier they are, the more they get swept away."

Maybe I was the one getting swept away, against my better judgment, because I'd been lonely for so long.

She urged me to blow off the Serenity Room and go instead to the garden where she could "cop a cig."

"Ruth is coming to visit," I said. "If she smells cigarettes on you, she'll get me fired."

"Oh, screw Ruth," she said. "I won't let them fire you. If she wants to get her titties in a twist, let her."

Ruth was her daughter by her first husband, Yitzy, and she came from Pittsburgh every two weeks if there was gasoline, never at the same time as her sister.

"You love Ruth," I said.

"I really do," said Mildred. "But why do young people have to be so uptight?"

Ruth was twenty years older than me, and I loved it when Mildred referred to her as a young person.

When Ruth arrived, I left the two of them alone to hug and kiss with all their obvious affection for each other. Mildred always took her daughter's hand while they talked, and Ruth put her hand over her mother's hand, and sometimes I walked by the room and looked in the door to get a glimpse of it.

When Ruth left, I found Mildred sitting by herself in Serenity, tapping her cane on the floor. She told me that Ruth had made a proposal. As the daughter of a Jew who had escaped Austria in the nick of time as a child, she was entitled to citizenship. She was applying for the passport, and it was going slowly, but well. Not only could she get citizenship for herself, but for her husband and immediate family, too. She intended to move there as soon as she could.

"You can't blame her," said Mildred. "Who wants to live in this farkakte country? People killing each other, losing their ever-loving minds over the most idiotic things."

"She's lucky she can get the passports," I said.

"My people are so *Mayflower* that I'm useless in that department," she said. "Her father was a horse's ass, but he did her right by ancestry."

"Won't you miss her so much?"

"She wants to bring me with her to Vienna," she said.

I felt—and tried to ignore—a pang.

"I hear Vienna's beautiful," I said.

"It is," she said.

✳

I returned to the office side of the village, back to the tiny room I shared with my colleague, Sarah. Not only did we share an office, we shared a desk, an L-shaped hulk that took up most of the room. It was an uncomfortable arrangement, and we'd tried a few different ways of placing our chairs, but it was always awkward. We each tried to be elsewhere when the other was using the desk, which is one of the reasons I spent so much time on the residential side of the village.

Technically, Sarah was my direct-report, and she was one of the most private people I'd ever met. She had no photos on our desk, she never made a personal phone call when I was there, and she told me nothing about her life. She kept our relationship professional, but I knew I liked her. Mostly. It was complicated, because she was a millennial, in her late twenties, with some of the stereotypical overconfidence of her generation. But she also seemed to have a soft spot for the elderly, spending almost as much time in the residential wing as I did. She had an obvious contempt for boomers, which sometimes showed up in tense moments with Ed; I often found myself in the middle.

I'd spent six months trying to get her to warm up to me. I opened up to her about my husband abandoning me. I made jokes about how I'd been dumped for a paramilitary group. I showed her photos of Ethan and recounted some of his silly stories about varnish. She humored me, but she never shared anything.

She was a gorgeous Black woman who had the Fibonacci thing nailed; everyone took note of her beauty. Aside from that, all I knew of her was that she had an Ivy League pedigree, she dressed impeccably, her makeup was perfect, and she had what sounded to me like a genteel Southern accent.

To fill in the blanks, I made up stuff. In my imagination, she was about to be engaged, no doubt to a person my mother would call "a good earner," probably a lawyer, and they were going to buy a Rodgers Forge town house with hardwood floors. She'd hang a framed "Live, Laugh, Love" poster on one of her stylishly greige walls.

When February 3 rolled around, the one-year anniversary of the Sedition and the start of the war, I made a bad joke about how the confederates had failed at killing Madame President but succeeded at killing my marriage. It didn't land. She flinched, and I felt bad.

I apologized—profusely—and she tried to brush it off as no big deal.

"Please let me buy you a drink after work," I said. "Do you drink? I don't even know if you drink."

She let out the biggest sigh, which I took to mean that she was giving in.

"I drink," she said.

We checked Safe Zones and agreed on the burgers-and-beer joint I'd been to with Ethan. On the walk to the bar, I told her about some of my dating mishaps, and she seemed genuinely horrified. We sat down, and before I could catch the bartender's eye, she came over and asked Sarah what she would like.

"That dude wants to buy you a drink," she said, nodding toward a blazer in Italian shoes.

The bartender looked at me and said, "You, too, I suppose."

Free drinks was a new world for me, and what's not to love? When Sarah ordered rosé, I followed suit. We both started to relax, and I asked her about *her* dating horror stories.

"I don't have any dating horror stories," she said. "Men treat me right, and the first time they don't, I release them."

"Nothing?"

"The most horrifying thing is that men always want to take care of me," she said. "They want to marry me, and they're always gorgeous or wealthy."

"Oh, shit," I said. "That is horrifying."

"It *is*, though," she said, and I had the sense that she might be warming to me.

"Are you on any dating apps?" I asked.

She named the two apps she used, which I'd never heard of.

"They're not really for . . . white people," she said.

"Got it," I said.

"Sorry," she said.

I told her that I didn't blame her for not wanting to date white people.

"Sometimes I don't want to date white people, either," I said. "It's a lot of work to find the good ones."

"You don't seem that bad."

"Black men never heart me on the apps," I said.

"Yeah, well," she said, and she drained her rosé.

The bartender refilled both our glasses, compliments of the same party, and Sarah raised hers toward the blazer in the Italian shoes. I think she was just being polite; she didn't look the least bit interested.

Sarah's phone lit up with a Conflicted alert, and mine did not. She was still getting the real-time alerts. The confederacy's president, the former Governor Rice of Florida, had just died mysteriously. Authorities suspected a poisoning by rivals, and Governor Water of Louisiana, the vice president, was calling off the investigation as he was being sworn in. Sarah did her signature eye roll.

Then she drained her glass and shifted gears.

"Not to bring up the office while we're drinking," she said, "but I ran into that guy again in the Café des Artistes."

"What guy?"

"That Tai Chi instructor," she said.

I knew who she was talking about. I overheard him teaching the class three times a week, with a voice that could lull a person to sleep. I called it his heroin voice. I'd noticed him cup his belly and talk about the "dan tien" in that soporific voice during class.

"He always tries to say hello when I'm making my coffee, but he ends up looking at my tits," said Sarah.

"Look, Sarah," I said, too tipsy to stop myself. "You have banging tits."

Immediately, I was concerned that I'd become too familiar, too fast, but she let it slide.

"I *know* that," she said. "But does he have to look like such a wolf?"

"Maybe he's lonely," I said.

"He has a creepy vibe."

"Have you ever been lonely, Sarah?" I asked.

She gave me a look that seemed to say, What do you think?

"There's all this leaky sexual energy coming out of him," she went on. "Ew."

I had pretty nice tits, too, or so I thought, maybe my best feature, but the Tai Chi teacher had never stared at them.

✳

The next morning, I went to the Café, and the Tai Chi guy was there, leaving as I walked in. He was skinny, with long hair parted in the middle and a woven belt around his too-big jeans. The belt looked suspiciously like hemp. He sported a deep brown flannel shirt, unbuttoned, and he was standing in one of the Tai Chi poses, his tail tucked and knees slightly bent, almost like he was sitting while standing.

"Hello," I said, and he walked out of the room, eyes on the floor.

Later that day, a freelance article I'd started just before the war was finally published, and I sent Ethan a link. "Hey, this is a thing I wrote," I said in the text. A week later I asked him if he'd read it, and he said he'd definitely do it soon. A week after that I asked him again and he said he'd read it a few days ago.

"You read it days ago? Why didn't you say anything?"

"Was I supposed to?"

I hadn't given him instructions to report back, that was true.

"What did you think?" I asked.

"It was good," he said. "That part about the ducks was funny."

I waited to see if he had anything else to say, but he did not.

※

Question 5: Have there been any moments during the war when you felt hopeful?

DOROTHY: *We all felt so bad for people in Atlanta, New Orleans, Austin. We knew that their vote to secede was not a real vote. There was so much voter suppression. They didn't want to be part of the New Confederated States of America, and we didn't want to leave them there. But what could we do? Every time we tried to take back a city, their army pushed back. In America, we wrapped yellow ribbons around trees for the good people trapped in bad states, like hostages.*

JEFFREY: *It warmed the cockles of my heart to see liberals finally grabbing their guns. I didn't do all those civil rights marches in the '60s just so we could go all pacifist and give away the store. We have to fight, fight, fight, and give the bastards hell.*

CLARA: *Oh, for decades, white people, liberals and conservatives, were terrified of "gang leaders" and "drug lords," in cities like Atlanta and New Orleans. Then all of a sudden, they were trying to get in their good graces, because they wanted their*

*guns. I guess the so-called drug lords weren't criminals any-
more, not once white people needed their guns. It was a new
brotherhood, praise Jesus. I'm being ironic.*

✳

In March, Madame President officially kicked off her campaign for reelection, and pundits predicted an easy win. In
our new America, a woman of color could run for president
with less scrutiny and hounding than before the war. She still
had to jump through hoops, but with less harassment. She
had no serious challengers.

The same month, Ethan drove his giant pickup to Connecticut for a box of condoms imported from Japan, which
had stopped shipping to Maryland because the ports here
were too unstable. They were the Japanese 004, ultra-thin, or
something like that, and he presented them to me with a
cocktail of pride and fanfare.

"They say it makes you feel like you forgot to wear a condom at all," he said, as I turned the box around in my hands.

"Is that a selling point?" I asked. "Because that sounds
like a panic attack to me."

He kissed me, which he did a lot, because he was an af-
fectionate person.

He told me the story of how he'd purchased them in Connecticut, and I silently estimated how much money he'd
spent on gasoline.

"I just walked right into the CVS," he said, "and there
they were."

"I hope you had a coupon," I said.

"I bought the whole shelf," he said. "I'm gonna resell them
to my buddies."

Naturally, it wasn't long before we tried out the new gift. He had such a joyful grin when he used the condom—holy cow, the look on his face.

"This is so worth it," he said.

One of the things I liked about Ethan was how much he enjoyed himself. Some men get such a serious look on their faces, *concerned* even, when they're having sex. But Ethan just loved it.

"Oh, man, I can really feel the heat from your vagina," he said.

A few moments later, when we were finished and lying on our pillows, he put his hands behind his head, the way he always did.

"I had no idea your vagina was so warm," he said, in his doped-up, postcoital tenor.

"You can say 'pussy,'" I said.

"I know," he said, "but I like 'vagina.'"

✳

When there was more violence than usual in public places, we hung out in my apartment. It was small, but tidy, and it had a nonworking fireplace that I confess to obsessing over. It rankled me that it didn't work, because being able to light a fire would have been so nice during the Baltimore winters, which, as far as I could tell, were only getting colder. The stratospheric warming events and polar vortices had seen to that.

I was always searching for just the right arrangement for the fireplace, and one early spring evening as Ethan and I lay on the floor, I realized I hadn't changed the arrangement since my husband had left, and that it was almost a year he'd been gone. It was still all white and off-white candles of different heights and widths, something I must have seen on Instagram. None of the candles were lit, and it struck me what a sin that was.

"Let's light the candles," I said, and we did.

They gave off a soft-enough glow, but they were a little taciturn. They didn't warm up the room at all. As pretty as they were, I thought: I should get rid of these soon.

Out of nowhere, Ethan asked about my husband.

"You never told me what happened to him," he said. "Did he die?"

"No, no," I said. "I don't think so."

"You don't *think* so?"

"He's out there fighting the fight, somehow," I said. "I'm sure he's still alive."

"Which side is he fighting for?"

"America," I said, insulted that he'd even wonder.

"Okay, cool," he said. "I was just making sure."

Yes, I thought, these candles are kind of soulless, a little too SoHo loft. I'll burn them all the way down, and then, when they are done, I'll try something new.

✳

April in America, fourteen months into the war, and Madame President was expertly steering her new ship.

In the first civil war, the United States put all its muscle into invading the seceded South, defeating the confederate armies, and reoccupying the territory. They did it with two goals in mind: emancipating the people who were enslaved, and preserving the Union.

But it was different this time around. Some Americans wanted to preserve the Union—but there were a lot of people who were just fine with letting the confederate states go. At first, Madame President made an attempt to "take it back," sending U.S. troops to the military bases we'd abandoned during the Purge. But their army held us off, and that project was back-burnered. More tactically, she sent our armies to fight for oil, gas, and coal, which we would still need for years to come, despite her enthusiasm for transitioning to renewable energy. We had some wins. But mostly we spent the first year putting out fires in our own states, responding to confederate terrorism taking place on our soil. We put our military energy into infiltrating their militias, confiscating their weapons, extraditing their leaders, and trying them in court.

As we found our groove with that, the United States tried to "liberate" people in the confederacy, but it was tricky. Anyone who wanted to leave, and had the money and wherewithal to do so, was granted citizenship in America. But the government didn't have the resources to relocate everyone. The refugees needed housing, jobs, transportation, and food, and we only had so much of those things. The only feasible way to liberate everyone who wanted out of the confederacy was to defeat the New Confederated States of America, and we weren't making much headway. We had to back off of that one, leaving them in a country they no longer felt was theirs.

At the same time, the confederates stepped up their terrorism game. They evolved from poisoning reservoirs and blowing up sewage plants to recruiting hackers who could create some serious chaos. You'd like to think that hackers would be too smart, too principled to aid and abet confederates—but you could always find a troublemaker for the right price.

On April 15, Baltimore lost power for two and a half

days. The terrorists had taken down a power grid, so we had no streetlights, no traffic lights, no light rail. There were accidents everywhere, and then people stopped driving, stopped going to work. Hospitals had to throw away medications by the dumpster-full, because they couldn't power the refrigerators with the generators they had on hand. Mercy Hospital, near me, had bags of expired medicines piling up in dumpsters, and they hired security guards to make sure people didn't go through the bags looking for drugs.

Sidewalks were lined with Hefty bags of rotting food discarded by restaurants. Everyone's phone was drained, except for the people who could charge them in their cars, if they had the gasoline. People who lived in high-rise buildings had to make decisions based on a gamble about when the elevators would work again.

With no electricity, there was no reason for me to go to work. The residential wing would be running on generators, but my wing would not. I wouldn't be able to update a mailing list or put new photos on our website without electricity. But I went anyway, because it was unsettling to be home alone in the dark, and the candles in my fireplace were bumming me out. I'd be able to make coffee in the Café des Artistes. The couple-mile walk did me good, and truthfully, it was kind of nice to see so many people outside, walking on the streets, *not* looking at their phones. Baltimore's gorgeous in April, and we marveled at the flowering cherry trees.

∗

I was surprised to find Sarah in the Café, and I wondered if she had been home alone in the dark, like me. She seemed a little embarrassed to be discovered there, and I tried to put her at ease, saying something about how it was nice that the village had Wi-Fi.

"We have to work these dating apps, right?"

"Why would you be using the app?" she asked. "Aren't you dating someone?"

"I am," I said, "but you never know."

She inserted a pod of hazelnut-flavored coffee into the machine, placed her mug underneath, and pushed brew. Then she relaxed a little and smiled.

"I actually met someone," she said. "I think he might be . . . he seems pretty great."

"Great how?"

"He's a tall drink of water," she said. "Handsome, too, and I think he comes from money."

Then she frowned.

"What's wrong with him?"

"I don't know yet," she said. "He's an environmental activist."

"That's not usually a bad thing," I said.

"He's big into salmon."

"Like, to eat?"

"No!" she exclaimed. "To save!"

She told me that he was anti-dam, as in, he wanted to help destroy the dams out West, because they were killing off the wild salmon populations, depriving communities of traditional, cultural food sources, and perverting the ecosystems in other ways. He had an advanced degree in engineering, which he hoped to use to blow up dams.

He sounded extreme, but I found it fascinating that in the middle of a civil war, a person could be passionate about wild salmon. Salmon are probably a much nicer species than humans, so there's that.

"Congratulations," I said.

She showed me his picture, and he was indeed very handsome, with a jaw that could cut glass.

By the end of the day, Baltimore had electricity again. The confederates threw Molotov cocktails through windows in city hall, but it barely made the news.

✳

Question 6: During the war, has there been anyone you feel especially badly for?

CHARLES: *My husband and I never had children of our own, but I've always been close to my nieces and nephews. I feel terrible for the children in the confederacy. Those states have a lot more poverty than we do. And now we're not sending them federal money for schools, food stamps, school lunches, welfare. I imagine they'll be hungry and skinny before long.*

DOROTHY: *I feel horrible for the children. I heard they have to memorize those horrible documents in school, that hideous "Declaration of Immediate Causes," where they pledge themselves to the Christian Creator. Why are they so hung up on being a Christian nation? I swear, theocracies are so boring.*

CLARA: *The New Confederated States of America wrote a constitution that talks about the self-evident truth that not all men are created equal, and that some men are better suited to rule, others to serve. The natural order of the sexes, of which there are only two. The fantasy lives of these people. Can you imagine? I feel bad for everyone who's not a rich, heterosexual, white man.*

✳

In May, our new Congress, which had lost most of its confederates, declared that our Supreme Court needed a do-over; so
many of the justices had been appointed by people we now
knew had been traitors. With very little opposition, a vote was
passed to reassess the nine justices. To fill the resulting vacan-
cies, Madame President nominated delightful, progressive
scholars, who were treated with respect in the hearings.

When Mother's Day rolled around, I did my daughterly
duty and took a train to Northern Virginia to visit my parents. I don't love taking trains; they're easy targets. But the
Washington metro area had good security. My parents lived
in Dumfries, just off the Capital Beltway, so it was within a
safe zone, if you want to call it that. Not all of Virginia
had seceded, only the southern and southwestern parts of the
state. Northern Virginia wanted to remain in the Union.
Growing up there, I'd thought it was chock-full of confederates, but I suppose it became more liberal over the years.

When my mother met me at the station, she seemed genuinely happy—or maybe relieved—to see me. She patted me
on the shoulder—never much of a hugger—and told me that
my jacket was flattering. It was cold, as it often is on Mother's
Day, and she was wearing the same beige puffy coat she'd
been wearing for ten years.

In the parking lot, we walked past a mild protest about
student debt forgiveness, one of the more milquetoast issues
facing the nation, and my mother sighed.

"You worked so hard to pay off your debt, Hestia," she
said. "We all did."

"Nancy," I said, "this isn't a big deal."

"But you worked so hard. Why should they get it for free?"

"I'm not the only person who works hard," I said, "and neither are you."

She exhaled powerfully through her nose.

"Everybody's working hard," I said.

"Oh, I doubt that," she said. "I doubt that very much."

This was what I called a "no-purchase" argument. I could recite facts, I could show them pie charts and bar graphs, about who would be eligible for forgiveness and who would not, and how the forgiveness would provide a desperately needed boost to the poorest among us, but none of it mattered. They were college professors, but even to them, "data" was a four-letter word. They'd already made up their minds. The only thing to do in these situations, I'd learned, was to change the subject. That's it, it's all you can do.

"Happy Mother's Day," I said.

She stood next to her car and looked at me quizzically.

"Oh, that," she said. "Is that what this is? You're here because of a fabricated, for-profit holiday?"

"Yes, Nancy," I said, "this is what people do."

My mother didn't go in for that sort of thing, holidays and celebrations. Once, when I asked my parents why they wouldn't throw me a birthday party after age ten, she said that if anyone should be throwing anyone a party on my birthday, I should be the one celebrating *her*, as she was the birth-giver. I should be giving thanks for another spin around the sun, not expecting accolades for it.

On the drive to their house, she asked about my husband, as if she wanted to get it out of the way before we saw my father. She wanted to know if I'd heard from him, and I told her what I always told her, that I had not.

"It's been more than a year," she said.

I agreed that it had been more than a year, and she pointed out some tulips on the roadside.

"He was always a weak man," she said.

"You liked him," I said.

"No, he *grew on me*," she said. "That's different. But he's abandoning his duty as a husband, and that's a sign of weakness."

"You were fond of him," I said.

"Because that's what happens," she said. "Some things you can't help."

"Well, for all I know, he's missing in action," I said.

I noticed her lower lip start to tremble, the way it did when she was trying not to cry. She hated to cry. She blinked and stared ahead, which was great, because she was driving.

"Nancy," I said. "It's all right. It's fine. I'm really, really fine."

That was our pattern: I comforted her on issues that were upsetting to me.

"You think those are nice tulips?" she said. "Wait until you see *my* tulips."

When we pulled into the driveway, the glory of her tulips was overshadowed by the enormous sign they'd placed in the middle of the yard. MAKE LIBERALS FEEL SAD, it said in block print, white letters on red, like my very own EXIT sign telling me to get out. I looked at my mother as she put the car in park, and we sat there, sinking into a few moments of silence.

"Do you have something you'd like to say?" she asked, looking for a reaction.

"Really pretty tulips," I said.

It started to rain a little, a bit of spit, and my father was moving lunch from the deck into the kitchen. Whenever possible, we ate outside; that was a thing about my father. We'd had so many meals in that kitchen, just the three of us, always the three of us, every day the three of us, that I think in some way we all wanted to set that kitchen on fire. But here we were again, swiping mustard onto bread while we watched rain slip down the windowpanes.

He asked about my job: "You can do better than that job," he said.

He asked what I was reading: "Make sure it nourishes your brain," he said.

He said, "I gather your husband is still shirking his responsibility to you."

"If you want to put it that way," I said.

"You don't need him," he said. "You know that, right?"

"Bill, I'm doing fine," I said.

He lifted up the top piece of bread on my sandwich and put an extra slice of turkey on it, then patted down the bread again.

"Bill," said my mother, "don't overfeed her."

"You call this *overfeeding*?" he asked. "This is called 'feeding.'"

He took off his fleece jacket, and then I saw his T-shirt. It said, "Fuck your feelings," superimposed over an image of a bighorn ram's head. The ram had become an unofficial mascot for the confederates, who were always complaining about people like me being sheep—which was weird, because a ram is a sheep. But there's no point in trying to split those hairs.

"Fuck your feelings, Bill?" I asked.

He smiled from ear to ear. "You like it?"

"Since when do you say 'fuck'?" I asked. "In forty-two years, I've never heard you say 'fuck.'"

"You're being evasive," he said. "Do you like the shirt?"

"It's rude," I said. "And vulgar."

"So, you don't like it?"

The way he smirked, while my mother sat next to him with a smug look on her face—they were goading me, and loving it.

"Not really," I said.

"So sensitive, Hestia," he said. "You were always so sensitive."

"When did you get like this?" I asked.

"Calm down, Hestia," he said. "Just relax."

My whole life, my father's been telling me to calm down. In his world, there was never a good enough reason for me to cry or raise my voice. He probably told me to calm down as I emerged from my mother's birth canal, and every day after that. Curiously, I'd never heard him tell another man to calm down. It was an instruction for women.

"You used to be pretty nice people," I said.

"You used to be nice, too," my mother said.

I'd only eaten half of my sandwich, which was a shame, because my parents bought the good stuff, the small-farm-raised, antibiotic-free, give-the-animal-a-name, humane-slaughter kind of meat. But I'd lost my appetite.

"We're moving," she said. "In a month. We sold the house."

I asked them where they were moving, but I already knew: somewhere deeper into the heart of darkness. Farther south, farther west. They'd be officially leaving America and relocating in the new wretched nation.

"You're moving to a different country," I said. "Aren't you worried that we won't be able to see each other?"

"So dramatic," said my father.

"Hestia," said my mother. "Do French people travel to Greece to see their families? Yes, they do. Do Swiss people travel to Italy to see their families? Yes, they do."

They thought they were making sense, but their vision seemed too easy to me, a kind of magical thinking.

"But those countries aren't hostile to each other," I said. "They're not at war."

"We don't have to be at war, either," said my father. "It's a choice."

"If the president would just stop trying to 'rescue' people who don't need to be rescued, we'd all be fine," said my mother.

Just like that, I lost both my parents. My whole life, I'd longed for a brother or a sister, felt the emptiness of being an only child. Now I felt like an orphan, but not the cute, plucky orphan who triumphs over adversity. I was the lonely orphan wondering if anyone had my back.

*

Back in Baltimore, I retreated to Ethan's bachelor couch—black pleather—which was deep and perfect for two people lying longways, side by side.

He'd called his mother earlier that morning; the Eastern Shore was too much of a drive for a one-day visit, and we weren't doing great on gasoline that month. I asked him what his favorite things about his mother were, and he told me that she always laughed at his jokes and always enjoyed his company.

Then I asked how his father had died. He told me it was during the Purge, the day after the February 3rd Sedition. I sat straight up. How had I not known that?

"Those were some real bad days on the Eastern Shore," he said.

I couldn't believe we'd been dating this whole time and I never knew his father had been killed in the Purge. He was so casual about it. I'd assumed something natural, a heart attack or stroke.

"There was a bagel shop, run by Jews, from Russia, I think, or maybe Israel, I don't know, and my father went every Sunday morning to get bagels for the family," he said.

I couldn't imagine his mother eating a bagel, she was so tiny.

"He was fixing to get an everything with cream cheese, like he always did, and three dudes walked in, a bunch of open-carry nutjobs, you know, and they started shouting at the people who worked there . . ."

He trailed off.

"Then what?" I asked.

"You know," he said.

He was right, I did know.

"Same old bullshit," he said.

I couldn't believe he was telling me this. I tried to tell him how sorry I was.

"They were asking the workers, 'Are y'all legal?' and saying shit like, 'Show me your birth certificate.'"

I put my hand on his arm.

"That's what the eyewitnesses say, anyway," he said. "I guess I'll never know for sure."

Also, according to those eyewitness reports, some customers tried to form a human wall between the workers and the shooters, while others scattered to the far corners of the shop. Someone called the police, but they came too late, of course. Ethan didn't know which type of customer his dad was—one of the ones who formed a human wall or one of the ones who retreated—because no one who was there remembered him specifically.

He nodded and pursed his lips.

"He did not live to tell the tale," he said.

I couldn't think of anything to say.

"He was a pretty good guy," he said.

"That's awful," I said.

"True," he said.

"How is it that we've been hooking up for five months and I just learned this about you?" I asked.

"I don't think about it that much," he said.

"What?" I asked, my incredulity obvious.

"Is that wrong?" he asked.

"No," I said.

"You look like you just caught me killing a cat or something," he said.

I answered carefully.

"I envy you," I said.

"What for?"

"Because something terrible happened to you, and you don't think about it that much," I said.

"It didn't really happen to *me*, did it?" he asked. "It happened to my dad."

I felt sad for him, and sad for the country, and sad for those workers at the bagel shop, and sad for Ethan's mom, and sad for anyone who ever gets a craving for an everything with cream cheese and has to remember that shooting. I guess I looked pretty bad, because Ethan took my face in his hands and kissed my forehead.

"It's all right," he said. "It's all right."

That made me cry, and he wrapped his arms around me and kissed the top of my head.

"This is ridiculous," I said. "I should be comforting you, not the other way around."

"It's all good," he said.

When he kissed me, it was tender and such a comfort, almost electric. One thing led to another, and I felt . . . so . . . *held* on that pleather couch. Later, he traced the scar on my stomach with his hand, which was warm and dry, and he looked up at the ceiling fan that had never worked since I'd known him.

"You said we've been 'hooking up' for five months," he said.

"Isn't that right?" I asked. "Five months?"

"Sure, but 'hooking up'?" he asked. "Is that what we're doing?"

I pulled away, trying not to panic. I went into emergency mode, preparing myself to feel like a fool. I could feel the skin prickling on my forehead, and I waited for him to tell me that he "didn't know" we were in a monogamous relationship.

"Is this going to be a conversation about whether or not we're exclusive?" I asked.

"I'm being monogamous," he said. "I thought you knew that."

"I did," I bluffed.

The relief made me suddenly sleepy.

"I am, too," I said.

"But I'm just a steady hookup to you?" he asked.

I curled into his side to take a nap and pulled the blanket up to my neck.

"No, you're more than that," I said.

"How much more?" he said. "Are we dating?"

"Yes, we're dating," I said.

"Am I your boyfriend?"

I was hoping to fall asleep before I had to answer, but I didn't, and I'm not a good faker, so I answered.

"That sounds right," I said. "You're my boyfriend."

✳

Question 7: Have there been any unexpected upsides to the civil war?

DOROTHY: *Right after the Purge, the United Nations sent peacekeepers to help us put down the traitors, and these peacekeepers brought a cosmopolitan breath of fresh air to Baltimore. I, for one, appreciate the Southern European male gaze.*

CHARLES: *When the peacekeepers came in, we suddenly started hearing French, Italian, German, lovely accents from Ireland, from Iran, from Azerbaijan.*

CLARA: *My daughter was so rattled by the Purge that she flew in from India to visit with me, and even spoke with me, breaking her vow of silence. It was such a happy week for me, and I know that's a strange thing to say.*

✳

In the first year of the war, the Triple Crown races were called off. But fifteen months in, Baltimore was undeterred. We had our Preakness in May. That weekend, the military presence in town must have doubled; it seemed that there were U.S. troops and UN peacekeepers stationed everywhere. It was probably an illusion, but for those few days, we all seemed to believe we could walk downtown without fear.

Ethan and I didn't care about the horse races, but we did enjoy being out and about. It was a beautiful late spring day, and the days were long, which meant curfew didn't come until late in the evening. Ethan and I strolled through Fell's Point, sometimes holding hands, although I never let it last too long. Something about the public display of affection had me spooked.

Every bar in town with a television was airing the races and serving Black-Eyed Susans, a slightly fancy screwdriver. A bar on Thames Street was serving them in plastic cups for carry-out—not exactly legal, but no one complained.

While Ethan placed his order inside, I stayed on the sidewalk, enjoying the weather. When he emerged with the drinks, he told me that the woman behind the bar had been flirting with him.

"She winked, too," he said.

Ridiculously, I felt jealous.

"That's nice," I said.

"Guess I'm not too shabby," he said.

"Not too shabby," I echoed without enthusiasm.

"Guess I got a backup plan," he said.

"Okay," I said. "The Fell's Point drinks lady is your backup plan."

"I got a fallback."

Why was he telling me he had options? Or was he just flirting, and he needed me to flirt with him, too? In hindsight, I could have been nicer.

"Was she pretty?" I asked.

"They're all pretty," he said.

"No, seriously," I said.

He paused, then said, "Yeah, she was cute."

I've been around long enough to know that when men

pause and say "Yeah, she was cute," what they really mean is "She wasn't pretty, but she wasn't ugly, either."

When we'd finished our drinks, Ethan stuffed our empties into his backpack. There were no garbage cans downtown—it was too easy to put bombs in them.

"You know, Ethan," I said, "it's okay to admit that not all women are pretty. Lightning won't strike you."

"I thought we were supposed to say that all women are pretty."

"Are all men tall?" I asked.

"No," he said.

"So, what if women went around saying that all men are tall?"

He was silent.

"That would be frustrating, wouldn't it?" I asked. "Because short guys have to be more interesting, and nicer, and maybe even rich. Short guys work so much harder."

Ethan was silent while he walked, patting a tree here and there.

"Okay," he finally said. "I guess not all women are necessarily *pretty*."

"Relax," I said. "No one is going to punch you."

"Okay," he said.

We walked a little more, and we held hands. But something happened inside me, and I couldn't let it go.

"So why do you say things like 'They're all pretty'?"

"You're right," he said.

"That was an actual question," I said. "Why do you say it?"

I wanted him to dig deep. He spent what seemed like a long time thinking about how to answer.

"Because you can always find *something* pretty about a woman," he said.

"So even if she's not pretty, you can tell yourself she's pretty?"

"Well, yeah," he said.

"Does that work?"

"Well, yeah," he said. "I'm not picky. It's all good."

I don't think I'll ever understand why that infuriated me, why I wanted him to be picky. But I may also never understand why I couldn't let this go. I watched myself, as if from afar, in horror. I thought: There I go again, punishing the wrong person.

"What lies are you telling yourself about me?"

"I'm not lying to myself about you," he said.

"How would you know?" I asked. "You're so good at gaslighting yourself, how would you *know* if you're gaslighting yourself?"

He was one inch from shutting down completely. I knew the signs. He leaned against a tree—maybe it was a sycamore?—and sighed and then sighed again.

"Hestia, you're pretty," he said. "You're one of the pretty ones."

"*That's not even what we're talking about,*" I said.

"But you *are* pretty."

I think I'm about 70 or 80 percent of the way to pretty. I'm a little plump, the only interesting thing I do is keep a kitchen herb garden, my hair is always messy, my clothes are wrinkled, I usually have crumbs somewhere on my person, but apparently I have a pleasing face, nice eyes, nice smile, and I usually look like I'm on day two of a camping trip—but that wasn't the issue. I didn't need Ethan to tell me I was pretty. I guess I wanted him to explain why men settle so quickly for a woman, *any* woman. It was a tall order, I know.

We kept walking and ended up back at his truck, which

made me angry because it had been so hard to find a parking spot. Now someone else was going to get our beautiful parking space. I couldn't blame him for his silence on the ride home. You can't force a person to examine himself, especially a person like Ethan, who had all that wonderful mental health that comes from not being too self-aware, or self-critical.

We barely talked, and that night we slept at our own apartments. I recognized the fork in the road for what it was. I had whiffed it. I'd pushed too far, made bad choices, not been my best self, operated from a scarcity mindset. It was time to either make a radical change by taking the scary, winding path toward the unknown, or time to hop off the ride.

✳

Question 8: Has anything shocked you about the Second Civil War?

CHARLES: *It's been devastating. I've felt so much grief over the war, more than the usual daily grief of being human, although it's nothing compared to the grief of losing my husband. But life goes on. Most people are still shopping for groceries, going to work every day, and grousing about traffic.*

JEFFREY: *My grandchildren aren't the least bit surprised by this war, and I find that shocking. Or maybe it's just sad. It's the world they've grown up in, and I wish it didn't have to be this way.*

DOROTHY: *I'm shocked that people will keep looking for love, no matter what the world throws at them. What's so grand about love, anyway?*

MILDRED: *Hestia, you've worn me down. I'll answer your Scribbles questions. I'm shocked that there aren't more people hooking up and acting out. There's a war on! What if it's the end of the world? You'd think people would let down their damn hair.*

✶

A couple days later, Ethan and I fell out while trying to decide if we had time to meet up with his friends at the bar. I didn't want to rush to the bar, only to have to hurry up and drink my drink before it was curfew, and then head back to his place, hungry and too drunk to eat a proper meal. I knew the night would end with sloppy sex and me eating crackers while standing at the counter wearing only a T-shirt, and I didn't want that. Ethan, on the other hand, wanted to rush out the door and meet his friends, a couple, who honestly were the best part of the whole equation because the one guy was perhaps the most humble person I'd ever met, and the other guy, his partner, always said things like "Oh my goodness, Hestia, you're hilarious."

As I explained to Ethan what I was thinking, how I'd end up eating crackers at midnight, he backed away from me a little on the couch.

"What do you have against crackers?" he asked.

"Crackers are fine," I said.

"Great," he said, "so let's just go to the bar."

I was realizing a thing that bothered me. He never discriminated, never compared. Everything was fine with him. Nothing was bad, and even the bad things ended up being all right, and while these might seem like nice traits in a person you hooked up with, they weren't what I wanted in an actual boyfriend. I didn't want him to think every option was just as good as the others. I wanted him to have preferences. I wanted there to be things that rankled him, people he couldn't stand, regrettable ex-girlfriends whose names, merely mentioned, made him shudder. I wanted him to be more particular, darker.

I wanted him to be more like me, I suppose. I always think it'll be easier to navigate a relationship if the guy is like me, but they never are. It's not even a fair request.

"Or instead of crackers, we could eat rice cakes," I said.

He shrugged. "Rice cakes are fine," he said.

"Or maybe some spelt balls," I said. "Dry, dusty balls of baked spelt. Should we have spelt?"

He stared hard at me, finally getting agitated.

"You know I don't know what spelt is," he said.

He waited for me to tell him.

"Is it some kind of wheat?"

Now I noticed that he was on the far end of the bachelor couch, as far from me as he could get.

"I'm sure your friends want to set you up with their friends," I said.

"Why would they set me up with their friends?"

"If something happened to me, they could find someone for you pretty fast," I said.

He hung his head now, because he knew what was happening. This was going to end, and it probably wasn't going to end well. He looked so defeated, and actually kind of sad, but I couldn't tell if it was because he didn't want to go through another breakup, or if it was because he had been looking forward to that drink with friends that he now realized wasn't going to happen.

"You should go and have the drink," I said. "They're waiting for you."

He shook his head and stayed put. He knew the etiquette.

"What do you mean by 'If something happened to me'?" he asked. "What would happen to you?"

"Well," I said, "we're in a civil war."

"You've got odds on your side," he said, "because they already killed my dad, they're not going to kill my girlfriend, too."

"I'm not sure I should be your girlfriend," I said.

He looked at his hands, cracked his knuckles, then looked back up at me.

"I was beginning to think that, too," he said.

We were quiet with each other for a few long, long minutes.

"I'm going to miss you," he said.

"But you'll get over it," I said. "You'll find someone else, and you'll be the same amount happy with her as you are with me."

He nodded, almost imperceptibly, and even looked confused.

"Is that a bad thing?" he asked.

Was it? In the world of evolved, mature, and emotionally resilient people, the answer would have been "No, no, it's not a bad thing, it's a good thing." But the answer, in the world of me, was "Yes." I didn't answer out loud.

"You're a nice person," I said.

"This is a fun relationship, isn't it?"

"It is," I said, "but you don't need me."

"I do need you."

"You don't need *me*," I said. "You may need *someone*, but you don't need *me*."

To his credit, he didn't argue. I don't know why he didn't argue, but if it was because he was tired and fed up—well, who could blame him? He was probably hungry, too, like I was, and I decided to leave quickly so that he could go to the bar.

"You're going to be all right," I said, and I ordered a rideshare on my phone.

He offered to drive me home, but I told him that was too much to ask.

"You really are going to be fine," I said. "Guys like you are always fine."

Ethan snorted.

"Guys like me," he said.

While we waited for the car, I kissed his forehead, sweeping his nice hair out of the way of my lips, and I was only an inch away from backpedaling the whole thing. I wanted to say I was sorry and let's try all over again, because somehow I was just realizing what I had done, that I had botched another thing, and my stomach dropped.

When the car came, I slid in next to the two other people with two stops before mine, and they seemed to be flirting with each other. I couldn't watch. I felt queasy. I looked out the window at Ethan's building, to see if he was headed for the bar, but the car left too quickly.

2

THE PEACEKEEPER

When we'd all grown quite tired of the civil war lived-history prompts, I moved on to questions about our childhoods, which met with varying degrees of enthusiasm. I found that my students were wild to reminisce about their childhoods, but they didn't want to *write* about them. Not nearly as much as they wanted to *talk*. Their thumbs had arthritis, they said, and their wrists hurt.

I let them interview each other, but no one took notes. Then they grew bored listening to each other's stories, because they were so impatient to tell their own.

"It's a zoo in there," I told Ed. "Everybody wants to talk, nobody wants to write."

I had just finished up class and met Ed at Taco Tuesday, which the events coordinator did twice a month. I liked Taco Tuesdays even more than ice cream socials.

"So let them talk amongst themselves," he said. "If they like it, if they take trips down memory lane, consider that a win. You're doing a great job."

"But what about the written product we're supposed to create?" I asked.

"There's more to this job than outcomes and outputs," he said. "Just write your own story, and let them do what they need to do. Don't pay 'em any mind."

We cruised the buffet, scanning all the tin trays perched above tiny burners.

"Black beans again?" he asked.

Being from Texas, Ed had strict feelings about Mexican food and beans. They had to be pinto, and it was better if they were refried, although he'd suffer them whole. Black beans were a deal-breaker.

"I can't do this," he said.

"Okay," I said. "Some rules must be upheld."

Dorothy, one of my students, had silently sidled up to us and was making her own taco, without the taco shell, without sour cream, without cheese, and without beans. Essentially, she'd made a pile on her plate of shredded lettuce on top of rice.

"I think all rules should be broken," Dorothy said. "Otherwise, what's the point? What is art, after all?"

Mildred stuck her cane between us and inserted herself next to me.

"I'm breaking a rule right now, Dorothy," she said. "I'm cutting the line. I guess that makes me an artist."

∗

Question 9: How did you get your name? Did you have a family nickname?

Both my parents were professors of Classics, hence the name Hestia, a goddess from Greek mythology. My mother was a scholar of Stoicism, and my father of the Spartans, and they lived those philosophies as well as they could. They'd both grown up in sad industrial towns past their heydays and somehow managed to emerge from them with advanced degrees and meaningful careers. I suppose they were a testament to the meritocracy that existed in this country, once upon a time, for some people. They wore their class mobility like badges of honor. And no, they never gave me a nickname, because that wasn't their style.

✳

After Ethan, I wanted to get right back on the horse. It was so easy to be single, so easy to be alone, but I knew it wasn't healthy for me. I could make an evening out of ruminating, staring out a window and playing the same scene over and over in my head. I could watch a drippy rom-com every night and never get bored. I was too good at listening to Joni Mitchell albums on repeat while eating cereal for dinner. Where other people might get restless and move past this stage, I would settle in and get comfortable.

Dating was my way of dodging this fate. I met Brandon online, and he piqued my curiosity by making a big deal about being "drama-free" and "eating clean" and exercising his "core." Also, Brandon was the first Black man on the apps to show interest in me, which compelled me to meet him. I'd hearted dozens of nonwhite men, but they never hearted me back. Not that I could blame them. It was hard enough for me, as a white person, to suss out the bad ones from the ones like me, who at least *wanted* to do better. There were clues, but I didn't always guess correctly.

It was a weekend morning in July, and we met up at a

take-out coffee truck on the south side of the harbor, both of us apparently experienced enough to know that for a first date, one cup of coffee is plenty of time. We found a table in Federal Hill Park, which had been a military outpost during the first civil war, and was once again a military outpost, although without the heavy artillery.

The place was lousy with peacekeepers, some of them on patrol and some off duty, hanging out near the tiny outbuilding the UN had erected for them, as they had throughout the city. It was nothing fancy, just a prefab toolshed or cabin painted in a mushroom color with a small UN flag tacked to the door.

Brandon's posture was so perfect that I couldn't help but notice his pecs before anything else. Right away, I got the sense that he was strident. He was wearing one of those American-flag shirts with "L-O-V-E" superimposed on it, to signal that he was true-blue.

At the coffee truck, I ordered with gusto, a huge bagel with cream cheese, and coffee. Brandon only drank coffee, with nothing in it.

"Do you not do dairy?" I asked.

I needed to find out, sooner rather than later, if he was a vegan.

He told me he wasn't a vegan, he was just fasting until noon, which he did every day, with the hope of going into ketosis.

Ketosis? I asked him.

"Well, *mild* ketosis," he said, resting his hand on his core. "Just to keep trim."

"You seem trim to me," I said.

"No one has the luxury of being out of shape these days," he said, touching his core this time with his other hand.

I patted my own core, which was several standard deviations removed from anything that would be considered a "sexy" stomach.

"I figure a little body fat is a good thing, in case of food shortages," I said.

"What an interesting perspective," he said.

"No one has the luxury of being too skinny these days," I said.

At the time, we were about three weeks into a national hunger strike by the Ursuline Sisters. They were protesting America's withdrawal of federal food aid from the confederate states, and while I'd seen some coverage on social media, the strike had been ignored by the television stations. I could've mentioned it to Brandon, showing that I was savvy on current events, but two things I didn't want to talk about were disordered eating and the war.

Instead, I asked him about his hobbies and creative pursuits, which he'd made kind of a big deal about on his profile. While he described them, I noticed that one of the off-duty peacekeepers was checking us out. Specifically, it seemed he was checking *me* out. He was relaxing on a stone bench, almost draped over it, actually, after a night shift, I assumed. He drank espresso out of a tiny ceramic espresso cup, which the coffee stand had invested in because they catered to so many of the UN guards. UN people like espresso, and they like it in ceramic cups, not paper—that was one thing of many that the war had taught me. The peacekeeper had olive skin and wavy hair under his uniform cap, and the gun strapped to his body looked perfectly natural on him.

"I make oboes out of invasive bamboo," Brandon said. "It grows in the alley behind my apartment building, and I feel obligated to make good use of it after I chop it down."

The peacekeeper did that thing where he sipped his espresso but kept his eyes on me. I liked it. Then he got silly. From his bench across the park, he started to mime a little, as if he were taking my hand and escorting me to his stone bench. He was dramatic, but self-deprecating and funny.

He must be Southern European, I thought.

"I'm a weed warrior, too," Brandon said, assuming that I knew what a weed warrior is. I wondered if it was a cannabis thing, but when I learned it was about invasive plants, I was glad I hadn't asked him to explain. It made him so sad, he said, to see English ivy choking out the native trees.

From across the park, the peacekeeper put his hand on his heart, then pointed to me, then crossed his hands over his heart and stuck out his lower lip as if to pout. I wanted to go to him immediately. I wanted to stand up and walk over there without even looking behind me. His display of interest was working.

I interrupted Brandon and put my hand on his arm.

"The truth of the matter," I said, "is that I'm not that interesting."

"We should explore that statement," he said, "because you might be fascinating."

"No, no, no," I said. "You're much more interesting than I am."

"Can you say more about that?" he asked.

"You're too interesting for me," I said.

"You don't even know me."

"That's true," I said. "But I know *me*."

"You seem great," he said.

"You make musical instruments out of bamboo," I said.

"I'm missing your point."

"I like to go to bed early," I said.

"That sounds very grounded."

"I think you want someone who's going to go to protests with you, and join the resistance, and be a badass," I said. "But I like things quiet. I don't like a fuss. I'm not your girl."

"Respectfully, you don't know what I want," he said.

"Let's quit while we're still strangers," I said.

"I beg your pardon?" he asked.

"Because years from now, we can bump into each other randomly, and it won't be awkward."

"Humor me for a moment," he said. "Would it be awkward if we dated for a while and then quit?"

"Yes, it would," I said.

Running into an ex can take such a toll. It can throw off your night, your week. I wanted less of that in my life.

Then he quoted his dating site profile: "I'm looking for someone like-minded and smart to spend quality time with."

"I know, I remember reading that," I said. "But I think you want a fighter, and I'm just a woman who wants to curl up on the couch and watch TV."

"Hestia," he said, "assuming that's your real name. Is that your real name?"

I nodded. He forced the words out of his mouth: "I like TV."

"Do you, though?"

Everything would be decided on how he answered. He took a few seconds to form his response.

"In moderation," he said.

And there it was. My decision was made.

I told him I was setting him free.

"Don't," he said.

"Why not?" I asked.

He paused and looked into his empty cup of zero-calorie coffee and sighed.

"Because you're cute," he said, "and you look soft."

A younger Hestia would have bristled so hard—Soft as in chubby? Soft as in you can bend me to your will?—but I knew men a little better now, and I gave him the benefit of the doubt. He probably wanted someone with a soft heart, and he thought that was me, and he probably hadn't even noticed that my body was slack and squishy and had never been in ketosis. I felt tender toward him, actually, for saying I looked soft, but I knew we would be terrible together.

"I'm soft in the wrong ways," I said.

From the stone bench, the peacekeeper cocked his eyebrow and held out his hands in an empty embrace, gave me an exaggerated frown.

"I really have to go," I said.

I put my garbage in my purse and stood up.

"It was nice to meet you," I said.

"Sure," he said, "I guess."

Poor Brandon. He walked toward the hill with his paper coffee cup crushed between his fingers, and I stood for a few minutes by myself, enjoying the sensation of being alone.

The weather was perfect. The trees in the park had leafed out fully, but nothing was dead yet. Some flowers had bloomed, and others looked like they were getting ready to bloom, and there were no dead petals anywhere. I extended my arms a few inches away from my body and took in a deep breath. Was that a breeze I felt circulating around my arms and hips? Maybe it was. I think I had one of those "You are here now" moments that people talk about, and I liked it. I felt my feet on the cobblestones.

When Brandon reached the bottom of the hill, the peace-keeper walked up to me and did a little bow.

"I am Marcello," he said.

He took my forearm in both of his hands, then slid his hand down to my hand, then brought my hand to his lips. He kissed my hand and let it go, where it landed on my thigh.

"What is your name?"

I told him it was Hestia, and he said, "Estia?"

"Yes," I said, "Hestia."

He tried again: "Estia? Is that it?"

"Perfect," I said.

"I've been watching you from that bench," he said.

"I know."

"There's something about you," he said.

"What do you suppose it is?" I asked.

He looked right into my eyes and said, "I think it's your eyes."

Then he tugged a piece of hair that framed my face.

"You are not dying your hair?"

It didn't sound judgmental, and besides, I only had a few grays.

"I am curious," he said. "Why do you let your hair turn gray?"

"I don't mind the gray," I said.

Also, it wasn't that easy to get hair dye, because of the war and the messed-up supply chains, but I didn't want to get into it.

"I like it," he said.

He was handsy in a way that I didn't mind—I kind of liked it—touching more of my hair, brushing my shoulder with his fingers.

"Are you some kind of hippie?" he asked. "Is that why you let your hair go gray?"

It was so European, the way he pronounced "hippie." Like "eepie."

"Hippie? Please. Hardly," I said.

"Why not?" he asked.

"Hippies are seventy years old," I said.

He traced his finger on my other shoulder. I looked at his finger sharply, and he pulled it away quickly.

"I forgot, I'm supposed to ask," he said.

"That's true," I said.

"I am still getting used to America," he said.

"Okay," I said.

He clasped his hands behind his back, in what looked like an attempt to keep himself from spontaneously touching me. I asked him where he was from, how long he'd been stationed here, and when he was going home. He said Italy; his first tour had begun the day after the Purge; he'd go home next April.

"And what makes you think I'm a hippie?" I asked.

"You look very . . . *natural*," he said.

I scanned the park and tried to see Americans, particularly the American women, the way Marcello saw them. They definitely had "hairstyles," and their shoes were "cute," and they had "thigh gap," and they did a good job wearing makeup.

"Do I look *messy*?" I asked.

He shook his head in a pouty way. "No, no, no," he said.

"But maybe a little?"

"Maybe," he said.

He pulled back and cocked his head, like he'd just had an idea that literally added weight to whatever was inside his skull.

"Have you ever been inside a United Nations courtesy cabin?" he asked.

We both looked at the tiny beige UN shed, and Marcello explained that it was for keepers to stash their changes of clothes, their bagged lunches, or whatnot.

He used a key *and* a code to get inside, which struck me as funny because the shed looked so flimsy that anyone who really wanted to get inside could probably just knock it over. Inside, there was a couch just big enough for someone to sleep on if they had to, a wall of lockers, a couple of folding chairs, and open shelves being used as a pantry.

"Macadamia nuts?" I exclaimed when I saw the tin on the shelf. "But where? How?"

Marcello smiled.

"We're the United Nations," he said.

"Holy shit," I said. "What else do you get?"

He reeled off some items that the war had made too complicated and expensive to import, and each word he spoke felt sexy, forbidden, racy. Olive oil. Prosciutto. Bourbon.

"Bourbon?"

I hadn't been able to get my hands on any bourbon for a while. Kentucky was still part of the Union, but the confederate presence there was strong, and they'd disrupted the bourbon trade out of spite.

"Oh, yes, bourbon," he said.

Facing me, he put his hand on my back and pulled me an inch closer.

"You like bourbon?" he asked.

I nodded, and he kissed me softly on my neck, just below my jawline.

"I can get you bourbon," he said.

He kissed me on the other side of my neck, also just below my jawline.

I wondered if we should sit on the couch and make out, but there was something nice about leaning into his body. He wasn't thin, but he wasn't fat, either. He was solid. I bet he weighed a lot, probably all muscle and bone. He seemed like someone who would have bones made of granite. I bet he drank a lot of milk as a boy. I bet his mother fed him a lot of mozzarella di buffalo, which might be my all-time favorite cheese, so moist, so sharp and creamy.

"Do you want me to get you Kentucky bourbon?" he asked, just before he kissed me on my lips.

"I do," I said, when we took a break from kissing. "I really do."

One thing led to another, and soon we were leaning against the open shelves while he ran his heavy hand over my ass and put his other heavy hand under my shirt. I unlatched my bra, and his kisses trailed down my neck.

I was about to be swept up by the moment, but then I remembered where we were. Anyone with a key and a code could walk in on us.

I pulled away and fastened my bra.

"We shouldn't do this here," I said.

"But . . . somewhere else?" he asked.

I gave him my number, and we made a date for later in the week. He said, "Va bene," and kept his hand on the small of my back.

He walked me to the ride-share that I summoned and watched as I rode away.

✳

Question 10: Where did you grow up?

I spent the first part of my childhood in Hickory, Virginia, emphasis on "hick." Then, when my parents were tenured at a new university, we moved to Dumfries, Virginia, and you can probably guess where the emphasis goes there. It's funny how those two cities can be so close to the nation's capital—less than an hour away—which was lined with embassies from all the countries of the world, and still feel like the sticks. Some days I wished my classmates would try being more worldly, but you know the saying: if wishes were horses, beggars would ride.

✳

I wanted to talk with Mildred about Marcello, but she was disappointed that I didn't have a dating profile to show her. I had showed her Brandon's profile, and now she was miffed that I didn't at least give him a fair shake.

"He had nice pectorals," she said. "My second husband had nice pectorals, and it was always so nice to look at him with his shirt off. You want a man who looks good with his shirt off."

"I don't know, Mildred," I said. "It's just a muscle group."

"Don't knock it till you've tried it," she said.

We were in the far end of the therapy garden, hiding out while the events coordinator ran a rug-hooking class indoors.

"I don't want to have anything to do with rug-hooking," Mildred said.

I'd just helped her stock up on cigarettes; the village employees wouldn't buy them for her. Ever since the war began, options had become complicated. You could buy expensive brands from Europe, made with tobacco from India, or you could buy Indian brands from India, which were a little cheaper and not as good, or you could get black-market cigarettes from the confederacy. "I'm not smoking any damn traitor cigarettes," Mildred said.

She leaned back in her chaise longue, and I presented her ashtray and Gauloises. I struck a match. But she blew it out and retrieved a lighter from one of her pockets. It was yellow gold, and she flipped it open and lit it with one hand.

"Deft," I said.

"Solid gold, baby," she said. "I bought it after my first husband died, to help me move on."

Was she trying to give me a hint about moving on? She took a long drag on her cigarette with her eyes closed, like she was remembering something good. Then she clutched the owl's head on her cane, which lay next to her, and moaned.

"Mildred?" I asked. "Are you all right?"

"Just living in the past for a minute, darling, thinking about pectorals," she said. "I know the best parts of the past to visit."

She said she liked that I was trying to date—but she didn't like that Marcello had been so forward, that he'd taken such liberties in the courtesy cabin.

"He unhooked your bra," she said. "And this wasn't even a date."

"No, Mildred," I said, "I unhooked my bra."

She waved her finger around in a circle in the air. "Whatever, whatever, whatever," she said.

"I didn't mind," I said. "I mean, I liked it."

"That's irrelevant," she said. "You're too passive."

"His hands were really nice," I said.

"You're too passive," she said.

"But it was fun and sexy."

"You're too passive."

"You've said that, like, three times already," I said.

"Don't try to make this about my dementia," she said. "You're making me a broken record, kid, and it's ticking me off."

"You don't have dementia," I said.

"How would you know?" she asked.

"Your mind is a steel trap," I said.

"Maybe you have dementia, too," she said, "which is why you can't remember if I have dementia."

I was about to bite back but something she said hooked me. Maybe I *did* have dementia. After all, I could barely remember anything about my childhood. The memories were so foggy. Same with my twenties—who was I, and what did I want? What did I do with all my time?—and it was even starting to be like that with my thirties. I remembered so little about how it all *felt*.

"You don't have dementia," I said, and she took another long drag of her cigarette.

"You don't either," she said. "You remembered to get me the 100s, and you remembered to get me the menthol."

She offered me a drag, which I declined.

"It'll burn through the cobwebs," she said, like a drug dealer.

"I think it's the nicotine that's keeping you so sharp," I said.

She made a sound like "pffft," and then lit a new cigarette on her old one, which she crushed into the ashtray I'd brought from my lower desk drawer. Chain-smoking was her daily delight: she knew she had limited smoking hours in the day, so she went for broke when she had the chance.

"Promise me you'll get a picture of this Marcello so you can show me," she said. "The next time he gropes you."

"It's not groping if it's consensual," I said.

"Po-tay-to, po-tah-to," she said.

✳

Question 11: Where were your ancestors from?

My real ancestors? I have no earthly idea. My parents met late in life, on the outer edge of my mother's reproductive years. It's a wonder they managed to come together at all, but that's a story for another day. They couldn't conceive the old-fashioned way, so they tried all the other ways. When that failed, my mother gave up on her own genes, and they searched for an egg donor by placing ads in the most elite college newspapers— above all, they wanted their child to be smart. Then they had to give up on my father's DNA, and they found a sperm donor the same way, with the same emphasis on engineering a highly intelligent offspring. My genetic package was put together for massive IQ. I was the embryo of their dreams.

✳

Sometimes guys don't know when to say good night, which is why I prefer that the first few dates end up at their homes instead of mine. That way, I can decide when the night's over. That's not a knock against the guys who want to stay, or *think* they should stay, and if I were the kind of person who could come out and say, "Hey, you should probably go home now," that would be better for everyone, but that might lead to talking about feelings I haven't processed yet, and I'm not good at that. Long story short: there are some postcoital hours that I enjoy more when I'm alone, and I'm no good at kicking people out.

But Marcello was living in barracks, so going to his home wasn't an option. Instead, he came to my apartment. We had texted about meeting somewhere, but then he offered to bring over dinner foods, including prosciutto. I thought he was being romantic, but I learned later that he didn't exactly feel safe eating in public. "Too many nutters," he said, using a word he'd picked up from the British guy who slept in the bunk above him.

There wasn't much to clean up—I keep a tidy home, which is in contrast to how I keep my person. Mildred said I kept a tidy life—"Too tidy." I didn't live with any cats, or even put out food for neighborhood ferals. I tidied up my herb garden on the back balcony and clipped some Italian parsley for dinner. I chewed some spearmint for my breath.

I buzzed in Marcello and stood in front of my door watching him ascend the stairs. My apartment was the third floor of a narrow row house, one bedroom with a smaller "study," one bathroom, a small kitchen. It was perfect for one person and decent for two. When Marcello reached my door, he immediately leaned in, pulled my face toward him, and kissed me on the lips.

"You look lovely, Estia," he said.

For a few minutes, we kissed on the threshold, and I invited him in.

He placed a bag on the counter and withdrew from it, one item at a time with great flourish, bread, cheese, and prosciutto. The last thing he pulled out was a bottle of Kentucky bourbon.

"This I found special for you, Estia," he said.

He placed the bottle in the center of the charcuterie.

There was no reason to hide how delighted I was. I felt like I was being spoiled.

I took out two glasses and poured. We drank it neat because it's easier than worrying about ice and whether the tap water is reliable.

Midway through the first glass, he scanned my apartment from his seat, nodding every few seconds.

"It's very nice here," he said. "It's like . . . Pottery Barn?"

He meant it as a compliment.

"You have these long pillows," he said, pointing to my couch.

"You have artistic colors," he said, sweeping his hands to indicate my walls.

"Everything is clean," he said.

"Yes," I said. "Thank you."

"May I pour you another?" he asked, and I told him to wait.

He was a good ten years younger than me, maybe more, and still drank like a young person.

"We need to take a picture of this beautiful spread," I said, and I held up the phone to capture not only the food, but also us, the two of us leaning our heads into each other, Marcello grinning ear to ear.

I knew Mildred would want to see more than just his face, so I made him pose by the counter with the food and took a longer shot of his body. In every shot, he was grinning, shoulders back, looking like he was ready for whatever came his way.

We drank more bourbon and ate that delicious food, and it was a late afternoon of sensory delight that turned into a summer evening of sensory delight. We had sex that I'd call vigorous, and only a little sloppy from the bourbon. I was right about his heavy hands—they were exactly what I wanted, and I loved the way he held me to him with the perfect amount of pull and pressure. At some point, he politely asked if we could do something "a little different," and when I ignored him, he didn't ask again. All in all, it was a good time, and despite my air conditioner, tiny beads of sweat broke out on his forehead.

"Do you always work that hard in bed?" I asked when we were finished and splayed on top of the covers.

"Was that work?" he asked.

A few seconds later, he asked me if I would massage his shoulders, and I said yes. He rolled over onto his stomach and lay waiting. While I massaged, he moaned in pleasure—the most profound moans by far that day—and told me I was amazing, incredible, the best masseuse he'd ever had. I'm good at massages. I go hard.

"With your skills, 'ow are you still single?" he asked, after a sigh and a groan.

I told him that was a story we could save for later, and he returned the favor of a massage, although he wasn't as good as I was.

Then I realized it was dark—sometimes in the summer you think you have all the time in the world before sunset, and then suddenly it's dark—and I became anxious because of curfew. If he got stuck at my apartment, would that be awkward? I tamped down an instinct to check my Conflicted app.

"It's dark," I said, trying not to sound panicked.

He stroked my collarbone and kissed the palm of my hand.

"Do not worry," he said. "I am above the curfew. I can leave anytime, if you want me to."

I suppose my relief was visible.

"Do you want me to leave?" he asked.

I was trying to think of a nice way to say yes, when he kissed the palm of my hand again, suggested that we lie there for a few more minutes, and then he'd leave.

"I must return to the barracks anyway," he said. "For the 'ead count."

When he left, about half an hour later, he said that he was very glad I'd enjoyed the bourbon. He kissed my fingertips in the doorway.

"Your fingers are magic," he said, and we made a plan for the next date.

✳

Question 12: Can you share a memory of your mother?

My mother told me that she loved, just loved my baby years. "You were so sweet, and so cuddly," she said. "You followed me around all the time. You hung on my every word." She even swooned a little when she reminisced. She crowed over my baby years: on line at the grocery store, in the pediatrician's office, at the hair salon where she finally, after a yearslong campaign on my part, agreed to pay a stylist instead of doing it herself. "Loved her baby years," she'd say, all dreamy, to the cashier. One time she followed up with, "And then, around age two, she learned to say no." She shook her head and said to the cashier, "And that was the end of that." Considering the lengths they went to, at their ages, to become parents, I'm surprised they didn't cherish the whole parenthood thing more than they did. Some people enjoy their children. But to be fair, people become parents for all sorts of reasons, and mine weren't in it for the adventure, or the personal growth journey, or maybe it wasn't their path. I guess they hadn't factored in the possibility that their child would be so contrary.

✳

Ed was old-school; he read the newspaper in print and bought a copy every morning with his coffee. Every now and then he'd stop by my office and place his newspaper on my portion of the desk, folded to something he wanted me to read. Usually, it was an obituary.

We both loved a well-written obituary. The good ones grounded a person's life in their time and place, so their stories had context. "What were they up against?" seemed to be the central question that a good obit answered. "How did they do something meaningful?" was another. In a good obit, time was relative, too: there might be five paragraphs devoted to one short but especially interesting period in the deceased's life, while several boring decades were collapsed into a few sentences. And the best part about an obituary is that you always get to know how the story ends. Birth to death. It's the ultimate satisfying story. Ed was the only other person I knew who felt that way.

Come to think about it, obits are the opposite of dating profiles, which tell you nothing. They're all lede, no resolution.

In the retirement village, obits were a constant source of frustration for us. Most of them were written by the deceased's children, who, it turned out, had narrow perspectives on their parents' lives. It's not their fault, and some of them were good writers. It's just—of course a child would center her parent's life as a parent. You can't expect them to do *research*, not like the professionals, while they mourn.

On the morning after my first date with Marcello, Ed dropped a folded newspaper on my desk and said, "Looks like the Ursulines have finally made the news."

One of the sisters on hunger strike had died.

"That's awful," I said.

"She had some preexisting conditions," said Ed.

"You look upset," I said.

He rolled his eyes toward the ceiling. "Me and the sisters go way back," he said.

"You're a Catholic school kid?"

"I'm a Buddhist these days," he said. "It's more peaceful that way. But there were a couple of real nice nuns in my life."

He promised to bring me the Ursuline's obit when it was printed.

Then he brought up a topic that we'd been over a couple times already. He thought I should offer to write obituaries for the villagers who died. And I always declined, because I thought it would be way too sad.

"It's your choice," he said. "I'm just saying—you have a gift."

※

For our next date, Marcello came over with dried porcini mushrooms and another bottle of Kentucky bourbon, a different brand, one I'd never even seen.

"Marcello," I said, "this is too much."

"Not for you, Estia," he said.

I wanted to ask him if this was how he always rolled, something like, "Do you bring every woman you date extravagant gifts, or is it something about me?" Even though I'd learned over the years that men have standard operating procedures, I wanted to believe that every now and then, one would deviate for me. But I decided not to poke the bear.

We made polenta with a porcini gravy—delicious—and we drank some and laughed some, and we had sex, in which he worked very hard again, and asked again, politely, if we could do "something different." Again, I ignored the question, or I *pretended* to ignore the question, because it was the kind of request that puts a woman in an impossible situation. If I asked him what he meant, specifically, by "different," and he told me, I had two choices: I could either be the cool girl who was down for whatever, or I could be the prude who said I'd rather not. I wasn't crazy about either option, so I let the question dangle.

He moved on, and asked me to massage his shoulders, groaning just like the first time. I started to wonder which he loved more, the sex or the massage.

Taking our time, little by little, we put our clothes back on, but truthfully it was quite nice to lie in bed with him naked. Usually I went for skinny guys, but his bulk and muscles, and the sheer heat of him, were alluring. I've read that men are warmer than women because of muscle mass, and Marcello was proving the rule. Not that I needed any extra heat in July, but it was a comfort nonetheless.

He told me about his childhood. He grew up in a tall, narrow house in a small city in Italy with a brother, parents, grandparents, occasionally an uncle who moved in and out depending on his employment status. He was raised by dozens of people, mostly his grandparents and their friends, busybodies who had no shame about interfering. One piazza was the center of his world, a statue of Garibaldi in the center, and he reminisced about the daily passeggiata, how the men and women walked around the piazza, the men in one group, circling Garibaldi, the women in another group. I pictured an atom: Garibaldi was the proton, the men and women its electrons.

I was an only child, I told him, born to older parents, late bloomers who found each other in the nick of time.

"I spent my childhood with old people," I said.

"I did also," said Marcello.

I told him about the summers the three of us spent in the RV, camping in a series of trailer parks at various beaches, with older people and retirees who were doing the same. Those fellow campers became our extended family, sort of, people we saw every summer in the trailer parks, and I was usually the only child there. In the late afternoons, someone would open up a folding table on an outdoor rug on top of the sand, and roll out an awning for shade, and the grown-ups drank gin and played gin rummy. For hours, they played cards and drank, getting louder as the evening progressed. Sometimes I watched, sometimes I played with them, but it grew dull for me. Naturally, I wasn't allowed to drink gin, and I walked up and down the beaches while they had their rummy. When their laughter became so loud I could hear it over the surf, I knew it was time to come home, that we'd all be going to sleep soon.

"That is lonely, yes?" said Marcello.

"I don't remember if I was lonely," I said.

"Estia, you do not remember if you were lonely?"

It was a good question, a question I've asked myself often.

"I didn't have anything to compare it to," I said. "How could I have known?"

I was dressed by now, pulling on a pair of shorts as we moved from the bedroom to the kitchen. His shirt was still off, and he asked me if I would squeeze the muscles that ran from his neck to his shoulders, just one more time.

"Your childhood story is so sad," he said.

I massaged his shoulders, then ate a few spoonfuls of polenta and gravy.

"Do your parents have the Err-Vee still?" he asked.

I told him they had sold the RV and moved to the New Confederate States of America. He was flabbergasted.

"They move away to a different country from you?" he asked.

I told him it had been a couple months since we'd talked, and he said, "Even social media?" I told him they didn't do social media. "'It's a toxic smorgasbord for pathetic attention-seekers,'" I said, quoting my mother.

What I'd told him was unthinkable, apparently. He wanted to know how it could possibly have happened, and I quoted my father: "'We've had it up to here with the elites telling us how to think. We have doctorates. We know how to think.'"

They thought I had been brainwashed, and I thought *they* had been brainwashed.

"And that's it?" Marcello asked.

"It's been brewing for years."

"But, in the end, your parents leave you?" he asked. "Over a war?"

"Yes," I said.

"That's very sad," he said.

"Yes," I said.

"That's worse than if they died," he said.

"Quite a bit worse," I said.

"Or even if they had Alzheimer's, that would be so much better," he said.

"It would."

"That's the worst thing I ever heard," he said.

This made me laugh out loud.

"If that's the worst thing you've ever heard," I said, "then you don't know much about America."

"This is true," he said. "I don't know about America. I'm just a soldier."

I ate another spoonful of polenta and gravy—so good—and he asked about my husband. Apparently, I'd mentioned that, at some point, I'd been married.

"Are you going to get divorced?" he asked.

"I don't know," I said. "Probably."

"How long has it been?"

I tallied up the months and told him it had been fifteen months. He clicked his tongue and shook his head a little.

"But do you still love him, Estia?"

"Oh, goddess, no!" I said, and I meant it.

"I don't understand," he said. "But I'm not that smart."

I told him that smart was overrated and put the newer bottle of bourbon back on the table with clean glasses. We drank a little more and fooled around a little more. He was one of those men who aimed to please. This time, I massaged his back without letting him ask first. It was growing on me, the way he moaned when I massaged him.

When it was time for him to return to the barracks, and he was putting on his shirt, we stood in the doorway and said good night. He exhaled deeply, as if blowing cigarette smoke into the hallway.

"Life is funny," he said.

"Is it?" I asked. "Or is it a joke?"

"Oh, it's definitely a joke," he said.

"Thought so," I said.

"But Italians 'ave always known this," said Marcello. "There's no question."

✳

Question 13: Can you share a memory of your father?

In middle school, there was a girl who I thought was the biggest idiot I'd ever known, and one day I was put in a four-person group project with her. She came up with all these fun, crazy ideas—balloons! glitter!—that everybody loved, and I was the one who had to say, "No, we can't do that, it's not possible." But did everyone ignore me and instead hang on that girl's every word? Yes, they did. When it came time to do the work, she choked. "I have no idea how to do this!" she said, pitiful, but laughing and fluttering her eyelashes. I was done with her—but the two boys in the group came running to her rescue. They did all of her share of the work, never became angry with her. The project sucked, and we got a C. "She's useless," I said to my father as I described the whole affair. "Why do those boys like her so much?" My father said that most males of the species find a damsel in distress irresistible. "Men worry that they're weak," he said, "and a woman who needs help makes them feel strong." I asked him if boys would like me if I pretended to be helpless. "Oh, come on, Hestia, you'll never be able to fake that," he said. "One thing is certain: No man will ever have to worry about you."

✳

"Why in the shade, Hestia?" asked Mildred. "You know I like the sun."

I pulled a little table next to her chair and placed her ashtray and pack of cigarettes within reach. She flipped open her yellow-gold lighter.

"I don't think we need to worry about me dying of skin cancer," she said.

"The reason we're in the shade is so I can show you photos," I said.

"Are we sending more 'Dear man' letters today?" she asked.

The day before, we'd spent my lunch break on the dating site calling out all the men who used the word "female" in their profiles. It was a foregone conclusion that I'd never date a man who referred to women as "females," so I had nothing to lose. Mildred and I crafted a pointed note and sent it to each of them: "Dear man, The preferred term is 'woman,' not 'female,' unless you're conducting a biology experiment with some species such as mice or fruit flies."

One man wrote back and said, "Oh your so high and mighty, Dating is a biology experiment dont you know that."

Another man wrote back and said, "I don't care about Biology, all I care about is Chemistry."

I told Mildred that we were not going to write more "Dear man" letters, but that I was going to show her pictures of Marcello. She was very excited about that.

With only a few pictures to show, she grew impatient.

"He's very handsome from the neck up," she said, "but I can't see what he's like under the clothing."

"There's a full-body shot right there," I said, pointing to the screen.

"But his chest," she said. "Tell me about his chest. How hairy is it?"

I told her it was smooth, and she scoffed.

"Smooth," she said. "That's not normal. A man's chest needs hair."

"There's nothing wrong with his chest," I said.

✳

After Mildred's smoke, Sarah and I sat kitty-corner from each other at our dumb L-shaped desk. We were preparing for a meeting to discuss brochure copy for the retirement village. At that job, I spent many hours writing brochures, composing and mailing monthly newsletters to family members, removing family members from the mailing list after people died, updating the website with photos of new villagers and removing the photos of deceased villagers, and crafting the ads we occasionally placed in the newspapers and online.

Sometimes Sarah drafted copy, which I edited, and sometimes I did all the writing, while she managed the mailing lists and website. It was mind-boggling, how many hours of a person's life it took to manage a mailing list. Naturally, it was important that we got it right when it came to taking down photos of dead villagers, and I always asked Sarah to double-check me on those decisions, because she knew almost all of them personally.

On this particular afternoon, some of the village's investors were going to be there, touring, which precipitated a fire drill for me and Sarah. The investors liked to "pop in" on meetings so they could feel like they had a hand in the operations, and we had to present as a high-functioning team. We had to sell the village as a haven.

But Sarah was distracted. She couldn't focus on our subscriber list or attend to newsletter subject lines. She'd been opening up to me about her boyfriend, the environmental activist, and apparently things were going very well.

"My parents met him this weekend," she said.

It was the first time she'd mentioned her parents, an unprecedented intimacy. It took me by surprise. I'd been careful not to mention mine, as I didn't want to have to explain that they'd moved to the confederacy.

"Do they love him?" I asked.

"They like him," she said.

"That's good, though," I said.

"They love that he's an engineer, but they don't love that he's an activist," she said. "They don't get the whole salmon thing."

She looked at me in a way that made me feel as if she were expecting something. Could she possibly be looking for advice? From me?

"The most important thing is how *you* feel about him," I said. "Right?"

"Do you really think so?" she asked.

She had that expectant face again, like she was looking for something from me. I wanted to advise her not to take advice from me.

"Sarah," I said, "I'm in my forties, but I'm no elder."

"But you know a lot about dating," she said.

"I promise you," I said, "I'm clueless."

She looked down at her left hand, where an engagement ring might go. She rubbed her temples and shook her head.

"It's a pretty crappy world and everything," she said, "but I still want what everyone wants."

What did everyone want? I was desperate for her to elaborate, but she did not. In my imagination, she wanted a pretty house with pretty gardens, good for entertaining friends and raising children. Maybe she wanted a she-shed where she could do her scrapbooking, or maybe she only wanted matching monogrammed towels. My sense was that people as put-together as Sarah could have anything they wanted.

"Parents don't know everything," I said.

She nodded.

"They just moved here from Charleston," she said. "Last year, during the Purge, their church was bombed, and they put their house on the market the next day."

We were still at our desk, and I wanted to reach over and hold her hand. But I didn't know if that would be all right.

"I'm so sorry," I said.

"Lots of people are," she said.

"I just want to hug you," I said.

"Let's not," she said.

I was nervous she'd ask about my parents, so I brought us back around to the boyfriend.

"I'm sure your boyfriend is great, but dating is hard," I said. "And this war makes it harder."

"You have no idea," she said, the truth of which smacked me.

I tried to be positive: Someday the war will end, I told her.

"But what if the problem isn't the war?" she asked. "What if it's America?"

✳

During the meeting, Sarah kept talking out of turn, even interrupting me a few times. Worse, she interrupted Ed, who was nearly forty years her senior and knew his way around a meeting with investors. In earlier conversations, she'd told me that it was the responsibility of women of her generation to lean in at the workplace and speak up.

She rolled her eyes every time Ed started talking.

"I think we should make it clear in the brochure what our political affiliation is," she said.

"The brochure says 'We're on the left side of history,'" said Ed.

"I think we could do more," said Sarah.

"Sarah, our residents are in their eighties and nineties," said Ed. "They want to know if the staff is nice, and whether the pool is heated. I'm not sure all of them care about politics."

"That's ageist," she said.

Ed did not roll his eyes.

"I think our prospective clients will be attracted to a staunch community of unionists who believe in progress for all peoples," said Sarah.

"I understand where you're coming from," I said to Sarah, "but I think Ed's right. First and foremost, these people want to know if there are seats in the shower."

"You're being ableist," she said.

"Say more about that," said Ed.

"We have a responsibility, a moral obligation, to take a stand on what's happening to democracy and uplift our own voices to make our stance clear," she said.

"I'm pretty sure," said Ed, sounding weary, "that no one wants to hear our voices."

He looked over at the investors and gestured, as if to say, What a lark!

"We have to speak truth to power," said Sarah.

I breathed deeply.

"But when a retirement village speaks truth to power," I asked, "does anyone listen?"

Ed said, "People grow old, they want to age in the care of kind people, in relative comfort. That's what they're thinking about."

"You're wrong," said Sarah.

I hated when she spoke to him like that. It was uncivil. Being confident is one thing, but being rude is another.

"Let's take it down a notch," I said.

"Oh, are we up a notch?" she asked.

"Yes, we are," I said.

"I think we should offer a lecture series for the residents," she said. "We can call it the Red Emma Conversations, after Emma Goldman. I already know which texts we'll start with."

"You want to lead a *lecture series*?" Ed asked. "The residents will be reading *texts*?"

Ed and I both looked at the investors to gauge how they were receiving Sarah's idea. But both were straight men, and they were under the spell of Sarah's youth and beauty. From my vantage point, a reading series with seminal texts was going to turn off residents who just wanted to goof off in their remaining years—but the investors were bewitched.

I was annoyed, and my ego was bruised because the investors weren't paying any attention to me or Ed. I looked to him for camaraderie in my irritation, but he only shrugged and smiled.

"Hey, how about we green-light the Red Emma lecture series?" he said. "Let's give it a whirl."

After the meeting, at the end of the day, he dropped off a

slender volume of Buddhist teachings for me, with a note that said, "Report back if you discover any noble truths."

✳

The next morning, I told Mildred about the meeting and how Sarah had behaved.

"She has no respect," I said.

"Damn," said Mildred, "listen to you."

"I know, I sound like 'the Man.'"

"But young people do have different ideas about respect," said Mildred.

"It's not fair," I said. "When *she's* a jerk, it makes *me* feel like a jerk."

Mildred rolled her eyes.

"Young people can be insufferable," she said.

"Right?"

"But she'll learn," said Mildred. "Time never stops teaching."

"She's champing at the bit for all of us to retire," I said.

"Well, then the joke may be on her," said Mildred.

The war was expensive, and some pundits were predicting that our national coffers would be depleted by it, depending on how long it lasted. At the retirement village, rumors flew among the residents: if money was running out, would social security be discontinued? Medicare? Other pundits tallied up the federal funds we were saving now that we were no longer bailing out the "taker" states, most of which had seceded. If we could stop spending so much money on the war, they suggested, we could make good on our intention to expand the social safety nets.

"Dear goddess," I said to the ceiling. "Please don't let them be the last generation to enjoy their golden years."

✳

Every Tuesday and Thursday, the Tai Chi instructor came, and I developed a habit of listening in when I walked past his classroom. Sometimes he'd teach about the dan tien, and how our qi was centered there. Sometimes he talked about yin and yang, and how the work of Tai Chi was to put your yang in the yang place so your yin could find its yin place. From what I knew about yin and yang, I wasn't sure I had enough yang to put anywhere. Or maybe I did, and maybe he was right about it being in the wrong places.

After class, his routine was to invite everyone to join him in the Café for a cup of tea. It was my understanding that he brewed different loose leaves every time, never using a bag, although I never heard him go so far as to use the word "artisanal." One morning Sarah and I were making coffee from pods when he brought in Clara, the lone student who wanted his tea.

"This is a tea I imported from China, before the war," he told Clara.

I was surprised by how chatty he was with her. Clara inspected him.

"Are you Chinese, then?" she asked.

He was bewildered by the question. Sarah and I caught each other's eye and stifled a laugh.

"No," he said. "I'm not Chinese. I'm just a white guy with a British mom who loves tea."

"So, your mother isn't Chinese, either?" Clara asked.

He shook his head. "Just British," he said. "I get my love of tea from her."

Clara cooed over the smell of the tea, how it reminded her of her time in the ashram, all those decades ago.

"My daughter's at the same ashram now," she said.

"Well, this isn't from India," he said, "this is from China."

Sarah leaned past him and put her coffee mug in the brewing machine.

"We'll be out of your way in two minutes," she said.

The instructor forced a smile and nodded his head and looked at the floor, tucking a strand of his hair behind his ear. Then he took equipment out of his backpack and put it on the counter, as if he were setting up for a lab experiment, being very careful not to do anything that would make Sarah feel like he was encroaching on her space. He boiled water in the kettle and prepared the glass teapot and filled the infuser with what looked like a precise amount of leaves.

"This is a special blend from the north of China, the Fujian province," he told Clara, barely above a whisper now, noticeably nervous. "It's a black tea, and it makes a lightly sweet, 'round' cup."

"That sounds lovely, sweetheart," said Clara. "What's it called?"

"It's Golden Monkey tea," he said.

"Speak up," she said.

This time he spoke a bit more loudly than necessary.

"Golden Monkey tea," he said, almost yelling.

Modulating his voice to be lower again, he said, "Because the tips of the leaves are golden."

Sarah had fixed her eyes on him and wouldn't drop her gaze. It seemed as if she were testing her powers. Her experiment was to see how uncomfortable she could make him. He turned to look at me, searching for an audience that wasn't so overpowering.

"It's highly prized," he whispered.

When our coffee was ready, Sarah and I added half-and-half, and I asked the instructor if I should leave it out for him.

"We don't use cream in this tea," he said quickly. "Or lemon, or sugar, or any product that would dilute the flavor."

He was looking at my chest, and he forced his eyes up to my face.

"We don't use any of that stuff," he said. "My teas are very fine."

Sarah baited him.

"Have you ever been in a band?" she asked.

It's a tried-and-true question for getting guys to open up, and he leaped at the opportunity. His face changed, as if he were suddenly comfortable for the first time.

"I played guitar in a punk band for a few years," he said, beaming at her.

"Punk?" asked Sarah. "Like Sid-and-Nancy punk?"

"Well, maybe not quite punk," he said.

He was looking into her eyes for what I think may have been the first time.

"No?" asked Sarah. "What was it then?"

I felt a little bad spectating. But he didn't know that Sarah was amusing herself with him and he probably never would, so perhaps there was no harm being done.

"It was probably more like emo," he said.

"Now that's funny," I said.

The sound of my voice snapped him out of his Sarah-trance. He turned toward me and cocked his head.

"Why?" he asked, genuinely confused.

"I'm trying to picture the outfits," I said.

"Oh, yeah," he said. "I'll show you sometime."

After he took a few sips of tea, he turned to me again.

"You remind me of an ex-girlfriend," he said.

I curled my lip and blurted, "Gross."

"What?" he asked.

"Why would you say that?" I asked. "Were you raised by wolves?"

"No," he said, answering the question earnestly. "I was raised by my mom."

"She should have taught you not to compare women to exes," I said.

"But she's a great mom," he said. "She's one of my best friends."

"Oh," I said, trying to convey in that one word that I was both sorry and envious.

✴

Back at our shared desk, I found Sarah reading her Conflicted alerts. The confederacy was running a campaign to malign electric cars, because states like Texas, Arkansas, Oklahoma, and Louisiana needed everyone buying gasoline, and lots of it. "Your country needs *you* to know," said the announcer in the commercial, "that God loves a car that runs on gas."

She closed her eyes and held her fingers in a mudra while she inhaled deeply.

I asked her if something was wrong, and her voice quavered as she told me that her boyfriend had headed out to Washington state to blow up some dams.

"You're kidding," I said, sitting down across from her. "He's actually doing it?"

"I didn't think he'd really do it," she said, her voice nearly breaking. "I thought it was just talk."

"You have to dump him," I said.

"It gets worse," she said.

She chewed on the side of her finger. I waited.

"Remember that he's doing it for the salmon," she said. "But he infiltrated a group—"

"—what kind of group?" I interjected.

"They're going out West to blow up dams so they can screw up the energy grid. If they can make the server warehouses go down, they can screw up the internet."

"Is it a confederate group?" I asked.

"I think so," said Sarah, "but he's not a confederate."

"Right," I said, "because he's blowing up dams for the salmon."

"Salmon are very sacred," she said.

I'd never seen her so nervous. She'd always looked calm and cool, composed. I made her show me her fingernails, which were bleeding, and I held her fingertips in my hands.

I told her she seemed anxious.

"Maybe a little," she said.

"You're dating a confederate sympathizer," I said.

"He's not a confederate sympathizer," she said.

She sipped her coffee, but it was cold, and she didn't want it anymore.

"Ugh," she said.

She stirred it with a pencil and said, "*My teas are very fine.*"

"Come on," I said. "He seems like a nice person."

"He's okay," she said.

"He told me his name is Tom," I said. "He said he was really glad to meet me."

"Monkey Tea Tom," she said.

I didn't like that nickname for him, but once she had christened him, it stuck.

"I'm sure he *is* very glad to meet you," Sarah said.

✳

For our next date, Marcello didn't text to ask what he could bring me. He just showed up with four gallon-jugs of water. I remembered that at some point I had complained to him about how I hated to buy bottled water, which I did out of fear of the reservoirs being poisoned again. This was his offering.

A gallon of water weighs eight pounds, which means he was carrying thirty-two pounds in four jugs with only two hands. I was impressed and grateful.

He'd invited me to a United Nations party, but here's the best part: instead of just meeting me there, which is what so many men would have suggested, he came to my apartment to pick me up, so we could go to the party together. I loved that.

When he knocked on my door, not only was he bearing water jugs, he also came with three ceramic bowls in his backpack. For me. "For cooking gnocchi," he said, "if you want to." The best way to prepare gnocchi, he insisted, was to bake it, like lasagna or ziti.

The ceramic bowls were wide and deep, in three different sizes, and they were beautiful. They looked like they might be handmade. They had ceramic handles. One was red, one was blue, one was green, the loveliest Mediterranean shades of each color. I adored them instantly. If things with Marcello don't work out, I thought, I want to keep these bowls forever. Breakups don't necessitate returning gifts of cookware, thank goddess.

UN peacekeepers know how to party. They start late,

after the curfew, and go deep into the night. They change into their civilian clothes, they bring women who dress up. For this party, they'd rented the Shot Tower, formerly a shotgun-pellet production site and now an event venue, and made it beautiful. They decorated it with yards and yards of fairy lights, with a fog machine in one of the corners, with votives everywhere. Not what I was expecting from a unit of soldiers. But these were *European* soldiers, so.

I felt like I was part of a secret, special underground club, but compared to the other soldiers' dates, I was shabby. I was the Cinderella of the ball *before* the birds and mice transformed her. But it was fine: Marcello was having fun, introducing me to everyone, drinking heavily, eating more than I could ever imagine eating, speaking loudly but miraculously without slurring.

It was weird to be out so late, after curfew. It had been a year and a half since the war began, and it occurred to me that there were billions of people living like this in the world. Millions of people partying until dawn. I'd done that, too, a long time ago, and was it the war that made me stop, or had I stopped before the war? When you're married and comfortable, is there any point in staying up so late?

It was at this party that I realized Marcello flirts with beautiful women as if it's an extreme sport. The goal didn't seem to be conquests—I think the flirtation was the point. It was fine. I didn't want to watch him do his sport, though, any more than I would want to watch if his sport were wild game–hunting. I roamed and observed, and let me say this: European men can dance. They understand things about the hips that have been lost to most of us in North America.

More roaming, and I found another room, and in this one there wasn't so much dancing as there were men playing guitar. Silly me. I had thought that man-playing-guitar-at-party was an American phenomenon. They played Bob Dylan and Beatles songs and sang with their sexy accents, French, Italian, Spanish. An Irish soldier did an Oasis song. One of the soldiers—Italian, I think—had brought an accordion, and he found a way to play along.

After the party, Marcello brought me home, and while I was fairly sober, he was drunker than Cooter Brown. All the flirting had revved him up, too—our fumbling had extra energy and urgency, and we had sex against my kitchen wall, or we tried to. The difference in our heights made that difficult, but we did our best. Afterward, as we leaned against each other, I ran my hand down his chest, to feel how smooth it was. This time I felt stubble.

"Do you shave your chest?" I asked.

He walked into the living room, toward a mirror, and looked over his bare-chested self. He flexed for the mirror and smiled approvingly.

"Of course," he said.

He flexed again for the mirror, in a different way, and again smiled approvingly.

He put some pants on—left the chest bare—and rummaged through my refrigerator. I couldn't believe he was hungry after eating so much at the party. Maybe he was bored, though. Sometimes boredom masquerades as hunger. He was one of those men who eats several thousand calories a day, and burns several thousand calories a day. His body was a well-oiled, high-powered machine, always running, always needing fuel.

"I can stay over tonight," he said. "I have permission."

As we lay down together, I wondered if he would ask me to massage his shoulders, as he usually did after sex.

"Oh, Estia," he said when his head hit the pillow, "my shoulders . . ."

A couple of times during the night I had to roll him onto his side, which took care of the light snoring. It wasn't bad snoring. If this was the worst his snoring ever got, it was no problem at all.

✳

The next morning, he asked me for my birth date, time, and year, and where I was born. My first thought was that I'd been had. Obviously, Marcello was a scammer and now he was trying to steal my identity. When I hesitated, he showed me the text thread with his mother, which I couldn't understand because it was in Italian.

"My mother wants to do your chart," he said. "She's into astrology."

Astrology had always struck me as a refuge for lonely women, but I couldn't imagine his mother, surrounded by so much family, could ever be lonely. I decided to learn more about it. Then I realized that Marcello had told his mother about me, and I was flattered. How nice this was—I didn't have to wonder if we were serious. Obviously, if he'd told his mom about me, we were.

"She wants to do my chart?" I asked.

"My last girlfriend—" he started to say, and then I stopped him short.

"Don't give me any details," I said.

"Not even her name?" he asked.

"Definitely not her name," I said.

The last thing I wanted was to be reminded of his former lovers every time I heard this woman's name.

As he lay texting with his mother, I had this idea that I'd like to know what went on inside his head. I asked him what he wanted from life, and he looked at me as if that was the silliest question. He didn't even seem to be hungover.

"I'll return to Italy," he said. "Make a family."

"What else?" I asked.

"You want more?"

"Yes," I said. "What will you do?"

"I'll work in my job, I don't know, maybe I'll be a waiter, that's a good job in Italy," he said. "I'll go to the beach on nice days. Raise my children."

"Where?" I asked. "Where will you make a family and raise your children?"

"I just told you," he said. "In Italy."

"But where in Italy?"

He seemed confused by my question.

"In Italy," he said.

Maybe that's how it was in Italy: the whole country was Italy. Unlike America, which was actually more like twenty different Americas.

I didn't get very far in this probe, and Marcello had to report back early. He was up and dressed and splashing water on his face and making coffee while I pulled myself out of bed, surprised by the extent of the hangover I didn't think I was going to get. He didn't ask me how to make the coffee, or where the coffee things were. He just found what he needed in the kitchen, as if piloted by a deep instinct, and he made a very nice pot.

He handed me a mug, stepped back a pace, and watched, as if he were framing in his mind a favorite photo: My half-dressed lover drinking coffee I just made. It was probably a good photo—my bedroom got really good light in the morning—and the coffee was strong and hot.

✳

Question 14: What was the role of religion in your childhood?

My parents were proud to be recovering from Catholicism and orthodoxy, and they patted themselves on the back for rising above the witchcraft and superstition. In fact, their defection was one of the things that brought them together; they met at a Young Atheists dance. I never really understood atheism, though. It seemed extreme, pompous, even. How could anyone be certain that there wasn't something out there? Dogs hear frequencies humans can't hear, and insects see colors we can't see. Maybe we modern humans are too limited to perceive what's out there. Sometimes my grandparents took me to mass, and I drank it up—the frankincense, the church bells, the candles, the call-and-response—but learned not to tell my parents how much I loved it. The thing they hated most about the Church was the doctrine of original sin. It infuriated them that they were supposed to believe they were sinners simply by the fact of being born.

✳

"I want to be like those penguins that mate for life," said Sarah.

We were eating the free potato chips at the bar, slowly, waiting to see if there would be free drinks coming our way.

"Which penguins?" I asked.

"Just about all of them," she said. "Chinstrap, emperor."

"Is that so?" I asked. "You've been watching the nature shows?"

"The pair bonding looks nice, I want to do that," she said. "And do you know that if the female thinks the male wasn't helpful enough sitting on the eggs, she'll dump him for a new mate?"

"That doesn't sound like mating for life," I said.

"Well, it's close," she said. "I bet most of the males do a good job sitting on eggs."

This was September, Sarah's birthday month, and as we became friendly—I'm pretty sure we were friends by now—she warned me that she was a birthday monster, one of those people who want to celebrate for the entire month. The whole month? Sometimes I was tempted to ask, What did your parents *do* to you?

There are few things in life I find more exhausting than feeling compelled to make merry, so my version of celebrating Sarah's birthday was to take her out for a drink at the beginning of the month, and again at the end. And by "take her out" I mean sit with her at the bar while she radiates the luminescence that will get us not only the first but also the second drink for free if we're patient enough. She did this routine so automatically that she didn't even know she had it down to a science, but I learned to follow along.

The bar was the tropical island place we'd made a habit of going to. It was a second-story bar, elevated over a parking lot, and you had to walk up a set of wooden stairs to get in. The elevator had broken years earlier, and the owner hadn't fixed it. Since the war began, there were no inspections to make sure things were to code.

I liked the bar because there was only one entrance, and I

could watch it. Sarah liked the palm trees in planters, and the neon palm trees, and the parrothead vibe. The furniture, including the barstools, was wicker. Most of their cocktails came as a frozen slush in wide cocktail glasses with a prop of some sort: umbrella, plastic palm tree, what have you. I could have done without all the steel drum–infused music, but then again, it had its appeal.

The first pitch arrived—the bartender asked us what we were drinking and nodded to the men across the room who were buying. Sarah told him she'd take any kind of fruit juice with vodka, but to go light on the vodka.

"Do you have bourbon?" I asked.

The bartender shook his head as if to say, Civil war, dummy.

"Maryland whiskey, then?" I asked.

"Rye, and it's not that bad, so don't ask," he said.

"Fine," I said.

He gave me the Maryland rye, stood back, and crossed his arms.

The smell of it brought me back to those summers with my parents, with their friends at the card tables. Sometimes I'd head toward the pines, away from the ocean and the campsite to watch the lightning bugs. When I returned, if my mother was buzzed enough, I'd grab one of her Frescas from the RV mini-fridge and secretly add a few teaspoons of sugar to the can. "Good girl, Hestia, watching your weight," she'd say, watching me drink the no-cal beverage. "Good girl."

"You're going to watch me drink it?" I asked the bartender.

"Just the first sip," he said.

He was handsome, in a straight-edge, short-hair, white-T-shirt-and-jeans kind of way.

"It's pretty good," I said.

"I thought you'd like it," he said.

Now he leaned in and almost whispered his next question.

"Who are the dude-bros buying the drinks?"

As unsubtly as I could, I looked over at the dude-bros.

"No idea," I said. "I'm not in charge here."

"Who's in charge?" he asked.

I pointed to Sarah, who was checking her phone.

Then I leaned over the bar and whispered to him.

"This is all way above my pay grade," I said.

The bartender decided to introduce himself to me.

"Alexei," he said, "and yes, it's Russian, and no, I'm not a confederate mercenary, or a spy. I've lived here a long time."

"Oh, that was a lot of information," I said. "Nice to meet you, Alexei."

"Nice to meet you, whatever your name is," he said.

I told him my name, and he said, "Like the goddess?"

"In the Greek pantheon," I said.

"An eternal virgin, right?" he asked. "Sworn to never marry?"

Sarah put her phone down and demanded my attention.

"So, Hestia," she said, tapping her fingers on the bar, "how's your little soldier boy?"

I turned on my stool and gave up on flirting with Alexei.

Sotto voce, I answered, "He's not that little. He's, like, two hundred pounds. Of muscle."

Her eyes widened.

"And sex drive," I added.

We'd already been over the basics—how many dates, what kind of kisser he was, the massage thing, and the shaved chest. I'd also told her about the gifts, the food, the UN party, and how hot he was. I'd showed her the same pictures I showed Mildred, and I think she was befuddled by why someone like him would want to date someone so much older.

I emphasized the gift-giving, and she wanted to know where I saw the relationship going. When I told her I didn't know, she looked as if she pitied me a little.

"You must have some idea of what you want," she said.

"I like having company," I said. "I like having conversations with someone, so I don't have to keep listening to my own thoughts."

"That's sad," she said. "Please tell me there's more."

"I like the idea of being able to count on someone," I said.

"My parents count on each other," she said.

"See? That's nice," I said.

"They have a good marriage and all," she said, "but there has to be more."

I told her that Marcello wanted to put gas in my car and check its oil and water levels.

"He wanted to put gas in your car?" she asked, and I knew that she was jealous.

She stared into the bottom of her cocktail glass and seemed to be thinking deeply.

"But wait," she said suddenly. "You don't have a car."

"I know," I said. "He was bummed about that. But when the summer's over, he's going to deal with my air conditioner window units for me."

I was deliriously happy about not having to lift the goddamned window units out of the goddamned windows this fall, and it seemed to make her more jealous.

Then Alexei came over breathlessly with his phone, to show us a headline with breaking news.

"The confederates exploded a dam out West," he said.

I put my hand on Sarah's arm and made her watch the

clip with me. We listened to the anchor, who said, through what seemed to be tears, "In what many pundits are calling a major turning point for the war, the confederates have hit their first major target in Washington state. This is the first time they've been able to pull off an attack of this magnitude, and experts wonder how this bodes for the future."

Sarah's face contorted, and her eyes filled with tears. Then she put both of her hands on her chest.

"Our Father in Heaven, he really did it," she said. "That fool really did it."

She looked at her hands on her chest. "My heart is racing," she said.

I urged her to take deep breaths.

"It's pounding through my chest," she said.

She looked scared, and tears rolled down her cheeks.

"Am I really dating a confederate right now?" she asked.

She fumbled with her phone, dropping it and picking it up, checking for messages.

I took the phone out of her hands and held tight.

"Block him," I said. "Right now."

She nodded furiously, and the tears kept coming. She pressed her hands into her chest again.

"Am I having a heart attack?" she asked.

I pulled her hands off her chest and held them in mine, and I did my best at maternal comforting.

"No, honey," I told her. "You're not having a heart attack."

"It feels like a heart attack."

"You're just mad," I said.

Alexei watched us, confused but fascinated, then returned to the work of the bar.

"Seriously, Sarah, block him," I said. "Block him on everything."

I gave her the phone, and she blocked him on text, email, phone, and all her social media apps.

Then she sank into a ten-thousand-foot stare, right past the dude-bros and into the streets. She had a cynical, wizened look, another face I'd never seen on her before.

"Has everything *always* been trash, and I'm just finding out now?" she asked.

Alexei delivered another round of drinks and pointed to the new set of gentlemen buying them. The dude-bros had given up. These looked like tech-rats, white guys with their stealth-wealth uniform: pricey haircuts that required straight razoring, dirty jeans, clunky eyeglasses, messenger bags.

"Our Father in Heaven," she whispered as she made the sign of the cross.

"Check this out," said Alexei, showing us his phone again. A new Conflicted headline announced that the confederacy's President Water had been accused by his vice president of having child pornography on his computer. Water protested that it had been planted there, but the pundits predicted his resignation. Vice President Pepper of Texas would be sworn in as the new president, they were certain.

"What is wrong with people?" asked Sarah, and no one answered.

✳

That weekend, there was more news. The intelligence community recommended a heightened terrorism alert level for schools and school buses. Madame President responded by stationing more soldiers on school grounds, and now there was a soldier on every school bus. But at the same time, she asked our mostly confederate-free Congress to increase funding for education itself, and they didn't even push back. They found the money, and suddenly, teachers were being paid fair wages. Without even having to fight for it, Baltimore public school classrooms got heat and air-conditioning. We began investing in students: more arts, more experiential learning, more time outdoors, and the school lunches got really good.

That weekend, I also burned down all the white and off-white candles in my nonfunctioning fireplace and had a new idea. I went to all the thrift stores in walking distance and shopped for ceramics. I bought pitchers and bowls that I thought would complement the gnocchi bowls Marcello had given me, in a range of colors, and scrubbed them clean at home. I arranged them in the fireplace and composed photos of them, which I posted nowhere.

And since his mother was doing my chart, I listened to podcasts with astrologers who talked alluringly about the astral bodies and what their positions decreed for the humans of this particular planet. Saturn squaring Uranus, or the trine between Venus and the moon—they all had personalities and force and intention, just like people, and there was a constant tension.

I liked it when they talked about the movements of the planets and asteroids, and how the movements created challenges or opportunities. The astral bodies are always moving, some quickly, like the moon, some slowly, like Pluto. Constant change: that was the currency. "There will be a new person." "There will be a new place." "There will be a new project." Everyone hopes for change. Everyone wants to believe that things will be different soon. What the podcasters never, ever said was, "Things will stay the same." Nobody wants to hear that. No astrologer could make a living telling you things will stay the same.

I think humans might be addicted to change, even though sometimes it seems that things hardly ever actually change. More or less, things stay the same. We reenact. We repeat.

Then again, the Buddhists say that nothing is permanent, and I always believe the Buddhists.

The more I listened to the podcasts, the more I became convinced that astrology was another deeply ancient tradition transmuted by Western ideas. It's too much of a stretch for me. But what I found addictive were the stories that astrologers tell. Each asteroid, each planet, each orbiting rock has a name and a personality, in tandem with mythology (Greek, to be specific), and all these personalities intersect and interact and have force and consequence. The stories of the three Liliths would be enough to keep me occupied, but there was so much more to be plumbed in the pantheon.

And maybe the astrologers are onto something. When you thought about how such tiny astral bodies—humans, I mean—affect each other minute to minute, just by coming closer to each other, or by pulling apart, maybe a shred of this made sense. Mars conjuncting Mercury moved cosmic energies; I knew that when Marcello and I conjuncted, we moved cosmic energies, too.

I asked Marcello how his mother was doing with my natal chart, and he said that it would take some time. I knew she must have been pretty serious about it, because anyone could go on the internet and get a natal chart in thirty seconds. I wondered if I'd ever meet her.

✳

Several times over my childhood, my mother explained to me that the reason I have an October birthday is that she and my father were waiting until the first of the year, when the insurance deductible reset, to start the process. Their insurance didn't cover the in vitro fertilization itself, only the consequences, and my parents wanted to get as much of that care paid for as possible, using only one year's deductible: all the prenatal visits, the scans, the bloodwork, the delivery. "We wanted what was owed to us," my mother said. It's the classic story of conception: donor sperm meets donor egg in a lab, fertilizes, and three weeks later gets implanted in a uterus.

This particular October, as I turned forty-three, my parents told me they were coming to Baltimore to visit me. They weren't worried about crossing the border; they hadn't even given up their U.S. passports yet. We hadn't spoken since they moved in June. I hadn't called them since then, and they hadn't called me. I thought that meant we were incommunicado, estranged. It was possible they simply hadn't noticed.

They'd already booked a room at the Leafy Greens Inn, their go-to hotel in Mount Vernon. It was near their favorite museum, which had a very good collection of ancient Greek art.

The hotel's restaurant served seasonal, local, and organic food, and the bookshelves were stocked with good books. It was Black-owned, and the owners were outspoken patriots, supporting all the progressive causes: reparations, civil rights, equal rights, gay rights, all the rights. "We're fine with the causes," said my mother, clarifying that they only objected to the government telling them which causes to support. Over the years, with their visits to me, they'd grown fond of the owners, a married couple about their age, who came from a tired industrial town not far from where my parents grew up. The four of them were on a first-name basis, and seemed to feel warmly about each other.

I checked the Safe Zones app, to make sure there hadn't been any activity there lately. It checked out as secure.

"Oh, stop with that app," said my father. "We don't need an app to be safe."

"Why are you so nervous?" asked my mother.

"You can't trust an app, anyway," said my father. "It's fake data."

"You have no idea where this data is coming from," said my mother. "You can't trust it."

They had reserved a table for three, outside in the courtyard, and I met them on my lunch break. The courtyard was elegant, with potted key lime trees and passionfruit vining on a trellis, herb spirals, and beautiful salad tables constructed from what looked like salvaged wood. The flooring was composed of a pattern of historic bricks and pavers stamped BALTIMORE BLOCK, salvaged from tear-downs that had been built during the city's brickmaking heyday.

"Happy birthday," they said in unison, handing me an envelope when I arrived.

As I sat down, my father urged me to open the card. Inside was a store-bought birthday card and a gift certificate to a plant store. I was genuinely surprised.

"We know you like to receive gifts on your birthday," said my mother.

Sometimes I thought they were aliens, trying to learn the ways of all these mysterious humans who do things like "exchange gifts on birthdays" and "tell white lies to make people feel good."

"You see, Hestia?" said my father. "We're trying."

I tried to give them the verbal pats on the back that they sought.

As we scanned our menus and ordered, my mother looked

me over and quizzed me on my weight; my relationship status; my dating life; my apartment. In trying to fend off her interrogation, I could barely focus on the words on the menu. Out of sheer exhaustion, I ordered a Caesar salad. They ordered interesting meals with braised carrots and brined okra and things like that, which I immediately envied. When we had finished with that, my mother took a long drink from her water glass.

"That dress is very slimming on you," she said.

Through the gates of the courtyard, we could see around the corner to Hamilton Street, where some of the courthouses were clustered. Usually, there was a mild-mannered demonstration taking place there. On this day, the protesters were upset about the reparations program proposed by the U.S. Congress. Confederate sympathizers had driven in from the rural counties of Maryland and Pennsylvania to slow-walk in a circle, holding signs that expressed their dismay. This group wore a lot of coonskin caps and camouflage cargo vests. One even wore a set of antlers. It was a warm day; I had to admire their dedication, wearing a coonskin cap.

IT'S NOT A CRIME TO BE WHITE, read one of the signs.

FAIR IS FAIR. NOTHING IS FREE! was another.

SLAVERY ENDED IN 1863, was the most common one.

Sometimes there'd be a guy with a shofar, because of the confederate obsession with rams' horns, and he'd blow into that for attention.

Everyone was behaving, and it was a fairly quiet day. Beautiful weather can breathe life into a protest, or take the wind out of it. Today was one of the latter: I think people just wanted to enjoy the fine temperatures before winter, without getting riled up.

When the food came, only a few minutes passed before

my father was slipping items off his plate onto my depressing Caesar. His pickled shishito peppers were delicious. The fresh coleslaw with apple cider vinegar, divine. Unfortunately, they had begun to interrogate me, which they had always insisted was done out of love.

"Just tell us one more time, Hestia," said my father, "why do you think your husband really left?"

"You know why," I said. "He was upset about the Purge. His sister was murdered in a ShopRite."

"But how was the marriage? Was it failing?" he asked. "*Before* all that?"

I didn't want to talk about my marriage or its demise, so I returned to what I thought was my more salient point. "The confederates have ruined everything," I said.

"All right, now," he said, "you can stop calling them confederates. This isn't the confederacy."

"Bill, come on," I said. "They named it the New Confederated States of America."

"Hestia, the word is 'confederated,' not 'confederate,'" he said. "Look it up in the dictionary. A confederation is a form of government."

"Did you know that Belgium is a confederation?" asked my mother.

"That's right," said my father.

"The Confederacy you're thinking of, in this country, only existed for four years, from 1861 to 1865," said my mother.

"It's long gone," said my father.

I put my elbows on the table, and my fork fell onto the ground.

"Let's change the subject," said my mother.

She asked me if I liked my salad, and I lied and told her it was delightful. All that big, hard lettuce banging into the roof of my mouth, what could be better? She told me she couldn't finish her meal and offered it to me. "But only if you're hungry," she said. I abandoned my Caesar and set upon her delicate grains and legumes festooned with herbs.

"Do you actually like your job?" she asked, and I told her that it wasn't the best thing ever, but that it paid the bills, and the people were nice, and I felt safe working there.

"But you're such a smart girl," she said.

"What are you saying?" I asked.

"Why are you doing this?"

"Because it's a living," I said.

"But you're better than this," she said.

"Who says so, Nancy?" I asked.

"Stop that," she said.

"You can always come live with us," my father said. "You can live rent-free, and you can do something worthy of your intelligence."

I told him that I couldn't do that, and he asked why not.

"Because you live in the confederacy," I said.

"Now you're just being stubborn," said my mother.

"Listen to me, Hestia," said my father. "This war is silly. You don't need to get caught up in it. The liberals are going overboard, trying to make everything equal, or equitable, or whatever. Things will *never* be fair, because we're human."

"Bill," I said, "you're oversimplifying."

"Just ignore them," he said, waving his hand.

"I think we should at least *try* to make things fair," I said.

"What you're forgetting, Hestia, is that humans are lousy," he said. "We like our tribes. That's from birth! You can't force new tribes on them. You can't force people to be nice."

"But maybe you can," I said.

He waved off my comment, so I tried a new tack and

turned to my mother, teeing up what I knew was a sore subject.

"Nancy, the confederates are arresting women for taking abortion pills."

"That does chafe," she said. "Did I ever tell you why I hate priests?"

She *had* told me this story, but I feigned naivete.

"When I was a girl, a pregnant woman came to our priest, after her doctor told her she couldn't survive a childbirth," she said. "She wanted Father's blessing for the termination, but he told her a termination would anger God. She had the baby, and they both died."

"He overstepped," said my father.

"Priests know nothing about women," said my mother.

"The confederacy is *literally* a bunch of Holy Rollers running the government," I said.

"America is being run by a bunch of holier-than-thous, too," said my father.

Tactical error: I fell for his red herring.

"It's not," I said.

"Yes, Hestia, it is," my mother said. "Your ruling party wants us to believe that we're bad. They want us to be ashamed of ourselves and atone for our sins. I didn't commit those sins! Your father and I have no reason to be ashamed. We're not guilty. No ancestor of ours ever owned another person—we were way too poor for that. In fact, we were *always poor*, right up until . . . now."

For dramatic flair, she checked her watch. (She and my father still wore wristwatches.)

"But there's this thing called systemic racism," I said.

"Apartheid is over, the Holocaust is over," she said. "They were terrible, but they're *over.*"

"But that's something different," I said.

"Hestia, listen to me. Listen. You can't be mad at people for not wanting to wear a hair shirt."

My father gave her a teacherly look, as if to say, Excellent point.

"How do you stand the sanctimony?" asked my father.

"Can you please look for the nuance?"

"That's goofy," said my father.

"You're goofy," I said.

"Now you're getting hysterical," said my father.

"Hysterical" was his Hail Mary pass.

"I'm not hysterical," I said. "I'm pissed off. There's a difference. And I know you know that men have used the word 'hysterical' for centuries to silence angry women."

"Relax," he said.

One of the life skills I had learned at an early age was how to manufacture my own inner quaaludes when my father told me I was hysterical. It was like magic. "Hysterical" was what flipped the switch and enabled me to segue immediately into sedative production. Sometimes I could go out of body as they talked at me. It gave me time to process things later, instead of having to do it in the moment, if I wanted to process them at all.

In this sedated state, in the elegant courtyard, next to a passionfruit vine, I thought about all the things I wanted to say to the confederates. Don't worry about women becoming too powerful. Don't worry about poor people becoming too powerful. Don't worry about history being "rewritten." Don't worry about your ancestors being called out. Don't worry about your new, Black boss. Don't worry about your children being passed over for jobs. Don't worry about your children not getting into college. Don't worry about people voting. Don't worry about rich people getting less. Don't worry about poor people getting things they need. Don't worry about women having abortions, because it's none of your business. Don't worry about giving a woman a compliment—if you keep it clean, she won't sue you. Don't worry about your opportunities diminishing—they've been diminishing for a long, long time, way before this war, and if you haven't noticed that before now, shame on you for your willful blindness.

But telling people not to worry is a lot like my father telling me to relax.

"Let's just all relax," he said, again.

I snapped out of my daze and placed my knife on my plate to signal to the waiter that I was done with my meal.

"That's a great idea," I said. "Why didn't I think of that? Thank you, Bill."

"Oh, you poor thing," said my mother. "Your life is going off the rails."

"Come live with us," said my father.

"We'll take care of you," said my mother.

I felt it was best not to see them again for some time.

✳

Question 15: Did you like school?

When I went to college, I found words to describe the distaste I had been feeling for years. I arrived with a mile-long list of things that filled me with despair—the founding fathers, shopping malls, Manifest Destiny, bootstraps, lawns and lawn mowers, pantyhose, trophy wives, and muscle cars. Within a few semesters—history, psych, anthropology—I put it all together and realized why I hated the story of the American Dream. But my parents, who had clawed their way into middle-class, comfortable lives, saw it another way: the liberal arts college experience had ruined me. Also, they'd made a critical miscalculation in choosing sperm and egg donors. They'd screened donors for IQ instead of character. My mother, the Stoic, said courage was the most important virtue, and my father, the Spartan, discipline. All this was discussed, when I was in my twenties, over barbecued ribs on the Fourth of July. I pulled the last bits of meat from the bone with my teeth and said, "They didn't donate anything. They had a product for sale, you bought it, and there are no refunds on this product."

✳

Mildred's daughter Annie visited as often as Ruth did, assuming there was gasoline. In contrast to Ruth, who was a very serious liberal, almost dour, Annie was more devil-may-care, unbothered by the status quo or the state of the Union. At fifty-something, she had big hair and fun earrings and she knew my name and sometimes even hugged me. She drove in from Philadelphia, the Main Line, where she'd been born and raised, younger than Ruth by ten years. She was the daughter of Mildred's second husband, whom Sarah had nicknamed Micky McIrish.

Annie found me and Mildred in the therapy garden. I had been showing Mildred photos of the meals I'd cooked with Marcello, and Mildred was vehemently questioning why she would want to look at pictures of food. She had just finished a cigarette, and the ashtray was on the table next to her chair.

"Show me something good," she said, "if you know what I mean."

Those words, coming from a man of any age, would have

been lecherous. But Mildred spoke with joy, and nothing she said ever sounded gross. Annie looked at her mother, then at the ashtray, then at me, then back at her mother.

"Mama," she said. "Really?"

"It's someone else's ashtray," said Mildred. "It was here when we sat down."

Annie leaned down and sniffed Mildred, then pulled back and shook her head.

"I get it, Mama, I really do," she said. "Cigarettes are fun. But you're in no condition—"

"Stop right there," said Mildred. "I love you like crazy, but you're not my doctor."

Annie turned to me.

"Be honest now, Hestia," she said. "Are you her accomplice?"

"I don't know what you're talking about," I said, and I told her that I had to return to my office. I didn't like lying to Annie.

"Was I able to answer your questions about those photos, dear?" asked Mildred, enjoying the charade. "I know we old people all look alike. I hope you have them sorted now."

"Yes, that was very helpful," I said, bowing out. "Thanks for the tip."

They moved into the Serenity Room, Annie holding Mildred's free hand, the one that wasn't using the cane. I liked to watch them, how they were with each other, holding hands just like Mildred did with Ruth. Like a doe and her fawn was how it looked to me, although Annie was older than me and hardly a fawn.

✳

The next day, Mildred told me that Annie was applying for citizenship in Ireland, which was possible because of her father.

"She's bailing on this place, too, just like Ruth," said Mildred. "It's a slow process, but she's getting citizenship for us."

"It's the smart thing," I said.

I'd thought about it myself, for a hot second, as my parents had recent European ancestry. But I always got confused because I wasn't sure how it worked when you're a donor baby, and whether my parents would need to help me with paperwork in seeking new citizenship.

"She wants to bring me to Ireland to live with her when she gets the passport," she said.

This posed a monstrous dilemma for her: Ireland with Annie, or Austria with Ruth? As Mildred explained with quite an ache in her voice, whichever daughter didn't get chosen would be hurt to the core.

"I'm going to have to choose," she said.

"I don't envy you that," I said.

"But if we're lucky," she said, "I'll die before that day arrives."

"Don't say that."

"We have to hasten my death," she said. "I only have a year or two before the paperwork is final."

"Maybe the war will end," I said, not believing my own lie. "Maybe you won't have to choose. Or die."

"Hand me a cigarette, dear," she said. "Let's get this show on the road."

✳

I was still going to Jamie's house for dinner once a month, to see the kids and help out in the kitchen if he'd let me. He'd started to allow me to load the dishwasher while he read to his son in bed. After, Jamie would come downstairs in his sweatpants, rubbing his eyes like he was trying to stay awake, and see the sink, empty and clean.

"Thank god for you," he said, in November.

"It's not like I even washed them," I said. "I just put them in the dishwasher."

"I don't think you understand how much this means to me," he said.

"Jamie," I said, "you're doing great. The kids seem great."

Twenty-one months after his wife's death, and they seemed to be finding a rhythm. The rhythm is working, I told him. Your children smile and joke all the time, I told him.

"Glass of wine?" he asked.

I stayed for a glass of wine, flattered that he was blowing past his bedtime for me. I wasn't sure it was a good idea, because he looked exhausted. We sat at the table, which I'd wiped thoroughly, and he ran his hand across it.

"It's so *clean*," he said. "There's no clutter on it."

"There's a pile of clutter on the couch now," I said.

His old, good dog, Bernadette, came over and sat on his feet. He scratched her head as if on autopilot, and Bernadette rested her jaw on her paws.

"You know," he said, "Liz died so suddenly."

"I know," I said.

There were still photos of her all over the house, which seemed right, including on the wall I faced while we talked.

"The children didn't get to say goodbye," he said. "I think it haunts them."

Would it have been better if she died slowly, grinding

toward death? There's no way to know. But, clearly, the swift-ness of it haunted Jamie.

"There's no good way," I said. "Either it's sudden, and you don't get to say goodbye, or it's slow and painful and you have to watch them suffer."

"I think they needed to say goodbye," he said.

"Maybe they have," I said. "You don't know."

We finished drinking, and I called a ride.

"See you next month," he said, as we hugged.

✳

The next time I saw Marcello, he had asked what he could bring me, and when I said nothing—niente—he brought me prosciutto. He also brought me a combination flash drive and ballpoint pen branded with the United Nations logo, which was disturbing, because the pen qua pen wasn't that good, and I wondered if the UN really used flash drives. I thought they'd be more technologically savvy than that. Then again, a flash drive might be a safer place to store data than the cloud.

Mille grazie, I said, and he asked me if I was learning Italian, and I told him I might have installed an app on my phone. It turned him on, and we ended up having sex right away, before dinner.

After, he asked if next time we could "do different stuff," and my patience was tried. Good goddess, what did he want, and why did he have to be so coy? Was it anal? It was usually anal. Maybe he wanted me to wear an outfit. Maybe he wanted me to do stuff with his butt. Straight men always think their little kinks are so *out there*—if only they knew how normal they are.

"Just tell me," I said. "Just tell me, with words in English, what you want."

"Maybe you would like to guess," he said.

No, I didn't want to guess. If he wanted something, he could tell me. But instead of talking about it, he asked for a massage, and what I gave him was really good.

"My mother says your Lilith is in Cancer," he said, while I dug into his neck with my thumbs.

He said "Lilith" with a hard *t* and long, drawn-out *l*'s.

"What does that mean?"

"I don't know," he said.

He checked his phone to reread her message and translated roughly.

"She wants me to tell you that it's all right if you need help," he said. "Because of Lilith."

As I massaged, he closed his eyes for a few moments and fell into the light trance of pre-sleep. While he lay on his stomach, I examined the eyebrow I had access to, to see if I could determine if it was waxed. He seemed like someone who should have more eyebrow hair, maybe even a unibrow. As I stroked his eyelid with my fingers, he woke up and turned over onto his back. He pulled me on top of him, looked into my eyes, and said my name.

"Estia."

"Marcello," I said.

"Estia," he said again. "Maybe instead of learning Italian, you should study Spanish."

I asked him why, and he said he wanted to take me on vacation to Mexico. I climbed off him and sat up straight in the bed.

"For real?" I asked. "Mexico?"

"Come with me," he said. "I can get you in, the visa is no problem. I have leave time soon."

We Americans had been banned from almost every country in the world. The problem was that any immigration official looking at a U.S. passport had no idea if they were looking at a terrorist. America had more documented recent acts of terrorism on record than any country in the world, and most of the people blowing things up were white. The new confederacy didn't even have new passports yet.

But with Marcello as my passport, I knew I could get away from this husk of a republic for a little while. It was a delightful, delicious idea. Mexico! I could daydream for hours about what a vacation in Mexico would be like.

"Let me think about it," I said.

We used the prosciutto with some gnocchi and cheese in one of the ceramic gnocchi dishes he'd given me. He had been correct: it was better baked than boiled.

The next morning, I continued daydreaming about a vacation in Mexico. He took me to the one and only coffee shop that he felt safe in, where the owners, very uniform-friendly, had a policy of letting peacekeepers tour the back of the shop so they'd know where all the exits were. Marcello had never talked about his experiences as a soldier, but I remembered that his first tour of duty began in the first days of the Purge. He must have seen carnage. He was sent to Washington, DC, where the body count was the highest: there were massive numbers of deranged confederates living just outside the Beltway. Marcello must have thought we Americans were animals.

In the coffee shop, he led me to a table with a perfect view of the entrance, and one of the owners came to greet us with free coffee. Actually, he brought us espressos—he knew what

Marcello liked. When he asked what we'd like to eat, Marcello ordered for me. He didn't ask me what I wanted, or if I wanted anything at all.

"You'll love the sfogliatelle," he said.

As it turns out, he was right, because I did love the sfogliatelle. And the fact that I loved it made me grumpy about him being so presumptuous. As I finished the pastry, I noticed a woman my age watching me over the heads of her children. Had she seen the whole episode, the full ten seconds, where Marcello ordered for me without even consulting me? I was mortified.

✳

Question 16: Are there any smells that take you back to your childhood?

The smells of saffron and cardamom take me right back to Thanksgivings in my parents' home. In hindsight, those Thanksgivings were multicultural, but at the time, it was simply my parents inviting over their students and teaching assistants who couldn't go home. The Indian and Pakistani students usually brought a delicious, spicy dessert. The Black students brought even more wonderful food. For me, an only child, it was one of the best days of the year. I was fascinated to see how appreciative the students were, and how much my parents wanted to help them with school and careers. But in the years while I lived away from home, the worm began to turn. My parents' invitations had to compete with stories about how they were celebrating the slaughter of native peoples, and that hurt their feelings. Thanksgiving had been the one holiday they truly loved, the holiday that allowed me to see them as generous.

✳

I had been managing to evade Marcello on the Mexico question by text and by phone, but the next time we saw each other, he pressed for an answer. I leaned into him, hoping to distract him while I bought time to think. I put my hand on his chest and it felt stubbly, so I took my hand off his chest.

And there it was, the feeling I knew well, but I told myself it was an illusion. Why on earth would I break up with a man who wanted to take me to Mexico? How cracked in my head would I have to be to do that?

I poured two glasses of bourbon, which we drank while we fooled around.

"Keep your shirt on," I said.

I told him it was sexy, but the truth was that I didn't want to feel the stubble.

We made love, and it was sweet, fun, tinged with charred oak barrel. When we were done, I noticed that he had sweat all over my bed. The sheets were clammy. Would it be rude, I asked myself, to change the sheets right now? I talked myself into waiting until later to do the laundry.

Marcello rolled onto his back and ran his finger along my neck.

"Beautiful," he said.

I noticed how especially lovely his eyes were when they were looking at me like that.

"So, is it yes to Mexico?" he asked.

My heart raced and I put my hand on his hand, which was still on my neck. I wanted to do the right thing. What was the right thing? I needed courage and discipline.

"You'll come with me?" he asked. "We'll swim with the sea turtles?"

I stood up and dressed—one should never be naked at a breakup—and handed him his clothes.

"Here, hon," I said. "Let's get dressed."

Then I told him that I didn't think we were a good fit, and that I'd feel terrible letting him take me to Mexico. He stood still and silent for a few moments, absorbing what I'd said.

"It's all right with me if you still want to go," he said. "We don't have to be in love for Mexico."

✳

The next morning, I walked into my office and found Sarah staring at the face of her phone, which lay on the desk. It was populated with many Conflicted red rhombus alerts, and she seemed a bit paralyzed. Without touching it, she leaned over so she could read the blurb on each alert, and she recited them out loud to me as I stood in the doorway.

"The governor of Michigan has disappeared," she said. "Three guards at a refinery in California have been poisoned. An Atlanta activist has—"

I covered her phone with my hand. "Stop," I said.

I picked up her hands and inspected her fingernails, which were bitten and raw. She let me hold them in mine as I tried to offer counterpoints.

"The other news is that today is election day, and a Black woman is going to win," I said.

"Madame President is a target," she said.

"We're going to have an actual federal law protecting our reproductive rights," I said. "And the ERA is getting added to the Constitution."

"The confederates will keep murdering us."

"Maybe you should delete that app."

"I can't do that," she said.

"Then do a daily digest," I said.

"I prefer to be informed."

"I prefer for you to breathe," I said.

For a few long, slow minutes, we did four-count breathing. Then she flipped the phone over. Then she asked me why I was being so nice, and I told her that Marcello and I had broken up. She took a fit.

"No one ever asked *me* to go to Mexico," she said.

She was genuinely angry, and she took the breakup personally.

"Honestly, why do you have to be so stupid?" she asked.

"I can't explain it," I said.

She glared at me.

"Tell the truth, Hestia, who *hurt* you?"

But *that* was a whole other story.

✳

When I told Mildred about Marcello, she shook her head and closed her eyes.

"Holy moly, baby, you're going to regret this," she said.

I watched her get lost in her memories. She was wearing a huge rabbit fur Russian hat, a scarf, and a sweater coat. I had to call her back to the present by waving my hand in front of her face.

"It's not the things I *did* that I regret," she said, "so much as the things I *didn't* do."

"Did Mark Twain say that?"

"Who knows?" she said. "He gets credit for all the good lines."

*

Now, in hindsight, I realize what an idiot I was. Literally, *What was I thinking?* Yet another decision I may never understand.

For weeks after we broke up, Marcello texted me intermittently to ask how I was, and if I needed anything. Two months after the breakup, when we had a blizzard in January, he texted, "are you in a safe place and have everything you need? let me know please."

All three of the ceramic gnocchi dishes he gave me ended up breaking, but I saved the pieces, thinking that one day I'd use them in an herb garden, with sage and basil.

3

THE TURNCOAT

Most oral history projects assume a happy, fruitful marriage.

"Describe your wedding."

"What were some of your happiest moments with your spouse?"

"What did you like best about raising children?"

When I wrote these questions on the whiteboard, my Scribbles students groaned. I found them pretty disappointing myself.

"I never had children, you goddamn fascists," Dorothy yelled at the whiteboard.

"Heteronormative poppycock," said Charles.

Jeffrey, who was a little crankier than usual, said, "Jesus Christ, we're old people, not fairy tales."

"Some of us were raped by Cossacks," said Clara, which brought the room to silence. "Not *me*, but some of us. People I know."

They spent the rest of the class recounting the horror-show marriages of people in their lives, the agony, the stuck-ness.

"Some of us married the asshole who got us pregnant," said Dorothy. "Not me, but some of us."

"Some of us spent years wishing our spouse would die," said Jeffrey. "Not me, but some of us."

Together, as a class project, we wrote a new set of questions for us, the disillusioned, disabused, and disappointed lovers in the world. I thought they were much more interesting than the ones you find online. They still centered on marriage (all of us had been married), but instead of exploring what was enduring about our marriages, they aimed at discovering what makes a marriage unravel.

This turned out to be another unit where I did most of the writing, while they mostly talked among themselves.

"Don't worry about them," said Ed. "Write your own story."

✳

Question 17: Why did you marry your spouse?

My husband and I met via the original dating app, when I was almost thirty: a blind date arranged by friends. I'd been bouncing around for a while, and I was worn down. We fell in love quickly, as fools do when they're raw. We loved the same books, movies, and music, and that seemed to matter. He was the kind of guy who liked people and thought well of them; he even liked my parents, and they liked him. He was the opposite of a misanthrope. Is there a word for that? "People person"? When we married, I finally felt like I had a family.

＊

After Marcello, I half-heartedly browsed the dating sites, but every profile I saw had a sameness. Everyone loves to travel. Everyone loves to laugh. Everyone loves animals and nature and food, or at least they say they do, and nobody likes drama. "But do you *really* love to laugh?" I heard myself ask out loud.

I took a break from dating, several months long, right past the new year, right past the second anniversary of the beginning of the war, right into the spring. I didn't look at a single profile or even make meaningful eye contact with handsome strangers in real life. Mildred was a little bored with me, I think, but we still had our daily smoke, which I never missed. During the winter months, I dragged over a giant propane patio heater (the retirement village had four of them) to our spot in the therapy garden, and we huddled under it.

"Anything's better than Yahtzee," she said.

The events coordinator was big on games during the winter. Yahtzee, bingo, UNO, and cribbage were the standouts, and Mildred had no truck with any of them.

"I'd rather freeze my tits off than play UNO," Mildred said.

I brought a fleece blanket for her, and sometimes she made me scooch my seat right up against her so we could conserve body heat.

The cigarettes made Mildred cough a little, so now, along with her ashtray, I brought a cup of hot tea to keep her throat soothed, with lots of cream and sugar. She liked Irish Breakfast, preferably from an Irish tea brand, because the American versions were weak, she said. She told me that when she was growing up, her parents hadn't allowed Irish things in the house. Irish things were "common," she said.

"But my second husband got me hooked on Irish Breakfast straightaway," she told me.

When April rolled around, she started nudging me to date again.

Before her first drag on a cigarette, she'd take some preemptive sips of her tea, to get her throat warmed up, then she'd speak to me over the rim.

"You need to learn how to like men again, dear," she said.

My response was quick: "But they disappoint me."

"That's only because you're an experienced dater," she said.

I tried to work out that logic.

"So, if I were less experienced, I'd be less disappointed?" I asked.

"Oh, on second thought, never mind, I don't know anything," she said.

"Come on," I said. "You know a lot of things."

"Hand to God, Hestia," she said. "I don't know enough to be incompetent."

That last part, of course, was a Woody Allen quote, so she affected her Maryland WASP version of a New York accent. It wasn't very good, but no matter, I loved it every time.

She settled her cup onto its saucer on the side table, and her arthritic knuckles looked cold and white, even though it was April.

"Sometimes it's too much," I said. "There are so many things to sort, especially with dating."

"I remember being a young woman," she said. "Sometimes it was torture. Sometimes it was exciting. It's a roller coaster!"

"It's making me seasick," I said.

"I promise you, if you live long enough, you'll get relief."

She was shivering, and her lips were turning blue. But I had tried—once—to cut short a smoking session because of the cold, and I learned to never try that again.

"Are you saying it's good to get old?" I asked.

"Am I old?" she said, but I knew she was teasing. "I rather like it. It's not exciting, but you know that saying, 'The suspense is killing me'? I think the suspense of life was killing me."

She was ready for her cigarette and handed me her lighter. The Gauloises were now forty dollars a pack. She was smoking a two-dollar cigarette.

"I don't torture myself anymore wondering how things will turn out. I know how the story ends."

"But do you ever miss the airplanes, the highballs, the pearls," I said, "the romance?"

"Oh, Hestia, sometimes I do miss that poor, distraught, gorgeous gal," she said.

"Were you gorgeous?"

"I was," she said.

"How did you know?" I asked.

"When your beauty starts to fade, that's when you suddenly realize how beautiful you were," she said.

"You don't miss it?"

"I miss my body," she said, "but that's all. I don't miss the opera."

I knew she meant the opera of life, not the actual opera. She started coughing. I held her arms up straight in the air like I'd seen other kids' mothers and fathers do for them when I was a child, and the whole time she kept her cigarette between her fingers. My hands circled her wrists, which were so small that my fingers overlapped each other. She was delicate, and I wondered if I should even be touching her, and what might be the difference, if any, between "delicate" and "fragile."

✳

During this time, Annie and Ruth both had the brilliant idea that their mother should take Tai Chi classes at the village. "For her mobility," said Ruth. "It could be fun," said Annie. They'd had the idea independently of each other, but at the same time, even though they never talked, which I found fascinating. I'd longed my whole life for a sibling, to have that kind of connection with someone, even if I hated them. I imagined it was easier to love a person when you didn't choose them. If they were annoying, or even awful, you could still love them without feeling that you'd chosen wrong.

Mildred didn't want the bother of fighting her daughters over Tai Chi, so she tried to rope me into going with her.

"I'm begging you," Mildred said, over another smoke, another day.

"I have no coordination and terrible balance," I said.

"I'll be your best friend," she said.

She was already my best friend, and for a couple moments that made me sad, even though I couldn't explain why. Mostly, my friendship with her filled my heart.

We went to a Thursday class, and Monkey Tea Tom took us aside and taught us beginners' moves.

"We'll start with Pushing Hands," he said in that ultra-mellow voice.

He tucked his long hair behind his ears, on both sides, and coached us while he lightly held Mildred's forearm in front of her to steady her stance. (She'd insisted on not using her cane.)

"Exhale *now*," he said.

"And now inhale," he said.

There was something about his voice that soothed me, and I was surprised to feel a little drowsy, but it was good. I think his voice lowered my blood pressure.

"You're a human narcotic," I blurted out, but he ignored me and kept teaching.

"Hold your wrists strong, but let your hands droop."

When Mildred almost stumbled, he insisted she use her cane.

"It's cheating," she said.

"Wrong," he said. "There's no such thing as cheating here. And the cane makes you look formidable."

*

While I stuck to my dating hiatus, Sarah was busy dating.

"The universe wants me to branch out," she told me across our desk.

Over the winter, she'd put her first poster on the wall, next to my poster of "Herbs of the World." It was a lotus flower in bloom, and when she said "branch out," she gestured to it.

Her strategy was to stick with the same dating apps she'd been using, but to be less strict in her criteria.

"Advanced degree no longer required. Alternative lifestyles considered," she said. "If I'm going to be out here dating, I might as well be down for whatever the world offers."

I admired her bravado but wondered whether she'd be able to truly chill. Then she showed me evidence.

From her side of the desk, she showed me photos of her

most recent fling, a man whose name she didn't bother to tell me. She referred to him as "Hashtag Vanlife." She was the master of nicknames.

What I gathered from the photos was a collection of nouns and adjectives: fairy grunge, yoga body, bare feet, drug rug. There were thousands, and it seemed that he wore a knit toque no matter the weather. He aspired to be an influencer. "Make me famous on Instagram" was one of his oft-used captions. I'd bet good money he sunned his perineum in the desert. But he was taking a break from the road and dating Sarah.

"He's gorgeous," she said. "And we say affirmations together every morning."

I asked her what she meant by that, and she told me they looked in the mirror together, and he encouraged her to say things like, "I'm a powerful and wise Black goddess," which she liked very much.

He introduced her to the music of Nina Simone and the poetry of Audre Lorde, and she pretended that she'd never heard of them before. He was helping to put her in touch with her Divine. As she spoke, I found myself smiling, happy for her and even happier that we seemed to be good friends now.

"I hope you find a man who helps you get in touch with your Divine," she said.

I asked her where Hashtag Vanlife lived, and she told me he was couch-surfing. A small alarm went off in my head.

"Don't let him sleep on *your* couch," I warned.

"He sleeps in my bed," she said.

"I mean, after you dump him," I said.

That pissed her off.

"You know, Hestia," she said, "happiness is an inside job."

✳

Gradually, the universe told Sarah that she needed to rescue dogs, and Hashtag Vanlife supported her whim. This being Baltimore, where all the rescue dogs are pit bulls, she found herself with one, and then two, animals that had been given up on. One had skin problems, and the other had hip dysplasia, and she was forever running to the vet's office on her lunch break for this skin cream or that skin cream, or worse, going home to pick up a dog to bring to the vet. When she walked them, she stuck to the shady side of the street so they wouldn't get sunburned. I went with her a couple times on these walks and noticed that other pedestrians crossed the street to avoid us. It was the opposite of what happened when we went to bars, where people were drawn to Sarah.

The first time someone crossed the street to avoid us, I was angry, but Sarah was cool and collected.

"I'm a Black woman walking pit bulls," she said. "What do you expect?"

We stopped going to bars, because the puppies, as she called them, needed dinner. Even bars that let you sit outside with your dog—no one wants you there with your mangy pit bull, regardless of how pretty you are.

Once, we went back to the tropical island bar with bartender Alexei, the flirty Russian, because I thought I might like to dip my toe into flirtation again. He had some kind of sexy energy that was hard to put my finger on. But the whole time we were at the bar, Sarah was anxious, wondering if the puppies were all right at home alone. She radiated nervousness, and no one sent us free drinks.

I tried to flirt with Alexei but there was a younger, prettier woman at the bar doing the same, so I was chopped liver. We weren't even there an hour.

As was destined to happen, it wasn't long before Sarah became overwhelmed with the care of her high-maintenance dogs. She'd had no idea it would be this hard, she admitted to me. They'd changed her life, and not necessarily in a good way.

"I just need help," she said.

✳

The next month, Hashtag Vanlife told her he wanted an ethically nonmonogamous relationship, and she dumped him, just like that.

"Who has time for that nonsense?" she said.

Her next man was "in real estate," and she showed me pictures on her phone. But they weren't pictures of him; they were pictures of house interiors, mainly kitchens. He remodels houses, she said. He has his own company, she said.

The photos she showed me were of the blandest, most sterile interior design that humans can achieve. Every wall was light gray. All the kitchens had the same black-and-silver-tile backsplash with granite countertops and melamine cabinets. There were pointless "bars" staged with empty liquor bottles, and the window frames were made of vinyl, with fake vinyl grids imitating panes. The front doors were either faux farmhouse or overly decorative. The first-floor floors were fake wood, and the upstairs was wall-to-wall ecru-carpeted. Some of them were even staged with an open book on the coffee table, and a pair of glasses next to the book.

I didn't want to keep looking, but I couldn't stop swiping.

"What do you think?" she asked.

I grimaced. I couldn't even be gentle about it.

"He's done awful things," I said.

She was taken aback.

"What do you mean?"

"He's a house-flipper," I said.

We were in the Café, making coffee, and while we'd been looking at the photos, Tom had come in quietly. He was drinking a glass of water on the other side of the Café.

"Can I show Tom?" I whispered to Sarah, and she acquiesced.

"Come here," I said, and he looked happy to be noticed.

"At your service," he said.

Sarah whispered "Ew" under her breath.

I showed him the photos: "What do you think?" I asked.

It wasn't fair to put him on the spot like that. He looked uncomfortable and took a long time scanning the pictures.

"Umm," he stammered. "I don't know what to say."

"Whatever comes to mind," I said.

"It's kind of a crime scene?" he said.

I softened toward him, but Sarah was annoyed. He hurried out of the room.

After Sarah dumped the flipper, she started seeing a doctor who'd relocated from Atlanta because he couldn't live in the confederacy one more moment, even though Atlanta was full of unionists. What he saw in the hospital's emergency department had done him in. There were too many patients who'd been messed up by explosions, armed skirmishes, and firearm accidents, especially children. Too many people had guns they didn't know how to use, he'd told her, and they were the worst.

She was excited to date a doctor, but in Baltimore, he gave up practicing, except for a gig with a humanitarian medical

NGO. The confederacy's federally funded health clinics had shuttered, so once a month, the organization escorted him and another doctor into Atlanta to provide medical relief from a van. Mostly, he took people's blood pressure and listened to their lungs, and gave out insulin and beta blockers if he had them. But on the down low, he distributed abortion pills, and once in a while he performed a vacuum aspiration on some distraught woman who was shit out of luck in the confederacy.

He also did a brisk import-export business with Viagra from Ireland, where it was manufactured. Ireland refused to export to the confederacy, so Sarah's doctor-man had it shipped to Baltimore, then sold it out of the van in Atlanta to a growing base of customers. He made bank with that business, but insisted it was a humanitarian act.

"He only sells to unionists," Sarah said. "He'd never sell to a confederate."

"Well, good," I said. "Let the confederates have erectile dysfunction."

"The fewer babies they make, the better," she said.

✳

Question 18: Were there any early signs of incompatibility in your marriage?

A few years before the war began, my husband and I were driving around my hometown in Virginia, and we came upon a peaceful protest about climate change. It was a garden-variety protest: we need climate action now; there's no Planet B; planet over profit, that sort of thing. And ringed around the protesters were parked pickup trucks—enormous vehicles. Their engines were running, and they were rolling coal. The burning coal blanketed the protesters in soot and black exhaust, and it made the air thick, dark gray. My husband was stunned. He was a Yankee from Rhode Island, and that was the first time he'd heard of rolling coal. He made me pull over so he could "engage" with some of the dudes, and I accompanied him to one of the less gigantic pickups. He asked the men inside if they cared about clean air and water, if they wanted to save our natural resources for future generations. "We all want the same things," he said to the driver, which made the driver laugh out loud. While my husband presented his points, ticking off his facts one by one on his fingers, they feasted on his frustration. For them, this was high entertainment, and they knew exactly how to make him dance a little more. Afterward, he demanded to know why I wasn't furious. I shrugged, because I was used to people like that, and I don't think he ever accepted that some people are just unkind.

✳

It was my dumb idea to create an online memorial destination for the retirement village, so I had no one to blame but myself when it sucked the life out of me. I'd spent more than a month researching what kind of software product—they're called "solutions"—we should use, and where it would live on our website, and best practices for getting enough site visits to get a decent return on investment.

My idea had been that when someone in the village dies, there would be a web page where we posted the obituary, and people who knew the deceased could post remembrances. My vision was a vibrant online conversation in which loved ones shared anecdotes and testified to the deceased's wonderful qualities. In hindsight, I suppose I wanted stories, and to be moved by how much people loved each other. Even if no one shared a single story, but said something like, "I'm holding you in the light," I would have been pleased.

What I got instead was a collection of nothing burgers, comments like, "I knew her in grade school," and "I have kidney failure, too," and "The same cancer killed my sister." One mourner wrote, "I played tennis when I was young, too" on an obituary that mentioned tennis exactly once.

There were some nicer comments, like, "I'll miss her every day," but those were rare. Most of the comments were the organ recital, people recounting how their own bodies were failing them. Why do people have to make other people's deaths all about them?

I kvetched to Ed about the mourners' tone-deafness, and he countered by insisting that the online memorial destination was a success. I asked him how he could think that.

"You're curating a community," he said.

"A community of self-absorbed people," I said.

"Well," he said. "People grieve in different ways."

I wanted to take the site down, and he said we should keep it, and that I should manage my expectations. Give yourself credit, he said: This is authentic.

"Stop hiding your light under a bushel basket," he said. "What's done is done, and you can't put the horse back in the barn."

I lamented that people are never as thoughtful as you want them to be, and Ed slowly took off his readers, leaned back in his chair, and looked at me with what I suspected might be a smile of paternal-type affection. It was not a look I'd seen on my own father, but I recognized it as fatherly. I expected him to say, "Bless your heart." But he didn't.

"Oh, Hestia," he said.

"Am I being a brat?" I asked.

He dragged out his next sentence, saying it in a slow Texas drawl.

"You . . . can't . . . change . . . people," he said.

"And that's exactly why I'm not dating," I said.

I hadn't meant to say it so vehemently, but I guess it had been on my mind. I was lucky to have Ed for a boss; he found my outbursts amusing.

"Look, I get it," he said. "As a person who's probably going to be single again, I'll admit there are some great advantages to it. You can go to the movies and get a great seat when you're only looking for yourself. You get to stay for the entire baseball game. You don't even need to buy vegetables."

"Are things that bad at home?" I asked.

"Indicators point to a poor long-term outcome," he said.

"So, is there some kind of prize for divorce number three?" I asked.

"Naw," he said sadly. "They discontinued the prize."

*

While Ed insisted on keeping the online memorial destination, he also helped Sarah get started with her rebranded Red Emma/Senior Socialists lecture series. He gave her a weekly slot in the Treehouse Studio and let her promote it on all the electronic billboards at the village and with table tents in the Café. Despite turning up fewer registrants than she expected, she followed through with full force, selecting passages from various seminal works of socialism and making a syllabus that looked legit.

Mildred made up an excuse to get out of attending the class, something about it happening on a day her daughters usually visited.

"Seminal works?" she said to me.

"Right?"

"I'm too old for this polka," she said.

After her cigarette, she insisted I follow her to her room, because she had something to give me. In her room, she dumped a bouquet of dying flowers into her garbage and handed me a vase.

"Here, have this," she said. "Annie brought this for me last week."

Mildred knew I was collecting vases for my fireplace. My earlier idea, to fill it with ceramics of different shapes and colors, had fallen flat, and now I was trying to fill it with vases, the uglier the better. Maybe I was going for shock value. I'd found one while thrifting that was smooth, white porcelain made to look like a pair of buttocks. I'd found another that was red, in the shape of an anatomical heart. I'd found another in the shape of an ugly baby-doll head, with blackened eyes and cherry-red lips, and then I thought, Maybe I could make my own vases out of ugly baby dolls, and I started looking for baby dolls, but thankfully lost interest before I'd acquired too many.

Unfortunately, most of the vases were simply the boring clear glass containers you get from the florist with a bouquet of flowers. All function and no form. This is what Mildred gave me now. The most functional vase you could ever ask for. The dying flowers in her trash can were far more interesting, and I thought maybe instead of vases, I should fill that empty fireplace with dead flowers.

"Sarah popped in earlier," said Mildred.

Sarah and Mildred seemed to have become fast friends, which made things cozy.

"She dumped the Viagra boyfriend," she said. "The doctor."

"I know," I said. "That's probably for the best."

"Is she all right?" asked Mildred.

"She's anxious," I said. "We're in a civil war."

"Yes, of course."

I asked if Sarah seemed all right with the breakup, and Mildred said, "They're all impossible."

"All who?" I asked.

"All the trifling little boys," she said.

*

Question 19: Was there a moment when you realized that you and your spouse had different worldviews?

One cold winter Sunday, about a month before President 46 died, my husband and I rented a car and drove into the Maryland countryside. It was my idea; I just wanted to drive. We drove past the picturesque rural areas—horse paddocks and old, falling-down farmhouses—into the poor rural areas—dogs in outdoor cages and the vinyl-sided rectangles that people lived in. When we stopped at a light, I noticed him bristle at the sight of an underfed dog chained to a tree, wearing a semicircle into the ground where it paced. Later, when I needed to pee, we pulled off at a wide shoulder. Something on a tree limb caught my eye, and I looked up. It was a noose. My husband was tall enough that he was able to jump up and bring it down; I guess it wasn't tied on very well. We promised to call the authorities the next day, but on the car ride home, we debated. The noose, we both agreed, was a symbol of hatred, a dark message, a

warning to everyone who wasn't white. "This isn't America,"
he kept saying, and I said, "Hon, I think it is, actually." In our
decade together, he always chose to believe in the goodness of
people. He couldn't abide the idea that some people are just
ugly, and I didn't want to convince him otherwise. I was try-
ing to be gentle with him; he had an unhardened heart. He
pulled the car over onto another wide shoulder, turned around,
strained against his seat belt to look at me, and said, "Do you
really think this is who we are now?" and what I said in my
mind was It's who we've always been, but what I said in real
life was "Hon, I'm so sorry."

✳

My dating hiatus came to a conclusion in late April, when I
received a message from my high school boyfriend. It had
been easily fifteen years since we'd talked, and he must have
been stalking exes on the internet, as one does, because his
opening salvo came via one of my social media accounts.

"Yo," he wrote.

I thought it was an impostor account, because "Yo" is not
who Christopher was. In high school, he was always the sweet
one, the fun one, the one who would drive across town to pick
me up because my parents didn't trust me to drive. He used
to make me mixtapes and sneak them into my backpack for
me to find later. He rewrote song lyrics that were funny and
absurd, and left them on loose-leaf paper in my locker. He
had memorized my locker combination, and I'd memorized
his. I can't imagine doing such a thing now—my locker was
my most private space. But I guess love is different when
you're young, and it's new.

I wrote lots of little stories and poems then, and he read

everything I wrote, and if a few days passed without me giving him something new to read, he'd tell me to get back to the keyboard. He loved everything I gave him, or at least said he did. Even at his tender age, he knew the number one rule about these things: you can give feedback on something that's not finished, but if it's finished, you're only allowed to say it's amazing. No question, he was my biggest fan. I had no idea how good I had it.

He was never moody, never vain, never prideful. He wasn't an athlete, wasn't an honor student, wasn't a music wank, wasn't a head who smoked on the back patio. It was perfect. He didn't have a tribe. His tribe was me, and I was good with that. His parents adored me (they didn't have daughters), and he navigated my parents' awkwardness with aplomb. They liked him, I'm pretty sure, despite their inability to show it.

When I think about it, I suspect that no partner has ever loved me the way Christopher loved me. Or maybe it's more precise to say that I've never felt loved by anyone the way I felt loved by Christopher. That might be splitting hairs. Or maybe not. What's important, I suppose, is that I never questioned how he felt, never racked my brain trying to figure out what he was thinking: I knew he was devoted to me. At that tender age, neither of us had exes, we'd never had our hearts broken. That was probably what made everything so wonderful, so easy. We were undamaged goods in the Department of Love, and we had no reason to be cautious.

What I'd always regretted, later, was that I was terrible to him in the end, as we went our separate ways for college. One minute we were at a petting zoo laughing hysterically as we watched poop fall out of goats' butts, and the next minute we were in his car, and I was saying something like, "Well, I guess I'll see you at Thanksgiving, if I even come home." I was resolute and unyielding, as I had been trained to be. My mother was always harping on courage, my father on discipline. In my defense, I was young and had zero clues, and I'd learned from "the literature," such as it was, that we were supposed to rip off the Band-Aid.

When Christopher dropped me off after the petting zoo breakup, I went to my room and cried for hours. I thought life was over. There was no way to recover from this breakup. When my mother came home, she entered my room and looked at me like I was a drowned rat, and she tried, in her way, to comfort me.

"Memento mori," she said, tilting her head. "Remember that one day you will die."

As a devoted Stoic, she often said, "Memento mori," but it was never comforting. I think she meant to tell me that the past is over, and to cherish the present, but it missed the mark.

A few months later when we came home for Thanksgiving, Christopher called to see if I wanted to hang out. I told him I was busy, and had to head back north soon, but we ended up at a party together. While there, I barely said hello. I knew that I needed to steel myself and keep my distance. At the end of the party, he slipped me a note. "Read when you're alone," it said on the front. I made myself throw it away before I left the party.

In the years after, I thought a lot about how badly I'd behaved, and I felt genuinely sorry. I wondered if there might be a good apology I could offer him. A couple times I started to write him a letter, but then thought better of it: What if he's doing just fine? What if he's better off without my apology? What if the letter is actually for me, and my guilt, and not for him at all?

✳

Question 20: Did you take steps to save the marriage?

By day, my husband was an account manager at a media solutions firm, but in the evenings, he tried to be a warrior. He went to listening sessions and workshops on how to be an ally. He reflected on his own contributions to what was wrong with the world and searched within for his internal bias. I was with him at every step. "Tell me more about what they said at the meeting," I'd say when he came home, but he didn't want to tell me, he wanted me to be there. I strongly dislike meetings, but I went to a couple of listening sessions. The women there were cute and friendly, and my husband seemed to hold some appeal for them as the older, wiser testosterone-person. I watched as they thanked him for helping to create a safe space, to which he said things like, "I want to show up for you." They held space for each other, and he made a point of decentering himself when he was there. At home, he re-centered himself, asking me what I thought of his new friends. "Do you think I'm uplifting their voices enough?" he asked, and I said, "Quite."

✳

When Christopher's "Yo" arrived, we exchanged a few messages and decided to meet up for dinner. What I learned from our emails was that he never married, had no children, was in between jobs, had been "doing art" for years but was about to throw in the towel, and was making a big move somewhere soon, but he didn't say where. I had the feeling he was living in Virginia and making the drive to Baltimore to see me, but he wasn't specific about those details. I'd filled him in on the bones of my life, as well.

We met at a sushi place on Aliceanna Street, and I found myself feeling nervous, as if I were going on a blind date instead of meeting up with a person I'd been so connected to once.

Normally, I didn't feel safe downtown. The historic cobblestone, narrow streets, and painted brick row houses were charming, but I worried about what might be lurking in every alley. What might pop out from behind a post or a pier.

But we'd been experiencing a strange, temporary peace. There had not been a single incident in Baltimore for two months—no military officers ambushed, no UN peacekeepers shot at, no local police officers kidnapped. The biggest news story that week was about how the New Confederated States of America had lost so much tourism revenue over the winter; Americans weren't spending their winters in Florida or Texas anymore. Nevada was taking the lead in appealing to snowbirds. So I relaxed into going downtown.

While I waited for him, one of my favorite Baltimore things happened: The 12 O'Clock Boys rode past. At least half a dozen young men on dirt bikes did high-angle wheelies down Aliceanna, trying to get their bikes nearly vertical, like a clock's hands at 12. When you saw them, you knew that winter was over.

As I approached from the east, I immediately recognized Christopher from behind. There was no mistaking his stance, his posture, the way he wore a ball cap—they were all unchanged. He'd grown thicker since high school, as we all do, me especially, but I was surprised by his dad-bod, especially since he wasn't a dad. I was unprepared to see him in a tucked-in shirt with a little belly.

I was reminded of something my mother said when I brought home my college boyfriend, who was a little on the heavy side: "Keep in mind, Hestia, they don't get smaller as they age."

I wanted Christopher to turn around, but also, I didn't. I wanted all the time I could get to observe and prepare. Instead of calling out, I waited until I was right up behind him and whispered, "Christopher."

He turned around. I could see that he was recognizing me the same way I was recognizing him: slowly. Simultaneously we updated our images of each other and tried to understand how they related to the images we'd stored in our brains for twenty-five years.

He said, "It's Chris now."

"Still Hestia," I said.

He pulled back for a moment, squinted at me, and then smiled.

"Yep, still Hestia," he said.

We hugged, but weakly, both of us unsure if we wanted to commit to it.

"It's good to see you," he said.

"You too," I said.

We entered the restaurant and busied ourselves with restaurant things. We pulled our chairs to the right positions at the table, we looked at our menus, we put our napkins on our laps.

"This seems like a nice place," he said.

"It does," I said, "but I never come down here. It's too scary."

"Then I'm honored you came here for me."

The waitress put bottled water and glasses on our table, and Christopher poured for both of us.

"Is your water supply compromised?" he asked.

"You never know," I said.

I took a sip, and he pointed at my chest and laughed lightly.

"What?" I asked, looking down.

"Your buttons," he said.

They were buttoned wrong. It happens all the time. He used to get quite a kick out of it in high school.

"Some things never change," he said.

"We should drink to that," I said.

"I don't do that anymore," he said.

"Okay," I said.

"I'm pretty straight these days," he said.

"Great," I said.

I fixed my buttons, and he smiled.

"Well, you were always . . . artless."

"That's a nice word for it," I said.

"They don't have buttons in the wild," he said. "When you think about it, buttons are one small piece of the cage we build for ourselves."

"Oh, so I'm caged?" I asked, trying to keep it light.

"We're all caged," he said, "and some of us are trying to break out. You're a wild creature—or at least you were. I don't know if you still are."

He started to read his menu out loud and suggested we order right away, so we could have more time to catch up.

He told me about art school, and his time on the circuit trying to sell big paintings in galleries, then scaling back and trying to sell smaller paintings at arts festivals, then scaling back even more to sell quirky miniatures at holiday crafts fairs. For a while, he found a niche with middle-aged women who wanted to adorn their empty nests with bright, idiosyncratic portraits of long-haired goddesses, but even that didn't pay the bills.

"Bottom line?" he said. "People don't want to pay for art."

"Well, yeah," I said.

"Money never liked me, anyway," he said. "If money sees me from across the street, it turns around and runs in the other direction."

I had always liked his sense of humor, and it seemed like he'd held on to it, thank goddess. He asked me if I was still writing, and I rolled my eyes and waved my hand and told him that I did some freelance work here and there but that mostly I'd given it up.

"But you're still a writer, aren't you?" he asked.

"I am," I said, "but is a writer really a writer if she doesn't have any readers?"

"I'm not smart enough to answer that."

"You're plenty smart," I said.

"Maybe it's for the best," he said.

"My failed writing career?"

He cupped his hands around his mouth and pretended to be yelling to an invisible, younger me across the room. "Save yourself while you stilllllll caaaaaaan," he fake-yelled.

I told him about my forays into various communications jobs, marketing this and marketing that, interfacing with various cogs and wheels, engaging with stakeholders, advancing various missions. The more I talked, the more it sounded in my head like I was saying, I'm in a cage, save me.

"But your job is writing, isn't it?" he asked.

"Honestly," I said, "it's selling."

"But you like it?"

"It's not the salt mines or anything," I said.

Talking with Christopher—or rather, Chris—was making me feel disappointed in myself. I wanted to get on with it and get to the apology portion of the evening, which I'd been looking forward to. Instead, he asked about my marriage, and I told him that my husband was a basically good person, kind, warm, large-hearted.

"A basically good person?" Christopher asked.

"Pretty much," I said. "Yes."

"So, did you get bored? Is that why it ended?"

"Why would you ask that?"

"You didn't say he was funny," he said. "You didn't say he was smart."

"I lost him to the war," I said.

"Oh, Jesus, I'm sorry," he said, "how did he die?"

"He didn't die," I said.

Christopher looked confused.

"He joined the circus."

"You're going to have to explain."

I explained that "the circus" was how I referred to my husband's efforts to take up arms and fight the good fight. Christopher took it in, nodding, giving off huge vibes of sympathy, or maybe it was empathy, I couldn't be sure.

I asked him why he never married, and he answered succinctly, "I never found the right person. I just had a series of disappointments, ya know? And I got really tired of getting disappointed."

I wanted to stand up and shout, Same!!!

But I did not.

Instead he gave me his wasabi—"Do you like wasabi? I can't eat it."—and asked me if I wanted his ginger, too.

"You'll get a kick out of this," he said. "My mother, at age seventy, beat breast cancer, and when she was one year into remission, she divorced my father."

I was stunned. I thought they were a happy couple, and I always preferred them to my own parents. They liked my company, and I enjoyed hanging out in the kitchen with Mona. She was a woman of many words, and I loved that. My mother barely spoke—or rather, she chose her words wisely and used them sparingly.

"I mean, who does that? Who gets divorced at seventy?" he asked. "Why bother?"

I thought of Mildred, and how much life she had in her at eighty-something, and for the first time that night, for the first time in my life, I thought Christopher was being a little mean.

"Seventy is nothing," I said.

"It's just so much paperwork, a divorce," he said. "Again, why bother?"

"Maybe she was in a cage and needed to get out," I said.

We reached a détente and ate our maki in silence for a few minutes. He liked the rolls with fake crabmeat, and I liked the rolls with avocado. We both remarked on how surreal it was to be able to eat sushi in a restaurant during a civil war. Not at all like the first civil war, we said, although what did we really know?

"I guess your parents are ancient by now. Are they still alive?" he asked.

"They're old but healthy," I said.

"They're too mean to die," he said.

I couldn't believe he said that. My parents weren't warm or bubbly, but what did he have against them? They didn't fawn over me, the way Mona did, or other moms of other boyfriends, but that wasn't my mother's style.

"You don't know my parents," I said. "We hardly spent time with them."

"I know what I saw," he said.

"What did you see?"

"I don't think they *believed* in you," he said.

I told him I wasn't sure what he meant by that.

"They didn't see the same magical Hestia I saw," he said. "They weren't dazzled, and they should have been."

"But you had on those big ole love goggles," I said.

He shook his head, as if to say, Hestia, you're so simple.

"They should have been wearing the goggles, too," he said.

I felt like I'd been punched in the chest.

"We've had a bit of a falling-out," I said.

"When was that?" he asked.

"I guess it started about twenty years ago," I said, trying to be wry.

"So, a slow simmer then," he said.

"They said that my liberal arts education had ruined me."

"You were *ruint*," he said.

"I was *ruint*," I said.

"Ruint" was one of many private jokes we'd had, and just hearing him say it with his exaggerated Southern accent made me laugh out loud. That's one of the sad things about break-ups, the loss of all those private jokes.

I'd left my phone on the table and noticed in my peripheral vision that my Safe Zones app was sending alerts: Suspects arrested for suspicious activity near Mercy Hospital. Union activist warns of impending attack. And so on. I decided I needed a drink.

I ordered a pot of hot sake, looking forward to how the warm ceramic cup would feel in my hands. I wished that

Christopher and I could share it, but I wasn't going to ask, since he'd been clear about his sobriety.

The evening was fun for a while. We reminisced about our friends and teachers from high school. We low-key gossiped to fill in knowledge gaps about people we knew, and we wondered about the ones we'd lost track of. We marveled over the teachers who had the most profound coffee breath—but we understood it now, too. There was our chemistry teacher's scandalous pregnancy, and our English teacher's Mercedes, which seemed incongruous to everything else we knew about her.

When we were done dragging the female teachers, we moved on to the men. Our civics teacher—ah, back when civics were taught in school—had been famous for his tirades. His favorite rant was about the first civil war, and how it wasn't about slavery at all, but about states' rights. "The War of Northern Aggression," he called it. Christopher had passed around a note that said, "The War of Southern Incompetence." We used to make so many jokes about how the teacher's bald head reflected back the ceiling lights. It was such a shiny head.

Our social studies teacher divorced his wife every December so they could pay taxes as single people and avoid the government's overreaching marriage tax, and then married her again in January. But government overreach was merely a sidenote he trotted out at tax time. Like our civics teacher, he went on tirades, too—these men loved to hear themselves talk—about how the first civil war was rooted in economic persecution. He never called it the civil war, not even on tests. It was always "The Lost Cause," and I got a D in that class because on the final exam I wrote about the raids on federal armories and the firing on Fort Sumter. He marked my exam incomplete and wrote at the end, "Reread the chapter about the burning raid of Shenandoah." His people were from the Loudoun Valley, so there was no arguing. He'd never let go of Shenandoah.

One of the things we did in class was place bets on how long it would take for the beads of sweat to break out around his mustache when he started one of his diatribes.

In hindsight, I realize that I had blithely assumed my fellow students knew those old goats were ridiculous. We never said anything in protest because the teachers' jackassery was obvious, right? But now it's clearer: some of those students must have believed the teachers, regardless of how ridiculous and embarrassing they were. I had overestimated my classmates.

"Can you believe those guys?" I asked.

"They were probably younger than we are now," he said.

"That blows my mind," I said.

"Those rants were entertaining, I'll give them that," he said.

"And the whole time, they were just racist fuckers."

"They were just ornery," he said. "They didn't like sheep."

"Sheep" took me by surprise.

"Sheep?"

"So many sheeple," he said. "That's why I'm moving farther South."

"Who are the sheeple?" I asked.

"You know who I'm talking about," he said. "People like your husband."

I realized that there had been a terrible mistake. Chris thought I was sympathetic to the lost cause. He thought I was estranged from my husband because he was fighting for America.

"I'm not a confederate," I blurted out. "I'm an American."

"Hestia," he said, "come on. You're too smart."

I tried to think of the most patriotic things I could say.

"I'm a patriot," I said. "Black lives matter. Tax the rich."

"Really? Tax the rich?"

"Correction," I said. "Eat the rich."

The buzz from the sake wasn't helping. I reeled back the last hour. How had I given Chris the impression that I was a confederate? The most clichéd thing happened: a shiver ran down my spine, and I put my hand on my forehead, because I must have had a fever.

"No offense, but you sound like one of those dimwit, liberal bigots from the peanut gallery," he said.

That was sudden. I couldn't believe he'd turned venomous so quickly.

"No offense, but you sound ignorant," I said. "Real nice words coming out of your mouth."

"I've been nice my whole life, and where did it get me? People telling me I'm racist, just because I'm white," he said, agitated and raising his voice. "I was nice to you twenty-five years ago, and where did that get me?"

I felt like I was melting, the way I imagined a computer's motherboard melts when it can't handle any more information. Christopher was one of the kindest, smartest people I'd ever known, fun and compassionate. I looked for the zipper on his neck, because surely aliens had snatched him and made a suit out of his skin. I looked at his ears to see if any froth from the brain-eating infection was leaking out.

"When did you get to be such a bully?" I asked.

"Oh, that's rich. *I'm* a bully? *I* am?" he said, even louder and more dramatically. "Libtards are the real bullies. They have so much anger in their hearts."

"I'm not the one raising my voice," I said, and I said it very, very calmly.

Finally, all those years of being trained by my parents to reject emotions and eat my anger, and above all *remain calm*, were paying off, in a sushi restaurant with an ex-boyfriend who was about to show his ass. But Chris tapped his fingertips together and lowered his temperature.

"You're so naive, Hestia," he said, and he sounded tender, as if he cared about me and worried about me being duped. "Do you hear yourself? Laugh till you cry, I guess."

"You're not being fair," I said.

"Oh, and you've always been fair?"

Yet another punch in my chest.

"Life isn't fair," he said. "What a stupid word. 'Fair.' 'Fair.' 'Fair.' Have you studied any history at all? Do you understand the Anthropocene *at all*?"

He was like one of those clowns at the rodeo, jumping up and down, ringing his bell, waving his flag, except he wasn't moving, and the flag was his words. I wanted the bull to gore him. Sorry, clown, life isn't fair, I'd say, while he lay there bleeding.

"I have plenty of ideas about the Anthropocene," I said.

"Fine, Hestia," he said. "But don't tell me that all of this isn't boring. 'Rights.' 'Voices.' 'Representation.' Taking down all those statues on Monument Avenue, which, by the way, we clambered on in the midnight hours when we were happy."

I tried to get my eyesight back in focus, because anger makes my vision blurry.

"They're only statues," I said.

"What I'm saying is . . . I'm sick of hearing about it. Nobody says anything interesting anymore. God forbid you say something with nuance. Nobody gets to play devil's advocate or have complex ideas anymore. It's social justice and safe spaces all day, every day. It's boring, Hestia, and you're smart enough to understand how boring it is."

I was still trying to focus my eyes.

"Do you disagree that it's boring?" he asked.

I had to think for a few moments, to gather my thoughts. I spoke slowly.

"I think that now . . . is not the time . . . for nuance," I said. "I think that now is the time for picking sides."

"Boring," he said.

"And yet, these are pretty interesting times," I said.

"Interesting like a bludgeon is interesting," he said.

"Maybe," I said.

"Be honest, does any of this light your brain on fire?"

"My brain's on fire right this minute, actually," I said.

Then we stopped talking. We stared at each other from across the table. I'd read articles about how to fall in love, and apparently, according to the latest science, staring into a person's eyes for four minutes straight was the fastest, most guaranteed ticket to intimacy. We stared for four minutes, maybe longer. I can't say it didn't feel intimate, more intimate than anything I'd ever experienced, actually. It was the deepest feeling, but the feeling was grief.

The human condition: confusion. Staring into Chris's eyes for four minutes, I had new insight into what I didn't like about relationships: I will never be able to truly know another person. The most intimate relationship of my life would be my relationship with me—which was wildly unappealing. This is why people believe in gods, so we can have intimate relationships with *them* instead of ourselves.

Chris was the one to break the silence.

"Look, I said some things I regret," he said.

"I hope so," I said.

"Can we forgive each other and move on?" he said.

Could I forgive him? In some ways, we were peas in a pod. When we looked at the world, we saw the same absurdity. But where life had befuddled me, it had made him bitter. I'd been slapped around a little; maybe he'd been slapped around a lot.

"What got you here?" I asked.

"I took I-95," he said.

My face went blank, and I couldn't stop myself from laughing out loud.

"No, I get it," he said, chuckling. "You want to hear what happened to me. You want my sad story so you can figure out how I became a monster."

"I don't," I said.

"We're old friends," he said. "We can get past this."

"But I don't know who you are now," I said.

"Isn't life supposed to be bigger than that?" he asked. "Aren't we supposed to try harder to love each other?"

"You're asking for unconditional love," I said.

"And?"

"I'm not sure I can do that."

"I understand," he said. "It hurts to give what you never got."

"Ouch."

I folded my napkin and put it on the table. He covered his plate with his napkin. I ordered a ride and put down cash for half the bill.

"Nah," he said, pushing the money back toward me. "Get me next time."

✳

Question 21: Can you recall a marital argument that seems particularly poignant in hindsight?

The more meetings my husband attended, the more energized he became. When I asked what he liked about the meetings, he said it was eye-opening to learn about other people's lived experiences. He said he wanted to do the work. I suggested he invite some allies over for a meeting at our apartment, and he did, and that's when I had an inkling of what was really energizing him. There was a woman there, my age but quite a bit newer to the world, if that makes any sense, who turned to him all night for help. She most especially needed help setting up the easel for the giant sticky pad, and at every stumble he came to her aid. The kindness I'd grown so used to was now being siphoned off to her. He said, "I know it's hard, but just breathe into it." And then she literally breathed, and he did, too, and they breathed together while he set up the easel. When the meeting was over and everyone was gone, I commented on how helpful he'd been to her, and he said that he liked being able to bring his expertise to the movement. I said, "So you're, like, the easel expert, then," and he said, "They need my help, and I like helping. Sue me." He accused me of calling him vain, and I told him that we're all vain, that's what makes us human, that's what makes us unique among all other species. "I'm making the world a better place," he said, and I held my tongue because I suddenly knew he was done with me and my way of seeing the world. I thought my self-restraint in that moment was admirable.

✳

The Baltimore cease-fire ended that night, after my "date" with Christopher. Actually, it was the early morning, when a pipe bomb exploded inside a van just outside of Mercy Hospital. It knocked out some of the electric grid and the radio signals down there, but my cell service, only a mile away from the hospital, was still working.

From my bed, I heard the explosion, felt the bed shake. All the things on my dresser rattled. Then the sirens began, and the helicopters, and men's voices over loudspeakers for hours. It was about 2:00 a.m. I put on a full outfit, checked all the locks on the doors, put on my shoes, brought my go-bag out of the closet, and put it by the back door. My go-bag was a backpack that held water, a flashlight, a sweater, extra socks and underwear, and some nonperishable food items high in protein and carbs. Even though it wasn't quite cold enough for it, I put on a highly functional army jacket with pockets everywhere, and I stuffed them with useful items.

I did the calculations in my head. Sometimes the terrorists just want to make noise and scare people, and if that was the case, I could wait it out behind my curtains. If they started banging on people's doors, I could go out the back door and sit under my deck. If they started breaking and entering, I'd take my bag, go out the back, and head uptown, north, using only the alleys, never the streets.

I kept my eye on the news coverage as a picture emerged. It was the same-old. Confederates were claiming the explosion, which was meant to protest the hospital's policy of performing abortions. Mercy was Catholic, and what I wanted to say to these people was, Dudes, if Catholic hospitals are doing abortions, you've already lost.

But it's never about reason. They were romantics, and they loved their cause.

Citizen journalists tweeted that the military had turned out to the bomb scene, and the local police as well. There were also reports of Russian mercenaries flocking to the scene to battle the military. Peacekeepers kept a respectful distance and let the military do their thing, but patrolled the neighborhoods.

∗

Question 22: Do you recall giving up on your marriage all at once, or did it happen gradually?

One night I took off my wedding ring to put on moisturizer, and I never put it back on. It wasn't a decision, it was just lotion. I just didn't put it back on, and about two months later my husband noticed. "You're not wearing your ring today?" he asked, and I said, "Yeah, not today."

∗

When someone posted footage of Russians smashing windows a few blocks south of me, I grabbed my bag and went out the back. It was almost dawn, still dark but getting lighter by the minute. I realized that I was hoping Marcello would text, just to check in on me, the way he had only three months earlier when there was a snowstorm. But he didn't. I guess he was too busy, or maybe he had a new girlfriend. I wanted to know he was safe, too.

I tried to keep to the darkest parts of the alley, slinking along the fences, staying in the shadows. I hadn't even gone two blocks when I came face-to-face with a Russian. I think we bumped into each other. He didn't understand English. He pointed a knife at me, which was telling, because why would you use a knife if you had a gun? This must have been a low-pay-grade Russian, if he was even paid at all. He looked all of seventeen, and teenagers, who have no impulse control, are the scariest soldiers.

The mercenaries had a reputation for showing no mercy. But this Russian, the kid with the knife, just looked tired. He held the knife close to my neck, and I wondered where the rest of his team, or whatever you call it, were. It occurred to me that he'd lost his posse, or could he have possibly defected?

Throughout history, mercenaries have gained a reputation for raping people, mostly women, and I ran through scenarios in my head about how to deflect it. All the trainings with my husband had come down to the same thing. The best defense was to throw up on your attacker. The grosser the vomit, the more likely you are to buy a few seconds to escape. I started thinking about things that make me gag or make my stomach feel queasy. I thought about getting my hand slammed in the car door; the sweet potato that rotted and the maggots that swarmed onto my hand when I picked it up; any number of dead and decomposing Baltimore rats that I've had to shovel up and bag for garbage pickup, in various stages of decay; the smell in the retirement village when someone dies in their room and it takes half a day to discover them.

The soldier looked directly at my chest, and I did the opposite of bracing myself. I loosened myself. It was something my husband had taught me during one of his manic phases. When someone is riding their bike, drunk, and they fall, they get fewer injuries than someone who falls off their bike sober. That's because they're loose, he said. The more you resist, he said, the deeper your injuries. He wasn't exactly like, "Lean into it," but more like, "You don't need to let it kill you."

I looked into the Russian's eyes and tried to get loose. I tried to loosen my stomach so I could vomit. I tried to loosen my bowels, even. I looked down at where his gaze was directed, my breasts, and saw that he was fixated on them. Or actually just one of them, the left one, and I realized that he wasn't fixated on my breast, but on my breast pocket. I had stuffed it with a cheese stick and turkey jerky, because protein.

I whispered, "Are you hungry, buddy?"

I guess he didn't like that I was whispering, because he put his knife a little closer to my neck. I used my eyes only to point to the food in my pocket and said, "Da?"—one of the words I'd learned during my husband's training.

He took the food, and I don't know what would have happened next because a peacekeeper discovered us and the Russian took off running. The peacekeeper could have chased after him, I suppose, but he didn't. I looked at his face, and it wasn't Marcello.

✳

Question 23: What were the last months of your marriage like?

Let's say the demise had three stages. At first, my husband was obsessed with getting a gun, which had become difficult to do, because people like us all had the same come-to-Jesus at the same moment. He went to shooting ranges every week, meeting up with the cute young lefties who hung on his words, and he took classes on hand-fighting and gun-cleaning. The next stage involved finding his way into groups that assembled in the evenings to talk about safe houses and escape routes. Find a safe house, he told me, by looking for the garden gnome wearing a hand-knit hat. The last stage kicked in during the Purge, when his sister was killed in a ShopRite parking lot, and two months later he was gone. He'd packed a duffel and left every-

thing else—including me—behind. He didn't even ask me if I wanted to go with him, which wasn't fair. I might have said yes, although I doubt it. Sometimes I'd like to know how he's doing, but I don't think I can take it on, the task of finding him.

✳

The morning after the bombing, only essential personnel reported to the retirement village, and although I was far from essential, I went. I wanted to check on Mildred, or maybe I just didn't want to be alone.

My first stop was for tea (I was too wound up for coffee), and I found Tom in the Café des Artistes. He was standing at the counter, his back to me, perfectly still. He must have been watching his tea steep. I've done it, too. There's something soothing about watching tea steep. But with his back to me, I had a chance to give him a good once-over. He was thin, not rippling with muscles, but fit. The flannel he wore over his T-shirt was fraying at the edges. His shoes looked like they probably had holes in the soles. I spoke softly so as not to startle him.

"Are you done with the kettle?"

He turned around quickly and forced his eyes up from the floor to meet my gaze.

"Yes, please, help yourself," he said. "It's your kettle, anyway. Not my kettle."

"It's not *my* kettle, either," I said. "But thank you."

He seemed unnerved, but was that because of me being there, or was that because of the evening's pipe bomb?

"It's dedicated of you to come in to work today," I said.

He exhaled through his nostrils rather forcefully and made himself smile.

"Soaring Crane isn't going to teach itself," he said.

"But you're a contractor," I said. "You could have taken the day off."

"I don't have anything else to do," he said.

His honesty caught me off guard. I wasn't sure I liked it, but it made me curious about him.

"I guess I don't, either," I said.

"And I don't get paid if I don't teach."

"Oh, right," I said. "That makes sense."

"I'm sure you have benefits," he said nervously.

"I do," I said. "They're not bad."

"That's lucky," he said.

Somehow, we had entered into a conversation that we both knew was tedious, but we couldn't figure out how to make it stop. Reflexively, I looked at my phone, and clenched my jaw when I saw all the red rhombuses.

"You can turn off the app completely," he said.

"I know," I said.

"I'm just saying, I turned mine off, and it's better. For me."

"It would probably be better for me, too," I said. "It's a weird day. I bet all the kids are really shaken up. Do you have kids?"

"I don't have kids," he said. "No one ever wanted to have kids with me."

The kettle stopped, and I poured steaming water into my mug.

"Was I prying?" I asked. "I'm sorry."

"You weren't prying at all," he said quickly, almost panicked. "I was trying to make conversation."

"Okay," I said. "I don't have kids, either. For what it's worth."

"Okay, thank you," he said. "Sometimes when I'm nervous, I don't talk enough, and sometimes I talk too much."

"You're just shy," I said. "It's not a sin."

He sipped his tea carefully; it was scalding hot.

"I wrote a song about that, actually, back in the day. One of the lines—"

"Stop right there," I said.

He held his mug in midair.

"Are you about to quote your own lyrics?" I asked.

"Is that bad?" he asked.

"It's pretty bad," I said.

"Oh, okay," he said. "Never mind, then."

"Like, kind of lame?" I said, to provide more clarity.

"I didn't know," he said.

But he was old enough to know.

I reached into the drawer next to him, brushing his hip to take out a spoon, and I put a sugar cube and cream into my tea.

"Does it bother you when people put sugar and cream into their tea?" I asked.

"How do you mean?" he asked. "Like, am I a purist?"

"Are you?"

"It's only a tea bag," he said.

There was a television mounted in one corner of the Café, almost always with the sound muted. Tom found the remote and turned up the volume. The news showed footage of the anti-fascists who'd come to Mercy in the wake of the bombing. I couldn't imagine what the anti-fascists thought they'd do there, how they'd be useful, but I watched carefully.

"Are you looking for someone?" Tom asked.

"My husband," I said.

"You're married?" he asked, his surprise apparent.

"Technically," I said. "Legally. I haven't heard from him in two years."

"But you're not divorced?"

Still watching the screen, I said, "It's such an ass-ache."

"What is? The legal stuff?"

"I guess," I said. "Yeah."

"People do it all the time," he said. "People a lot less smart than you."

I took my eyes off the screen and looked Tom in the eye, which made him turn away after a few seconds.

"See you in class?" he asked.

"Maybe," I said, and using the water that was still hot in the kettle, I made another cup of tea to bring to Mildred.

✳

I found her in one of the game rooms, reading a book. She said she'd never been able to read in a quiet room. She liked to read in the rooms where people played the most rousing games of spades and poker, the more raucous the better, because she concentrated best when she was blocking out noise. "I've had a lot of practice blocking out noise," she said. "Three husbands, two children."

She had her fleece blanket wrapped around her as she read.

"I brought you some Irish Breakfast," I said.

She looked up, startled.

"What are you doing here?" she asked. "Why didn't you take the day off, like a normal person? Aren't you trauma-tized by the night's events?"

I pulled a chair next to her and sat down.

"You mean my date with Christopher?" I asked.

"We're calling it a date now?" she asked.

I told her all about it, recounting all the words I could remember, and describing the contempt in his voice the best I could. Then I told her about the encounter with the mercenary.

"Oy vey, I don't know which one is worse," she said, "the date with the schmuck or the run-in with the Cossack."

"Oh, I know which one is worse," I said.

"Yes, you're right," she said. "The schmuck."

I asked her earnestly what is wrong with people. She laughed, until she realized I was serious. "Oh, Hestia," she said.

She held the mug between her hands and warmed her fingers, and when she was finished, I asked her if she'd like more tea.

"No, let's put a thirty on it," she said, because Micky McIrish had worked in the newspaper business, and that was a thing he used to say.

I asked her if she'd like to smoke, and she said it was a little too cold for her today, she'd be just fine reading in the game room. I realized I'd tired her out. I pulled the blanket up to her neck and stood up, getting ready to leave. She beseeched me to go home and get some sleep, and I decided that she was right.

But before I left, I asked Mildred how she felt when her children learned to say no.

"Oh, dear God, the No Years," she said, and I could tell she was searching in her brain for the memories. "That was one of my favorite stages."

"Why?" I asked.

"Oh, Ruth was serious, even as a little girl, she was always worrying. When she said no, I laughed out loud. It was hilarious. It was like, she was finally becoming herself. I was finally getting to know her."

"That's sweet," I mumbled.

"Then ten years later, Annie did it, and I loved it even more. She never concerned herself with serious matters, always wanted to sing and dance, you know? When she said no, I was getting to see her dark side. It was delightful. What a treat."

I thought about how lovely it must be to have a mother who loves you like that. Imagine: a mother who loves you *more* when you show her who you really are.

"You're such a good mom," I said.

"I'm all right," she said. "But I must've done something wrong. My lovely Ruth is a unionist, and my little Annie is a confederate, and I swear I raised them the same. The rub is, they're both good girls."

"It's a shame they don't get along," I said.

"Worst schanda there is," she said.

"They both love you."

"Vive la différence," she said.

4

BROTHER JAMIE

Two years into becoming single again, I felt it was time to start a Scribbles unit on love. We'd already moved through prompts about the war, our childhoods, and our marriages—and my students had flat-out refused to write about the latter two. "Feh," was the general consensus on both topics. But when I said we'd be writing about *love*...
Oh, how their faces lit up.

Mildred stood up from her desk and held her cane high, like a torch welcoming the downtrodden.

"Let's tell Hestia Harris about love!" she said.

Jeffrey stomped his feet in approval.

"Hear ye, hear ye!" said Dorothy.

"Finally," said Charles. "I get to impart wisdom."

"Settle down, everyone," I said. "Hestia Harris is doing fine."

While the class tried not to laugh—I saw Mildred coaching them to zip it—Clara stood up, put her hands on her heart in prayer, and bowed to me.

"Of course you are," she said.

We spent a couple of weeks reading women's magazines, in search of love quizzes with interesting questions. The five of them agreed on a list of prompts, from which I removed the queries about sexual techniques, despite how eager they were to share what they had learned.

"You're no fun, Hestia," said Jeffrey.

"Your children and grandchildren are going to read this," I said.

"Are you kidding?" he balked. "They can handle it."

But I held my ground. "Rated PG," I insisted. As a compromise, we spent a class session sharing out loud.

"I was late to the party," said Jeffrey, "but I learned to do some things with my tongue."

Clara gave us some insight into tantric practices. Charles insisted that communication was the best lubrication, and Dorothy concurred, wishing that she'd learned to use her words earlier.

"What I'd tell any young woman is this: Be the boss in the bedroom," she said.

Mildred listened carefully. "This is what our readers want," she said.

✳

Question 24: What should someone look for in a romantic partner?

JEFFREY: *Find a mensch. Watch how they treat waiters and cashiers.*

DOROTHY: *I always looked for men who were brilliant or interesting. Then a light bulb went off—I could date men who were nice to me.*

CHARLES: *My husband thought I was the most astonishing creature he'd ever met. Aim for that.*

CLARA: *Partners should help to heal each other.*

MILDRED: *You have to love being around them, dear.*

✳

When I met my husband, his sister and Jamie were already married, with three children. Right away, Jamie and I hit it off. At family gatherings, we were often the bystanders watching the drama unfold. My husband and his sister came from a close-knit United Methodist family that was always taking up one cause or another, and singing hymns. Family gatherings were boisterous and sometimes contentious. "Let's agree to disagree" was something they said often. You might, at a large family meal, have someone respond to your request to pass the salt and pepper by singing, "O food to pilgrims given, O bread of life from heaven," as they handed you the shakers.

Jamie referred to me as his "outlaw," because we had both married into the family and were a step removed from being in-laws. There were times when I thought Jamie and I understood each other better than our own spouses did. I suggested this to him once, drunk on Easter wine, and he said, "You're onto something, sister."

For the last two years, since his wife died and my husband left, I'd been having dinner with him and the kids once a month. It was a habit that was easy for both of us to keep up. I was happy to let someone cook for me, and he was happy to have the company of someone who wasn't a picky eater.

"You can't imagine how much I miss having another adult in the room," he said often.

Every time, he made grilled chicken. The goal was to cook the blandest, least seasoned meal he could so that no child could object to a spice or an herb. He didn't even so much as marinate the chicken in lemon. One of the twins was a "super-taster," he said.

"There will come a time in my life," he said over the grill one evening, "when I never eat a piece of chicken again."

He served salad, too, usually romaine lettuce with ranch—on the side, of course. His son didn't like tomatoes, one daughter didn't like cucumbers, and the other daughter didn't like avocados or carrots.

"You try making a salad in this house," he said. "I dare you."

Sometimes he called me Sister Hestia, and I called him Brother Jamie, a tradition from the before-times.

He loved his children so much. When dinner was over, and they dispersed to their bedrooms, and he finished nagging them into dental hygiene, and he finished reading to them, and I finished my rendezvous with his dishwasher, we'd sit on the couch. He'd tell me about the problems they were having. Then he'd ask my advice, which was both ridiculous and flattering.

"As you know," I said, "I don't have children, so you should probably ignore all my ideas."

"I'll take anything," he said.

Usually I said things like, "The kids are doing great. They're wrapped up in your love," because that's what struck me when he talked about them. He cared *so much* about what they were going through—that was the most obvious thing about him.

Sometimes he seemed sad, or overwhelmed. After the incident with Christopher and the pipe bomb, I asked him how *he* was doing. He thought I was talking about his son.

"No," I said, "I mean *you*. How are *you* doing?"

He shook his head.

"You know the saying," he said. "A mother's only as happy as her least happy child."

"But . . . you're not their mother," I said.

"I know," he said, "I know. It's awful."

He put his head in his hands and actually cried a little. It was a reflex—I hugged him, and he hugged back, and we held each other for a few moments. I hadn't meant to start anything, but when I felt the electricity, I hightailed it out of there.

"So sleepy today," I said, yawning, as I scooted out the door.

✳

Question 25: Do you think humans are meant to be monogamous?

JEFFREY: *I don't care how many sex-at-dawn books people want to write, they're all going to get debunked eventually. Everybody wants their one special person.*

CLARA: *I tried an open marriage with one of my husbands, but it was too much work. There were so many rules: who we were allowed to sleep with, where we were allowed to do it, what days of the week. It was such a relief to just cheat.*

CHARLES: *My husband and I always said we'd try an open marriage, but we never found anyone else we liked enough to*

*go through with it. We're wired for pair-bonding, for survival.
Going solo exposes you to predators; a triad leaves your loyalty
split. Pairs are safest.*

DOROTHY: *Men love a comfortable rut. But women get bored.
We want adventures, and that's exactly why the patriarchy
invented monogamy.*

MILDRED: *Monogamy, shmonogamy. I was pretty good at it,
although who knows if my husbands were. In between marriages, I did enjoy being a merry widow.*

✳

The next time I had dinner with Jamie, when we sat on the
couch to discuss the children's problems, he made a point of
asking me about *my* life. I told him we didn't need to talk
about that dreariness.

"It's not even close to interesting," I said. "Not like yours."

"My life is interesting?" he asked. "My life is as cookie-
cutter as they get."

"But you have all these people," I said. "You're never alone."

"Hestia, what are you talking about?" he said. "I'm always
alone."

I was taken aback.

"I'm confused," I said.

"You and me both, sister," he said.

"I'm the one who's alone," I said. "I mean, look at me."

"You look great," he said. "You look like you're doing
great. You're dating."

"You could be dating, too," I said. "You're a catch."

He held up his hands in protest.

"Not even close to ready," he said. "Not like you."

At some point after my husband left, I congratulated myself on how well I'd "moved through it." I'd told myself that it really was like the billboards said: you can't go around pain, you have to go through it. I felt I'd done some very good work, some honest healing. Now, sitting next to Brother Jamie, as I replayed that conversation with myself in my head, I could hear what a crock it was.

"How are your herbs?" he asked. "You grow cilantro, right?"

"You seriously want to know about my cilantro?" I asked.

"I've always been impressed by your potted herbs," he said.

"It's too early for cilantro," I said, "but my lemon balm is perking up. I think we can say it's spring now."

"Spring," he said, and he sighed deeply.

I nodded and sighed, too.

"How's your love life?" he asked. "Anything of note?"

From time to time, he'd asked this question, and I'd told him only the bare facts about Ethan and Marcello. Neither of them held a candle to Jamie.

"It's embarrassing," I said.

"What's embarrassing about dating?" he asked.

I answered carefully.

"I guess that Ethan and Marcello weren't really what I wanted," I said. "I knew it from the beginning, but I went with it anyway."

"Ah," he said. "But what *did* you want?"

I thought about how hard my marriage had been those last years.

"I think I wanted to remember what it was like to have fun."

"Do you need a boyfriend to have fun?"

"It's easier."

"Are you one of those people who can't stand to be alone?"

I flashed back to the summer nights of my childhood when I walked up and down the beach by myself, while my parents played gin rummy with their friends. The Atlantic always smelled like loneliness to me.

"I don't like being lonely," I said. "So, I lower the bar."

"You *are* the daughter of a Stoic," he said.

"That's the truth, Ruth."

"Those guys were lucky to have you, though," he said.

That sentence felt like voltage. He put his hand on my knee, and I put my hands on his cheeks and pulled him closer to me. Then I kissed him on the lips.

He kissed me back, putting his hands on my cheeks, just like I'd done to him. We'd always had chemistry, but I was surprised. And after a kiss like that, we couldn't not have sex.

It was carnal, like the sex you have at a wedding or a funeral, when you're feeling so many things about the human condition, and you need to be reminded that you're just an animal. I felt as if Jamie were devouring me.

We had to be quiet, stealthy even, because of the children, which entailed some creative problem-solving. We couldn't do it in the living room, obviously; we couldn't do it in his bedroom, which was next to the children's bedrooms; we tried the bathroom, but it was too bleak; we ended up in the mud-room, filled with the household's shoes, boots, jackets, backpacks, tennis rackets, and a skateboard. We made love on a bench, where people sat down to tie their shoes, with a couple of winter coats hanging on hooks over us, and we held our hands over each other's mouths to muffle the moans. When we were finished, he laid his head on my heart and listened.

"Does it always beat this loudly?" he asked.

"Honestly, I have no idea."

He wrapped his arms around me, and I felt wrapped up in his love. It had been a long time since I felt so close to someone. We lay on the mudroom floor, on the utility rug, for what felt like a long time. Neither of us wanted to move into whatever came next, I think, because nothing could be as good as what had just happened.

But we did move, and there was no question of me staying the night, because of the kids. Brother Jamie was clear: The kids couldn't find out. It would be too confusing, it would be *too much*, and I agreed. I dressed and went home, and that night I lay in bed, unable to sleep, wondering if he might love me someday, and how much, and in what way, and how his feelings about me compared to his feelings about his wife, who was also my sister-in-law, and if he thought about her when we were having sex, and if he said her name in his head, by accident or on purpose, when he came. I had a special knack for draining the joy out of beautiful things, which I'd been perfecting for more than forty years.

✳

Question 26: What's difficult about looking for love?

CLARA: *Dating is a perpetual cycle of revising criteria and second-guessing what you want. Sometimes it's hard to even know who you are.*

DOROTHY: *Sooner or later you realize that dating is performative. You have to perform how interesting you are. Perform how kind you are. Perform what an emotional grown-up you are. And then—it gets worse. Because when your performances* *get his attention, well, then you've got his attention, and do you actually want all that attention? It's exhausting.*

✳

Finally, we had some warm spring days, and the retirement village came alive. I was happy for Mildred; she was tired of being cold. We drank a cup of tea before heading out to the sunny garden.

"This Café sucks eggs, by the way," she said.

"I know," I said.

"Splenda on every table," she said. "And why are the lights so bright?"

"People have been asking that question for a couple hundred years," I said.

When we'd first met, I asked Mildred how she liked the retirement village, and she'd said, "When you're a young woman, it doesn't take long to realize that you'll spend your whole life cleaning the kitchen. But in this village, I haven't washed a damn dish in years."

"Sounds like a relief," I said.

"It's glorious."

In the garden, the sunlight was perfect. I begrudgingly lit a cigarette for her, feeling guilty because she'd been coughing more than usual, but also feeling like I wanted to be a good friend to her. Almost immediately, Mildred started coughing. I held her arms up in the air and patted her back, as had become our habit.

"Do you really need the cigarettes?" I asked.

"I like them a lot," she said.

"I'm concerned about your cough."

"It's just a winter cold," she said. "Cigarettes make me happy."

"But the coughing."

"The heart wants what the heart wants," she said. "It doesn't have to make sense."

She'd recently switched from French to Indian cigarettes, because of the prices. The Europeans were gouging us on imported tobacco. Add on Mildred's requirement that the cigarettes be menthol and 100s length, and the cost was getting out of control.

"Is it really worth it, Mildred?" I asked.

She beat her chest and rolled her eyes.

I hadn't told her about Jamie. I was nervous about it, afraid that I'd crossed a line. More importantly, I didn't want her to tell me to break it off. Jamie and I had seen each other a couple more times, and it was just as hungry and passionate as it had been the first time.

Instead of telling her about Jamie, I showed her Ethan's profile on the dating app.

"Remember Ethan?" I asked.

"Oh, yes, of course," she said. "I remember his harness."

I swiped through his series of photos on the profile, and her eyebrows raised with each one.

"They're good photos, right?" I asked.

"Very charming," she said.

"They're *my* photos," I said. "Photos I took of him when we were together."

"He's a good-looking boy, and you're a good photographer."

"That's *my* gaze making him look so good," I said. "We broke up, and he put *my* photos on his profile."

"If I recall, Hestia," she said, "*you* broke up with *him*."

There was too much ash hanging off her cigarette, so I took it from her, tapped it into the ashtray, and gave it back. She held out her pack to me, offering me a smoke, but I waved it away. I slumped deeper into my chaise longue and leaned all the way back, so the sun could bathe my face.

"I don't like it," I said. "It feels shitty, and I don't even know why."

"Life is like that," she said.

"Would it trigger you if I said I was triggered?"

"Yes, dear."

"Okay."

She offered me the pack again and said that if I smoked one cigarette with her, she'd tell me how to cope with the shitty feelings.

"Mildred, that's a three-dollar cigarette," I said.

A pack of menthols was close to sixty dollars.

"Take it, please," she said. "I'm dying to give you advice."

I didn't want to, but I smoked the cigarette, both of us in our chaises, faces to the sun. Every now and then she commented on the breeze, and how it felt on her face with the sun. I stubbed out the butt in the ashtray.

"So," I asked, when we'd finished our smoke, "what's the secret?"

"It's more of a deal than a secret," she said. "You accept that you're always going to feel shitty about something. You'll never get rid of the shitty feelings, because you're human. You submit to it. If it's not one thing, it's another, and you live with that."

"You said you were going to tell me how to get rid of shitty feelings," I said.

"No, I told you I was going to tell you how to cope with them," she said.

"You tricked me," I said.

"Hardly."

"I'm not mad, though," I said.

"Dogs get mad, people get angry," she said.

"Yes, thank you for that," I said.

She patted my hand between our chairs and told me I was quite welcome.

✳

When Sarah wearied of her dating adventures, she decided to try a new tack. Instead of aimlessly browsing the aisles, she'd decide what she wanted before entering the store. Then she'd make a beeline for it. It was time, she decided, to use the law of attraction, and she asked the universe to send her the perfect boyfriend.

One morning, she brought her new vision-board to the office and hung it on our wall, next to the lotus flower. It was foamcore, with pictures of good-looking men cut out from magazines and glued in a collage.

"I'm setting an intention," she said. "I'm calling in my man."

After that, she repeated key phrases to the board every morning with her eyes closed, creating vibrations that would radiate into the world and manifest the boyfriend.

How is manifesting different from praying, I asked, and she insisted, It's different!

"I am a lovable, powerful goddess who deserves to find a true love," she said six times.

"My love will be tall, handsome, and serious, and he'll spend money on me," she said three times.

"I'll feel safe with him," she said nine times.

I asked her how strict she'd be about the money part, because so many rich people had moved to their second homes in peaceful nations to wait it out.

"Oh, Hestia," she said, with pity. "It's just as easy to fall in love with a rich man as a poor man."

Silently, I disagreed. Rich men and me were like magnets with our north ends facing each other.

I wondered, also, what she meant by "safe."

"Anyway," said Sarah, "I'm manifesting the shit out of this."

At that moment, a red rhombus from the Conflicted app appeared on her phone screen. She picked it up and read aloud, very pleased, as if the good news confirmed that she was on the right path.

"'America passes its most comprehensive gun laws to date,'" she said. "'Gun safety reform sails through Senate and House.'"

✳

Question 27: How important is alone-time in a relationship?

CLARA: *Something must be said about solitude. Rilke said our highest duty is to guard each other's solitude. But it's difficult, because that's when we see ourselves most clearly.*

DOROTHY: *We'll probably always be alone, whether we like it or not, whether we're single, married, or deeply in love. You never really know anyone but yourself.*

✳

Once we'd started our affair, I had dinner with Jamie's family more often, two or three times a month, and we waited until the kids were asleep before we made love. We'd upgraded to the bedroom, agreeing that the trade-off was worth it: we had to be quiet, but the bedroom was so much nicer than the mudroom. On nights when I didn't dine with the family, I'd wait for him to text me that the children were asleep, and then I'd come over. He'd quietly escort me upstairs, we'd tip-toe into his bedroom, close the door, put our hands over each other's mouths, and undress.

Most of the time, I'd go home afterward. Jamie worried about one of the kids coming into his room in the middle of the night and discovering me there. But every now and then, he was so tuckered out that he fell asleep right afterward, as did I, and I stayed until we woke up with the sun. Whenever that happened, I whooshed out of there at the crack of dawn, which was really early. We were at the summer solstice, and the days were as long as they get.

Some people get turned on by the secrecy of an affair. But not me. Sneaking around, making up stories, thinking fast and coming up with lies under the gun—it felt wrong, especially because we were lying to children.

But the sex was so tender. I never questioned my desire for him. And for a father of three, he had a surprisingly good dirty-talk game. When he whispered what he wanted to do to me, and what he wanted me to do to him—the desire in his voice drove me wild. Not only did he tell me what he wanted, he told me how to do it, and how much he wanted it. And the words he used . . . surely, somebody's mother wanted to wash his mouth out with soap. It was pure gold. Irresistible.

After, as we lay together and talked, we'd let in his old dog Bernadette to stop her whining. She had been with the family since before the twins, and she was long in the tooth, slow and creaky. And so devoted.

Jamie told me about his day, and I told him about mine, and we discussed the children and what might help them, until it was time for me to go.

One evening, while we lay there, Jamie told me that he'd looked up my website and read all of my articles on it.

"All of them?" I asked.

"Every single one," he said.

"Oh my goddess," I said.

"Come on, Hestia," he said. "They're fantastic."

That moved me, and I loved that he was a reader. I wondered if one day we might be the kind of couple that reads novels together and discusses poems in *The New Yorker*. Maybe we could be a book club of two.

"Do you have more I can read?" he asked.

It had been a long time since I'd dated anyone who'd taken an interest in my writing, let alone thought it was fantastic. I hardly knew how to respond.

"You want more?" I asked.

"Of course I want more."

I was lying faceup, and before I knew it, there was a tear rolling out of each eye, dampening my hair under me. I didn't dare move, for fear that I would slip into a shaft of light from the street and he would notice.

✳

We fell into a routine. On weekends, we met at Robert E. Lee Memorial Park, which was renamed Lake Roland Park, but so recently that everyone still called it Robert E. Lee. His children had reached an age where they were beginning to sleep in, or at least didn't need him immediately if they woke up early. We'd meet at seven o'clock and walk through the park holding hands, choosing the yellow trail, a fairly untraveled path, so we didn't run into anyone he knew. Jamie brought coffee in travel mugs for both of us, and we marveled over summer's early morning light through the trees.

We always chatted with Khalil, a peacekeeper from Algeria, whom we befriended. Sometimes Jamie brought him coffee in a paper cup.

"Mr. Jamie," he said, which was a very Baltimore thing to say, "good morning to you and your wife."

Neither of us corrected him.

Lake Roland was where we were most romantic: kissing, hand-holding, looking into each other's eyes. He still wore his wedding ring, and if it had been any other man, that would have been a deal-breaker. But I'd known Jamie for so long, and his wife for nearly as long, that I didn't see the ring as an affront. I mean, dysfunctional, probably, and it would have to come off at some point, but it was all right for a while.

On one of our early morning walks, we were talking about our former spouses, and he said about Liz, "I still miss her sometimes."

I understood.

"We weren't always happy," he said, "but we were building something."

"I know," I said.

"It was bigger than me or her," he said.

Building something together—maybe that's what had been missing from all my relationships.

It was so much easier having known her, I realized. If I'd just met Jamie and had to contend with the enormous shadow presence of his dead wife, the mother of his children, I might not have ever felt comfortable. But I knew her: I knew how annoying she could be, how dumb in certain moments. I'd seen them bicker a hundred times. I'd seen how drunk she got on Christmas Eve, and I'd seen him get grumpy about it, and I'd seen how she looked for real, in person, which was nothing like what she looked like in any of her photos. She had been real and flawed, so my mind couldn't torture me with a fantasy. There was no mystique to wrestle with.

Jamie asked about my husband.

"Do you ever hear from him?"

"Never," I said. "Do you?"

"No," he said. "It was the strangest thing, him leaving you."

"I saw it coming," I said. "And then when Liz died . . ."

"The final straw," Jamie said.

"He held on as long as he could," I said.

"Why haven't you divorced him yet?"

The eternal question. Every time someone asked it, my answer changed. I told Jamie I felt bad asking for a divorce. For all I knew, he was impaling confederates, or surviving by eating bugs, all for the cause. How can you present paperwork to someone who might be battling gangrene?

Jamie asked if I thought the civil war was more crushing for some people than for others, and I said, "Hell yes, it's harder for optimists. They're maladapted for times like this."

"Because optimists hate to be disappointed," he said.

"And people are disappointing," I said.

"Then you must be an optimist," he said, "because I think you're always disappointed in people."

That blew my mind.

Jamie admitted that he'd found my husband insufferable for about a year before Liz died.

"He was full of hot air," he said.

"Mildred says he sounds like a blowhard," I said.

He asked who Mildred was, and I changed the subject because it felt strange to tell him that my best friend was an eighty-six-year-old nursing home resident.

"Hey," I said, "I invented a joke after he left. Do you want to hear it?"

He said he did.

"How do you know when a white man is woke?"

"How?" he asked.

"Oh, don't worry," I said. "He'll tell you."

That got a nice laugh out of Jamie. I hated saying goodbye to him at the end of those walks. He was going home to begin a long day of chauffeuring, nagging, and cleaning the kitchen, and I was going home to make coffee and take pictures of my fireplace filled with vases and dead flowers.

✳

One Saturday morning in July, before we went on our walk, I helped Jamie tie a yellow ribbon around the maple in his front yard. It was for the hostages trapped in the confederacy—citizens who didn't want to live in that theocracy, but couldn't afford to leave. His whole block had trees with yellow ribbons.

The same day in Lake Roland, we rounded a bend on the trail and saw a suitcase. It was in the middle of the path, all alone, no nearby human connected to it. We stopped walking and stared at it. Then we started to back away, slowly and carefully.

"Goddammit," said Jamie, emphasis on "damn."

"We should tell Khalil," I said, and then all at once, everything felt urgent.

Why were we backing away slowly? We should be running. I grabbed Jamie's hand and pulled him with me as I ran.

When we told Khalil, he looked in all directions, standing perfectly still. Then he called it in to his partner.

"Another grip," he said. "Yes, a valise."

"Suitcase," I said.

"Yes, man," he said into the radio. "Another suitcase . . ."

In hindsight, it didn't make sense that the suitcase would contain a bomb. There were only a few hikers, no electrical substations, no cell towers nearby. It would have been a lot of trouble for a minimal return on investment.

"Yes, man," said Khalil. "A middle-aged couple."

Jamie and I ran out of the park and back to his car. (Were we really a middle-aged couple?)

The next day, I pored over the Conflicted digest for news of the terrorist suitcase, but there was nothing. We were so embarrassed, that we never went back to the yellow trail. We adopted the red trail, which was the most remote the park had to offer.

✳

Finally, the man Sarah called in arrived. He was twenty years her senior, fairly well-off, and devoted to her. They'd met while she was walking her dogs, and he told her he was drawn to her because he used to rescue dogs, too.

"I meant to call in someone younger," she told me.

"I think he's what you manifested, though," I said.

"He's tall and rich, but I also asked for handsome," she said.

"He's handsome," I said. "For a fifty-year-old."

She smacked her forehead.

"I never said *young*, did I? I totally forgot to say *young*."

He spoiled her, mainly with acts of servitude. He drove her dogs to the vet. He gave her dogs baths. Whatever wish she expressed, he was at her command.

I asked her if she was attracted to him, and she said she wasn't, not really.

"But he thinks I am," she said.

"He's buying it?" I asked.

"Oh, I'm a really good actress," she said.

"Brava," I said.

"I just pretend I find him sexy, and he does all this stuff for me. Does that mean I'm using him?"

"I mean, yes?"

"Do you think it's wrong?"

I told her I'd have to think about that one. On the one hand, in the relationship pie chart of hours that couples spend together, sex is just one tiny slice. And people pretend all the time. They pretend they like a partner's haircut, or a partner's taste in music. Is it any different to pretend to be horny for someone so they'll drive your dogs to the vet? On the other hand, that felt really cynical, even for me.

"Do you think he'll figure it out?" Sarah asked.

I told her she had nothing to worry about. A lonely man will be whatever kind of chump he needs to be to stop being lonely.

"Wow," she said. "You don't think highly of men, do you?"

"I have reasons," I said.

"Why do you even date them?"

"I'm not dating right now," I said, lying because I hadn't told anyone about Jamie yet.

"Should I feel bad about using him?" Sarah asked.

"Come on, Sarah," I said. "You're hardly the first woman to use a man. The world is full of transactions."

"I guess you're right," she said. "I was hoping you'd tell me it could be love."

"Does it feel like love?" I asked.

"No," she said.

"Maybe you should hold out for love," I said.

"Mildred says you're a closet romantic."

I scoffed.

"You two are discussing my love life?"

"Don't worry," she said. "Mildred's rooting for you."

✳

In August, while I clipped my mammoth dill, my mother called. I thought about not answering. It had been months since we lunched at the Leafy Greens, and a smarter woman might not have answered. But I was feeling good, and I suppose my guard was down.

"Hestia, is this still your number?" she asked.

"Hello, Nancy."

"Are you doing all right?"

"I'm fine," I said.

"That's good," she said. "We're fine, too."

"That's good," I said.

"Things went off the rails in our last conversation," she said.

"Yes, it was pretty bad," I said.

"I'm sorry you felt hurt," she said.

Neither of my parents had learned to apologize properly, and I didn't hold out hope for them learning at their ages. Like all the gurus say, You have to *want* to change.

"I'm calling to remind you about your father's birthday," she said, almost whispering. "He'd appreciate a call."

I told her that if he wanted to talk to me, he could call me himself—and also, since when did birthdays matter to them? She asked me when I got so hard, and I laughed.

"And this time, Hestia, don't make up some story about how it's the war," she said. "The war has nothing to do with our family. We can still respect each other, even if we don't agree."

"But you don't respect *me*," I said.

"Because you're so naive," she said.

"That's not a nice thing to say."

"You do not have to get upset if you don't want to," she said.

"Is there anything else you need to tell me?" I asked. "Because I'm pretty busy."

I had potted herbs to pinch, not wanting them to go to seed.

"Your father and I want to see you," she said. "We want to visit you."

"But you'll have to cross enemy lines," I said, mostly being sarcastic because it was so close and the border in Virginia was so permeable. But I thought "enemy lines" sounded appropriately dramatic.

"We can make it work," she said. "The war doesn't have to be a big deal."

It totally tracked that the war wasn't a big deal to her. Our democracy was crumbling because of spite—but it wasn't one of her concerns.

I stayed vague about a visit and said goodbye, then returned to my business with the mammoth dill. I kept the dill outside, on my window ledge, and every year, the black swallowtails laid their eggs on it, and the caterpillars ate all the leaves. I'd leave the house in the morning with a nice healthy dill plant and come home from work to find only the stems. If the butterflies needed my dill, I could share, but I just wanted a little for myself. I make a great egg salad, but it doesn't work without the dill.

✳

Question 28: Do breakups make you stronger?

JEFFREY: *Nietzsche said that whatever doesn't kill you makes you stronger, and certain types like that line very much—extreme athletes, inspirational speakers, businessmen. The Nazis liked that line, too, I recall.*

CHARLES: *I have an old friend from the commune, an anti-vaxxer, who believed that measles would make his son's immune system stronger. But the measles gave his son permanent heart damage. I feel the same way about breakups.*

DOROTHY: *Rejection is a bitch. It damages you, no matter what.*

MILDRED: *Hestia, why are you so heavily defended? Your armature is debilitating. You poor bird.*

✳

The affair with Jamie was so sweet that I *almost* didn't mind having to keep it a secret from his kids—but I did mind. I wondered out loud when we might give them the big reveal, and he said it was way too early. Like, how much time has to pass, I asked, and he said quickly, Oh, at least a year, I think.

"I just don't want anything to be weird for them," he said. "Everything is hard enough as it is."

In the meantime, we came up with ways to integrate Aunt Hestia into the family. I asked them to stop calling me Aunt Hestia—Hestia would do nicely—but they couldn't break the habit.

I'd had an idea that I could fill my empty fireplace with birdhouses—so I bought cheap, unpainted birdhouses and painted them with the kids. We used big jars of tempera paint, just like in elementary school, with fat brushes. We painted out on the grass, hardly any cleanup necessary.

Back in May, we took the kids to a pick-your-own farm where we harvested strawberries and paid for them by the pound. Then we made strawberry pie. We picked peaches in June, and in July we picked cherries. By August, the kids were sick of picking fruit, and Jamie worried that they were going to see through the ruse. We were pretty good about not touching each other in front of them, but we both knew that the first time one of us slipped, they would see it.

Bernadette the dog became more arthritic and had a hard time even walking, so sometimes we'd make a weekend afternoon out of putting her on a red wagon and pulling her around the neighborhood. The kids had entered the eye-rolling phase of their lives, but they refrained from that when we wheeled Bernadette through the streets. I think they enjoyed it. We made her a paper crown, and sometimes draped a small red blanket over her, like a queen's robe. It was a treat to walk around the neighborhood like that, the three kids adjusting her crown, fawning over her, even waving her paw at passersby, like the queen that she was.

*

At my desk, every morning, I scrolled though the Conflicted digest while Sarah manifested things. Iran, a "sister theocracy," was trying to form an alliance with President Pepper, who had successfully championed the popular anti–income tax crusade. So now the confederacy was broke, and when a thousand points of light failed to keep the lights on, Pepper said yes, please, to the Supreme Leader's big, fat loan.

We had our weekly check-in with Ed in his office, and Sarah could barely contain her eye rolls when he spoke.

She liked him in general, and over the summer, he'd been joining the three of us—me, Sarah, and Mildred—in the therapy garden. When Mildred offered him a cigarette, he'd say, "Woman, you're a godforsaken temptress," which delighted her. He and Sarah bonded over shrimp and grits, as Ed had lived in Charleston with his second wife. And Ed always asked to see photos of Sarah's dogs.

"Dogs are the best people," he'd say, to which she'd say, "Amen."

But when it came to work, they were like oil and water. Sometimes it's so hard to work with people you like. Or maybe I have that backward, and it's hard to like people you work with.

Sarah questioned why we were still doing the written history project, with only five students who could barely be bothered to write. Ed insisted it was worth doing.

"But it's so twentieth century," she said. "It's so much writing and reading."

She had become convinced that we needed to have a presence on social media.

"We could record the students and post sound bites online," she said. "Or short videos, under twenty seconds."

The village didn't have any social media accounts, and I liked it that way. I'd tried to make a Twitter page for us once, but the two-factor authentication felt like a slow death.

"The residents don't like social media," I said.

"But their children and grandchildren use it," she said.

Ed leaned back in his chair and spoke to the ceiling.

"They'd have to sign media releases," he said, in a wearier drawl than usual.

I wanted to high-five him, because media releases could stop anyone in their tracks.

"Besides some children and grandchildren, who would even look at these videos?" I asked.

"There's a nursing home TikTok!" said Sarah. "They have all these sassy old folks on there, giving out advice and being feisty. People love it."

"Lord, just take me now," said Ed.

"I can record them on my camera," said Sarah. "Research shows that people prefer unprofessional videos because they look authentic."

"Any time now, Lord," said Ed. "Take me to the Great Big Texas in the sky."

They both looked at me for resolution, and I felt caught in the middle.

"I think we've covered enough for today," I said.

"Oh, right," said Sarah, "let's put a pin in this until the next meeting."

Like many millennials, she hated meetings and had even suggested that we have stand-up meetings where we set a timer, so we wouldn't waste so much time with useless questions like, "How was your weekend?" and "Is your mom feeling any better?" And her using the office jargon we mocked, like "Let's put a pin in it," let me know she was annoyed.

"We'll circle back next week," I countered.

"We'll ring the bell on this again," she said.

"Let's get another bite of the apple," I said, and she made her exit.

With Sarah gone, I remained in my seat across from Ed and shook my head.

"I think she thinks it's her duty as a young person to speak her mind," I said.

"It's all good," he said. "She thinks I'm a dinosaur, and she might be right."

"But she's a little rude sometimes," I said.

"I thought we were calling that 'outspoken.'"

I asked him what he thought about asking the residents if we could record them, and he said it was fine, but we also needed something written for the children. "That generation likes books," he said, "and those books are their inheritance."

"You know what's funny?" I said. "When I was a little girl, my parents made it clear there'd be no inheritance for me. They said inheritances should be illegal, because they make people weak and dependent."

"Your parents sound like a piece of work," he said.

He'd heard a few stories from me about my parents.

"I guess they tried," I said.

"I don't know about that," he said. "It doesn't sound like they tried *that* hard."

✳

I started looking forward to Tai Chi. Tom's heroin voice smoothed out my edges, and he went easy on me and Mildred. While he advanced the rest of the class on Shoulder Strike, he gave us the Standing Bear lesson, a pose in which we stood with our legs slightly bent and moved our arms very moderately from hip to hip. It was basically standing, plus a small, gentle movement.

"Slower," he kept saying to me. "Go more slowly."

After class, I found Sarah at our desk, pouting. She had a couple of seminal texts in front of her, and she was staring at the wall. I sat in my chair kitty-corner to her.

"How's the Red Emma lecture series going?" I asked.

"It's trending," she said.

"Really?" I asked. "What's the enrollment?"

"I started with a soft launch," she said. "This way it gathers steam."

I asked again what the enrollment was, and she waved away my question.

"Do you have some good students?" I asked, and she ignored me.

"Oh!" she said, remembering something.

She opened one of her drawers and pulled out a plastic baggie with a note inside. She waved it in front of my face and grimaced.

"Your little friend left this for you," she said.

I had no idea who she was talking about.

"The Tai Chi guy," she said. "You should read the note."

The bag contained a few seeds, and his handwriting was surprisingly beautiful, almost old-fashioned. The note said, "I found these in my chicken curry last night, and I know you like to grow herbs. I thought you could grow cilantro from these coriander seeds."

I read the rest of the note: "Don't worry! I washed the seeds before putting them in this bag!"

I didn't know what to make of it. Tom had gifted me seeds plucked from his curry, and somehow believed that they'd still be viable.

Sarah sat with her arms folded, with a shit-eating grin on her face. She watched me refold the note, enjoying herself.

"It's sweet, isn't it?" she asked. "He likes you."

I decided it was time to tell her about Jamie; keeping the secret had been hard. When I explained the nature of the relationship—that Jamie was my husband's sister's widower—she pulled her head back and tried to raise a single eyebrow to indicate her archness. She didn't have the eyebrow muscle to pull it off, but she tried.

"Ew," she said. "Isn't that kind of . . . wrong?"

"Is it?"

"He's your *brother-in-law*," she said. "It sounds . . . *gross*?"

"I think I might be falling in love."

"Our Father in Heaven," she said.

"Is that bad?" I asked.

"I don't even know," she said.

"I'm worried it's bad."

"Look, Hestia, I'm just a girl who lets an old guy drive her puppies around town."

"He loves your dogs."

"We should get a drink," she said, "because I'm worried that Hestia is in love."

I agreed.

"Honestly, though, going to bars is not as much fun as it used to be," she said.

I asked her to elaborate.

"You know how fun it is to sit at a bar when you're hot and single?" she asked.

I ignored the question, because I definitely did *not* know what that was like.

"It's not nearly as much fun when you're not single," she said.

I asked her if she had started turning down the free drinks, and she said that men weren't buying drinks for her anymore.

"At first, I wondered if I had become unattractive," she said. "But I'm still hot."

The problem, she deduced, was that she wasn't giving off single-girl vibes anymore.

"Who knew that single-girl vibes were a real thing?" she said.

"Who knew?"

"I guess it was never about the alcohol for me," she said.

"Huh," I said. "It was always about the alcohol for me."

"Why do people have to be so complicated?" she asked.

"Humans are complicated."

"Who said, 'Hell is other people'?"

"That was Sartre," I said.

"Right," she said.

✳

The next day was sunny, but not too hot, a perfect summer day for warming the crown of your head. It seemed as if the village residents were using every available square foot of outdoor space. The therapy garden overflowed with villagers basking in the sun. Some days are like that, so beautiful and unexpected. But because she liked to be discreet, Mildred couldn't smoke out in the open per usual, and she was put out.

"Get me into the wheelchair and let's bust out of here so I can smoke," she said.

"Why the wheelchair?"

"Have you not noticed how slowly I walk these days?" she asked. "I'm getting slower, you know."

"I shouldn't take you out of the facility," I said.

"I know it's frowned upon, but . . ."

"Mildred, it's against the rules."

"Sure, some people might see it that way," she said.

As the war had escalated over the last two years, the village had decided that only family members could take residents out of the building. But Mildred talked me into breaking the rules. We went back to her room, I helped her into her wheelchair, and we left the building.

"Mildred," I said, taking her across the street so we could be on the sunny side, "if anyone asks, would you just tell them we're related?"

"Of course, dear," she said. "Are you my daughter or my granddaughter?"

We had about forty years between us, so it could have gone either way.

"You pick," I said.

She went with daughter, preferring a late change-of-life pregnancy to being a teen mom. I loved the idea of having Ruth and Annie as my older sisters. I parked Mildred's chair next to a bus stop and stood beside her, holding her ashtray, like a butler statue, while she smoked. I tried to imagine how we looked to passersby, amused by the optics of it, and I told her about Jamie.

Mildred seemed to take a great deal of pleasure in smoking out in the open, on the street, not hiding from anyone. She also seemed pleased to hear about Jamie and wanted to know more.

"He texts me good morning," I said, and she nodded.

"He texts me to say good night," and she nodded.

"Good. Make him work for you," she said.

"What?"

"Men don't always know they want you—until they have to work for it," she said. "The hard work is what penetrates the skull."

The last thing I wanted was to make Jamie work. He worked so hard already, all the time. I wanted to make things easier for him.

"He's a really good person," I said.

"Look at how you're smiling," she said. "Hestia, your face!"

"I'm not sure I can stop smiling," I said.

We both waved to the peacekeeper on the corner, who tipped his hat to us. This was the French (or was he Belgian?) keeper who used our restroom. He approached and offered to light Mildred's next cigarette; she put her cigarette between her lips and stuck out her face toward him with an ease that spoke of how many thousands of times she'd done this. He seemed curious about the brand.

"No Gauloise today?" he asked.

"No, I switched," she said. "I'm anti-colonial."

"At the harbor, I see some guys selling cigarettes," he said. "Black market."

"Over my dead body," she said. "I'm not smoking any traitor tobacco."

He lit her cigarette, and she checked out his ass.

"One hundred percent beefcake," she said right to his face, as she took her first pull on her second cigarette.

He posed for her, and she laughed, and he posed again.

Mildred took another pull on her cigarette and exhaled for a long time, dragging it out.

"When you spend all your days in the death warehouse," she said, "you forget that in the real world it's still perfectly legal to smoke."

The peacekeeper chuckled.

"It's not a death warehouse," I said.

"To-may-to, to-mah-to, dear," she said.

"Oh, but death doesn't want you," said the peacekeeper.

"I think he does want me," said Mildred, squinting her eyes as she took her next drag.

"You're not his type," he said.

"Now you're just blowing smoke up my skirt," she said.

He laughed, saluted us, and returned to his corner. Then Sarah started to walk past without seeing us, holding a paper cup of coffee, and when she walked through Mildred's cigarette smoke, she waved it away dramatically, as if she were trapped in a fire and fighting for her life.

"Stand with us a minute," Mildred said. "We're all friends, right?"

Sarah's shoulders relaxed.

"Hestia was telling me about Jamie," said Mildred.

"Did she tell you he's her brother-in-law?"

"I think she really likes him," said Mildred.

"But look at her track record, Mildred," Sarah said. "She likes them, and then she breaks their hearts."

Sarah waved away a plume of smoke.

"That's not my pattern," I said.

"Look at how she's smiling," said Mildred. "Have you ever seen anything like that?"

"What about the fact that they're practically related?" asked Sarah.

"They're not, though," said Mildred. "And it's juicy that she's schtupping the brother-in-law."

"It's icky," said Sarah.

"It's complicated," I said, "but that doesn't make it wrong."

"The heart wants what the heart wants," said Mildred.

"You always say that," said Sarah.

"Because it's always true," said Mildred.

Sarah and I debated what the worst-case scenario could be with the kids, but it became laughable because, as Mildred pointed out, neither I nor Sarah had children.

"Tell us more about him," said Mildred, and I obliged.

"He's kind, and tender, and I feel relaxed when I'm around him," I said.

"Nice," said Mildred.

"He's a grown-up who makes good decisions, and there are people he loves and takes care of," I said.

"Excellent," said Mildred.

"I love being one of the people he looks out for," I said.

"Fine, fine," said Sarah, "but tell us about the sex."

I threw her a bone and told her he was great at dirty talk.

"Like, what does he say?" she asked.

"What do you mean?" I asked.

"Tell me some of the things he says."

There was no way I was going to repeat the things he said, but I told her that he was skilled at telling me what he wanted, how he wanted it, and when he wanted it.

"Like he's ordering off a menu?" she asked.

"No!" I said, loudly, because she wasn't understanding at all. "It's the way he says the words, the way his voice sounds when he wants me."

She looked at me and shook her head.

"Hestia," she said. "You're such a *writer.*"

There was pity in her eyes.

"It's my cross to bear."

"I still don't know how I feel about him being her brother-in-law," she said.

"Feh!" said Mildred. "Who's even around to judge? Hestia's husband is gone, her parents are out of the picture, she has no brother, no sister, and except for us, she's totally alone."

"Ouch," I said.

"That came out differently than I meant it," she said. "You're not 'totally alone.' I was being hyperbolic."

"I know, Mildred," I said. "I love your hyperbole."

✳

Question 29: What do you know now about rejection that you wish you'd known when you were younger?

CHARLES: *Sometimes rejection has nothing to do with you. People go through things, and you can't understand them.*

JEFFREY: *Sometimes rejection is as simple as you're not his cup of tea.*

MILDRED: *When someone rejects you, don't argue with them, no matter how much you want to. If they believe they don't want you, that's all you need to know.*

✳

Sarah told me that she'd started wearing a blindfold during sex: "It turns me on," she told him, "it's my kink," and he bought it.

To me, she admitted the truth, which was that the folds of skin on his neck made him look like an old man, and she didn't want to see that during sex. Sometimes when they went out together, people mistook him for her father—and she stopped bothering to correct them. She started giving him blow jobs because it was faster than intercourse, and there was less overall touching.

He began taking her dogs to doggie kindergarten while she was at work, but then she dumped him.

I was relieved for both of them. Their relationship made her feel yucky, and she deserved someone who made her feel good. Also, it must have been humiliating for him. No one should have to bear that much humiliation just for a warm body at night.

After they broke up, he asked if he could keep walking her dogs, and she said yes.

"Poor guy," I said.

"He keeps 'loving' all my photos on Facebook," she said.

"That's embarrassing," I said. "But some people have trouble moving on."

"Why do I even still have Facebook?" she asked.

"Fair question," I said.

"He just posted a picture of himself with some old woman," she said.

She showed me several photos on her phone. The woman looked to be about his age, and they were smiling wildly.

"Look at her cankles."

"Sarah," I said, "literally, straight guys *never* notice cankles."

"How can they not care about cankles?"

"Why does it bother you?" I asked.

"It's just . . ." she said. "How could he go from me to *her*? It's like he doesn't have standards."

"He'll probably never have another girlfriend as pretty as you, and he knows it," I said. "But thank goddess you released him."

"What if it was a mistake?"

"Stop it," I said. "Now he's free to find someone who loves him, and you are, too."

We swiped through some more photos.

"Does he look happy to you?"

I reminded her of how this works: "However hard someone is trying to look happy on social media—that's exactly how miserable they are."

✳

Jamie and I were taking it slow, mostly because of him. I looked forward to the two or three nights a week we spent together, but by the end of summer, I wanted more. I wanted to curl up with him on the couch and watch TV with him and the kids. I wanted to make coffee with him in the morning, instead of running out of the house before the children woke up. I wanted all of us to be honest with each other.

"I hate being your secret," I said.

"But if they find out about you," he said, "they might see you as a potential stepmother."

That seemed like a leap, from girlfriend to wife, but I didn't probe. The topic was sensitive.

"Maybe they could handle it," I said.

In September, I got a bee in my bonnet to plant some spring-flowering bulbs. My mother was obsessed with tulips, so I planted daffodils and hyacinths. I'd never done it, but Jamie's yard was perfect for it. With his blessing, I bought dozens of bulbs and planted them, by myself, on a weekend when he chauffeured the kids to playdates and birthday parties. I suppose it was an act of faith. They'd bloom in April, and I really wanted us to still be together then.

At the same time, Bernadette became miserable. When we tried to lift her into the wagon, she cried. Sometimes she panted for no reason, and sometimes she couldn't even stand up. She barely ate and had started to look unclean.

Sometimes when I came over after the kids were asleep, Jamie did late-night chores before he carried the dog upstairs and we went to bed. One night, while he was putting away clean dishes, I suggested that it might be time to let Bernadette go. "We could show her some mercy," I said.

He became angry, the first time I'd ever heard him raise his voice. The kids can't take another loss, he said, slamming a cabinet door.

"If you had kids, you'd know," he said. "But you don't."

That seemed unnecessary and even mean, but I tried to put myself in his shoes. They were all still missing Liz, even if it looked like they'd gotten on with their lives. She'd been killed in the Purge, and I couldn't imagine that kind of grief, although I was certain it could make you mean on occasion.

"But what if she dies in front of the kids?" I asked.

"At least they'd get to say goodbye," he said. "They were never able to say goodbye to their mother."

"But what if it's a painful death?" I asked. "You can't let them watch that. It would be unspeakably cruel."

"You think I'm *cruel*?" he asked, angry.

I told him I could find a mobile euthanasia unit that would come to the house.

"You could put Bernadette down in comfort," I said. "A win-win, because she could go in peace and the kids would say goodbye."

"I *can't* put her down," he said.

He slammed a mug on the counter with such force that it cracked, and chunks of ceramic flew onto the floor.

"Great," he said, staring at the shards on the floor. "That's just great. That's the mug they gave her for her birthday before she died. Thank you so much."

I put my shoes on and headed for the door.

"*You* broke the mug," I said, and I left.

I summoned a ride-share, and on the way home with the windows down, I could smell the change of seasons.

The next morning, he texted.

"I'm sorry for being so emotional," he wrote.

"Don't apologize for being emotional," I wrote back.

I didn't want Jamie to be sorry about having feelings. I wanted him to be sorry for being an ass.

I didn't like it when people apologized for having emotions. My parents had always tried to coach me away from feelings. "Now, Hestia, I see you're getting emotional," they'd say. "You don't have to let that happen." As a result, other people's emotions were like nectar to me, and I wanted to drink them up.

I wanted to make a new rule for the world: No more apologizing for getting emotional. The addendum to the rule would be: Apologies for *not* getting emotional will be taken under consideration.

"See you Thursday?" he wrote.

"Sure thing," I wrote.

✳

The next morning, when I told Sarah about the mug, the fight, and Bernadette, she suggested I break up with him.

"Just tell him it would better for everyone," she said.

"What?"

"Do you even know why you want him?"

"Because I love him."

"But why do you love him?"

"Because we're good together."

"I think you're afraid," she said.

"The world is frightening," I said. "Have you seen it? I need people."

"You have me and Mildred."

"I need someone who's more than a friend."

"Okay, answer me this, and don't think too hard about the answer," she said. "If you had to choose between (a) having a lover and no friends, or (b) having friends and no lover, what would you choose?"

I knew the answer so quickly it startled me.

"I'd choose friends," I said.

"See?"

"But can't I have both?"

"I'm digging the single life."

"What's happening?" I asked.

"I think I've had an awakening, Hestia," she said. "I'm going solo."

"An awakening?"

"I'm going to find some answers," she said.

✳

Ruth and Annie made visits to Mildred in the same week, which made me wonder if something was going on. I had assumed that if there were medical concerns, Mildred would not tell me. Lately, she'd seemed more frail than usual, but it's hard to see change when you watch it happening every day.

While Ruth visited, I slow-walked past the Serenity Room to see if I could overhear anything important. But Ruth's a low-talker. When Annie visited, I did the same, and even though she's quite a bit louder than her sister, I heard nothing. Annie was her mother's compatriot in Irish Breakfast, and they sipped together while Annie talked about things that seemed to concern her, judging by the look on her face. When she was finished talking, she went to Mildred's room and came back with a hairbrush, and then brushed and fluffed her mother's hair until she was satisfied with how it looked.

Before then, I'd never seen anything close to serenity in the Serenity Room, but I saw it on Mildred as her daughter brushed her hair. For those couple of minutes, her body seemed different, her face seemed smoother.

Later, Annie found me at my desk, while Sarah and I were working.

"Hestia, I know you and my mother are good friends," she said. "Can we talk in private?"

Sarah stood up to leave, but I motioned for her to stay.

"Sarah and Mildred are very close, too," I said. "The three of us are."

Annie seemed a little surprised, but she proceeded.

"I'm so grateful for you," she said. "My mother never had a lot of friends that I knew of."

"She had a lot of husbands," said Sarah. "That probably got in the way of friendships."

"Probably," said Annie.

"She's a very good friend," I said.

"She made me swear that I wouldn't talk to you about her medical condition," Annie said, "and I'll keep that promise."

"But you're trying to tell me something?"

"See if you can figure it out," she said. "My mother says you're very smart for a young person."

I took both compliments.

"Let's keep her healthy," she said. "No more smoking. She has to make it to Dublin, as you know."

"Dublin, right," I said.

Sarah and I exchanged a glance. Apparently, Mildred hadn't told either daughter about the other's plan.

We chatted about the Tai Chi class and about Scribbles, which Mildred only participated in to humor me.

"I look forward to reading the product someday," she said. "Although she said I have to wait until she's dead."

As Annie left, she hugged me and Sarah, and the hug lingered in the room for hours.

"Thank you again," she said. "I'm counting on you."

As soon as Annie was gone, Mildred tried to talk me into aiding and abetting her in a "wee smoke." Having just been told, more or less, that Mildred had health problems, I refused.

"You *refuse*? What kind of narrischkeit is that?" she asked.

"Maybe tomorrow you can smoke," I said. "If you're not coughing."

"Well, shit," she said, crossing her arms.

I told her about Jamie and the dog, describing the pain the dog was in. I told her how badly I felt for the children, who were going to lose the pet they loved only two years after losing their mother, and how angry Jamie had been.

"This sounds like a slow-motion disaster," she said.

"The dog?"

"I meant the relationship," she said. "But sure, the dog."

"You think the relationship is doomed?"

"I've buried three husbands and two dogs," she said, "and from your description, I'd say that dog's time has come."

"He has to let her go, right?"

"He's got to get off the dime with that dog," she said. "Hestia, you go there today and tell him it's euthanasia or bust."

*

By the end of the day, I had resolved to go to Jamie's after bedtime and make my case for Bernadette. My basil plants were peaking, so I clipped all the leaves, bought some cheese and some nuts, and drove to his house. I thought we could make pesto with his food processor while I convinced him to be as humane as possible with the dog. When I arrived, unannounced, I couldn't find him in the house.

"Where are you? Here with pesto stuff," I texted.

A few minutes passed before he replied.

Then, finally, "In the alley."

I walked through his backyard and found him leaning against his back fence. He was weeping. I'd never seen him cry like that, not even at his wife's funeral. I'd never seen any man weep. I wasn't sure if I should hold him or give him space, lean in or lean back. I liked it when people leaned in, but not everybody does. I put my hand on his back and felt his spine shuddering.

"Hey," I said.

He said nothing, so I rubbed his back and tried to hug him from behind.

"Bernadette died," he said, still leaning over the fence. "It was bad."

"I'm sorry," I said.

"It was cruel," he said. "Just like you said."

"It's not your fault," I said.

"It is my fault. The kids were traumatized," he said. "Just like you said."

"Where is she now?" I asked.

He'd moved the body into the shed and planned to take it to the vet in the morning.

I asked him why he was in the alley.

"The kids finally fell asleep," he said. "I don't want them to wake up and see me like this."

After a little while, I coaxed him back into the house, and he moved through his hysterical misery until it became numb silence. When he was calm enough to go upstairs without waking the children, I put him into his pajamas and into bed. I spooned him, wrapped my limbs around as much of him as I could.

In the early morning, after a fairly wretched night, he seemed finally to be sleeping. I really wanted to look in on the kids while they slept, but I couldn't risk it. Even though I didn't have a food processor, I took the basil, cheese, and nuts home, figuring I'd crush the pine nuts with my mortar and pestle. I didn't leave a note, because I didn't know what to say.

✳

Question 30: Who was the one that got away?

    CLARA: *I didn't agree to this question. Did you slip this one in, Hestia?*

    JEFFREY: *We vetoed this question, Hestia. Why is it still here?*

    CHARLES: *If you want to torture yourself, tell yourself that there's "one that got away."*

    DOROTHY: *What a crock. "The one that got away." Who invented that? Hollywood?*

    MILDRED: *Lovers don't "get away" from you. You end it, or they end it. It's a choice. Spend your life regretting it if you want to, but what's the point?*

✳

The day after Bernadette died, I texted Jamie and said I was coming over with dinner. I arrived at his house bearing plain cheese pizza, unsauced chicken wings, and bottles of soda.

    Maybe it was too reminiscent of those visits when Liz died, and my husband and I brought over take-out meals and milkshakes. Back then, we mopped Jamie's kitchen floor and opened his mail for him, sorting out all the junk. We even cleaned the bathrooms; my husband was good that way. We watched the children as they processed, at various stages, the realization that they were motherless. My husband helped plan the memorial, and I helped Jamie with some of the paperwork; it was complicated, during the Purge, to get a death certificate. The medical examiners and morgues were so busy.

The kids ate the pizza and wings. When they were asleep, I asked him if it was all right that I'd brought over the food.

"It's all right," he said. "You're a good aunt."

When he said "aunt," I got a bad feeling and waited for the rest.

"You were Aunt Hestia long before you were my girl-friend," he said.

I waited.

"And I hope you always will be," he said.

"Aunt Hestia," I said. "But not your girlfriend?"

There was no way I was going to make it easy for him to break up with me.

"You'll always be their aunt."

"They might like to have me be more," I said.

"They've been through so much," he said.

"Kids are resilient," I said.

"They've been through so much," he said again.

"I think the odds are good that they'd adjust," I said.

"But I don't want to gamble with my kids."

He had ideas about how to be a good father, and who was I to say otherwise? I didn't want to argue with him about how much he should love me.

Actually, I did want to argue. He should have loved me madly. I wanted to yell at him and say, I know you love me. Don't be an idiot. I almost did. But I was afraid of how his grief over Liz's death might have damaged him, and I didn't feel equipped.

"Can we keep our monthly dinner ritual?" he asked.

I ordered a ride and sobbed in his arms until the car arrived.

"See you in a month," he said.

✳

The next day I brought my mug of coffee into my office and sat on Sarah's side of the desk. She tried to rescue her papers from under my ass.

"You don't look so good," she said. "What happened?"

"You were wrong," I said. "I didn't break his heart. He broke mine."

I started to cry, and she retrieved a box of tissues from a desk drawer.

"It was kind of ill-fated to begin with, don't you think?" she asked.

"Fate," I said, scoffing at the concept, as I had been trained to do.

I stayed on her desk and cried some more.

"Hold on," she said, closing the door. "Blow."

She handed me a tissue, then shook her head and rested her hand on my shoulder.

"Poor Hestia," she said.

She squeezed my shoulder and used her fingers to lift my chin up.

"Maybe he did you a favor," she said.

"I doubt that," I said.

"You never know," she said. "Let's just see."

✳

I took my mug to the Café, my eyes good and swollen, face red and splotchy. And there was Tom, cleaning up while he watched the TV in the corner. The national news channel was running a story about priests, Baltimore Jesuits, going on a hunger strike to protest the war. It had been three weeks, and they were just starting to look ill.

When the Ursuline nuns did the exact same thing, it made local news only after one of them died. But the priests were getting national coverage. Of course: when a woman starves herself it's barely news, but let a man stop eating . . .

The priests were beseeching our Madame President and the confederacy's President Pepper to meet and mediate, to reconcile and reunify. But neither side wanted to betray their own causes, so the priests were beginning to be hospitalized.

I caught a glimpse of Tom studying me. My puffiness and tears seemed to make him uncomfortable. He packed his bag faster.

"It's all right," I said. "It's not the end of the world. I've been crying."

"About the Jesuits?"

"No," I said. "My boyfriend broke up with me."

"I'm sorry," he said.

"It sucks, because I really liked this one."

"That does suck," he said.

"I hate it," I said.

He looked like he might want to comfort me, if he weren't so painfully shy.

"I'm usually single," he said.

"Oh," I said.

"When I go through a breakup, I write a song about it," he said.

"I don't write songs," I said. "Did I say that I write songs?"

"No, you didn't say that," he said.

"Do you ever write songs about your girlfriend *during* the relationship? When things are going well?" I asked.

"No," he said. "That would make a boring song."

Suddenly, instead of being sad about Jamie, I was annoyed by Tom.

"Some of the most beautiful songs in the world are love songs," I said.

"They're flukes," he said. "To be beautiful, a song needs yearning. Conflict. Suffering."

"Forgive me," I said, "but that's really stupid."

"I don't make the rules," he said.

"You *do*, actually," I said.

"I'm just saying, people want to hear songs about pain."

"So, you'll write about a girlfriend after you've broken up, but not while you're together?"

"More or less, yeah," he said.

"No wonder you're always single."

For a moment, we glared at each other. He looked pained.

"Ouch," he said.

"Sorry," I said, but I wasn't sorry.

Like, at all.

"So, this boyfriend of yours, why did he break up with you?" he asked. "Did he say why?"

I thought the question was overly forward of him, but for some reason I didn't mind.

"He said it was bad timing."

"Oh, yeah, *timing*," he said, like he knew the word well. "*Timing* is a cock."

His use of the word "cock" startled me, but I turned my attention back toward the news program.

"In Connecticut, a confederate sympathizer entered a yoga studio wearing a vest of explosives, killing five. In Maryland, a Kent Island lynch mob is apprehended. And tech companies are relocating from Texas to Wyoming, but Wyoming residents are dismayed."

Tom found the remote on the counter and turned off the television.

"You're welcome," he said.

✳

Hours later, I met Mildred in the therapy garden, told her about Jamie, and cried again.

"Oh, now this chaps my ass," she said. "You actually loved this one."

"I'm so embarrassed."

"He's the one who should be embarrassed," she said.

"I should have known better."

"People who know better end up alone," she said.

I asked her, in earnest, why I did this to myself.

"That's a mystery," she said. "But the good news is, you'll get over it."

"You're making it worse," I said.

"Can I paraphrase Woody Allen to you now?" she asked, and I gave her permission.

"Life is full of misery, loneliness, and suffering, and it's all over much too soon."

That reminded me of when my mother used to try cheering me up by saying, "Memento mori, remember that someday you will die." I told Mildred, and she looked pained.

"Well, then, I'm very sorry for saying that. Forgive me?"

"It's all good," I said.

"Oh dear, Hestia, you fell in love, it's not the *worst* disaster. It'll pass," she said. "It always does."

"That's for sure," I said.

"We're very adaptable creatures," she said. "And Jamie can pound sand."

5

JOHNNY PUPPETS

A fter Jamie broke my heart, people were patient with me, for about a month. Then they grew tired of my moping, and I got tired of it, too. I could barely stand to hear myself talk, and I even considered taking some time off to relieve them from me.

I'd thought about Jamie so much that he wasn't real anymore, and I couldn't distinguish very well between actual memories and imagination. Had he really whispered all those things in my ear, or had I imagined the things he might whisper someday? The brain will do that to you. Memory is the worst.

Sarah did a lot of compassionate listening while I pined over Jamie, and she was patient. And then she couldn't listen any longer. In October, she stared at me from across our desk and aggressively sighed.

"I'm begging you," she said. "Come to my singles group and get inspired."

She'd told me about the group. It was called Single Best Life.

"Why?"

"I'm learning so much," she said.

"Like, what are you *learning*?"

"There's so much freedom in being single," said Sarah. "I don't know why I waited so long to try it."

In the almost two years since I'd met her, I'd never known Sarah single. She had fended off plenty of suitors and dated men who meant well but stressed her out. As a single person, she seemed to have a little more bounce in her step.

"Freedom from what?" I asked.

"Freedom from dysfunction!" she said.

"But I don't want to be single," I said. "It doesn't bring me joy."

Sarah reached across our desk and patted my hand.

Sometimes her Single Best Life group went deep. They chatted about how reality is an illusion. They discussed the ideas of couple-hood that we're attached to, and how unhealthy attachments are delusions that control us. They talked about how liberating it was to come home from work and slip into sweatpants for the rest of the night.

"Have you ever noticed how uncomfortable real pants are?" she asked.

"I have!"

"You can evolve, Hestia," she said. "There's still time."

✷

When our Scribbles unit on love and relationships ended, Sarah convinced me to listen again to her idea about short videos.

"My vision," she said, "is to tackle something weighty, but do it light."

To that end, we prepared questions about the civil war and filmed the students answering them for TikTok. She promised a report that would measure the depth of our online engagement.

When I told Ed, he looked pained. He hated all the newer social media platforms, especially videos.

"Are we really going to do this?" he asked.

"I owe Sarah," I said. "She's been doing a lot of listening."

"I guess I need to let it go," he said.

"It's just a few months," I said.

"Nothing is permanent, including my suffering," he said.

"You're a really good Buddhist."

"Thank you," he said, "but there's no such thing as 'I.'"

✳

Question 31: Do you feel traumatized by the Second Civil War?

CLARA: *Being an American is so difficult for anyone who's not rich. Most of us have been trying to survive America our entire lives. Is that trauma?*

DOROTHY: *My friend was telling me about GoFundMe, where you get on the computer and beg for money to pay for medical treatment your insurance won't cover. Would you call that trauma?*

JEFFREY: *America hasn't felt safe for a long time. For years before this war started, my daughter has had mornings she's* *scared to send her children to school. She's terrified of a school shooting. Does that qualify as trauma?*

CHARLES: *The question was about the war, and I think we're having a collective experience with it. I don't know if it's trauma, or if it's something else. Maybe we need another word. What's a word for when you're scared, disappointed, and grieving?*

✳

About the same time that Sarah lost her patience with me, Mildred did, too. They had become close, and they ganged up on me. Apparently, they'd made a plan, intervention-style, and Sarah met us in the Café after Tai Chi. While Tom steeped his teas, they told me a thing or two.

"About your long face," said Mildred.

"I know," I said. "It's enough already."

"Do something, anything," said Sarah.

"May I say something crude?" asked Mildred.

"Of course," I said.

"You have to get under someone to get over someone."

"Wow, that *is* crude," I said.

"But not wrong," she said.

I was touched by her concern.

"You don't need to fall in love, dear," said Mildred. "But you do need to get out there again."

"Or blow it off entirely," said Sarah. "You don't *need* a partner."

"Oh, I think she might," said Mildred.

"I disagree," said Sarah.

"Fire up the dating app, Hestia," Mildred said. "Please."

"I could take up macramé instead," I said.

"I've done that," she said, "and I can assure you, it will leave you wanting."

The next day, Mildred and I spent my lunch break reading profiles on the app. Baltimore is alluring in October, rich with fall foliage, and the harbor doesn't smell so ripe. Everyone puts on sweaters and socks and enjoys relief from the heat, and the way the light slants makes the harbor water dance. We sat with my laptop facing the sun so we could read the screen in its own shadow.

We pored over the opening gambits in the profiles, collecting our favorites. "Beer and chocolate enthusiast" was good. "I'm an indoor cat" was pretty good, too. I hearted them, but they didn't heart me back. The really handsome ones never hearted me back. Ditto with the really funny ones. But "Taking applications for a cuddle buddy" was too much. "Please message me if you don't have a problem with body hair" was scary. "Looking for a partner in crime" was just, no.

"Looking for a woman who doesn't use Snapchat filters on her profile pics," held a lot of appeal. He followed that with, "I don't need to see you with puppy ears or a crown of flowers," which spoke to me.

"Yes," said Mildred, "I like that one."

I wasn't interested enough in the transaction to compose a message, so Mildred wrote it for me. She had a flair for it, and he messaged back.

Mildred asked for a cigarette, and I thought about the medical condition Annie said she couldn't tell me about. I'd made a deal with myself: if Mildred could sit for fifteen minutes without coughing, I'd let her have one. But she rarely passed the test.

"I don't like the sound of your cough," I said. "No cigarette."

"I have a chest cold," she said, "so what?"

"I'm trying to be disciplined about this," I said.

"Aren't you a hard-hearted Hannah," she said.

✳

With the weather so nice, Ed joined us sometimes. He had never stayed long before, because Mildred's cigarettes were too tempting. But he was coming more often and staying longer, and where the cigarettes were concerned, he seemed less committed to staying quit. With his marriage on the rocks, I think he was looking for company and a vice.

"Oh, looky, one of the suits is joining us today," she said.

"I'll have to loosen my tie," he said.

"Will you have a cigarette, young man?" she said.

He knew well and good about the exception that was made for Mildred's smoking, but he liked to tease her.

"There's no smoking allowed in this village, ma'am," he said.

"Who are you calling ma'am?" she asked. "Is my mother here?"

"I'm sorry, miss," he said. "A nice-looking dame like you is no ma'am."

She asked again if he'd like a cigarette, and he said yes.

I loved watching people flirt when they were good at it, and they were both so skilled. When he finished smoking, Ed took out his phone and asked Mildred to pose. "It's for the website," he said.

I told him we already had photos on the website.

"We should update them," he said, and I realized it was his

way of having a little fun with Mildred. I wondered if Annie or Ruth had informed *him* about the medical condition.

When he put his phone away, he told us that he'd learned that morning that his second wife had died.

"The news was out of the blue," he said.

"Heart attack?" I asked.

"No, no," he said. "She'd been ill for some time. But I hadn't known that. Not until today."

He'd found out about it from Facebook, from a mutual friend who posted a tribute.

"We didn't have kids together, not even pets, and we didn't get along that well," he said. "So we fell out of touch."

"I'm so sorry to hear that," Mildred said. "My second husband was my favorite husband."

"My second wife was my least favorite wife," he said.

"But still, it stings, I know," she said. "All three of my husband's deaths threw me for a loop."

"Will you go to the funeral?" I asked.

"Probably not," he said, and that sent a pang of sadness to my gut.

Mildred patted my hand and said, "Hestia here is still on her first marriage."

"How long has it been?" Ed asked.

"He left two and a half years ago," I said.

"I know the paperwork takes time," he said, "but two years, Hestia?"

October was when we renewed our benefits packages, and he'd reminded me about the deadline just that morning.

"You don't carry him on your health insurance, do you?"

I lied and told them that I did not. But the truth was, I had enrolled him in my plan, even though I started the job after he left. I knew it was maudlin, but every time I had to fill out the form, I thought about how he might get injured defending the Union. I let myself believe that my insurance policy could ease the suffering of one soldier. But in the sunlight of the therapy garden, I realized how ridiculous this was—he had no way of knowing that he was insured.

When I went back to my desk, I logged on to my portal and changed my insurance package so that it covered me only. I was pleasantly surprised by how much money I saved by taking care of no one but myself.

✳

The no-Snapchat-filter guy and I arranged a date at the bar with the tropical palm trees. To be honest, I didn't have high hopes. The tropical palm tree bar was his idea, though. He said he was "kind of a regular" there, but I'd never noticed him. I'm not even going to describe what he looked like. We made small talk. It was fine.

I could tell he was trying to make an impression as an evolved man. In the middle of our first drink, he said, "I'll always love my exes."

Something fizzled inside me. Melted. Drooped. I knew I didn't have the energy for that kind of theater.

I heard Mildred in my head saying, He wants you to think he's sensitive. I heard Sarah saying, Why would you want someone who still loves his exes?

"I'm sorry," I said. "I have to go home."

I counted out some cash for the drink and a hefty tip, and I put it on the bar.

"I just can't," I said. "It's not you. It's me."

That was a lie, mostly, because it *was* him. But I wanted to be kind.

I walked out of the bar and headed down the sidewalk, but halfway down the block, someone tugged on my shoulder. I turned around to see Alexei, who must have abandoned the bar. It took a moment for me to get my bearings. I'd never seen him anywhere in the wild.

"What's wrong?" I asked, almost panicked. "Did he stiff you?"

I patted my pockets to make sure I had my phone.

"Did I forget something?"

"No, nothing like that," he said. "I just thought that was hilarious, and I had to tell you."

"What was hilarious?"

"You just walked out on that dude in the middle of a date, right?"

"Well, yes," I said.

"What did he do to make you walk out?" he asked. "I'm dying to know."

I took a deep sigh, certain that Alexei wouldn't understand, but too tired to do anything other than tell the truth.

"He told me he would always love his exes," I said.

For a moment, Alexei's face went blank—and then he burst out laughing.

"For real? He said that?" he asked.

"He did," I said.

"What a poser."

"You're humoring me," I said.

"No, I mean it," he said. "That's one hundred percent duck fat."

I relaxed. I hadn't realized that Alexei and I shared a wavelength. Maybe compatibility wasn't a lost cause. And I liked seeing him from this new vantage point, not behind a bar, for the first time.

"Right?" I asked. "Why would I want to date someone who can't get over his exes?"

He was still laughing, and he looked down at the sidewalk and shook his head.

"You know," he said, "some guys just say stupid shit."

"Yes," I said, "I know."

"They think it makes them sound deep," he said.

"I know."

"Half of them don't even know what they're saying," he said.

"I know," I said.

"Those guys don't deserve you."

Now I looked down at the sidewalk, because I felt flattered. Not only had he chased me, but he was giving me a compliment?

"Did he at least leave a good tip?" I asked.

"Oh, that guy's still drinking," Alexei said. "I'm sure he'll be drinking for a while."

He had to get back to work, and just like that, we hugged. It was quick and light, but it counted. For a few seconds, we were close enough that I was able to smell his shampoo, or maybe it was aftershave.

"Thanks for chasing after me," I said.

"I'm looking forward to the next time," he said, jogging off.

✳

Question 32: Why do you think America is so polarized?

CHARLES: *There's an America that some people never see. It's not just the ignorance, it's the hardness. Some people grow up hard, and all that hardness makes them mean. They're people who, if they see you slip on ice, what's the first thing they're*

going to do? They're going to laugh. They may eventually help
you, or they may not—but first they're going to laugh.

CLARA: *We're on different wavelengths. Some of us think life*
has an infinite number of riches to offer us, and others think
the riches are finite.

MILDRED: *It's so simple. America's polarized because some peo-*
ple like change, and some people don't. And everything is
changing. And change is everything.

*

"Work in progress," was the first line of Johnny's profile,
which is the first line of so many profiles. As an opening salvo,
it's not great, but it's not terrible, either—at least it's honest.
Also, according to the profile, he aligned himself with Raven-
claw, which is another thing you see on the apps; I was always
surprised by how many grown-ups publicly align themselves
with a Harry Potter house, especially in the wake of Rowling's recent infamy.

"You can't go out with him," said Sarah.

"He probably doesn't even know about Rowling," I said.

I wanted to meet him because of the killer line at the end
of his profile: "I don't do threesomes, so don't even ask. If I
wanted to make two people cry at the same time, I'd have
dinner with my parents."

When he messaged to tell me that he thought I was
pretty, I decided to give it a go. It hardly ever happens that
someone goes out of their way to tell me I'm pretty, and nov-
elty is an intoxicant.

He had a funky vibe, with an almost handlebar mustache

and a pointy goatee. I said to Mildred, "I might be able to work with this." She was satisfied with how he looked in the profile photos: "Just shy of handsome," was how she put it.

He was one of those people who cultivated a look, through facial hair and head hair, through hair products, through well-placed pieces of jewelry, that did not flatter them, but made them look interesting. It was definitely a tactic. I was curious to see it in person.

For our first date, he wanted to meet at Lithuanian Hall, which had continued its monthly dance party throughout the war. I didn't want to go on a first date that would last for hours, but Sarah and Mildred convinced me. "You're in danger of being boring," Mildred had warned me. "Drink the viryta and have fun," said Sarah.

The neighborhood was in Southwest Baltimore, far enough from the ports to not worry about them, and something about being among Lithuanians assuaged my fear. They hated Russians, and because the confederates hired Russians as mercenaries, the Lithuanians hated confederates. As far as I knew, if there was any safe haven, it would be a Lithuanian bar. It checked out on the Safe Zones app, too.

When I agreed to meet Johnny, he replied, "Maybe John Waters will be there," and I had no idea if he was being sincere or sarcastic, but it didn't matter.

The social club was a typical dive bar, a bit damp and dark, and it smelled like the day after a house party. The ashtrays were full, and the bar was sticky, but the drinks were cheap, and for two dollars each, Johnny and I bought the honey-mead drinks that Lithuania was famous for. It was loud enough that we couldn't talk very much—normally a source of irritation on a date, but this time I found it a comfort. I was able to enjoy the viryta, and even dance, which I hadn't done since at least before the war. Johnny had an awkward way of dancing—as if he were primarily in the business of stomping, like those Irish troupes that don't use their arms—but I liked it because his awkwardness relieved me of my own self-consciousness. I wasn't a great dancer, either, but next to Johnny, no one noticed me.

Weirdly, John Waters did show up, in a three-piece suit, and he took a seat at one of the little tables by himself and drank his drink as if he were in his own living room. He seemed by turns oblivious to and mildly amused by the shenanigans going on around him. The whole time we were there, nobody bothered him, and he was eventually joined by a friend. Everyone in the club was way too cool to acknowledge the presence of a celebrity.

When we left, we chatted on the sidewalk before summoning our rides. I told Johnny I had had fun, but that I felt like we didn't really get to know each other. I yelled it actually, because I hadn't adjusted back to a normal volume after the club.

"Let's call tonight a chemistry check," he said.

"Okay, chemistry check," I said. "What's your verdict?"

Just like that, he kissed me, in the middle of the sidewalk. The kiss was mediocre at best, but I liked the swiftness and decisiveness of it. People don't get better at kissing, no matter how much you tell yourself that they can. But I decided it would do, and that's when I knew I was even more lonely than I'd thought.

For our next date, he invited me to a puppet show at a puppet theater—for adults—and I thought that surely "puppet theater for adults" was code for "burlesque," which I thought could be exciting. But no. When I met him there, I realized it actually was a puppet theater for adults. It was freezing inside because they couldn't afford heat, and that's where Johnny told me that he was "involved in the puppet scene." Which, I thought, explained the bad kissing.

"Puppetry, mainly," he said, "but I'm also a mime."

I could have left right then.

"And I do clown work, too," he said.

Amazingly, I didn't leave. After the show, we went for a drink with a couple of his puppet friends, and they talked about this "scene" and that "scene." One of them, a fellow clown, was heading to Boston on a grant.

"I hear there's a great clown scene up there," he said.

The other friend was actively recruiting Johnny to go with him to New Orleans, where he was going to do guerrilla performances.

"I have an artist's visa to bring the troupe down there," he said. "All those people in New Orleans, trapped in Louisiana, they could use some clowns to cheer them up."

The proposal was to bring relief to the war-sieged city and do impromptu skits in busy parts of town in November and December. For the holidays. Maybe they'd even be able to bridge some ideological gaps with their clown art, they said. You never knew if some confederates might find their way to the shows, and if Americans and confederates could stand together in an audience and share a laugh, they reasoned, there might be hope.

The amount of fun I had with him was indirectly proportional to the amount he talked about his art. That is, on the dates where we talked about the civil war or television shows or food, the sex was decent. On the dates where he talked about his art or "the scene," I could barely will my libido into action. But pridefulness has its advantages: he needed to think of himself as an artiste in the boudoir as well as in real life, and he had a palette of techniques he liked to deploy. "I'm not stopping until I find the move that lights your fire," he liked to say.

He had some other important skills, too. He could do a perfect imitation of Van Morrison, from both the skinny and the fat phases of his life. He knew all the words to a dozen songs, and he performed them for me in my bedroom. He had a nice set of pipes! He sang "Moondance" and "Brown Eyed Girl" and "Crazy Love," looking right at me, like he was singing the songs for me, like they were written for me, and he was singing them to me alone. Which I guess he was, since I was the only other person in the room, but it seemed bigger than that. He did the strut, and he scatted like Van, and he did all that other stuff that makes for great entertainment. When he sang as Fat Van, he stuffed a pillow under his shirt and I swear, it was spot-on. Johnny had a tattoo on the tender part of his forearm with the words "No regredior," meaning "I can't go back," which were lyrics from "Saint Dominic's Preview."

He did an amazing Edith Piaf, too. He'd hug my hairbrush like a microphone, wrapping his body around it, curling his lips and gazing at the ceiling, effecting her mournful, nasal voice as he sang about how he had no regrets. He only had one verse, but it was in French, and that was enough.

Sadly, the kissing never improved, but I solved that problem by telling him I didn't like to kiss. "I prefer nuzzling," I told him. So we had kiss-less evenings together, which worked, mostly, but I think we both knew it wasn't going anywhere. I'm pretty sure he thought I was funny and smart, and he messaged me a lot during the day with this thought and that thought, as they occurred to him. I left him on read way more often than a real girlfriend would have.

One of my freelance articles came out in a national magazine, a glossy, which was a big deal in my small world, and when I told him about it, he asked which magazine. When I told him, he remarked casually that the magazine was the corporate rag of establishment white supremacists.

"But it's great they published your piece!" he said, and he never asked to read it.

The same day, Jamie texted me a note of congratulations about the article, but all I could do was reply "thank you." His rejection still hurt so much that this moment of attention and kindness stung.

Johnny's social media accounts were a nightmare. He and his friends were not exactly rigorous intellectuals, and he had a knee-jerk (but passionate, I'll give him that) political ideology. It was as if his ideas about the world had stopped developing in ninth grade after reading his first *Mother Jones* article, which he only half-understood. He also posted a lot of memes about "clown life."

One day in the therapy garden, I showed Sarah and Mildred his page. Mildred clucked her tongue and shook her head.

"Cringey," said Sarah.

"All hat and no cattle," said Mildred.

But I kept seeing him. My birthday was coming up at the end of the month, number forty-four, and I reasoned that on my birthday, what I needed was some fun in the bedroom, even if it was with Fat Van.

＊

My parents called on my birthday, which surprised me but touched me a little, too. I hadn't reached out to them in quite some time, and I suppose they were trying to give me some space. But maybe they missed me.

Since my mother's last call in June, my father had sent a few postcards, pictures of Renaissance paintings with a few words written on the back. "We're thinking of you, Love, Nancy and Bill," and things like that. The week of my birthday, I received two postcards, one penned by my mother, and the other by my father. My mother's said, "We miss you, won't you come visit?" and my father's said, "I remember the day you were born. You cried so much, what a racket, you wouldn't stop. Even so, it was the best day of our lives." As I read it, I could picture him holding his hands over his ears the way he did whenever an ambulance passed by.

The day of my birthday, I received another card in the mail, this time in an envelope. It was from my mother, and it said:

> I know you don't want to visit because you think we live in the confederacy. But it's just a country. It's only a place, like Latvia, or Togo. It doesn't mean anything. I know you think that the whole country we live in now is spiteful. And I know you'll be embarrassed to visit, because of your beliefs. But they're only beliefs. You can't trust them. And anyway, Hestia, since when do you care what other people think about you?

It felt like a dig. I could picture her looking me up and down, disapproving of my appearance, and saying, Well, at least you don't care what other people think of you.

So when they called in the evening, I let the call go to voice mail. Johnny Puppets was with me, eating the food I'd bought for us because he never had a job, and that was a good distraction. I ignored the phone and let him pour me another glass of the bourbon I still had left over from Marcello.

✳

At the village earlier that day, I had found a note inviting me to the Café. Mildred was waiting for me there, seated at a table, and when I entered, she sang "Happy Birthday." On the table in front of her was a plate with four French cream puffs, with the cream practically tumbling out of them.

"I'm going to eat two of these," she said, "and you should eat the other two."

"They're huge," I said.

"Did you eat breakfast?" she asked.

When I shook my head, she said, "What are you waiting for?"

She rapped her cane on the chair where she wanted me to sit, and walked to the counter. She leaned her cane against the counter, withdrew two K-Cups of coffee from the dispenser, held them up, one in each hand, and placed them over her breasts as if they were falsies.

"Breakfast Blend or French Roast?" she asked, using a seductive voice.

I pointed at each of her breasts, back and forth, and said, "Eeny meeny miney moe . . . I'll take the left breast."

"French Roast," she said. "Good choice."

As we waited for the machine to brew, she leaned on her cane and smiled at me.

"I know you probably think you're old," she said. "But trust me. You're a baby."

I gave her the benefit of the doubt and assumed she meant it as a compliment.

"A *baby*!" she said.

Later that day, there was a Halloween party in the village, and we were all invited to it. For some reason, the events coordinator had thought piñatas would be fun and had hung them in the party room. But when the villagers started beating them with poles she provided, we realized that none of the villagers had quite enough strength to break them. "This is a disaster," said the events coordinator, who was paralyzed with guilt. "All's well that ends well," Ed said, as he cut down the piñatas and slit them open with his pocketknife.

I brought home the donkey piñata, as well as the cactus and the sombrero and put them in my fireplace. The birdhouses went onto the street for whatever poor soul wanted to collect them.

✳

Question 33: What do you think about the divide between progressives and conservatives?

JEFFREY: *Progressives are hopeless optimists, while conservatives are hopeless optimists. Progressives assume that everyone believes that a rising tide lifts all boats. Conservatives assume that people will treat each other fairly, without any laws forcing fairness. Joke's on all of us.*

DOROTHY: *Progressive, conservative, whatever. We all delude ourselves into thinking we're so rational. We have that much gall. But we're all emotion, all the time. Just pure emotion.*

✳

The next day, after work, Sarah took me to "our" bar for my birthday.

"Happy birthday, if you believe in that," she said.

Alexei was at the bar that evening, and he overheard.

"It's your birthday?" he asked.

"Not a big one," I said.

"I'm buying you the next round," he said.

Sarah looked put out all of a sudden, and confused.

"Yes, Sarah," I said, "every now and then someone like me gets a free drink."

"But—"

"I know," I said. "It's crazy."

"It's all good," she said. "This is all an illusion anyway. None of this is real."

"Right on," said Alexei.

I waited to see if any strangers would buy Sarah a drink, but no one did. I guess she was putting new energy into the world, and it was having an impact. She was blossoming into hyper self-sufficiency, and the fact that she didn't need a man must have been obvious.

"Tell me more about this Johnny person," she said.

I told her about the puppetry and the upcoming trip to New Orleans and the Van Morrison and the tattoos.

"But do you like yourself when you're with him?" she asked.

I sighed. "Maybe not," I said. "I cringe so hard when he talks about 'the scene.'"

Alexei popped over again when he heard this.

"He talks about 'the scene?'" he asked. "Act it out for us."

I told them that I would not act it out for them. So Sarah acted it out for him, and she and Alexei had a good laugh.

"Oh, man," said Alexei, "he should be brought before the tribunal."

So, obviously, Alexei was my soul mate. It was a ridiculous torch to burn for a man I only knew from the bar, but we seemed to be in sync on everything. He was exactly the right amount of judgmental, and I never found myself disagreeing with him. It was as if we recognized each other instantly.

"Which tribunal?" Sarah asked.

Alexei laughed, because he thought she was joking, but she wasn't.

"He's kidding about the tribunal," I said. "There's no tribunal."

"Oh," she said, looking embarrassed. "Well, either way, I'm glad I'm not dating any losers or fools or little boys. I have so many hobbies now. I just started making my own candles."

"That's new," I said. "Candles?"

"They smell gorgeous," she said. "I infuse them with essential oils."

Alexei pretended to stifle a yawn.

"So you're not dating at all?" he asked.

"I'm solo and loving it," she said.

"We'll see how long that lasts," he said.

"You don't know me," she said, bristling.

"That's true," he said. "But I know you'll be dating again someday."

"Seriously?"

"Most people like to be with people. They're hardwired for it."

"But you don't know *me*."

She was offended; Alexei had been presumptuous. And I was uncomfortable.

"It's true that we don't know how Sarah's wired," I said.

"But I know people," said Alexei.

"Listen," said Sarah. "Let's shut this down. You're all right, more or less, and I don't want to see you making an ass of yourself."

I liked that idea very much and waited for Alexei to respond. He nodded, left to help some other customers, and Sarah rolled her eyes.

"White man telling me how my brain works," she said. "Like I need that?"

"Yeah, no," I said. "Nobody needs that."

He returned with the two drinks he'd promised and left again quickly. I looked at him wistfully.

"But . . ." I said.

"But what, Hestia?"

"But he *is* kind of cute, right?"

"Our Father in Heaven," she said.

✳

One morning after Scribbles, Mildred stayed behind in the Treehouse Studio, and I knew she was going to twist my arm about getting her cigarettes. But I'd heard her coughing in class, and she didn't look well. While I cleaned up the whiteboard, she sat on a table, not speaking, and tapped her cane against a table leg. When I couldn't take it anymore, I sat in a chair across from her and returned her silent stare.

"Pipe down, you're talking so much," she said.

"Mildred," I said, "don't even start."

"What?" she asked.

"You know," I said, "with the cigarettes."

"Who did this to you? Was it one of my daughters? Did Ruth come for you?" she asked.

"I just think your color's off today," I said.

"My *color* is off?"

"You were coughing."

"I coughed four times, that's nothing," she said. "I love Ruth, but she can be such a pill."

"I can't let you smoke today," I said. "And anyway, it was Annie."

"But you do realize, don't you, that I plan to die before I have to choose between my daughters?"

"You're not going to die," I said.

"I'm not going to yank your chain, dear," said Mildred. "I won't bore you with my diagnosis. But the fact is, not only are we all going to die, but I'm not going to make it out of this place alive."

I knew it was true, but hearing her say it hit me hard. To distract myself from tearing up, I tried to think about other things: what time it was, the brochure copy I had to edit, how many minutes were left in the workday.

"Okay," I said.

"This is my last vice, Hestia, the last thing I have left to rebel with," she said.

"Who says you have to rebel?" I asked.

"Camus," she said.

"What?"

"He said that's how you know you're alive."

I offered to make her Irish Breakfast, and she followed me to the Café. When we were comfortable, sitting and sipping, I showed her more pictures of Johnny on my phone.

"He's not bad," she said.

"That's about right," I said.

She blew on her hot tea and shook her head.

"So, what's wrong with him?"

Without missing a beat, I reminded her about the adult puppet theater and the cringey Facebook posts.

"You disqualify people too quickly," she said.

"I should disqualify them slowly, instead?" I asked.

She rolled her eyes heavenward over the tea.

"Sometimes you learn to love a person," she said.

"I don't think Johnny's that person," I said.

"Then why waste your time with him?" she asked. "Give him the hook."

She had me there. I sipped my tea.

"It's just nice to have someone," I said.

"But you have *me*!" she said. "I haven't gone off to my great reward yet."

Mildred was too casual about her own mortality for my comfort, and I tried to think of a way to change the subject. All I could think about, though, was the diagnosis, which surely was cancer. Why can't people just say "cancer"?

"Which reminds me," she said.

I waited.

"I want you to write my obituary," she said.

Without pausing to consider it, I told her I couldn't do it.

"But why?!"

"That's your daughters' domain," I said.

"But they're not beautiful writers," she said. "They're going to write about what a good mother I am. Blech."

"But they're right," I said. "You *are* a good mother."

"They're good daughters, the best a mother could hope for, and I'm a nice mother," she said. "But so what? You see the *real* me. You'd write about the real me."

"I can't," I said. "I won't."

"I'm going to grind you down," she said.

I didn't know what to say, so I sipped my tea. Of course she would grind me down. Everyone and everything grinds me down. And still, I knew it wouldn't be right for me to do that, and I liked Annie and Ruth too much to intrude.

✳

The week before Thanksgiving, I accepted an invitation from Jamie for dinner with the family. It was against my better judgment, but I wanted to be there for the kids. I missed them so much more than I had anticipated. So maybe I was doing it for me, and not them, although at the time it felt like I was doing it for them.

One of the twins answered the door, and we were so happy to see each other that we hugged, no small thing for a preteen. I'd been wondering how Jamie and I would greet each other. We had a cordial but short-lasting hug, the kind where you don't lean into each other, the kind where your arms never really pull the other person in.

Naturally, we had grilled chicken.

He was as handsome and appealing as I remembered him, and I wanted him just as much as I always had. Before we'd even sat down at the table, I knew I'd made a mistake in coming. It had only been a couple of months since we broke up.

But then—there were the kids. They were so funny. Delightful, even.

There was a no-phones rule at the table, and the conversation was sometimes lively. Jamie did very little talking; he let the children run the show. I put all my attention into engaging with the kids, which relieved me of having to make eye contact with him. Toward the end of the meal, he said that having me there as a guest had inspired him. He'd been working on a limerick during dinner, and asked if we wanted to hear it.

The kids and I agreed: let's hear it now. I could see how much they loved to see their father like this—playful.

"Keep in mind how masterful it is," he said. "Especially the rhymes. Pay close attention to the rhymes."

"Recite it already," said one of the twins.

> *There once was an aunt named Hestia,*
> *No one could believe her name was Hestia,*
> *Best aunt we'd ever seen,*
> *She was never, ever mean,*
> *And that's how we rolled with Aunt Hestia.*

It took the kids a minute, but when they understood how silly it was, they were amused.

"Yeah, great rhymes, Dad," said the boy, who, at age ten, was fairly new to sarcasm.

By the end of the meal, I was crushing all over Jamie again and wished I hadn't come. I'd brought ice cream for dessert, and I held it together through the eating of the Moose Tracks. When Jamie started clearing the table and loading the dishwasher, I offered to help, and he said, "No, you should visit with the kids more."

With phones allowed at the table again, my nephew showed me the latest video to go viral, and we all marveled over it. It was a vlog of a confederate rogue operator who'd posted footage of himself on a mission.

"I'm driving my truck out to the West Coast," he said into the camera.

"I'm in a hurry to start some wildfires," he said.

He promised his audience he wouldn't stop for anything except gasoline, not even a bathroom break.

"I'm heeding an urgent call to burn those liberals' ancient forests," he said. "And I'm wearing a diaper right now, because I don't want to waste one precious second."

My nephew and I gave each other a look.

"Couldn't he pee in a bottle?" he asked.

"For real," said one of the girls.

My nephew read out loud some comments on the video, and we were fascinated by how many people celebrated diapers for the cause. Some commenters questioned how burning down forests furthered the confederate cause, but they were ignored. The act didn't have to make sense—it was the meanness that mattered, the nonspecific fuck-you.

My sweet nieces. They looked up how to donate money to the firefighters out West and asked if I could help them with the transaction. They gave me their cash—five dollars each—and watched me Venmo it. When Jamie came back into the room, they scampered upstairs. He sat down across from me, with his dishpan hands.

"I should go," I said.

He looked a little disappointed, but not *that* disappointed. I wanted him to convince me to stay awhile, but he didn't.

"I understand," he said.

If I'd been reading the situation correctly, he wanted me, or at least, some part of him wanted me. But this passivity—his and mine—was irritating.

"I mean, I have somewhere to be," I said.

"I get it," he said.

Would it have been so hard for him to say, I'd love it if you could stay a little longer? I knew he wanted me to. I could have offered to stay, but he was the one who'd broken up with me, not the other way around. And I was at his house. It was his turn to make a move, and he was failing the test. His silence plucked my last nerve.

"My boyfriend Johnny's in a performance," I said.

I didn't mention it was a *puppet* performance, or that I'd never called him my boyfriend until that moment, or that I didn't love him the way I loved Jamie, or even love him at all. Jamie was polite about it. Again with the passivity. I can't remember what he said, exactly, because my ears were ringing with anger, but whatever it was, it was mild. We hugged goodbye, same as when we hugged hello, concave and barely touching.

✳

Nearing the puppet theater, I checked Safe Zones, to make sure everything was all right in the neighborhood. "Incident has been managed by officers. No present danger," it said. The incident turned out to be a guillotine, set up in front of the free clinic next to the theater. A news crew was packing up their van, and two peacekeepers were dismantling the guillotine. They had already set up barriers and police tape, and they were shooing people away.

"Nothing to see," said one of them in a European accent.

"Don't pay it any mind," said the other, with a bit of a brogue.

Inside the unheated puppet theater, I pulled my wool cap

over my ears and checked my Conflicted app. I was behind on my national news digest, and this seemed like a good time to catch up.

Before I could stop myself, I chuckled: Texas had tried to secede from the New Confederated States of America, and the New Confederated States of America had said, in a word, "No, sir." The headline read: "Pepper in a pickle, as NCSA president, former governor of Texas, contends with Texas secession."

"It's not funny," I whispered to myself, "Don't laugh."

The other headline was simply grim. A new report showed that public executions were making a comeback in the confederacy, and that sex offenders were now dead men walking.

During the show, I bought three glasses of shamelessly overpriced boxed chardonnay, doubled up my scarf for warmth, and tried to pay attention to skits about a parrot who found his true voice; a bottle cap that decided to take up his rightful space in this world; and a donkey who turned into a rock, the plot of which I think was lifted directly from a children's book. I couldn't believe how sweet and fruity the chardonnay was. Had chardonnay always been like that? No wonder I liked whiskey. I didn't want to spend the evening thinking about Jamie, but the wine made me weak.

I felt wrecked about the kids, because I knew I'd have to pull back and they would lose an aunt. If I had behaved differently, back in April, if I'd been less selfish, I could have avoided all this. But no. I had been lonely. Boo-hoo. Sad, lonely Hestia *had to* jump into a tricky relationship with her brother-in-law without any thought to how it would affect three sweet children if things didn't work out. I'd followed my heart and taken a leap of faith—what a load of bunk.

Glass One of Boxed Wine: You messed up.

Glass Two of Boxed Wine: Your loneliness is not an emergency.

Glass Three of Boxed Wine: Every love affair ends, every single one, whether through death or divorce or disappearance.

Why did this feel like a revelation?

I had to stop flailing.

"Suck it up, Hestia," I said to my chardonnay. "Stop grasping. Don't hurt anyone else, including yourself."

When it was Johnny's turn onstage, I watched with a drunken remove. I was dating a clown, and he rarely earned a dime. I told myself it was fine. It would end, I knew that, probably fairly soon, and it wouldn't even come close to breaking his heart. Nothing ventured, nothing lost.

✳

Question 34: Do you think racism is the underlying reason for the Second Civil War?

CHARLES: *Racism is the problem that gives birth to every other problem: capitalism, war, environmental destruction, you name it. Every time you decide that it's all right to treat one group of people more terribly than you treat another group of people, that's racism—and once we have decided to live with it, we can justify going to war, or doing capitalism, or tolerating climate change.*

CLARA: *When we pollute a river, we're saying that the people who live near the river are not as important as other people. When we desecrate land, we're saying that this land is less* *important than other land. That's racism. Can you imagine what this world would be like if we decided that every person, and every river, and every meadow was sacred?*

✳

Still feeling badly about the piñata fiasco, the village's events coordinator ushered in December by throwing an elaborate lunch forum for the villagers. The forum topic was "Understanding Your New Benefits," and it featured a slideshow that explained America's new Universal Retirement Income program. It was a multiphase overhaul of social security, which would now be more equitable and guaranteed in perpetuity. She made it a build-your-own-pizza event, which was popular.

Ed and I attended with great interest, and Jeffrey showed off his bespoke pie.

"Who ordered the large sausage?" he asked.

"Do they ever grow up?" said Mildred, shaking her head.

A few days later, the weather was unseasonably warm, and Tai Chi was held outside in the pavilion. Mildred dressed up for it; she wore a blouse and skirt. I did no such thing. In fact, I took some photographs of the villagers in their forms because the website loves photos of elderly people doing outdoor Tai Chi.

Tom led the class and spoke so softly I could barely hear him.

"There's nothing like doing Tai Chi in the fresh air," he said.

I joined the class, and we were to focus on moving healing qi energy throughout our bodies. He reminded us how to move through Brush Knee into Playing Guitar, and end in

Single Whip. As usual, I was hopeless. I rushed through everything. Mildred, on the other hand, was brilliant at it, and she delighted in besting me. She was using her cane when she needed it, so I told myself that had something to do with her superior balance. She winked at me and gave me the thumbs-up when I did something rudimentary, like Standing Bear, which was only slightly more challenging than simply standing.

Tom spoke in his heroin voice to the class, "Everyone is invited regardless of experience." It made me sleepy. He walked around the pavilion as the class moved and gave special attention to me and Mildred, whom he still treated like the newbies. I did need some help, but I was embarrassed about being so bad. So I came up with the best line I could at the moment.

"Sorry, I didn't really want to be here," I said.

It wasn't a great way to ask for help, which I realized as soon as I said it.

"What I mean is, I don't want to do this," I said, because some part of my brain thought that would make it better.

Tom was unfazed.

"Look, everyone," he said, waving toward the sky. "Birds and trees are included in today's class. Free of charge."

Then he came back to me and Mildred and put his hand gently on my wrist and placed my arm where it needed to be.

"Your front hip," he whispered, "move it here," and he held out his other hand for me to move toward. He asked me, whispering, if I could feel the qi moving, and I told him I could not. He adjusted my arm, putting a bend in my elbow, and asked if I could feel it now. Still no, I said.

He returned to the front of the class and led us into our next movement.

"Tai Chi is the art of yielding," he said.

He explained, as he always did, that it's a martial art, the point of which is to help you defeat your enemy.

"You win by yielding," he said.

Which enemy was he talking about? By my count, there were so many.

"You step aside, you lean back," he said. "You let them lunge and fall, and they defeat themselves."

He swept his arm over his head and leaned back, turning slowly to the side as he did so.

"You yield," he said. "Yield, and you win."

When class ended, Mildred was eager to partake of his tea. We were the only two students who joined him in the Café, and he started immediately to get the kettle boiling. She flirted with him, and it seemed as if he flirted back.

"Nice job in there, young man," she said.

"I aim to please," he said.

"You're smooth," she said. "A smooth operator."

"Smooth is my middle name," he said.

"Oh really?" she asked. "I would have thought your middle name would be Danger, or some such."

"It is," he said. "I was lying."

"I knew it," she said.

I'd never seen Tom so at ease, so *not* at a loss for words. His conversation with Mildred was effortless. It all happened while he infused tea leaves and did pour-overs for the three of us, which he placed on a table. Mildred sat down first, and we followed suit. She took the first sip.

"Thank goodness we're sitting," she said.

"Were your dogs barking?" he asked.

"Indeed they were," she said.

Why was he talking like this? He wasn't an old man.

"Mine too," he said.

"Aren't you a sweetheart," she said, taking another sip and crossing her legs.

She adjusted her skirt.

"Nice pins," he said.

Did she smile. Oh boy, did she smile.

That moment was cut short, however, by the sound of sirens outside.

Then my phone blew up with red rhombus alerts. Next: the helicopters overhead. Ed's voice come over the PA system, and he told everyone, in his Texas drawl, to remain calm.

"We are being told to shelter in place," he said. "It's nothing to worry about, but there's been an explosion."

Immediately, chaos came to the village. Our head of security took over for Ed, and our two security officers raced from room to room to alert and relocate the villagers. The preferred locations for sheltering in place were the Treehouse Studio and the Serenity Room, because they were interior spaces without windows to the outside.

I told Tom that I was taking Mildred to Serenity, and he stepped aside for us. He said he was going to help the security guys knock on doors and get villagers to safety.

"I'll meet you in Serenity," he said.

Sarah found and joined us as we helped more villagers get situated. Ed arrived, too, with Dorothy on his arm, a little out of breath.

"This kind of thing really makes you feel your age," he said.

We needed more chairs in the Serenity Room, and when Ed started to lift them, Tom said, "Here, man, let me do that."

For a skinny guy, he lifted them with so much ease. Ed

stood back and watched, then whistled that it's good to be young.

"I do core work," said Tom.

"When I look in the mirror," said Ed, "I don't see the old guy with the beard and the belly. I see the twenty-year-old me. I'm my own skinny mirror."

"Nothing wrong with being your own skinny mirror," said Tom.

Mildred, who was listening, said men were lucky to be so delusional.

"You know it," said Ed.

When everyone was safe, we tried to make sense of things. The news on our phones gave us bits of information. The explosion had occurred only one block away, at the World Trade Center on the harbor, but that was all we knew.

Sarah sat on the floor with her knees to her chin and her arms wrapped around her legs. She did breathing exercises to stay calm.

"This fucking country," she said again and again.

I put my hand on her shoulder, but she swatted it away.

"I know reality's a giant illusion," she said, "but this fucking place."

I'd never heard her say "fuck," but this wasn't the time to point it out.

We heard more sirens and helicopters outside, and more news came to our phones. There had been a "freedom rally" scheduled, with a permit, and now it seemed that the rally had been organized by confederate sympathizers within Maryland. There were pre-explosion photos of the rally: MARYLAND, SECEDE NOW, said the banner.

Mildred tried to lighten the mood by joking that her bony ass was going to secede, and the confederates could have it.

That got a smile from Sarah, who seemed to have found her breath.

We watched videos on our phones of people with two-by-fours storming the building and destroying things.

"Did they have to smash the art installation?" asked Dorothy.

"Why do they break all the windows?" asked Jeffrey.

"I don't get it," said Tom. "Why do they hate bike racks so much?"

The rioters had dumped all the bike racks into the harbor.

"Is it the bikes they hate, or the bike racks?" asked Ed.

Two hours after they began, the sirens stopped. Thirty minutes after that, the head of security announced over the PA that it was safe to return to normal. We staffers helped the residents back to their rooms, and when we were done, we stood in the lobby, dazed.

Sarah looked like she was about to cry, and I asked if I could walk her home. She lived about a mile from the office.

"I'll come with you," said Tom. "Safety in numbers."

"Count me in, too," said Ed.

We walked north, away from the water, and dropped off Sarah at her place. Then they began walking me home, about another mile, and Ed turned toward his place. Tom and I kept walking, and when we reached my stoop, I turned to him and said, "The art of yielding, huh? That's how we win?"

"It's open to interpretation," he said.

✳

The next time Tom had class at the village, I found an old book on my desk. It was clothbound, starting to tatter, with pages that smelled like dust. The typeface struck me as old-fashioned, and it had a tag from a nearby thrift shop. It was about asteroids.

It had been left open to a particular page, and marked with a bookmark, too, in case I lost the spot.

It read: "46 Hestia is a large asteroid orbiting between Mars and Jupiter in the main portion of the asteroid belt." There was an arrow pointing to where in the solar system 46 Hestia was located.

Also, Tom had underlined, "NASA has not classified Hestia as potentially hazardous," as well as the line, "Not a Near Earth Object."

On the bookmark, he'd written a note in his shockingly beautiful script: "Check out the orbital eccentricity rating! —Tom."

I left a note for him—"Thank you for the asteroid book"—inside the mug he used, which he always tucked into the farthest reach of the mug cabinet.

*

Johnny and I kept seeing each other right up until he left for New Orleans.

Because of the trip, there was no need to go through the pains of a breakup. Had either of us been keen to do so, we could have discussed how we might sustain the relationship during and after the trip. He was going to be gone for three weeks, maybe four—we could have made it work. But neither of us cared enough to bring it up. It was no big deal. We didn't talk about it, didn't anticipate, didn't plan.

In those remaining weeks, we had fun.

He was nervous about going down there, even with the

artist's visa. Getting across the border was one thing, but fitting in was another. It was bad enough that he was a puppeteer, which would come with its own harassment. He didn't want to get the extra hassling on the buses on account of looking like a unionist.

We studied videos from the traitors' rallies and riots, and he let me help him pull together an outfit.

We went to thrift stores with our research photos on our phones and tried to match the confederate garb. The shops inside Baltimore city limits could only get us as far as the hoodie. He found a good one, though, thick material, in a camouflage of varied grays. We also picked out a heavy metal T-shirt, size XXL, large enough to wear over the hoodie.

For the rest of the wardrobe, he borrowed a car, and we drove out to the suburbs. We found him a baseball cap, and he was more than happy to practice his look in front of the store's mirrors. He put on the cap and pulled the hoodie's hood over it. We found a field coat in brown and layered that over the hoodie, and he tried on some cargo pants, too. It was weird how well he nailed the look, as if he'd replaced his eyes with cement to achieve the required hardness. He set his jaw; he clenched. It was so dead-on that a couple of shoppers steered clear of us.

"I don't know," I said. "The cargo pants are good, but maybe you should wear shorts. Cargo shorts."

"Hestia," he said, "it's December."

"Exactly," I said.

"I think we need to sew a raccoon tail onto my hat," he said.

As good as that idea was, I told him, no one would see it with the hoodie over it. Put the rattail down, I told him.

"Do I need a hockey stick?" he asked.

"Tiki torch," I said.

As he preened at the shop mirror, he was getting scary good at the confederate's stance and walk. He really did have a talent. It all fell apart when he opened his mouth, though, because he was shit at the Southern accent.

"Just don't talk when you're there," I said. "Get on the bus and sit with your arms crossed. Grunt if you have to communicate."

Back home, he put the outfit on again and strutted around the living room. I sat on the couch and watched, with the sombrero piñata in the fireplace behind him. On the sly he'd bought not only the raccoon tail, but also a hunting vest in blaze orange.

"You should wear the vest," I told him.

"I'm *wearing* the vest," he said.

"No," I said. "You should wear *only* the vest."

Quick as a bunny, he undressed and put the vest back on.

"Can I wear my raccoon tail, too?" he asked.

This was weird territory we were entering, but it was *my* weird territory, which meant I had to be in charge.

I told him he could wear the hat, but only at the end, after he'd put on the condom. All foreplay would happen with the hunting vest only, and we'd save the raccoon tail for the climax.

"Now show me what you're all about," I told him.

He ducked into the kitchen and returned with my broom, which he held like a weapon. He thrust it not *at* me, but *near* me. His penis swung with each jab of the broom.

"I'm holding a hockey stick, and I'm not afraid to use it," he said.

"What are you going to do with it?" I asked, trying to sound coquettish. I couldn't believe the weird role-play I'd found myself doing. I was going to take this to my grave.

"I'm gonna break the windows of Northern oppression," he said, pointing the broomstick close to my window.

"You're a dirty fucking seditionist," I said, using my lowest voice.

He came closer, his penis more rigid, less swingy. He made the cement eyes.

"I'm gonna smash socialism," he said.

"I should smash *you*," I said, using my meanest voice.

Who was I?

He pressed himself against me, pushing me toward the wall, and pinned me there. He was so forceful, and I was breathless. He put his mouth near my ear.

"Smash the patriarchy, you filthy patriot," he whispered hotly.

"Pull my hair, you pathetic confederate," I said.

He dropped the broom and grabbed my hair and pulled back my head to expose my neck. He kissed me, hard. My knees started to give.

"Can I put on the coonskin now?" he asked, but he used the mean confederate voice.

"Not yet, traitor," I said. "You have to wait."

"This is torture," he said.

"The punishment for treason is torture," I said.

The sexual buildup was almost too much for him. The role-play was almost too shameful for me. But I was making him work for it, for me—that was new. I'd never made a man do that.

After a minute, he asked again. "Is it time?" He sounded desperate.

I loved hearing him plead. I mean, *loved*.

"Yes," I told him, "put on the raccoon tail."

He deployed the pièce de résistance, and afterward we lay on the couch, panting. I turned my head and stared at the cactus piñata; the donkey seemed to wink at me. When we caught our breath, he confessed that he hadn't known he was so freaky until today. He asked me if I'd known all along.

"How did you not know you're a freak?" I asked.

"I'm an artist," he said. "People love artists."

I couldn't stop myself in time: I laughed out loud. Leave it to Johnny Puppets to bring everything back, full circle, to "his art." I wondered if I should kiss him, quick, before he mentioned "the scene," except that I didn't love kissing him.

If I had been more invested in the relationship, I would have debated the idea with him, or let him down gently. Maybe I would have tried to disabuse him of his notion that artists walk on some kind of hallowed ground. But what was the point? He was leaving soon, and all this would be over.

In mid-December, he joined his troupe in New Orleans, riding an American bus to the border, then catching a confederate bus from Virginia to Louisiana. We texted each other several times a day, and he sent me photos from Louisiana that made it seem so foreign, so exotic. This was me and Johnny at our best: friends who texted while in different countries. Experiencing his trip through him, I realized how long it had been since I'd had an adventure.

New Orleans was more or less under permanent siege, with rural Louisiana militias making modest gains into city establishments, only to be pushed back by urban militias who'd gotten their shit together. The confederates would "take over" grocery stores and gas stations, maybe a volunteer-run health clinic, by scaring off their owners, and then twelve hours later the urban militia would reclaim them. American military forces defended and held on to things like banks and power grids and oil refineries. Johnny said you had to be careful about every public space you entered because you never knew who had control.

But it was the holiday season, and the people of New Orleans were trying to make the city festive. Some people strung up lights across the streets, some put wreaths on their doors, and others caroled. Johnny sent me a video of one cheerful caroling group, his spirits obviously buoyed by the small crowd that gathered for the singing. The carolers shifted location after every song, for safety.

And finally, it was time for the puppet troupe to perform. They felt the French Quarter was the right place, given its historic fondness for flair, and they took turns livestreaming the shows on Facebook. Nervous for Johnny, I watched the livestream from my desk, hoping to see likes and other positive emojis floating upward across the screen. Sarah watched with me, keeping an eye on her phone for alerts. Truthfully, we were riveted.

Their costumes were impressive, full of color and gold. They juggled in front of an oyster bar. They sang and danced and hammed it up—it was like ten Johnnys doing Van Morrison and Edith Piaf all at once, with capes and glitter and funny voices. To my relief, they drew a modest crowd, especially children. Oh, those poor children of New Orleans. As much as we tried, it was hard to get humanitarian aid that far South. Their school lunch program was gone; their supplemental nutrition assistance was gone; their free breakfasts were gone. Did they even go to school, and if so, was it just like Christian Sunday school? Their heads were shaved because of lice, and they were too skinny, but on the livestream I saw them smiling as they watched the show. Maybe, I thought, Johnny was more heroic than I'd given him credit for.

The troupe brought out the Hula-Hoops. And then they set the Hula-Hoops on fire. I hadn't known that fire dancers were part of the show. The children drew closer, and heart emojis fluttered upward on the screen. But I remembered reading a news story about how some of the families whose kids had lice used kerosene on their scalps, instead of oil, which was so hard to find. From what I gathered, it was a decent preventive measure, and kerosene was cheap, even if it burned a little at first. But this was a bad combination, kerosene and fire.

I typed in all caps into the comments section: "KEROSENE ON KIDS HEADS. PUT OUT FIRE!!!" and many other versions of that same message. Wide-eyed, Sarah chewed her nails and kept checking her phone. I texted Johnny, hoping that someone was watching his phone. Please don't let the children's heads catch on fire, I prayed, please don't let their little heads catch fire. I gave up on texting and called Johnny, who was no longer visible on the screen. Maybe he'd answer. When it went to voice mail, all I could do was scream into the phone, "THINK OF THE CHILDREN."

The troupe got lucky. A peacekeeper who had been watching from a corner botanica recognized the danger and swooped in to save the day. She rushed into the dance, putting her own body between the flaming Hula-Hoops and the children, pushing them back behind her, shouting all the while at the dancers. The livestream captured her cursing a blue streak at the troupe.

"Eejits!" she shouted. "Stupid wankers!" she screamed.

And then whoever was recording the performance hit stop.

✳

Sarah and I went to the Café and made some soothing herbal tea. Tom was the only one there, and Sarah told him the whole story. She made sure to emphasize that Johnny was my boyfriend, and that he was a fool.

When she was finished with the story, he turned and tried to look me in the eye. He could barely manage eye contact with me, but in his defense, I *was* wearing a tight sweater, one of those ribbed turtlenecks with lots of Lycra.

"That's quite a story," he said.

"Yes, thank you, Sarah, for that," I said. "I hadn't been embarrassed enough."

He was packing away his tea kit, and he had his coat on already.

"If you don't mind my asking," he said, wrapping his scarf around his neck, "why do you date men you know are wrong for you?"

Sarah tapped her fingertips together. "Yes, tell us," she said.

When had this happened, this intimacy between us, that he could ask me such a question? Was it because I'd cried in front of him over Jamie?

"That's a great question," I said. "Maybe it's habit."

"Maybe you're an optimist," he said.

"That's rich." I snorted.

"You think these guys will surprise you and turn out to be great, against all evidence to the contrary," he said.

"So, I'm delusional?"

He closed his eyes and put his hands together, thinking. Sarah leaned in and listened, enjoying herself.

"You must really want company," he finally said.

"Fine," I said. "What's *your* habit?"

Again, he closed his eyes and inhaled before he spoke.

"I find that being with the wrong person is not worth the company," he said.

Before I could stop myself, I found I was nodding.

"You can't stand to be alone," he said, "and I can't stand to be with the wrong person."

"That might be accurate," I said.

"There are a lot of fools out there," he said. "I never learned how to suffer fools."

"I suffer them all the time," I said.

I'd meant it to be funny—*I suffer them all the time! Ba dum dum!*—but neither of us laughed.

6

THE WEDNESDAY MAN

I n late December, I helped the events staff with the holiday party. It was outside my scope of duties, but I had nothing else to do, and I enjoyed being around the villagers. "I hope you're getting overtime," Ed said, which was one of our jokes, because full-timers never get overtime.

It was a good time of year to update the website with new photos, too. Snapshots of residents involved in holiday craft-making went over well. We did an activity that involved sticking cloves into oranges, which was fun for about the first three cloves, then became painful for everyone's fingers. But it made for good pictures.

There was a cookie-decorating activity, as well, which I photographed. Dorothy became absorbed in her art and bartered with other residents for certain colored sugars.

"Do you think you'll use that green sugar?" she asked Jeffrey, several times, until he relented and handed over his stash.

Midway, Jeffrey refused to decorate any more cookies,

exclaiming that this was a form of brainwashing, and Clara hopped on his bandwagon.

"It does have the smell of Judeo-Christian hegemony, doesn't it?" she asked.

Charles told Dorothy that her cookies were beautiful, and she swooned.

In Scribbles, I gave prompts like, What is a holiday tradition you remember fondly? And, What was your favorite holiday party ever? The most popular prompt was, What is your favorite holiday food?, although it's possible that was *my* favorite prompt and the students went along. It was the right time for cheerful memories; the Scribblers were quite done with writing and talking about love and civil war.

They wrote about babkas and bûches. Filets mignons with horseradish sauce, hams with spicy mustard, and geese. And of course, the cocktails, adorned with fruits that looked like jewels.

Not that all the memories were cheerful. Clara wrote about being so exhausted from throwing parties that she couldn't enjoy them, and Dorothy wrote about how depressing it was to forgo the holiday treats so she could avoid becoming "sturdy" or "stout." (The men enjoyed the parties and treats just fine.) Jeffrey wrote about how he couldn't understand, as a child, why Santa gave such wonderful gifts to rich kids and such modest gifts to him and his brother. But mostly I read about holiday lights and bombastic uncles and the bustle of large families, of which I knew nothing. There were no Dylan Thomases in the Treehouse, but everyone had a tipsy-aunt story to tell, or a tale about the snow.

For Christmas, Annie took Mildred to her home in Philadelphia for almost a week, and then Ruth took her to Pittsburgh for the new year. By the time she was settled back at the village, she was pale as a ghost.

"It's all the traveling, dear," she told me, but I knew she was very ill.

"We'll get you rested up," I said.

"Oh, please, Hestia," she said. "The doctor told me I'll be dragging this out for years."

✳

In the new year, I did some more seasonally appropriate Scribbles prompts such as, Have you ever fulfilled a New Year's resolution?

My answer to that was, I stayed up until midnight this year, composing texts to people from my past before I came to my senses and deleted them. It was shameful and true. I wrote one to Jamie about how much I missed him, and I asked if he missed me, too. Thank goddess I deleted it before hitting send. I simply texted "Happy new year."

But I did have a New Year's resolution, which was to finally divorce my husband. I'd have to track him down somehow, and I knew that would take time. I didn't really want to see him or speak to him, but it was a necessary part of the process.

After making that decision, I took a couple of months to hibernate, as some humans want to do before major change. I spent my time at work and home, drew a small winter circle around my life and stayed inside it. At home, I streamed videos of burning yule logs, both the classic and the birchwood. I wore *all* the sweatpants and slept a lot, and I pondered, slowly, how to make contact with my husband.

I developed a pastime of watching movies back-to-back: the first would star an actress when she was young, and the second starred the same actress when she was older, and I surveyed the aging process. It was simultaneously disturbing and uplifting. All the young actresses' beauty was identical; same collagen, same brightness, same sharp hip bones and clavicles; it was almost generic.

But faces and bodies became fascinating as the actresses aged. It was as if they became Real, like velveteen rabbits. Watching them age on the screen, I felt some degree of outrage, too. How can our corporeal cages betray us like that? How is it that Time is allowed to write, without our permission, on our faces and bodies like that, in all caps, for everyone to see?

I remembered the Tolstoy line about how all happy families are alike, and every unhappy family is unhappy in its own way. It was the same with aging: beautiful young people all look alike, and every old person is striking in their own way.

Late in winter, Sarah reported that the TikTok experiment had not yielded any encouraging metrics. She had hoped to keep the content light and fun, but we kept doing prompts about the civil war and trauma. "It wasn't the right energy," she said, and one of the users commented, "Take your sadness to another platform." We decided to return to the written format. Our new unit would feature pearls of wisdom from the students about the human condition.

"Give me strength," said Dorothy. "Is there any human who's not a narcissist? We're obsessed with our condition."

Mildred chuckled.

"But enough about me—what do *you* think of me?" she asked.

"My mother always said, 'No one's looking at you,'" said

Jeffrey, "but what the hay? Let's drop some truth bombs—for the children."

✳

Question 35: What is human intellect?

JEFFREY: *We're apes with overgrown brains that have cracked the code on black holes, the large intestine, chakras, gravity, ions, and neutrons—but for what? We keep killing each other.*

DOROTHY: *Our brains are an accident of evolution. If they were smaller, we'd be happier, and if they were bigger, we'd be happier. They're just big enough to make us miserable.*

MILDRED: *There are many kinds of intelligence, and very few of them concern the brain.*

✳

I didn't have the foggiest idea how to find my husband, but my desire for a divorce persisted. He had lied, probably cheated, definitely abandoned me, and, as far as I could tell, turned into a new person. It was tedious, and I wanted it to be over.

"I've never been divorced," said Mildred, almost wistfully, enviously.

This was one of the most exciting days of the year at the retirement village—a March day when the village entertained small pets. Twice a year, the events coordinator arranged for someone from a rescue organization to come in with abandoned animals so that the villagers could spend time with them. Mildred liked the guinea pigs the best, and she made sure she arrived early enough to get one. The effort of walking across the room with her cane to grab a guinea pig seemed to take the wind from her.

"I prefer the chinchillas," said Dorothy, bringing one of them to her chest and holding it there.

"That makes perfect sense," said Mildred.

"Of course you would," said Clara, scooping up a bunny.

Clara stroked her bunny, and Dorothy held her chinchilla to her chest, whispering to it, "The world is such a peanut gallery, isn't it?"

Mildred and I sat while we enjoyed the guinea pig. She asked for a cigarette, and I told her that I would be giving her cigarettes under no circumstances. She tried to catch her breath, and I returned to our earlier conversation.

"Do you wish you'd been divorced?" I said.

"Aren't divorcées glamorous?" she asked.

I looked down at my work pants and my office-appropriate low boots. Recently I'd realized that I needed reading glasses—"Forty-four is the magic age," my optometrist had said—and had decided to wear them on a chain around my neck because they kept getting tangled in my hair when I kept them on my head.

"Let me look it up," I said, and I put on my readers and pretended to be looking up information on my phone.

"Yes, you're right," I said, tapping my phone, squinting through my glasses. "Divorcées are glamorous."

"Stop it, you're glamorous, and I know it," she said.

"What's so great about divorce?" I asked.

"Divorce is *hard*," she said. "Not easy, like when your husband *dies*. When your husband dies, it's like you've just been given a 'Get Out of Jail Free' card."

"It doesn't sound *that* easy," I said.

"Much easier than divorce," she said. "You have no choice in the matter."

"But what if you love him and he dies?" I asked.

"Well, that's different, if you still love him," she said. "That's less easy."

"Divorce is an ass-ache," I said, thinking about the paper trails I'd have to follow to make it happen.

"That's what I'm saying," she said. "All those *decisions*. Divorce is *bold*."

Mildred suggested that I go back to those safe houses he'd told me about and leave notes for him there. "Find him through his KAs," she said, meaning "known associates." (Her third husband had been in law enforcement.) It struck me as a good idea, so I did it. I remembered three of the houses and left a simple note at each, in a sealed envelope. "We need to talk about the future," I wrote. "You owe me a divorce. You know how to find me."

A few weeks later, I still hadn't heard from him, and I wondered in earnest if he'd died. This wasn't the first time I'd wondered about it, but it had been more abstract before. It occurred to me that his parents might know how to find him, or know if he'd died, but I didn't want to open up that line of communication.

When my husband left, his parents were so deep in their grief over Liz that they couldn't pay attention to what was happening with him. Or me. The mysterious departure and disappearance of their adult son was not the worst thing that happened to them that year, and I wanted to give them their space.

If he had ever made contact with them, nobody told me

about it. The person most likely to know was Jamie, whom I had not texted since New Year's Day. I didn't want to text again without a good reason, but I thought this was one.

He asked how I was doing. I told him, "Fine, just in the mood for a divorce," and he replied with a laughing-crying-face emoji, followed by a double-heart emoji. I hadn't expected to feel my heart race, but it did, in the privacy of my kitchen, where I was making a meal for one. He need never know that my heart had raced.

"Come to dinner soon?" he texted. Chicken-leg emoji. Baby-chick-hatching-out-of-egg emoji.

"Not sure about this month, pretty busy," I lied. Flamenco-dancer emoji. Disco-dancer-man emoji. Mermaid emoji. What a whopper.

"We miss you," he texted. Glass-of-wine emoji.

For the girls' birthday a month earlier, I'd sent them each gift cards. "You're teenagers now!" They'd texted me their thank-yous.

"I miss the kids, too," I texted, which was only half the truth.

As to the question of finding my husband, he said that he'd seen him a couple months ago at Liz's grave site. Before Jamie could reach him, though, he'd hurried off.

It had been more than three years since she died, and I realized that I hadn't visited the grave since the funeral. I decided to go, and if I happened to run into my husband there, great, although I didn't believe I would.

Approaching her grave, I saw the headstone for the first time; it hadn't been in place at the funeral. I was struck by how elegant it was. It was her name, her birth date, and her death date. There were no DEAR MOTHER or BELOVED WIFE engravings, nothing like that to box her in. No SISTER or DAUGHTER, as there were on the graves of the young. The stone listed simply her name and the dates that she'd been alive. She was free to be anything to anyone, any memory at all.

Predictably, I didn't see my husband there, so I returned to the houses of the known associates that I knew about, and I left more notes for him.

At the cemetery, I'd noticed that daffodils were starting to poke through the ground, and I remembered the bulbs I'd planted at Jamie's house in the fall. For days, every time I saw a hyacinth or a daffodil, I felt a surge of anger about Jamie. How could I have been such a fool? How could he have been so afraid? And most infuriatingly, Why didn't he love me enough to try?

I sank to a new depth and hired a ride one night to Jamie's house, bringing my little trowel and a sack. It was late, and the street was quiet. Bernadette was dead, so there was no dog to bark at me as I committed my trespass.

I knelt in his yard and dug up every bulb I could find. I didn't want him to know what I'd done, so I smoothed out the ground after I removed the bulbs. I wasn't trying to hurt him. I just didn't want him to enjoy the flowers I'd planted if I couldn't enjoy the flowers, too.

As I waited for my ride, I felt a pang of remorse and canceled the car. I imagined Mildred telling me, Love is love, baby. I imagined Sarah saying Let the kids have the flowers. I replanted all the bulbs except one, and smoothed out the ground once again.

I took home one bulb, which I hoped was a hyacinth, and set it up in a glass of water on my windowsill. When it bloomed, it was, in fact, a hyacinth, a blue-purple, and I enjoyed my own sweet-smelling micro-garden.

✳

When I was finally hit with the urge to crawl out of hibernation, I asked Sarah if she'd go to the bar with me. She'd been going on outings with people from Single Best Life, and she'd found someone to look after the dogs.

On our way out of the retirement village, she let herself into the events closet and grabbed a half dozen leis. (The village did a luau every year for the residents. The leis were cheap and flimsy, but we reused them every year, our attempt at sustainable practices.) I didn't ask.

When we got to the bar, I realized that not only had she come with festive leis, she'd come with something to prove—how happy she was. She placed a lei on herself, and one on me, and she flirted with a couple of guys who were powerless to resist her charms. She was warm with Alexei, despite the friction with him on my birthday in the fall, and she ordered a fruity drink. When he brought it over, she asked him to wear a lei, too. He was reluctant, putting up a good fight. But in the end, he donned the lei.

"What's up with the festivities?" he asked.

"I need a little color in my life," she said.

"Rough day?" he asked.

"Rough country," she said.

"Understatement," he said.

"America's so busted."

"It's better without the confederates, though, yeah? Now they have their own country to mess up."

"I don't know about that," she said. "I see a lot of haters living right here."

He nodded forcefully and said, "But there's nothing to do about them, is there?"

She chewed the maraschino cherry from her drink.

"My parents miss Charleston so much," she said. "They lived their whole lives there."

"But they're lucky they got out, yeah?"

Sarah shrugged and told Alexei that she didn't want to dwell on misfortune. She proceeded to upgrade her mood by sheer force of will, and he plugged in some multicolored holiday lights that were still strung across the ceiling. With Sarah smiling and laughing, the free drinks started rolling in.

Alexei asked me where I'd been all winter, and I told him I'd been wearing a lot of sweatpants. He said he'd missed me, and I didn't know what to say in response, so I stumbled over some nonsense.

Sarah saved me by trying to take a group selfie.

"No, no, no," said Alexei. "Move along."

"Come on," said Sarah. "You're the star here."

"Nah," he said. "*You're* the star here. Your third round of free drinks will be coming any minute . . ."

"I'm never the star," she said. "I'm a Black woman in America during a civil war."

Overall, I thought a lot about whether there was some way I could make America safer, kinder, or smarter, and most days I specifically thought about Sarah and wondered about the load she carried. Her fears, her worries—I only knew what she told me, which wasn't a lot, because she rarely shared her feelings about the war, and I didn't want to pry. I had so little to offer, and one well-meaning white woman wasn't going to change the world. I admired her resolve, and how she'd pulled off an evening of lights and leis. I liked seeing her have fun.

She tried again to take a group selfie, and Alexei protested.

"I don't do photos," he said.

"That's a shame," I said.

Maybe it was the alcohol, but I felt pretty in the lei. The colored lights became a little fuzzy, and I felt warm looking at the palm trees. People were laughing and smiling, and I almost forgot that there was a war. I stopped checking the door every few minutes. Sarah flicked one of the flowers in my lei.

"What can I say, Hestia, I love being single," she said. "I have zero entanglements. Zero unhealthy attachments. Zero codependence."

I stopped myself from mentioning the pit bulls, who seemed like unhealthy attachments to me, but what did I know about dogs? She loved her puppies. She took selfies of the two of us—no Alexei—and we both looked pretty. They were a little out of focus, and the colored lights and leis made our world look merry.

She told me how healthy she was feeling. In addition to all the uncoupling, she was doing ice baths ("cold thermogenesis") and taking essential amino acid supplements ("EAAs"). She had a Spiritual Discipline Journal, which she wrote in every day.

"I've got a face yoga routine, too," she said.

"Alexei," I called down the bar, "I'm ready for that third drink."

Sarah excused herself for the bathroom.

"I don't think that's a good idea," he said. "About the drink."

"I'm not drunk," I said.

"You're a little drunk," he said.

"But that's all right," I said. "What does it matter?"

He looked around the bar, scanning, then looked back at me.

"I have a proposal for you," he said, leaning close, because the bar was loud and he was almost whispering.

"You're proposing to me?"

He laughed.

"No, not marriage," he said. "Another kind of proposal."

"A romantic proposal?"

"More sexy than romantic," he said.

"Are you asking me out on a date?"

"I don't date," he said.

I cocked my head and asked him with my eyes what he meant by that.

"I'm a little different," he said. "I don't date, not the way regular people do."

"I see," I said.

"Do you?" he asked.

"No," I said.

"Do you want to hear my proposal?"

I did want to hear the proposal, but even though he leaned closer, he was talking so low that I couldn't hear him. To remedy this, he took a pen from his shirt pocket and wrote on a bar napkin. I appreciated his commitment to clear communication.

He wrote: "I want to come to your home, pleasure you, and leave."

I read the napkin and reflexively crumpled it up, afraid that someone would read it over my shoulder. Putting the napkin in my pocket, I looked at him with both eyebrows raised. There are so many ways that a woman can interpret "pleasure you."

Pleasure me? I mouthed.

He leaned over the bar and put his lips near my ear, to make sure I could hear what he said.

"I want to give you oral pleasure," he said. "And then go home."

My neck caught fire. My face burned. If I could find some ice, I could cool down my skin. Sarah's cold, slushy cocktail was still on the bar, and I held it against my cheeks.

"Just, like, while I'm sitting on a chair, or something?" I asked, putting the daiquiri on my neck.

"Chair, bed, tabletop," he said. "Up to you."

"I have questions," I said.

"I promise, I'll get out of your way as soon as you finish."

I pulled back and looked around the bar, checking the exit, thinking that maybe Alexei was a Russian spy after all, and that this was a setup. But everything looked exactly as it had. Sarah was on her way back from the bathroom. The colored lights blinked.

"Wednesdays are my days off," he said. "I could come over then."

"Wednesday's tomorrow," I said.

"Should I come over tomorrow?" he asked.

I couldn't think of a good reason to refuse.

"When do you get home from work?" he asked.

"Like, five thirty?"

I was already tingling at the thought of it. It was unusual. No-nonsense, but sexy.

I was also confused. Did he like me, but only kind-of, sort-of like me? Had my body, unbeknownst to me, been putting out some kind of vibe? Was I somehow undatable? Or was he one of those damaged people who can't manage emotional intimacy and can only do physical things? Maybe he was a freak with a fetish. I was in no mood for a man with a fetish. What if he was into cosplay and wanted to wear a costume? What if he wanted *me* to wear a costume? There was no way I was going to put on anything with fur just to have a guy go down on me. I had my limits. I had standards.

"I'll be there at five thirty tomorrow," he said.

He gave me his pen and a new napkin and asked for my address.

"So, you're just going to come over?" I asked.

"Tomorrow," he said. "Which is Wednesday."

I was so discombobulated that I had to either leave immediately or have another drink so I could stay longer. I ordered another drink, but I soon realized that Alexei had made it weak. I watched him work at the bar, and we didn't say another word to each other the entire night, but he did help me summon a ride-share when it was time to go home.

＊

The next morning, I knew that I'd made a terrible, drunken mistake. I'd told Alexei to come over too early, and I wouldn't have time after getting home from work to shower or wash the dishes. That evening, I tried to quickly wash in the bathroom sink, but it didn't go well, and then I heard the downstairs buzzer.

I buzzed him in and waited at my front door. He arrived empty-handed, which was fine, because there was no need to bring me gifts.

"Good evening, Hestia," he said, waiting to be invited in.

"Good evening," I said, wondering if we were supposed to hug or kiss.

I stepped aside so he could come in. We didn't kiss, or even touch.

"I hope you didn't have too much of a headache this morning," he said.

"I did," I said. "It was ugly."

He smiled and stood there.

"Are you feeling better now?" he asked.

"All better," I said.

He continued to smile and stand there.

"Would you like a drink?" I asked.

"No, thanks," he said.

"A piece of cheese?"

He laughed and turned down the cheese.

"There's no need to be nervous," he said. "I don't bite, ha ha."

I wanted to be able to laugh at his joke, but I was too tense. We stood there, and I looked around the room. He looked around the room. I smiled at him.

"So . . . ?" I said. "Should I . . . ?"

"Why don't you tell me where you want to be?" he said. "Then you can take off whatever items of clothing you want to."

I had actually given this some thought earlier that day, and I had decided that the couch in the living room would be best. I double-checked the curtains to make sure they were drawn, and took off my business casual jeans, which I folded over the arm of the couch. I noticed that Alexei was watching my every move, but also taking long, hard looks at his surroundings.

I took off my underwear, and placed them, folded, on top of my jeans. Who on earth folds their underwear? I was such a fool. I sat on the couch, legs together, and Alexei looked at me, took me in with his eyes, took in the whole scene.

"It's like you're committing this scene to memory," I said.

"I'm very visual," he said.

"Everyone's visual," I said.

"I was a cinematographer," he said, "before the war."

I was genuinely surprised. I'd never considered that he'd had a life before bartending.

"That's so interesting," I said. "What kind of films?"

"Wildlife programs. Nature shows."

He knelt on the rug, close to my legs, and placed his hands on my knees.

"I guess the work dried up because of the war?"

He ran his hands up and down my calves, then my thighs, taking in all of my legs with his eyes.

"War is kind of its own nature show, isn't it?" I said.

He put his hands on my knees again and began to spread my legs. He took another long look, and he came closer.

"A lot of lions eating gazelles and stuff, right, I guess war is a lot like the wild," I said.

What he did next made me shut up, finally, thank goddess, because I was prattling on. He moved in even closer. He was confident and focused, almost virtuosic. I closed my eyes, and an image of Yo-Yo Ma playing his cello flashed through my head—he was a virtuoso—but I really didn't want to be seeing Yo-Yo Ma just then, so I opened my eyes and watched the top of Alexei's head. He was gentle. Patient. Indefatigable. He didn't talk. I didn't talk, either, but it did occur to me, at some point, that this had not been the worst decision I'd ever made.

When I was finished, he kissed each of my knees and stood up. He squeezed my thigh.

He asked about the bathroom, and I listened to him wash up as I pulled on my clothes and tried not to see the donkey piñata in my fireplace. When he emerged, he looked fresh as a daisy.

"I can let myself out," he said.

"I can see you to the door," I said, trying to sound casual.

As we stood in the doorway, he told me he'd had fun.

"I also have Sundays off," he said.

"Sundays are good for me," I said.

"Good then," he said. "I'll see you Sunday, same time?"

I wondered if he was going to kiss me goodbye, and what all of this might mean. He squeezed my shoulder, which I hadn't expected, and walked away. There was nothing left to do but make myself dinner.

✳

Question 36: What is the ego?

CHARLES: *"I think, therefore I am." We're the only species that thinks about our thinking. We think and we think about it. How perverse.*

DOROTHY: *We spend our lives believing there's a unique, spectacular "I." I'm calling bullshit. Eventually, you realize that "I" is just a tiny lump of the universe stuffed into a random meatsuit, for a finite number of years.*

MILDRED: *That guy who said "I am"—let's arrest him. That was a crime.*

✳

Sarah told me and Mildred that she was thriving without a man and loving her single life, and we detected no lies. She was still making essential oil–infused candles (which we couldn't burn in the office because of fire codes) and had expanded into guerrilla gardening. She and a few other women planted perennials in vacant lots and dedicated the small plots to the families of the fallen. They painted wooden signs to mark their memorial gardens, and Sarah christened each one by nestling a candle in it.

"That's amazing," I said.

"I know," she said.

After Alexei had visited me a few times, I decided to tell them about him, but I didn't want Sarah to know it was Alexei. If she knew, things might be awkward at the bar. So I told them it was a person I'd met online. "He drives in from Parkton," I said, a good thirty-minute drive. "All the way from Parkton?" Mildred remarked, looking sleuthy, as Parkton was one of her old stomping grounds. Naturally, they were both titillated.

In hindsight, it wasn't my best lie, as Baltimore's gasoline supply was tenuous and expensive. Would someone really use all that gasoline for such a short sexcapade?

Sarah's disappointment in me was palpable.

"Whyyyyyy?" she said. "This attachment is so unhealthy."

"Is it?" I asked.

Mildred piped up: "It *might* be healthy."

"This isn't what you want," said Sarah.

"It's not?" I asked.

Mildred made a mustache-twirling gesture, and offered, "It *might* be what she wants."

Sarah literally threw up her hands and said, "You and your entanglements," and she henceforth referred to Alexei (without knowing it was Alexei) as my "Wednesday man." As in, "Did you get a visit from your Wednesday man?" or, "Maybe you can get your Wednesday man to help you with that," or, "Who told you that, your Wednesday man?" I didn't tell them about Sundays. Wednesdays were one thing, but Wednesdays *and* Sundays seemed, I don't know, overindulgent.

Beyond being annoyed at the lack of visual information (she wanted photos of his face), Mildred didn't know what to make of it. Neither of us had any predictions about how long things would go on as they were, or if they would change at all.

"People certainly are strange," she said.

"Pics or it didn't happen," she also said.

✳

With winter receding, I should have felt energized. Instead, every day, it was just a little bit harder to get out of bed than the day before. Even with Alexei, my life didn't feel that interesting. What was there to look forward to, except Wednesdays and Sundays at five thirty, for half an hour?

In this time of civil war, we were all urged to practice self-care. From the human resources departments to the doctors' offices to the posters on the insides and outsides of buses: Be gentle with yourself. But how? No side of a bus ever tells you how, exactly, to be gentle with yourself as you watch confederate shitlords—your former countrymen—throw hissy fits over some hallucination they once had about America.

We were supposed to go high when they went low, and remember that we are all stardust. We were supposed to look for the helpers. We were supposed to squint our eyes and see the arc of progress. We were in the grips of a collective, national delusion, and we convinced ourselves that in one of the Chinese languages the word for "crisis" is the same as the word for "opportunity." We were drowning in toxic positivity.

What if I could walk into a meeting and someone would say, How are you? and I could say, Feeling rather crap, thanks for asking, how about you? and she would say, Same, feeling rather crap today, I could barely bring myself here. That would be better.

Walking home one day, I noticed a pile of items on the sidewalk, household things that someone was getting rid of. "Life's a Beach" said one of the wall hangings, and I took it home with me for the fireplace.

To my surprise, there were some moments during Tai Chi class when I felt lighter. I think I harnessed qi and held it between my hands, sensing its gentle buzz, which pulled my palms together while also pushing them apart. I might have moved the qi into my dan tien, too. It felt big. And I liked being in the class with Mildred. I hadn't realized it before, but she was a big man on campus at the village. Everyone knew her and wanted to be near her, and she knew everyone. I'd never been part of the popular crowd.

"Smaller movements," Tom told us in his calm voice.

"Put more weight in your legs. Make smaller circles with your arms," he said, hovering his fingers over my biceps to help me focus.

"Think about your center," he said. "Let your dan tien guide you."

＊

Over the winter, Mildred and I had begun joining Tom for tea after class, although sometimes, if one of her daughters was visiting, she'd have to skip it. As her health deteriorated, they visited more often, and I found myself alone in the Café with Tom, waiting while he steeped his tea.

I'd loaded a meditation app onto my phone, which was supposed to make me less moody. I was giving it a whirl, reading the menu while we waited. When the guide's voice popped on, Tom said from the counter, without turning around, "I know that app."

"Tamara thinks I should notice my feelings," I said. "But not engage with them."

"She means well," he said, bringing two hot mugs of tea to the table.

"She says I shouldn't judge my feelings," I said.

"I think that's difficult," he said.

"No shit," I said.

"Cognition is so overrated, though," he said.

I agreed with him.

"Why does everyone have to hate on depression? It's a perfectly sane response," he said. "Life is rough."

"Especially now," I said.

"This is a raw pu-erh made from trees along the Bulang Mountain," he said.

I sipped it gingerly, because the water, Tom told me, had been heated to exactly 208 degrees.

"Did you get this tea before the war?" I asked.

"Of course," he said. "When I was barely making a living importing tea."

"And now you barely make a living teaching Tai Chi?"

"That's correct," he said.

He took his phone out of his pocket and leaned toward me.

"This might cheer you up," he said.

He showed me photos of a band onstage, and he was holding one of the guitars. Emo punk, he explained. While the other band members were gloriously adorned in emo punk wear, he looked the same. Long hair, slight hunch, flat belly, tattered clothes.

"Are you in a band now?" I asked.

"Oh, no way," he said. "That's too dangerous for me."

I liked that Tom remembered the world was dangerous. Sometimes I forgot about the risks of daily life, distracted as I was by dating.

We sipped from our mugs, and I thanked him for showing me the photos. He said that he'd thought I'd find them more amusing, and I told him that he looked exactly the same in them as he did now. He told me that I must be crazy. In his mind, he looked completely different. He took another sip of pu-erh and spoke softly.

"Speaking of crazy," he said, "do you think you might ever want to go out with me?"

His question took me by surprise, but I faked calm.

"On a date?" I asked.

"Yes," he said.

"I'm kind of seeing someone," I said. "I think."

"Say no more," he said, taking a long sip.

"It's complicated," I said.

"It's all right," he said.

"I'm sorry," I said.

"This isn't my first rodeo."

"I feel bad," I said. "Badly."

"We can stop this now," he said, annoyed.

I wondered if I was actually "seeing someone." Did Alexei count? I tried to backpedal.

"Maybe we could—"

"It's all right," he interrupted. "Timing is a cock, and it's as simple as that."

"You've said that before," I reminded him.

"Well, it's almost always true," he said.

Later, I thought about Tom for a while, in a way I'd never thought about him before. He was kind and decent, smart in his way. He had that heroin voice, and when I was near him I felt myself becoming a little more calm, a little more balanced. But he was also poor. Scared. Awkward. What turned me off most about him was his honesty. He seemed like a person who couldn't stop himself from telling the truth, and I knew myself well enough to know that I needed some pretty lies. A whole bunch of pretty lies, actually, except that I needed them to be mostly true. Magical, pretty lies, like, You're the woman of my dreams, or I've waited my whole life for you.

I didn't think Tom had it in him to do that kind of magic. If I were with him, I'd have to give up on being romanced and find a way to love someone who was blunt and graceless, like me. I'd have to believe in myself and trust that he loved me—the thought of doing all that emotional work made me sleepy.

I didn't tell Mildred or Sarah that he asked me out, because I didn't want to hear it from them. Mildred would probably say that I was a fool for turning him down. "Get out of your comfort zone," she'd say, but I didn't want to be uncomfortable. Sarah would congratulate me on staying untethered, but I didn't really want to be untethered, either— I worried I'd float away.

✳

The weather got warm, Alexei continued his Wednesday and Sunday visits, and my husband left a handwritten note in my mailbox. The handwriting was conclusive: it was definitely him, and he was still alive. The gush of relief I felt at learning he was alive surprised me, because I hadn't known that I was worried.

"Dear Hestia, I'm so sorry. If it's any consolation, time wounds all heels," he wrote. "We can meet up anytime you'd like."

He didn't write anything about the divorce I was asking for, but he left a phone number and said I could text to arrange a get-together.

I showed the note to Mildred, and she checked the envelope to see if there was more.

"This is it? After three years?" she asked. "What a putz."

She asked me for a cigarette, knowing I'd say no. But she had to ask. It was our tug-of-war now.

"The fact is," she said, "I'm having surgery soon. They're going to try to cut out the cancer from my body. I wish them luck."

So my hunch was correct. It was cancer. I didn't let myself cry.

"I'm surprised you're letting them take heroic measures," I said. "You told everyone you didn't want that."

"I was heaved into existence," she said, "and I wanted to fade out of it."

"So, how did this happen?" I asked.

"Why does anything happen? It happened because of my children."

"Why can't they let you go on your own terms?" I asked.

"They're attached to me," she said. "Imagine that."

"Imagine," I said.

"So now you see why you should let me have that menthol 100," she said.

"I promised Annie I wouldn't," I said, "and I like Annie."

"I paid through the nose for those cigarettes," she said, "and now they're getting stale."

I stonewalled her.

"I'm going to die whether I smoke that fag or not," she said.

"I promised her," I said.

She made an eloquent case for how if she had to suffer indignities, she should at least be allowed to enjoy a smoke now and then. I held fast, though. Annie was too sweet for me to betray. Mildred rolled her eyes heavenward and held her hands as if in prayer.

"Christ on the cross, the food is terrible here," she said. "And such small portions!"

✳

A few weeks' worth of thrifting had paid off for my fireplace display. In addition to "Life's a Beach," I added plaques and embroidered hangings with inspirational slogans like, "You Got This" and "Relax." While I sat on the couch during Alexei's visits, I found "Relax" to be especially helpful.

Despite my intentions, I was getting attached to him. They say that the orgasm is powerful that way: have enough orgasms with someone, and you'll fall in love with them. Or at least become very fond of them. I wanted to get to know him a little more, and twice a week, before our dates on my couch, I'd ask as many questions as I could before his hands touched my thighs. Once his hands were on my knees, conversation was futile. But until then:

"Where did you grow up?"

"Have you ever been married?"

"Do you speak Russian?"

"Who's your favorite Beatle?"

"Where were you when the president died?"

With these icebreakers, delivered as I removed the appropriate garments, we conversed a little more each time. The de-pantsing period grew longer, a few minutes here, maybe a few minutes more the next time. He told me once, "I really do enjoy these afternoons with you," but something about the way he said it, the "I really do" part, sounded to me as if the lady doth protest too much.

"I enjoy them, too," I said, and he said, "I know."

I wondered if I should offer to return the favor. By now, I was beginning to feel terrible, like a taker. I wanted to offer him pleasure . . . but I stopped myself. If he wanted more, he could ask. No one was forcing him. I needed to get better at receiving.

✳

I came home from work one day to find a package in the foyer of my building, under my mailbox. At first, I was afraid to pick it up off the floor. Using my foot, I turned it around on the floor so I could see if it was for me—it was—and what the label looked like.

The return address was one I didn't recognize, a town in what I could only assume was confederate Virginia, but the handwriting was my mother's. I relaxed a little. My parents wouldn't send me a bomb, or anthrax, or a sheep's head, of that I was certain. It was hard to describe them, but they weren't monsters. I took the box upstairs.

Inside was a "book" I'd made as a child. I'd made so many of them, or at least that was my recollection. They were stories about animals, because I used to dream about animals, and I remembered the dreams. The pages were 80 percent illustration and 20 percent words, stapled together into a crude spine. Back then, I was big on foxes. And deer. Also, chipmunks.

But it wasn't the original book; it was a reproduction, stapled-together color copies of the pages.

In her note, my mother wrote, "We wanted to hold on to the originals a bit longer."

It was surprisingly sentimental for her. This was a woman who seriously thought there should be eight, not seven, deadly sins, and that Clutter was the eighth, belonging in the lineup between Pride and Greed. After all, she'd argued to her priest as a teenager, according to the story she'd told me, what is Clutter if not a greedy attachment to something that makes you feel prideful? And now I learned that this same woman "wanted to hold on to" all those childhood books of mine.

Half of the note was in my mother's handwriting, and half was in my father's.

From my mother:

It occurred to me that you might like to be reminded of more virtuous, innocent times, so I've sent you this reproduction of one of your little "books." You worked so hard on them. Some might call it a labor of love. You were a passionate child, but many children are. We wanted to hold on to the originals a bit longer, although as our life shrinks, so must our possessions. It feels courageous, to slough off the materials of our lives. When we meet again, I can give them to you. Your father and I think of you often. Shall we save the little books for when we meet?

From my father:

Do you have a thing called FaceTime? We have that now, and we think it would be a good way for us to communicate. Can we set up a time this month? We can have a no-politics rule. For example, Your Mother and I will not mention what we think to be flaws in your critical thinking skills, and you will not call us "privileged" or, worse, "racists." (We believe that you know, Hestia, that we are neither of these things.) If we are disciplined, we can adhere to this rule, and the FaceTime will go smoothly. There does not need to be any yelling, crying, or blame. Your Mother and I would like to know that you are doing well.

He left a phone number, which was the same as the one I already had, and wrote, "This is the number to use for the FaceTime." He suggested a date and a time, and I felt all the power sucked out of me, the power to resist, the power to think straight, the way an encounter with a parent can do. I entered the date on my calendar.

Naturally, I brought my little book to work and showed Mildred, who lingered and cooed over every page.

"Look at this, the lady fox is wearing a pink scarf!" she said.

I remembered that I had been pleased with that scarf, back then.

"And the opossum. She has babies on her back, and a tiara on her head. A tiara, Hestia, what a thing, to put a tiara on an opossum."

"As you know, Mildred," I said. "I've always been fashion-forward."

When she finished the book, she asked me why I filled it with animals, and I told her they were what populated my dreams as a child. Maybe I hadn't known a lot of people back then.

"I used to dream about animals, too," she said. "I'd like to do that again."

"I would, too," I said.

"Hestia, dear," she said, and I prepared myself, because it sounded like she was going to ask me something.

"Have you thought any more about writing my obituary?"

"No," I said. "I haven't."

"You should," she said. "I really wish you would."

✳

Question 37: Why do we feel so discontented?

CHARLES: *We give ourselves names, like "doctor" or "husband." We're always defining ourselves. We think that if I'm an uncle, and he's an uncle, we can bond on being uncles. But we were already bonded by being human, and those labels just carve us away from each other.*

DOROTHY: *We spend our lives giving ourselves names and stories. What a trap.*

CLARA: *When you believe in your "self," you separate from the sacred source, and that's why we feel bad.*

JEFFREY: *It might be because of the christofascists.*

✳

Tamara, from the meditation app, wanted me to send loving-kindness to myself. Her segment on failure, which I considered one of my areas of expertise, was one that I listened to often. Every time I listened, she said the same thing: you can reframe failure as a victory, because you tried, because you had the courage to try. She invited me to think differently about it, and I tried out various acts of self-compassion. Tamara was a bot, but in my mind we had conversations.

"It's okay that you've utterly failed at your creative pursuits," I said.

"That's not what I meant," Tamara said.

She invited me to try again, and I tried to be more kind.

"It really is okay that you failed, sweetheart," I said.

"Still not getting it," said Tamara.

"What am I supposed to say?" I asked, and she said, "Don't use the word 'failure,'" and I said, "Oh, Tamara, you really don't know me at all."

✳

After a Sunday visit, as Alexei and I said goodbye at the door, he stopped in his tracks, turned around, and asked me if there were other things I'd like him to do. I nearly joked, Yes, mop my floor, but I stopped myself because what if he didn't think it was funny?

"Like, what do you mean?" I asked.

He shrugged his shoulders, and I shrugged my shoulders.

"Like, if you took off your shirt, I could kiss more of you," he said.

"Right now?" I asked.

"Sure."

I led him back into the living room and took off everything. I was naked, and he was clothed. He knelt and stared straight at my chest.

"Tell me what you had in mind," he said. "Tell me *exactly*."

The more detail I provided, the better. He wanted to get it right. I narrated the sex scene as if I were writing a soft-core porn romance, in past tense and third person. As the novelist of this scene, I controlled his every move.

"And then he ran his lips along her neck, down to her breasts," I said. He acted out the scene. "He stroked her gently with his fingertip," I said, and he complied with what was on the virtual page.

The heroine never touched the hero; she barely moved a muscle. He kept all his clothes on and pleased her in every way the novelist could think of.

"He stood back and beheld her naked body," I narrated.

I liked the way the hero looked at the heroine, the way it's supposed to happen in the romance novels, with a mixture of anticipation and admiration.

"He closed his eyes and thought deep, sweet thoughts about her," I said.

He closed his eyes and took a long, dramatic breath, which was not on the page, but I liked his willingness to improvise.

Then I got to the *hard-core* stuff—the stuff women want the most, but never ask for.

"He told her that she was the most amazing, beautiful woman he'd met in his entire life," I said.

He hesitated. "What?"

I repeated the line, and the hero mumbled, "You're amazing, yeah."

I went full potboiler.

"He whispered that he wanted her more than he'd ever wanted anyone," I narrated.

The hero kissed her ear, and she could sense that he was flummoxed.

"He wanted her more than he'd ever wanted anyone," I repeated.

He stammered, and then substituted a different compliment, a lame one.

"I love your wavy hair. It's . . . really, really wavy," he said.

After that, I gave up on the game and rushed to the finish. I put on some clothes and offered him some water, leading him into the kitchen. All this time, and he'd never been in any rooms other than the living room and bathroom. He squeezed the plastic water bottle.

"You do know that these don't actually get recycled?"

"Yes, my husband made sure I knew."

Oops. Mentioning the ex, *any* ex, in a moment like this—what terrible form. And it was weird, because I hardly ever mentioned my husband to anyone. Who wants to hear about all that nonsense?

"I didn't know you were married," he said.

"I haven't seen him in years," I said. "The marriage is a technicality. There's nothing between us."

"It's all right," said Alexei. "You don't need to explain anything."

"Aren't you curious?"

"It's not necessary for us to talk about these things," he said.

"But it might be nice if we did," I said.

He crunched the water bottle. He sighed. He sighed again.

"What do you want to know?" he asked finally.

I looked away while I asked my questions, because I hated to look at the face of a guy who didn't want to talk about the relationship.

"Who else do you visit like this?" I asked. "How many people?"

"I only have two days off," he said.

"Okay," I said, focusing on my herbs outside the kitchen window, "but can you answer the question?"

He sighed again.

"No other people," he said.

"Is that true?" I asked.

"Yes," he said, "it's true."

"Thanks," I said. "I just needed to know."

"We don't need to explain anything to each other," he said, and I nodded.

✳

Question 38: What makes us human?

JEFFREY: *Kafka said that the meaning of life is that it ends, but I think that's only half the story. What really makes us human is that we know it's going to end.*

CLARA: *And we can't figure out what happens to us when we die. We're obsessed with that. No other creature does that.*

MILDRED: *Can you imagine? If we spent our lives having no idea that we're going to die?*

✳

When it was time for Mildred's surgery, Annie and Ruth had to face each other, had to be in the same room. As I understood it, they hadn't spoken for years, because of the war. According to Mildred, the girls had loved each other way back when. Ten years older, Ruth doted on Annie with attention that was almost maternal. She dressed her up, taught her about makeup, and showed her dance moves. When Ruth went to college, Mildred would pick a random weekday, keep Annie home from school, and drive them three hours to visit for the day.

"Annie thought her big sister hung the moon," said Mildred.

Now they lived on opposite ends of Pennsylvania, and while Ruth stridently supported the Union, Annie expressed nothing but disdain for it.

Mildred's plan for the hospital was that Annie would pack the clothing, and Ruth the toiletries. As they packed, I walked past her door once—okay, it was twice—to see if I might be needed, but the daughters had everything under control. Ruth refilled the weekly pill case, and she braided Mildred's hair into one long side braid.

"You've kept a thick head of hair your whole life, Mama," she said.

"It's been one of my proudest achievements, giving you girls good hair," Mildred said.

When I was back at my desk, Annie stopped by my office and invited me and Sarah to join them in the lobby.

"My mother asked to see you before we left," she said.

As we walked to the lobby, she told us that she expected to have all the citizenship for Ireland worked out within the year. "Next spring, I'll be taking my mother to Dublin," she said. "God is good," she said.

When I reached the lobby, Mildred was in a wheelchair.

"They insisted on wheels," she said. "I walk too slowly for them."

"Mildred," I said, "you'll be back here in no time."

"You'll be banging that cane so soon," said Sarah.

"This may be it for me, dears," Mildred said. "I've been playing with house money for some time now."

"Stop it, Mama, Jesus is watching over you," said Annie.

Ruth rolled her eyes at the Jesus reference.

"I guess I'm canceled for saying 'Jesus,'" Annie said.

Ruth looked heavenward.

"God give me strength," said Ruth.

"Girls," said Mildred. "That's enough."

Annie wheeled Mildred out of the room, and Ruth lingered a moment to whisper to me: "I'll have the Austrian passports ready to go in six months' time." She then knocked on her forehead three times, and also said "Pu pu pu" to the ground.

∗

Ruth texted me from the hospital the evening after the surgery: "Too much cancer. They opened her up and closed her right back up again." As I was trying to compose a reply, she texted again: "Peek and shriek." I tried again to text, and she wrote, "LOL," but I knew it was a sad, sardonic LOL.

The next day was one of those searing Baltimore summer days: hot, muggy, stifling. Sarah and I visited Mildred in the hospital, and when she saw us, she tried to sit up straighter. "Pillows, dears, pillows," she said, and we propped her up until it was almost normal.

"Are the girls gone?" she whispered. "Check the hall."

Sarah checked and confirmed that Ruth and Annie were not in sight.

"Get over here, before they come back," she said. "I hate

to be the skunk at the picnic, but I don't think I'll make it past the summer."

I had to grab on to the bed railing, and I felt my face go cold. Sarah's eyes became dead fish. Mildred told me to get Sarah a chair, and she sat down while I leaned on the bed rail.

"No, no, Hestia, you're not understanding. This is good," said Mildred. "Listen to me.

"Number one, I'll be returning to the village sooner than expected. Number two, you can let me smoke all the cigarettes I want. And we're going to go big. The French cigarettes, not the cheap ones, and none of that traitor tobacco. And number three, I get out of having to choose between Dublin and Vienna."

Sarah and I looked at each other. I tried to shake off a shiver. It was freezing in the room, and I wrapped my arms around myself, rubbing my arms to stay warm.

"It's a godsend," Mildred said. "My death will be a miracle. Can you get me some water? No ice, please. It's freezing in here."

She changed the subject and asked Sarah if she was still solo and loving it. Sarah told her she was.

"No unhealthy attachments, then?"

Sarah was quiet for a moment and then answered. "I think my only unhealthy attachment is my idea of myself as an American."

Mildred nodded immediately.

"Yes, I understand," she said. "But, may I ask, can you think of yourself as anything *other* than an American?"

"I might be able to leave America," said Sarah. "Like you."

"I'm not *leaving*, dear," said Mildred. "I'm *dying*."

Surges of anger flickered through my body. I felt my skin get prickly. I glared at them, and Mildred noticed.

"What is it, dear?" said Mildred.

"Sarah never told me she was thinking about leaving America," I said. "And you? Do you have to sound so happy about leaving?"

"Our Father in Heaven, Hestia," said Sarah. "Not everything is about *you*."

Mildred changed the subject, asking about my Wednesday man.

"Well, he's Sundays, too," I said, and Sarah looked miffed.

"Why didn't you tell me?"

"Do I have to tell you?"

"I tell *you* things," said Sarah.

"Apparently not," I said.

"Girls," said Mildred. "That's enough."

She said it exactly like she said it to Ruth and Annie when they bickered.

Then she wanted to sleep, and Sarah and I walked back to our office in silence. I couldn't believe how awful Mildred looked, but I didn't want to talk about it. I also didn't want to put that weight on Sarah. And I didn't want to say out loud how ugly the process of dying was. You want something like that to be more beautiful.

✳

When Mildred returned to the village, her daughters brought a wheelchair and told the staff that she'd had to give up her cane. With her in her new chair, we went to Tai Chi, which I'd been doing in her honor. Before class started, Tom showed her how to position her arms for certain poses while sitting.

Ever the skeptic, I doubted there was any such thing as Tai Chi for people in wheelchairs.

"I call it Chair Chi," he said.

She squeezed his biceps and laughed, almost girlishly, as he clasped her wrist. When he moved her arm into position, she beamed at him.

"Oh, Hestia, come here," she said. "Tom said he'd teach me some modifications for the chair."

"That's nice of you," I said.

"How could I not, for one of my best students?"

She giggled. He corrected the way she was holding her wrist. "Like this, fair lady," he said while he positioned her. I didn't understand how he could be so suave and gallant with Mildred, but so labored with me.

After class, I told Mildred we should go to the gardens.

"Why, Hestia?" she asked. "Don't you want some tea?"

Tom was coming toward us.

"I brought an oolong today," he said. "Soft and milky."

"The weather's too beautiful for the Café," I said, which was a lie, because it was a beastly summer day.

If Tom tried to hide his disappointment, he did a poor job of it. But I wasn't sure if he'd even tried.

When we were outside, Mildred gushed about how nice it was for him to modify the poses.

"It's kind of his job," I said.

"Well, he's nicer than he has to be."

I put her chair in a spot under a tree, and she complained about being in the shade.

"Life's too short for shade," she said.

"Mildred," I said, "it's good to have you back here."

"Hestia, listen to me," she said. "When people want to do nice things for you, just let them."

"Okay," I said.

"Tom wants to do nice things for you," she said. "You should let him."

"Why?"

"You're exasperating," she said. "It's just nice when people are nice. Let it happen. Promise me you will."

✳

Alexei continued to come over twice a week, never missing a day. I asked him more questions about his life, waiting until he'd answered to my satisfaction before I'd take off my pants. Sometimes I asked him to tell me about one of his films, and he'd try to recall it scene by scene. His memory was impressive. I liked how he described not so much the animal itself, but the way he had captured the animal on film: a zoom-in or a pull-away or a pan of a post-kill feeding frenzy.

I asked him about his childhood, and he told me that his parents had emigrated from Russia when they were young adults.

"So I grew up scoffing," he said.

He described walking into stores with his mother and facing, say, a wall of shelves lined with different brands of toothpaste. "Who needs all this choice?" his mother would ask, and scoff. He'd been trained to sneer at the mediocrity that the vast majority of humans seemed to crave. Architecture, poetry, music—these were painful subjects for his parents, and then for him.

"People want mediocrity, though," he said. "They like the middle."

Sometimes, when we were done and standing at the door,

he gave me a compliment out of the blue. "You have a great sense of humor," he said once. "You've got a lovely bosom," he said another time. It was analytical and kind, never gushing. He definitely was not trying to win me over, or land me, or lock that shit down. I had no idea what either of us was doing, but the habit was easy.

I don't know what I was thinking, but one time I asked him if he'd like to have dinner together sometime, and he said, "I could go either way." That was the last time I invited him to share a meal.

✳

The day came to FaceTime with my parents, and I didn't know what to expect. I wanted them to repent. It would have been wonderful to hear them say that they'd had a good think and finally realized nobody really pulls themselves up by their bootstraps; that rugged individualism was a stupid story; that middle-class security was a lie; that trauma was real. I would have loved to hear them say, We should all take care of each other.

But I knew that wouldn't happen. When I saw their faces on my screen, I self-soothed. It was a reflex I'd learned over many years.

They'd aged only a little. There was no small talk. No "I've missed you." We didn't tell each other we looked well. Because of climate change, we couldn't even talk about the weather.

"We want to mend some fences," my mother said. "Tell her, Bill."

"We care about you very much," said my father.

"We do," said my mother.

"We'll come to Baltimore," said my father. "What do you want from us?"

That was an interesting question. We had a few moments of FaceTime silence before I answered.

"Can you just give people the benefit of the doubt?" I asked.

"We always do that," he said.

"But you two seem to think you're working harder than everybody else," I said.

"There are a lot of grifters," said my mother.

"We busted our asses to get where we are," said my father. "But some people want things for free."

"Everybody's busting their ass," I said.

My mother put her hand on my father's shoulder, and they both stopped talking.

"We can come in a month or two," she said. "Does that work?"

"It will be hot here in August, over a hundred degrees," I said, "and I only have the window units."

"We'll stay in the hotel," said my father.

"That makes sense," I said. "That's probably for the best."

I told them I'd look up the Leafy Greens on my app and see if it was safe, as there had been a lot of demonstrations lately.

"We're older than dirt," said my father. "Forget about the app. We've lived this long."

"And Hestia, it's always hot in August," said my mother. "It always has been."

"The Earth has a natural warming process," said my father. "You know about the Milankovitch cycles, don't you, Hestia?"

When I was with Mildred, I knew that she was enjoying

my company, because she always made that clear. But my parents? I never could tell. We used to be able to laugh together. When I was young, we watched funny movies every Sunday, Charlie Chaplin or the Three Stooges, and we laughed until our ribs hurt, eating popcorn seasoned with nutritional yeast. But that was a long time ago, and I wasn't sure we could ever do it again.

"I wanted to tell you, Hestia," said my father, "that you look beautiful today."

"I think she's finally grown into her face, Bill," said my mother. "You *do* look well, Hestia."

"We'll have a big meal together," he said.

What I felt for them, mostly, was sympathy. They were old people, somewhat misled, who had created me out of a feeling they believed was love. They loved me the way they thought it was supposed to work. But it wasn't going as planned. They were confused. Instead of enjoying their golden years surrounded by cheerful grandchildren, and cared for by a devoted daughter, they only had each other. Had I been too hard on them? Did they deserve more mercy?

At certain moments, when I saw them on my screen, instead of seeing my parents, I only saw old people. Confused, thrashing. Trying to figure out a smartphone, wondering what to do about the mortal coil.

✳

A few days later, my husband buzzed to be let in, as scheduled, and he sat down at my kitchen table. Or was it still *our* kitchen table? We'd agreed to "settle some things" and, because there were cameras everywhere, and facial recognition, and cell tower pings, we had to avoid being in public.

For a moment, I wondered if I should embrace him, but I did not. He hesitated, too, but then walked in and made a beeline for the refrigerator, where he put his phone. He drew the blinds. He asked me to turn on music when we talked, just in case, and he said, "Wait a minute, holy shit, you don't have an Alexa, do you?" I took offense at the question, and he backed off.

I think I was expecting him to be a train wreck, kind of bedraggled and muddy, but he looked all right. He was thin and weathered, and I couldn't help staring at him, as if I'd forgotten what he looked like. I kept asking myself: Had he really looked like this all along?

I put cheese and crackers on the table, adorned with chives I'd just cut from one of my plants. He stared at the table, then pieced together a few crackers with cheese to make tiny sandwiches with chives sticking out of the edges. When he bit into them, I couldn't help thinking he looked like a squirrel. He seemed at ease, and it bothered me, as if he were simply picking up where he left off, which he had no right to do. The way he leaned back in the chair, the way he helped himself to a napkin—it was too familiar.

I asked him what he'd been up to, and he said he'd spent some time in Portland, blowing things up, as one does. But mostly he'd been in places like New Orleans, Atlanta, and Austin, training the resistance.

"And how's the resistance going?" I asked.

"It's all right," he said.

"Is it what you were looking for?"

He closed his eyes and sighed deeply. *Now* he looked tired.

"It's not bad," he said, "but it's not great."

I asked him how it wasn't great, and he described tiffs with compadres, ego trips, and annoying colleagues who jockeyed for status. Everyone wanted to be a hero. Everyone wanted to be a star. Nobody wanted to take out the trash.

"People," I said, with my most misanthropic sneer.

"Some days it just feels like a job," he said.

"What will you do when the war's over?" I asked.

"This war's never going to end," he said.

"That can't be true," I said. "All wars end."

He rubbed his eyes with both hands.

"I'm not sure any civil war ever ends," he said. "But this one especially."

This was more cynicism than I'd ever heard from him. Maybe his three years away had changed him.

"You're in the thick of it," I said.

"I'm not even sure I want a revolution anymore," he said.

I laughed out loud. Was revolution the goal, then? That was a new one. I hadn't realized he was full-bore for revolution.

"I'm no history scholar," I said, "but I know that no revolution has ever helped anyone who really needed it."

"Revolutions have changed the course of history," he said.

"Sure," I said. "But the poor stay poor, and the powerless stay powerless. Revolutions only switch around which rich people run the show."

"I disagree," he said.

"It's what happens when the upper classes move the deck chairs," I said.

"Were you always like this?" he asked.

We stared each other down for a few minutes, until I took away the platter of food. From the sink, I asked him how long he'd been in town. He told me a couple of months, but that he'd been coming and going over the years. It was summer, but I shivered from the coldness of it. He never once tried to contact me.

"Have you talked to your mom?" I asked.

He shook his head.

"I'm sure she'd love to know you're alive," I said.

"I know," he said. "I should."

"I look for your name in the papers," I said. "I'm sure she does, too."

"I need to make some changes in my life," he said.

"How about your nieces and nephew?" I asked.

"I'm going to contact them," he said.

"You should," I said.

He stood up, took a glass from the cabinet, and turned on the faucet.

"I think the water's safe to drink today," he said.

I took a bottle of water from the fridge. "Drink this," I said.

He grimaced, and I knew what he was thinking about the plastic.

"You seem angry," he said.

"A little bit," I said, hoping he took the sarcasm.

He put the glass back in the cabinet and sat down again. He stood up and paced the room, peeked outside through the blinds. His face got tighter, his jaw clenching. He sat down, then decided to stand up again.

"But isn't your life better now?" he said. "You're free now to do whatever you want, with whoever you want."

I did some of the four-eight breathing that Tamara had taught me on the meditation app.

"You got the young Hestia," I said.

"You're still young," he said, and I laughed.

"I didn't take anything from you," he said.

"I *gave* it to you," I said. "That's what makes it so bad."

He said nothing, and I decided to have the conversation I'd been wanting to have for three years.

"You left me for that . . . girl," I said.

"I left you for the movement," he said.

"No, be honest."

"Fine," he said.

"Why did you do it?" I asked.

"She needed my help," he said.

This sent me straight back to the childhood conversation with my father about how men are drawn to helpless women, because a damsel in distress makes them feel strong. I actually tasted bitterness in my mouth.

"And you couldn't resist a woman who needed your help," I said.

"I couldn't."

"Because you're weak," I said.

He clenched his jaw so hard that the air in the room changed. My mouth tasted like metal, the light was too bright, and his face got shiny. I think he wanted to punch me. It was no small thing to call a man weak, and I knew that. I'd been waiting three years to do it.

"I wanted to do one big thing in my life," he said. "I just wanted to make a difference."

"It would have made a difference if you stayed."

"You didn't need me, Hestia," he said.

"Was that the problem?" I asked. "I didn't need you?"

"You don't need anyone," he said.

That stung, because I was the neediest person I knew.

"Well, I guess you don't know me at all," I said. "I need *everything*. I'm a goddamned mess."

He curled his lip and looked at me quizzically.

It was pointless. I'd thought that maybe we could move on, maybe laugh, maybe feel something like friendship. But I wasn't interested in whatever this was. I presented him with the paperwork, and he signed everything at the kitchen table, with flair.

"Let me know when it's over," he said.

I told him I'd text him the court date.

"You look good," he said at the door. "I don't think I mentioned that. I hope you're happy."

I reminded him to call Jamie, to visit his nieces and nephew. Visit your mother and father, I told him. They love you and miss you, I told him, which I knew was true. They don't care about all the other stuff, I said, which I also knew was true because they were like that.

"They adore you," I said.

"I know," he said.

"They believe in you," I said.

It was not my intention, but that made both of us cry, although for different reasons. He cried because he felt guilty, and I cried because I envied him more than I could stand.

✳

Question 39: What is the primal human need?

MILDRED: *People are always doing one of two things. We're either loving, or we're crying out for love.*

✳

The last time I saw Alexei was a coincidental run-in. We didn't do outings, and I'd stopped going to the bar because it was awkward. It was a Friday, the end of the workday, the day after my husband signed all the paperwork. I was leaving my office, and I noticed a rally at the harbor. I wondered if it was another gathering of confederate sympathizers, so I went closer to check it out. Yep. They held signs complaining about "tea" and "taxation" and "overthrowing." Mother of goddess, I thought, another tea party. I would have turned around and walked home, except I spotted Alexei in the sea of unionist counterprotesters. I was drawn to him; I wanted to see him in daylight, outdoors, anywhere other than my living room.

I realized that the traitors were throwing tea bags into the harbor. Didn't they understand there was no king, no troops being quartered in their homes, and that their grievances were silly? Tea bags. This was just embarrassing. They looked ridiculous, but did they know it? I didn't think so.

Alexei and his crew mocked them, which they deserved. I felt a surge of pride, and I wanted to be near him. As I was making my way toward him, the confederates had another idea. The tea bags were so light that they couldn't be thrown far, hardly making it to the water. So they tied rocks to the tea bags to give them some heft, and that's where things got ugly.

Some of the rocks tied to tea bags hit people in the head. They landed on peacekeepers and counterprotesters. But the peacekeepers had come with riot gear, having learned their lesson at the World Trade Center, and they subdued the worst offenders. They used handcuffs and zip ties, and they pulled the detainees out of the crowd. I had just arrived at Alexei's side when things took a darker turn.

"Hey," he said, when he saw me.

"Hey, there," I said.

"Fancy seeing you here," he said.

"I know, right?"

As arrests were made, the protesters grew angry and started throwing their tea bag rocks at the peacekeepers. The peacekeepers became angry, and unlike the police, they didn't give anyone the benefit of the doubt. They didn't see "white men behaving badly." They saw dumbasses wrapped in snake flags throwing rocks at people's heads, and they were not going to stand for it. In addition to zip ties, they started using rubber truncheons to beat back the rioters.

Emboldened by the support from the peacekeepers, Alexei and his group of counterprotesters advanced on the confederates.

"Fuck you, police!" yelled the confederates.

I stayed just on the edge of the clash while Alexei dove in. I guess he really wanted to punch some traitors. The peacekeepers tried to pull people apart, but by then Alexei was being held against his will by some ugly confederates in Gadsden flag ball caps. I lunged for him, but I was shoved around.

"Run, Hestia!" he shouted.

I glared at the confederate who was holding him.

"Let go of my boyfriend!" I shouted.

"Honestly," Alexei said, over the roar of the crowd, "do we have to label the relationship?"

I didn't know who I was anymore. I screeched at the traitors to give up and go home. I cried. "Give me back my country," I yelled, before I even knew what I was saying.

They pointed their fingers and laughed at me. Alexei had been pulled backward into the crowd by the rioters, although I saw him break free soon after. He didn't come to find me. I still had my backpack on, and I took it off so I could look for the mace I kept attached to my key ring. I wanted to mace some traitors so badly, and I was going to rush up really close so I could get it into their eyes.

But someone pulled me back and wrapped his hand around my hand. It was the Belgian, the peacekeeper who frequented the retirement village.

"Give me my mace," I said.

"I won't let you spray it," he said.

"Give it," I said.

"You'll get arrested," he said.

"I don't care!" I yelled. "Why won't you let me spray the mace?"

He put his hands on my shoulders and shielded me with his body, trying to shuffle me out of the crowd.

"Why won't you?" I asked again.

Someone tried to punch the mace out of my hand, and the Belgian blocked the punch with his enormous biceps.

"Because we're not animals," he said.

He pointed to the men with the snake flags. "They are."

7

REPULSE MONKEY

There was no question about it anymore. Mildred was dying, and sneaking or not sneaking her cigarettes would make no difference. Either way, she wouldn't live long enough to make it to Dublin or Vienna, and that was the way she wanted it.

"Another fag, dear," she said, from her wheelchair in the garden. "We have work to do."

Her "work" was to advance her illness such that she might die in her sleep, in her room at the village, instead of in a hospice bed with a shunt in her vein.

"Don't get me wrong," she said, "I think a morphine drip could be quite nice."

It was summer, and in an attempt to keep Mildred cool when we were outdoors, Sarah and I made fans of printer paper. It was a campy scene, like some old Hollywood flick: Sarah and I sat on either side of her in our work clothes and fanned the starlet while she smoked menthol 100s.

"Darlings," Mildred said. "Peel me some grapes, won't you?"

She delighted in being the center of attention. It was one of her many skills.

Sarah and I ditched work more often to spend time with Mildred, and Ed joined us sometimes, too. As he'd anticipated, his marriage had finally unraveled, and he appreciated having company. "I come for the esprit de corps," he said, "and the cigarettes." Mildred liked to let him light hers.

There was a hollow inside me that needed to be filled with hours of Mildred's company. And yet, regardless of how many hours I poured into it, it remained empty.

Mildred was blithe about her imminent death, but I struggled with it, mostly by being silent.

With Ruth and Annie, she delved into the details, insisting on cremation. Ruth found a business that planted trees in memory of the deceased, and she purchased the Remembrance package for her mother.

"Will you visit my Remembrance Tree?" Mildred asked us, once.

Every now and then, Mildred pointed her finger at me or Sarah and said, "Don't be so glum, lass. This is the best-case scenario. This is how the universe is *supposed* to work."

"I know it's just your body leaving the earth," said Sarah. "You're only taking a different shape."

Sarah was so much better at this than I was. She believed in vibrations and energy, in consciousness beyond the brain. She was the type of person who could see a butterfly or a bird and believe that it was a loved one with a message for her. She had a friend from Charleston who had died by suicide at the age of thirteen. Sarah saw her constantly; she took the form of a Carolina wren.

What I talked about was cigarettes. I found different brands of imported menthol 100s and brought them to Mildred to sample.

"I like the packaging on this one," she said, tapping a box of Pakistani cigarettes. "But bloody hell, the green."

It was an unspoken challenge, for me to find a pack of menthol cigarettes that wasn't green. There were packs in teal green, emerald green, sage green, and an almost-aqua green. You'd think that other countries might have other ideas about how to package menthols, but, no, green was the rule. I think I convinced myself that Mildred would stay alive as long as I kept finding new brands that were green.

"Listen, people, I'm here today, goon tomorrow," she said, emphasizing "goon."

"You can't trick death or taxes," she said.

"You can stall on both," said Ed. "But you do have to pay, eventually."

She begged us to tell her something good, to regale her with tales, so I told her that Tom had asked me out earlier that spring.

"And you turned him down?" she asked.

I nodded, and she said, "That was dumb."

Sarah came to my defense: "My father's a weird man, and my mother always warned me about marrying a weird man."

"He *is* weird," said Mildred. "Life isn't easy when you're with a weird man. But they have good qualities, too."

"My parents still love each other," said Sarah.

"I think Tom's a good fella," said Ed.

Sarah shot him a look, and he said, "I'll stand on my mother's grave in my cowboy boots and say that."

Sarah shook her head. "I don't even understand what's so great about having a partner, anyway," she said.

"It's nice to have a person who's your number one," said Mildred.

"I love having the bed to myself," said Sarah.

"It's nice to have a person who knows what's going on in your life. When you have good news, you want to tell them first," said Ed. "Same with bad news."

"That's what friends are for," Sarah said.

I told them that I wasn't sure about Tom, because he was too strange and way too shy, and Mildred said, "We all have our flaws."

"I know," I said. "I'm critical and judgy. I get jealous, and I expect too much."

"Every love affair is a shot at the Great Revision," said Mildred. "You're a writer, you should like that. With Tom, you could be whatever kind of lover you want to be."

"He'll never be able to sweep me off my feet," I said.

"Ouch," said Ed. "Every time I get swept off my feet, I break my ass."

"Great point," said Sarah. "Check it out, Ed and I agree on something."

"You know what?" said Ed. "In the end, the person you end up with is you. You are your only soul mate. The rest is gravy."

Sarah curled her lip at the word "gravy." To me, it sounded like grave-y.

"But hey," said Ed. "I'm outta the game, what do I know?"

Mildred slid her gold lighter across the table to Ed, and he lit her another cigarette. She dragged on it a few times and stubbed it out to avoid a coughing fit.

"Young lady," she said, pointing her extinguished cigarette at me. "I'm lighting a fire under your ass to give him a try."

✳

Question 40: What advice would you give to someone who wants to live a happy life?

JEFFREY: *We think we know so much and that our ideas are good. Not true. Our ideas are garbage, and as long as you remember that, you have a shot at happiness. Don't ever be certain. Stay confused. Always be curious.*

✳

During Tai Chi, Mildred seemed less mobile, despite the Chair Chi adaptations.

The latest form we had worked on was Repulse Monkey, which should have been easy enough to do from a chair. It was mostly arms and wrists and scooping qi into the palms of our hands.

After class, Tom helped Mildred with her form while he made tea. He'd hold her arms and move them for her, so she could see what it felt like to do it correctly. When he did that, I imagined him doing that with me, and it made me feel so calm.

The hardest part about spending time with Mildred as she got on with dying was knowing that she welcomed it.

One day, as she took her tea with Tom, a fine pu-erh, no milk, no sugar, she savored each note that Tom pointed out. This one was woodsy, earthy, peaty.

"It's bursting with petrichor," she said.

Then she looked at me, looked at Tom, and said, "Look at this one with the long face."

I tried to fake a smile, and she clucked at me, told me it was all right that she was dying, perfectly normal and fine.

She paraphrased Woody Allen: "'I'm not afraid of death, I just don't want to be there when it happens.'"

"Not helping," I said.

"You're sulking," she said.

"You act like you're relieved to be dying," I said.

"Well, it's a huge weight off my shoulders," she said.

I objected, and she explained that with death so imminent, she didn't have to worry about keeping her shit together for an indefinite amount of time, like you do when you're younger.

"Now I know how the whole thing is going to end," she said. "No more worrying."

I offered that what she described didn't sound great.

"No, no," she said. "The pressure's off. For example, I can stop wondering if I'm ever going to learn how to play the piano. I won't."

But it upset me to know that Mildred would never learn to play the piano.

She distracted me by badgering me about writing her obituary. At this point, even though I didn't want to do it, my subconscious had written and rejected so many ledes that my head was already in it.

"Don't worry about that," Mildred said. "Start writing at paragraph three."

I had tried that, too, but realized eventually that it wasn't the substance that was difficult, it was the tense. Writing about her in the past tense was too upsetting.

"So, write it in present tense, you goose," she said.

One morning before Tai Chi, I tried out my latest lede on her.

"Mildred is a wild woman who's doing the best she can in a world that doesn't want her to be wild."

"Decent start," she said. "Go on . . ."

"She didn't choose to be a mother, but she was lucky, she was a natural. She took to it like a duck takes to water. She has two daughters and several stepchildren, all of whom adore and admire her."

She grimaced.

"Less duck, dear," she said.

"Got it," I said.

"And you can move all that motherhood stuff down, so it's later in the piece."

"Less motherhood," I said.

"I'd like to hear more about the wild woman," she said.

Another thing that made it hard was that Annie and Ruth were around more and more, every day. They took turns visiting, so I never felt crowded, but I wasn't getting that much alone-time with Mildred, and it bothered me because somewhere in my lizard-brain I imagined that she would be adopting me as her third and youngest daughter. The baby, the late-in-life love child. I'd been hoping to brush her hair and help her use the bathroom. I thought I'd be the person to help her with her morphine. Somewhere underneath rational thought, I imagined that she was signing up to be my mother in her remaining months, and that now, at the age of forty-four, I'd have a doting parent for a little while.

Seeing Annie or Ruth every day disabused me of those ideas, and Mildred's stream of visitors wasn't limited to those two. Stepchildren came to visit, as did nieces and nephews, and some children of her friends who had already passed. I should have been happy for her, because she was so loved.

What a thing, to be in demand. But on the other hand, the *real* hand, I was jealous, and I felt displaced. She knew it, too.

One stifling afternoon, post–Tai Chi, we gathered in our usual spot: Mildred, Sarah, Ed, Tom, and me.

"Darlings," she said, "I have something to tell you."

As Mildred drew a cigarette from her pack, Ed reached for her lighter, but Tom stepped in and said, "Here, let me."

He pulled a pack of matches from his jeans pocket and—with one hand—lit a match from it. I hadn't seen that move since high school, where the heads smoked on the back patio.

"Nice," said Mildred. "Very good, don't you think, Hestia?"

"Actually, yeah," I said, surprised by how much it impressed me.

She pointed at Tom: "Have you been practicing?"

"I have," he said.

Then she put her burning cigarette in her ashtray and took my hand in one of hers, and Sarah's hand in the other.

"As much as I'd like to have you girls with me at my deathbed," she said, "I don't think I'm going to have any control over it."

"We don't need to discuss your deathbed," I said.

"My daughters will keep a vigil, I'm certain," she said. "I'll ask them to include you, but I don't know that they'll let you be there."

All the energy in my body rushed to my throat, trying not to cry. I put all my effort into stopping it.

"That's all right," I said. "I don't need to be there."

"You should be with your daughters," said Sarah.

"It's going to be glorious," said Mildred. "My spirit will be released from this cage."

"It sure will be glorious," I lied.

"I'll come visit you," she said. "After."

"Find me, too," said Sarah.

"Oh, I will," she said. "I'm going to find you all."

Then the lights went out—and a few seconds later, there were sirens. Our phones buzzed simultaneously, and the Safe Zones app alerted us to a power failure. "Unclaimed attack on a Baltimore power grid," it said. The director of security's voice came over the PA and told us that it would be a few hours until power was restored.

"Sounds like he's telling us the workday is over," said Ed.

I was still holding Mildred's hand.

"Go home, dear," she said. "I have to nap, anyway, and it's easier in the dark."

As we did when the World Trade Center was bombed, the four of us walked home, heading north from the village.

Along the way, we passed a blood drive for victims and soldiers, and I realized that blood drives had become part of the fabric of daily life. There were row houses with their curtains drawn and signs on the windows memorializing soldiers who'd been lost to the cause. More fabric of daily life. We passed a small group of nuns in black, gathered in a circle and holding signs as they prayed for the souls of the young people who'd died battling the new confederacy. Still more fabric.

When had all of this become so routine? The more we walked, the sadder I became. I wished it were dark, so no one would have to see the sorrow on my face, but it was July, and there was plenty of sunlight left in the day.

"You okay?" asked Tom, and I told him I was fine.

We reached Sarah's home first, and then Ed peeled off, leaving me and Tom to continue.

I told him that I had a crazy idea, and he asked what it

was, and I told him that I had groceries that would spoil if I didn't cook them tonight. The gas stove would work without electricity.

"The refrigerator will only keep the food fresh for so long," I said.

He accepted my invitation for a home-cooked meal. When we were inside, I checked all my windows and the door to make sure they were locked, pulled my go-bag out of the closet just in case, and placed the tapered candles on the table for when it got dark.

"We need to light the stove," I said.

"That sounds like a call to action," he said, doing the match trick, and a teeny-tiny bit, I swooned.

While I made rice, he chopped parsley and garlic for the beans, and tomatoes, onions, and cilantro for the salsa. He complimented me on the freshness of my herbs and admired my plants. He set the table, and while I plated the meals, he stood in front of my fireplace.

"What's going on here?" he asked.

It was still filled with kitsch I'd collected from thrift shops and sidewalk throw-aways. There was a laminated-wood sign proclaiming HAPPY WIFE, HAPPY LIFE, and another promising that LIFE IS GOOD. Tom cocked his head toward IT'S FIVE O'CLOCK SOMEWHERE.

"Does it work?" he asked, meaning the fireplace, and I told him it never had, not since I'd been living there. He asked if we could put on some music, and then remembered that the power was out.

While we ate, he asked me a lot of questions about myself, and I told him about the things I felt like explaining. When it finally started getting dark, I lit some tapers, and he said that he had a better idea. He pulled a curtain and looked outside, to the sky.

"With all the streetlights out, you can see the stars," he said.

"You want to stargaze?"

"Do you have roof access?"

It sounded dangerous to me, but with a blanket in hand, I led us to the roof of my building. There were three other couples doing exactly what we were doing, seizing the rare opportunity to look at the stars in the middle of the city, and I wondered why they weren't more afraid. Tom and I settled onto our backs, and he told me that it was a little too early for the Perseids—"That's a meteor shower," he said, in case I didn't know—but that he could show me a few planets. It was so dark we could see the Milky Way.

"I know about the Perseids," I said.

I hadn't done any stargazing since my childhood summers on those lonely beaches, but I still remembered the constellations my parents taught me after everyone else had passed out. For all their emphasis on self-control, they had been passionate about the stars. When they recited the stories of the gods and goddesses, the mythic animals, the heroes and symbols in the night sky, I could hear how much they loved the cosmos, how they adored its mythologies. On those nights, the universe felt really close.

I told Tom a few tales about the stars, and he listened well.

We were the last couple on the roof.

"You're really quiet," he said. "Are you bored?"

"No!"

"You are," he said.

"I am, just a little," I said. "But I don't know. Maybe I'm just feeling peaceful."

"Yeah," he said, "I get those things confused, too."

"I might like it, though," I said.

"Well, just see if you do," he said. "No pressure."

Maybe this was the Great Revision. My opportunity to reinvent myself, to become someone who felt calm and hung out with a sweet man who was kind of special. Maybe I didn't need witty repartee or banter or, as Mildred might say, *frisson*. "Witty repartee is only witty for so long," I could hear her say. Tom seemed like a man who would ask me for nothing but acceptance, and if I could learn to see that as a feature, not a bug, I might be able to embrace it.

I can't explain what came over me, but I invited him into my bed. He said, Yes, please.

I'd forgotten how nice it was to kiss, and with someone who was good at it. He didn't seem to have an agenda, or a technique he deployed: kissing him was like a call-and-response. We did that for a long time.

One of the joys of July is that you can take off all your clothes and not get cold, so we did that, all at once, and I pressed against him. After a long clutch, he hung his head and backed away.

"Fuck me," he said. "I'm so sorry."

When I realized that he had come, I told him it was all right.

"I just got so turned on," he said.

"I'm flattered," I said.

"Yeah, you *would* say that," he said. "Because you're so nice."

I laughed out loud. "That's hilarious," I said.

"This is fucking embarrassing," he said.

But it *was* fine. I didn't even care about the sex. I liked hearing his voice, and I felt calm next to him. Unfortunately, he mentioned that my unshaven underarms reminded him of his ex-girlfriend, who had the same.

"It was really sexy on her," he said.

"I should punch you right now," I said.

"What?" he asked. "What did I do wrong?"

His confusion was earnest: he had no idea what he'd done wrong. But instead of getting mad and giving up on him, I told him that he wasn't allowed to compare me to an ex. I could practically hear the mental-note-to-self as he wrote it: Don't compare current girlfriend to ex-girlfriend.

✳

In August, I told Mildred about Tom, and Sarah, too. Mildred was pleased, and Sarah was indifferent. "I guess he's all right," she said.

We went to a bar, a new one, because I couldn't risk running into Alexei, who had never texted again. This one billed itself as a speakeasy and had good Instagram cred. They kept the lights low and the music jazzy. The Wi-Fi was excellent, and Sarah checked the alerts on her Conflicted app.

"They blew up another dam out West," she said.

"But there are good things, too, you know?"

"What are you talking about?"

I reminded her that Madame President was pushing for a national health care program. She reminded me that the war was expensive and we'd have to wait for it to end before we could implement anything like that.

"Besides, if we do national health care, we'll never re-unify," she said. "The confederates will be wringing their hands about free-loaders."

"They can love it or leave it," I said. "Besides, be honest, do you *want* to reunify?"

Sarah let out the mother of all sighs.

"I don't even know," she said, sighing again. "This country. These countries."

"You're cynical for thirty."

"I'll be thirty-two next month," she said.

"Oh," I said, embarrassed that I'd lost track of her age.

"I'm too old for this shit," she said.

"You're not that old," I said.

"I want to be like Mildred. She seems happy."

"Mildred's dying," I said.

"Oh, Hestia," she said, "we're *all* dying."

True as this was, I was surprised to hear it from Sarah. She got lost in a ten-thousand-foot stare, right through the window and into the streets.

"Sarah," I said. "You're still so young."

"Not really," she said.

"This country's still so young," I said.

"Please don't give me the speech about growing pains," she said. "I've heard it."

The bartender came over and announced that the gentle-men in the corner wanted to buy us drinks. Sarah turned to them, waved, and ordered something fruity. I ordered a Maryland rye.

"Don't worry, I'm not dating," said Sarah. "But if a man wants to buy me a drink . . ."

I'd been waiting to ask her for a favor.

"I finally have a court date for my divorce," I said. "And I need a witness."

"What for?"

"To tell the judge that the marriage is a lost cause."

"That can't be real," she said.

"But it is. It's a relic of patriarchy," I said. "I need someone to swear on a Bible in the courtroom that the union should be dissolved."

Sarah looked outside, again with the ten-thousand-foot stare.

"Are you asking me to be your witness?" she asked.

I told her I was.

"I've never even met your husband," she said.

"That's true," I said.

"Don't you have any other friends who could do this?" she asked.

Our drinks arrived, and she took a sip of hers, which didn't have a paper umbrella this time, because there were no more paper umbrellas. Sarah sipped hers while looking at me.

"We have a weird kind of friendship, don't we?" she asked. "We're work friends, and bar friends, but I've never even been to your house."

"It is a little fucked-up," I said.

"A little bit," she said.

She took a few more sips and told me she'd be my witness.

"Thank you," I said. "I swear, it's for the greater good."

"I know," she said. "Some unions are better off dissolved."

✳

Over the next couple of weeks, Tom and I made a lot of dinners together. Every time, I liked him a tiny bit more. The kissing was reliably great, and the sex was getting better, too. When I was with him, I felt like a fist that was finally letting go. It was disorienting to feel so unclenched, but I was pretty sure I liked it.

One night, he took a picture of me and sent it to his mother. "Why?" I asked.

"Because she worries about me," he said.

"And she's your best friend," I said.

"Maybe not my *best* friend," he said.

By the time we'd finished dinner, she'd texted back that I reminded her of Barbara Stanwyck, which was not helpful, because I had no idea what Barbara Stanwyck looked like.

"Oh," Tom said with authority. "She was hot."

I washed the dishes, and he stood next to me, handing me dirty plates and forks. I asked him what he'd told his mother about me, and he checked the text thread before answering.

"I told her that you're really smart, and that we have a connection," he said.

"Okay, but what did you tell her about *us*?" I asked.

"Can you clarify?" he asked.

"What did you tell her about our relationship?"

He read from his phone again, checking the thread.

"I told her we're dating," he said.

"Okay," I said, and decided that was good enough.

"Then she asked if you were my girlfriend," he said.

"And what did you tell her?"

He read from the text thread on his phone.

"She said, 'Is she your girlfriend?' and I said, 'I don't know,' and she said, 'Do you want her to be?' and I said, 'I hope she will be one day,' and she said, 'I hope so, too,' and I said, 'If that happens, I'd like her to be my last girlfriend' and I put the word 'LAST' in all caps."

I almost dropped the knife I was washing but grabbed it before it fell on the floor. Luckily, there were only a few drops of blood that beaded on my skin.

"You put 'LAST' in all caps?"

"I did," he said.

What a strange sensation, to be pleasantly surprised by someone. The civil war had lowered my already low expectations of people. Keep going lower, I kept telling myself.

You spend all that time thinking that your parents, your fellow humans, your fellow Americans can't possibly get any worse—and then they do actually get worse. You learn to expect disappointment. And while this seems like a sensible coping mechanism, the problem is that when you're in the habit of being crushed, you forget how to look forward to anything. It feels impossible to be excited.

But here was this nice man, telling his mother that he wanted me to be his LAST girlfriend, and I barely knew how to receive the sweetness of it. When we had sex that night, it's possible I felt some qi moving through my hands.

✳

Question 41: What advice would you give to someone who wants to live a happy life?

DOROTHY: *Let go of the idea that you're important or special. Decide that you belong here, and that being ordinary is the most beautiful way to be.*

✳

The next morning, Mildred, Sarah, and I met in the therapy garden, and I brought Mildred's cigarettes, but she was already ecstatic.

"I had what they call an end-of-life experience," she said.

That gave me a start, because I thought she was saying that she'd almost died, but no. She'd had visitors from the spirit world, as plain as the nose on my face. I thought they might have been her husbands, because that seemed right to me, but that was not the case.

"I've seen neither hide nor hair of those fellows," she said.

Her visitors had been her parents.

"My father held out his arms toward me and said, 'What a gal,'" she said. "My mother smiled on me and said, 'Millie, you're remarkable.'"

I don't think I've ever seen anyone so at peace, so happy. I knew that if I said anything, I'd ruin it. I put my hand on Mildred's shoulder and squeezed. I lit a cigarette for her and put the ashtray in her lap. "Godspeed," I said to myself, as she took her first drag.

I patted Mildred on the back as she had a coughing fit. She stubbed out her cigarette in the ashtray.

"I think we can trust Tom," she said.

"I think so," I said.

"He's honest," she said.

"Maybe too honest," I said.

Mildred beckoned for her second cigarette, and I lit it. She smoked it gently, barely pecking it with her lips to get the faintest bit of smoke into her mouth. She kept smoking and remained silent, even though she must have known that I wanted more pronouncements about Tom. Finally, she finished.

"He wears his heart on his sleeve, doesn't he?" she asked.

"I think he does," said Sarah.

"What do you think of him, Sarah?" asked Mildred.

Sarah emptied the ashtray into a nearby garbage can, then handed it to me. She put her fingers in a mudra over her third eye, then exhaled.

"I think he's harmless," she said.

"That's high praise, dear," said Mildred.

"Yes, it is," said Sarah.

✳

Back at my desk, I texted my husband: "Court date next Tuesday at 10. You're not required to be there."

✳

That night, as Tom and I lay together, I asked him what he thought about the spirit world, and he told me, then asked me what I thought. I told him about my grandparents and the masses they snuck me into, and how thirsty I'd been for it, and my parents' insistence that there was nothing after life, and the spiritual deficit I'd been left to bear.

I told him that I was getting divorced in a matter of days, and about the upcoming meetup with my parents at the Leafy Greens Inn.

I told him I was worried that Sarah was giving up on America, and how that made me simultaneously terrified and weepy.

I told him I prayed for Mildred, although I had no idea how to pray.

We were eating cookies in bed, which I considered the height of indulgence. Every now and then, he picked a crumb off me and didn't make a big deal about it.

"You know what?" he asked. "I love your mind."

I tried to remember if anyone had ever said that to me before. I was pretty sure the answer was no. On top of that, he'd said the word "love," and I wasn't sure what I thought about that. Things were going well, and I didn't want him to jinx it.

He continued. "Sometimes, when I'm going through my day, something will happen, and I'll think, 'What would Hestia say about this?'"

I stood up and brought the cookies into the kitchen, and sat down on the couch. He followed me.

"Everything okay?"

"Everything's great," I said. "I just kind of hate this fireplace right now."

I sat on the rug in front of it and picked up the I WOKE UP LIKE THIS sign, holding it next to my face. He picked up LIFE IS TOUGH BUT SO ARE YOU and grimaced.

"I've hated these signs since the first time I saw them," he said, which made me so fond of him.

❋

Valiantly, Tom tried to teach me and Mildred the form known as Carry Tiger Over Mountain, but it was a flop. Mildred was in no position to lift her arms anymore, and I was hopeless.

"Get your head in the game, dear," Mildred whispered in class, when I failed to embrace the tiger before carrying it.

"Get *your* head in the game," I whispered back.

Tom snapped his fingers and clucked his tongue at us.

"The tiger is the ego," he said in his heroin-voiced monotone to the villagers. "And the tiger has a lot of energy."

Slowly, he moved his back foot to the front and pivoted at his hips.

"But we're going to turn over the tiger energy and give it to the mountain," he said.

He moved his hands up and away from his heart.

"We're converting the ego energy into stability," he said. "The mountain has enduring energy."

We prepared to move into the next form, and he talked about how the mind is like a tree full of monkeys, jumping and chattering.

"Step back into Repulse Monkey," he said. "Observe the monkey mind, stay detached."

We repulsed the monkey five times in a row. Mildred crossed her arms and watched, the best she could do.

At the end of class, we skipped out on teatime and went back to the therapy garden.

I told her I had a new lede.

"Hit me," she said.

I pulled it up on my phone and read: "'Mildred was always a rebel—'" but she interrupted.

"Let me stop you right there," she said.

"Why?"

"I'm no rebel," she said.

I insisted she was, in fact, a rebel. She'd had the gall to take up space, have opinions, send daughters to college, gain weight, get old . . .

"Boring," she said. "You're a better writer than this."

Mildred leaned her head back against her chair. She stared at the tree canopy.

"I wish I'd known you when you were little, Hestia," she said dreamily. "I bet you were a delight."

"I was all right," I said.

"I would have enjoyed being your mother," she said.

I almost cried right there. If I could have moved my tiger energy into the mountain, I would have, but I still hadn't mastered the form.

✳

Question 42: What advice would you give to someone who wants to live a happy life?

CLARA: *There are people on the internet who tell a story about Albert Einstein. They say that he said the most important question facing humanity is this: "Is the universe a friendly place?" Think carefully before answering.*

✳

One morning later that month, Tom gathered my inspirational hangings from the fireplace and took them outside. "I'm leaving them on the sidewalk, yeah?" he asked, and I told him to go for it.

That evening, he suggested we try books in the fireplace. We tried different arrangements, ranging from stacking vertically to stacking horizontally, to a combination of both, and we color coordinated. We put the reds and darker spines on the bottom, escalating through orange, yellow, green, and the blues.

He asked me how I was doing with the imminence of Mildred's death, and I told him I was getting used to the idea, although I didn't know how I'd ever get over it.

But there was one bright spot, if you can call it that: When you're watching someone die, there's no uncertainty. You know how it will end.

He agreed that uncertainty makes things so much worse.

"Like falling in love," he said. "You never know how that's going to end."

Instead of telling him that every relationship ends, either through death or breakup, I held my tongue.

He turned a stack of books ninety degrees in the hearth and examined his work.

"With Mildred, there's no reason to hold back," he said. "You can let yourself feel everything."

"Because you know what's happening," I said.

The books looked all right, not great, a titch too Pinterest. I added my watering can. I added a vase and a ceramic bowl, but everything I added made it worse, not better.

*

A few days later, the fateful moment was upon me—the meetup with my parents. Oh, how I'd dreaded it. Was there any bridge that could be built to span the gap? I laughed at my own self-talk. *Bridge?* It wasn't as if we were on opposite banks of a river; we were on different planets.

It was a Monday, and I'd taken a vacation day because I knew I wouldn't be able to work. Tom made me breakfast and tried to distill some Tai Chi advice for me, but my brain wasn't having it.

"I should ride the tiger of ego?"

"Make it serve the intellect," he said.

"And that's when I break the lotus?"

"*Sweep* the lotus, don't break it, and let your ego be absorbed," he said.

"Into the nothingness?"

"Into the Wu Chi," he said.

"I thought this was Tai Chi," I said.

"Tai Chi is born of Wu Chi."

"We need to stop now," I said.

As I stood near the front door, he moved my body into a form that he thought would ground me.

"Tuck your tail," he said.

He adjusted my wrists, fixed the bend in my knees.

"There's a golden ball in your dan tien," he said. "There are tree roots growing from the soles of your feet, down into the earth."

He pushed my shoulders down my back and pushed my ribs toward my spine. When we got to the door, he offered to go with me for moral support.

"We're not there yet," I said. "As a couple."

"Oh," he said.

"I mean, right?"

"Mildred said I should do nice things for you, and you should let me."

I went by myself, but he promised to meet me afterward and walk me home.

＊

As I walked onto the hotel's courtyard, I saw my parents sitting at an iron table, on iron chairs. I had a sensation that was becoming familiar: I couldn't quite attach myself to them. Were they *my* aging parents, or just *someone's* aging parents? My mother squeezed lemon into her glass of water. My father inspected the salt and pepper shakers. They looked like normal people. Nice. To look at them, you wouldn't know that they were sympathetic to the confederate causes.

I realized that in my nervousness I hadn't done any reconnaissance, forgetting to check the Safe Zones app. But my mother noticed me in the doorway, and she waved me in. My father stood up and started toward the door, but he moved slowly. How old they'd become. I headed out onto the brick patio and met them at their table. Thankfully, they'd been seated in the shade. My father signaled to the waitress to bring a chair.

"I can get it," I said.

"So can she," he said.

I wanted to tip the waitress immediately.

"We weren't sure you'd come," said my mother. "That's why we didn't have three chairs."

"But here I am," I said.

"Here you are," she said. "And look at you! I would have never expected you to look this put together!"

All hail Nancy, the master of the backhanded compliment.

They were both standing, and we were all squirming, trying to gauge whether or not to hug. I put my arms around both of them lightly. Sweep the lotus, I told myself, convert the qi. They gave me tentative hugs, and my mother brushed my cheek with her lips. Dry, so dry. That's what happens when you age, I told myself. I started to wonder if that would happen to me, if I would desiccate as she had, and then I reminded myself that I share no DNA with my mother—except for the 97 percent of DNA that *all* humans share with each other.

It was an awkward time to meet, too late for breakfast, too early for lunch, and I wondered if they had requested this time because they didn't want the complication of eating a large meal with me. But in her attempts at small talk, my mother mentioned that they'd slept very well in the hotel bed, that they'd been sleeping later these days, in their retirement, and that they had tickets to the Aquarium in the afternoon.

"Let me check the app," I said, because the Aquarium was on the harbor, and there'd been some demonstrations there lately.

"Put that thing away," my father said, pointing at my phone. "We don't need to check anything."

"You should order lunch," my mother said. "Order a lot, enough for a doggie bag. I can't believe how expensive food is now."

"You can thank your Madame President for that," said my father.

"Yes, Bill," I said. "Everyone at the table knows you don't like her."

"That's exactly right," he said. "Am I allowed to have an opinion, here in America?"

I muttered under my breath, "Petulant."

"Speak up," said my mother.

"I said you were petulant."

"And why is that?" asked my mother.

"Because you're okay with letting democracy die just because you don't like the person who's in charge of it."

The waitress brought over a basket of rolls, and my father generously buttered one, which he put on my plate.

"Eat, sweetheart," he said. "Please."

"I remember, back when Bill and I were poor, we took all the free meals we could get," said my mother.

"Nancy," I said, "I'm not poor."

"Yes, that's right, honey," she said.

"Watch yourself," said my father, almost under his breath, to my mother. "Watch."

This was how they coached each other. Or, more accurately, this was how he coached her. She rarely told him what to do, but he was generous with his advice for her.

It was as if we were following some unwritten rule: we would do small talk until the food arrived, and then, once we started eating, we could talk for real. It was a terrible rule, a recipe for indigestion. Both my parents were terrible at small talk. We chatted about the *temperature* (yes, it was steaming hot in August in Baltimore), although not the *weather*. My mother told me about a few people from home who'd died or become ill, but only the ones who could point to natural causes.

This time, I did better than a stupid Caesar salad, and I ordered cured meats on artisanal bread, with a kale salad. When the waitress brought our food, my mother ignored her and looked directly at me. "You look well, Hestia," she said.

"Yes, you do," said my father. "Are you well?"

I told them I was doing well.

"I'm getting divorced tomorrow," I said, because after all, the food had arrived.

"Tomorrow?" said my father.

"The final court appearance," I said.

My mother's eyes started to tear up, and I said, "Please, don't. It's fine."

"It's just so sad," she said, dabbing at her tear ducts.

"Come on, Nancy," I said. "You'll get over this."

My father asked which court, and what time, and when I told him, he said, "Oh! It's just around the corner!" He said that they'd be in the hotel packing up to check out. "We could meet you there if you'd like," he said.

"It's all right, Bill," I said. "It's already done. This is just a formality."

"We should be there for you," he said.

"It's done," I said.

"Have some rye bread," he said, putting a nice seedy slice on my plate. "We don't have to let our failures define us."

"Thanks, Bill," I said, "that's helpful."

It was hard to think and eat and talk at the same time, but I had some thoughts, and they wouldn't go away. Maybe I should ride the tiger of ego. But my tiger was roaring, and it was trying to say something to my parents: Acknowledge me. I was sitting right there, in front of them.

The waitress refilled our water glasses and brought another small plate of lemon wedges for my mother's drink. This time, my mother looked at her, and said, "Thank you, honey," with affection, which threw me for a loop.

She took another bite of her small meal and put her fork across her plate to signal that she was done.

"Is your meal not good?" I asked.

"It's delicious," she said.

"But you don't want to eat it?"

"I suppose I do want to," she said, "but I won't."

"It's called self-discipline, Hestia," my father interjected.

Now we were getting close to the molten core. I waited. My mother folded her hands in her lap. My father looked like he was in a hurry to eat more of his meal before he had to stop, and I put another slice of salami on a piece of bread and filled my mouth with it.

"We see now, Hestia, the hubris of what we did," she said.

"The audacity of it," said my father, wiping mustard from his mouth. "We plucked you into existence, and for what?"

"We created you," said my mother, squeezing more lemon into her water. "And why?"

"This world is a meat grinder," said my father. "It's no place for tender souls."

"But we wanted company," said my mother.

"We did it because we could," said my father.

"We were selfish," said my mother.

At last, they paused, and I could catch up with their words. It seemed that they were apologizing for bringing me into the world; they might have been saying I was tender; they seemed to think they had made me, that they were responsible.

"You did *what* because you could?" I asked slowly.

"Made you," said my father.

"Made me?"

"You know, Hestia, we went to a lot of trouble to make you."

"Like Dr. Frankenstein," I said.

They looked at each other and nodded, and looked back at me. My father dipped a breadstick in oil and ate it quickly.

"We wanted a baby. We wanted something cute and cuddly," said my mother.

"But instead . . . you got me?"

"You're not a monster, Hestia," she said, "that's not what we mean."

I placed my hands on the table and stared at my fingers, my nails. I should start using lotion every day, I thought. I'm so dry.

"The world is a wonderful place," said my father, "if it weren't for all the people."

"We wanted to share the world with someone," said my mother. "But we forgot how awful people are."

"People thrash," said my father.

"They flail," said my mother.

"When you think about it," said my father, "is it fair to bring a child into the world? Is it rational?"

There it was. In their minds, I was *their project*, and it was getting a failing grade. With them, I was never just me. I was always an extension of them.

Acknowledge *me*, said the tiger of my ego. My mother put her hand on my hand. Let your ego be absorbed into the nothingness, I told myself. There are roots growing from the soles of your feet.

"I don't belong to you," I said.

"We know that," said my father. "You're a grown woman."

"I *never* belonged to you," I said.

"You were always independent," he said. "We knew that right away. But we *made* you."

"You didn't," I said.

"We did," he said.

"And the doctors," said my mother.

"Well," I said, "I absolve you."

My mother stuck her hand into the air to call for our waitress, and before she could get to our table, my mother yelled across the room that we would have sweet tea, all three of us. The server cleared our plates, and we waited for tea. When it arrived, my parents drank theirs with straws. I tried mine, but I didn't really want it.

"When you're expecting a child," said my mother, "you imagine yourself with a baby."

"I understand," I said.

"There's a failure of imagination," she said. "You never imagine being the mother of a forty-five-year-old woman who's alone."

I saw how they pitied me, how terrible they felt.

"Nancy," I said. "I'm forty-four."

They looked at each other and pursed their lips.

When the waitress came with the bill, my father took it and thanked her for her commendable service.

And that was the meal. We stood up and walked toward the exit, and my father suggested we go for a little walk before they headed to the harbor.

"If you have time," he said, and I told him I did.

As we walked into the hot street, I heard the all-too-familiar sounds of a shofar and men shouting.

"Something smells terrible," said my mother as we walked down the block.

My father started to gag, and the smell hit me, too. At the corner, in front of the art museum, police were taping off the steps and trying to control a growing crowd. My father wanted to know what was going on, so he wormed his way into the crowd, my mother and I behind him.

There was a severed sheep's head on the steps of the museum. The blood had clotted, and it was almost a hundred degrees. Confederate protesters in animal skins and snake flags marched back and forth in front of the barricades with tissues stuffed up their noses. Some of them wore swimmers' clamps on their noses to keep the smell out. One man started to gag because of the smell, and another screamed "Snowflake!" at him. I overheard an officer calling for backup as the crowd grew.

They carried the usual signs. FAIR IS FAIR and NO REPARATIONS and that sort of thing. My father was busy reading the signs held by the demonstrators, and he tried to talk with one of them, a man wearing antlers. "Young man," he said, "a word, please."

"Fuck off," screamed the antlered man in my father's face.

"Rude!" shouted my mother at the man, but he didn't give her a second thought.

They started to ease backward out of the crowd with me, and my mother repeated herself. "So rude," she said.

"Yes, Mom," I said. "That's their *whole* thing."

I meant it, and I wanted to explain that rudeness *was* the whole thing. America was unaccountably rude, and we didn't used to be. Americans say out loud things that should not be said out loud. We tell people their feelings are wrong, or impossible. We get messed up in everybody's business, instead of just saying, Okay, whatever, you do you. *E pluribus unum* was proving too difficult.

For a moment, I thought that if my mother could see the rudeness for what it was, she might be able to shift her alliances. My father still looked puzzled by being told to fuck off by one of the "rebels" he claimed to agree with.

What with the heat and the shofars and the antlers and the odor of a decaying sheep's head, we bailed on our outdoor stroll. We retreated to the lobby of the Leafy Greens and decided to part ways for the day. Tentatively, we agreed to try another get-together in a month or two. They were going to head down to the Aquarium when things calmed down, and tomorrow they'd pack up while I became officially divorced. My father offered again to accompany me, and I told him that I had it under control.

I thought about Annie and Ruth, and what a curious thing it is to love people you didn't choose. It's one thing to marry an asshole: your mistake. It's another thing to have them as a parent, or a sister: not your fault for picking an asshole, but you do have an opportunity to rise above something.

All the mystics tell you that love is the largest thing, the supreme thing. The thing that conquers all, although I'm not crazy about that word, "conquer." If love is so big, why is it so easy to mess it up? What happened to "too big to fail"?

My parents were trying. Even I could see that.

I remembered my mother talking about my soon-to-be

ex-husband, and how she loved him in spite of herself, because sometimes loving someone you don't like is the right thing to do. In hindsight, it seemed remarkable to me, that my mother would have risen to that.

The heart wants what the heart wants, and the heart has nothing to do with the mind. I can be bigger than my mind, I told myself, bigger than my stupid ideas. I can grow roots from the soles of my feet. I can be the mountain.

✳

Question 43: What advice would you give to someone who wants to live a happy life?

> **CHARLES:** *I like what it says in the "Desiderata": "With all its sham, drudgery, and broken dreams, it is still a beautiful world."*

✳

The next day, Tuesday, Sarah and I pushed past a confederate rally to enter the courthouse, where a family magistrate would render a judgment on my marriage. The protesters were loud and indignant, many of them bare-chested, dripping with sweat, their tattoos damp, their neck-beards moist. The magistrate wore fleece under her robe, because it was so cold in the courtroom, air-conditioned to an unnatural temperature as long as the power grid was working.

I scanned the room for my husband, but he wasn't there, which was fair. After all, his presence was unnecessary, and I'd told him not to bother. There were a few marriages on the docket ahead of us, and Sarah and I sat silently on the wooden benches and listened, freezing, as each plaintiff stated their grounds for divorce. My grounds were simple—abandonment—and as it turns out, so it was with several of the other plaintiffs.

Although I was petitioning for "absolute uncontested divorce," I still needed a witness, and that's where Sarah came in. Nervous, she'd dressed up, wearing a little lawyer outfit, a skirt with low heels, a blazer, classy earrings. She studied the other witnesses and plaintiffs as they were sworn in, and when it was her turn to take the oath, she nearly lost her voice.

The magistrate spoke directly to Sarah.

"Do you have any reason to believe that the plaintiff and her husband could be reconciled?" she asked.

Sarah looked at me, looked down, then looked at the magistrate.

"I do not," she said.

The magistrate said she'd make her recommendation for divorce, and I'd receive confirmation by mail.

"I'll be divorced by mail?" I asked, but she had already moved on to the next plaintiff.

It felt good to have it finished. As we were walking out of the building, I actually took Sarah's hand and swung it in the air, like Mary Tyler Moore flinging her hat.

"I'm single again," I said. "Like you!"

"Yeah, right," she said.

"But you've been encouraging me to be single," I said.

"But you're not single," she said. "You're rinsing and repeating."

"Ouch," I said.

When we walked onto the street, we found ourselves up against the rally, which had grown larger and uglier. More damp, bare-chested men had gathered, wearing confederate flags as capes. They wore snake flags wrapped around their heads like turbans, and some of them wore the pelts of small animals attached to their hats or their belt loops. They blew into horns and pounded on drums covered in animal hides. Goddess, I thought, those poor animals. To have had their lives taken for *this*?

I knew my parents were in their hotel around the corner, packing up, and I hoped that they'd gotten wind of this, maybe even that they were watching from their window. I wanted so badly for them to see their allies behaving this way. I wanted them to look at each other and have a come-to-Jesus moment. I wanted them to ask, *Are these our people?*

It might have been the heat hitting my nearly frozen body, or maybe it was the whole civil war: I became furious.

What flipped my switch the hardest was this: Some of the ignorant dumbasses were carrying American flags. Right alongside the other stupid flags they wrapped around their bodies. *American* flags. As if the confederate flag and the American flag were not cancellations of each other. As if these confederates could claim one ounce, one shred of allegiance to the American flag.

I shouted at one of the protesters.

"Hey, that's *my* flag," I said.

From a few yards away, a police officer shouted at the counterprotesters, like me and Sarah, who weren't moving through the crowd quickly enough.

"Do *not* engage with the protesters," she said. "Do *not* linger."

Sarah removed her blazer and put it over her arm, but one of the confederates grabbed it and tossed it backward into the crowd. She locked eyes with him and said, "That's my jacket!"

He mocked her. "That's my jacket," he said.

I'd never seen Sarah so resigned. For the years I'd known

her, she'd been rocking the eye rolls, but this time she stared straight ahead. She held her tongue and tried to inch past, but the confederate kept saying "That's my jacket." She looked at me, dead in the eyes.

"I hate them," I said.

"Same," she said.

But she put her head down and kept moving, and I followed her lead.

The next confederate we passed was waving an American flag, and I put my face right up to his.

"Hey, *dumbass*," I yelled at him.

"That's *my* flag," I said. "That's an *American* flag."

He started to speak, but he changed his mind. Instead, he spit on me. Right on my cheek. Please let my parents be watching, I thought.

I spit back.

We glared at each other, and then I tried to grab the flagpole out of his hand.

"This is *my* country," I screamed.

"You're *ruining* it," he shouted.

He tried to pull his flag back, but I wouldn't let go. He growled at me. I snarled at him.

"It's *mine*," I said, almost barking, pulling the flag toward me.

"Walk *away*," shouted the police officer from behind me. "Walk *away*."

"Hestia," said Sarah, tugging on my forearm. "Let's get out of here."

But the confederate and I were locked in a tug-of-war, and I have no idea how it would have ended if it had been allowed to play itself out. But it did not play out.

There was an explosion, a huge one, very close to us. We

were thrown backward by the force of it, and Sarah and I tumbled onto the pavement.

Our bare arms were scraped and bleeding. Dust and debris rained over us. I wondered if we'd gone blind. Sarah and I felt around and found each other's hands.

I heard her say, "Let's go," and we stood up. As my vision returned, we ran to the end of the block, then turned around and looked at the scene.

When we paused, we discovered that we were covered in dust, and we saw other dust-covered people running, panicking, looking frantically for each other. They were shouting theories about what had happened, where the bomb had gone off, and what the target had been. A few people seemed to be trying to make phone calls. I hadn't looked at my phone since texting my ex-husband that the deed was done.

We ran back to my apartment, only a few blocks away, and sat on the stoop to catch our breath. We watched dusty, traumatized people running past us.

Eventually, I thought we should get some water, and I invited Sarah in. This was her first time in my apartment. I watched all the wheels clicking in her brain as she assessed my living quarters.

"It's cleaner than I expected," she said.

I knew it was a compliment.

That morning, I'd put two cans of soda in the fridge to chill, as a treat for me and Tom. I offered Sarah one while I drank the other.

She was reading her phone, searching for the same information we all wanted. Her eyes grew wide, and then tears streaked the dust that was still on her face.

"Hestia," she said.

"What?"

She gave me her phone with the flashing red rhombus: Confederates bomb Leafy Greens Inn in Baltimore, killing at least thirty.

✳

It's such a cliché, but when I saw that the Leafy Greens had been bombed, I lost my sense of time and space. I didn't know that I was drinking soda. I couldn't feel my feet on the floor, or that my hand was clasping a can. I didn't know if I was upside down, or if I was going to float up and hover over the city. I might have been a candle, melting in the Baltimore heat, falling into myself, collapsing around my wick. I felt that I might have come to the very end of myself.

The next few hours were a blur that barely happened to me, as far as I remember.

While I sat on the couch, numb, Sarah called Tom and Ed and sat next to me. She was with me when I got the phone call about my parents, and she wrapped her arms around me while I cried.

She read me news reports from her phone, editing as she did so. The body count was growing, but so was the number of people needing amputations, intubations.

"Maybe it's better that they died," I said.

"Hush, Hestia," Sarah said. "Just hush."

When Tom arrived, he sat on one side of me while she stayed on the other, and they each held one of my hands. That was a blessing, because I might have floated away, lost forever, without them tethering me. I wished Mildred were with me, but I knew she was too sick to come.

Tom went with me to the coroner's office and told Sarah she should go home.

"I'll come back in the morning," she said.

He must have done a million things for me, but I don't remember any of them. All I know is that he was there.

The day ended. The next day started, the first day of my bereavement leave, and it was only a tiny bit less awful. Tom made coffee, and I tried to remember the people I'd seen at the Leafy Greens—our waitress from the day before, the clerk at the desk—and wondered if they'd died also. I thought about the owners, too, and tried to imagine who all of them had left behind.

Midmorning, Sarah returned, and this time she came with Ed and a few candles she'd made. They were infused with lavender oil, for the grieving process.

"I wanted to bring Mildred," said Ed. "But her wheel-chair . . ."

I lived on the third floor, with no elevator.

"She sends her deepest sympathy," said Ed. "And this, too."

He handed me her yellow-gold lighter and said that I was supposed to "light some shit on fire." I slipped it into my pocket, surprised by how heavy it was. He put a newspaper on my kitchen table, and I scanned the articles about the explosion.

"Still too early for the obits," he said.

I realized that I'd have to write obituaries for my parents, so I decided to start right away. It was something to do. But I only wrote one, a joint obituary. Their lives had been so similar, so parallel, up until they married, and then nearly identical for forty-five years—there was no point in writing two.

I wrote about their childhoods in the melancholy towns where they were born, their constant striving, their achievements, their good intentions. Their work ethic. I wrote about their devotion to the American dream and how much they believed in it, for themselves and others.

My mother and father became parents in an era before "parent" was a verb. They didn't do parenting, they simply were parents. I wrote about that, too.

Ed helped me edit. He kept me straight. He made sure I didn't veer. He struck through anything that wasn't kind. He struck through every hint of ideology.

"But why be secretive?" I said. "Shouldn't I tell the world they were confederates?"

"Maybe someday," he said. "But right now, you don't know what you want to do."

"But I know what they were," I said.

"No, you don't," he said. "You only know what they told you."

While we wrote and edited, Sarah and Tom fussed with my fireplace. First, they removed the books.

"Too stuffy," Sarah said.

Tom cut sprigs of herbs from my kitchen garden, put them in vases of water, and arranged them in the hearth. Sarah placed her lavender candles among them and called me over to look at it. It was just right. I pulled Mildred's lighter from my pocket.

"Do it," said Sarah, and I lit the candles.

She took a breath. "Smells better," she said.

As we inhaled the new air, Sarah glanced at the newspaper on the table and said, "This fucking country."

I remembered that she'd been talking about leaving.

"I guess Ghana's looking even better," I said.

"Ghana, sure," she said.

"Or Germany?"

"Also good," she said.

I asked her if there was any chance she might stay here in America, and she asked me if I could give her a good reason to stay.

"Spite?" I asked.

"That's not actually a good reason to do anything," she said.

"Goddess, don't I know it," I said.

Ed looked up from my draft and said, "Sarah, will you let an old man give you some advice?"

She granted her permission.

"Stay," he said, "because look at this here. You're in a room full of people who love you."

The room went silent. I looked around.

"True," I said.

"True," said Tom.

Sarah pouted.

"I'm not very good at this," she said.

I didn't know what she was talking about, but it didn't matter.

"Me, either," I said.

✳

I should have spent the rest of the week on bereavement leave, but I wanted to get back to Mildred. I was worried that she'd die while I was gone. On Friday, I went back, and until then Tom spent every minute with me that he wasn't working. I went to sleep with him holding me, and I woke up with him holding me.

When the herbs in the vases wilted, he replaced them with fresh cuts.

His constancy made me suspicious, and I asked him one

morning, my first day back to work, "What do you want from me?"

He was making tea for himself and coffee for me. He took a piece of toast from the toaster and buttered it carefully, slowly. I knew he must be making it for me, because he didn't like bread.

"I want to come over every evening and tell you about my day," he said, "and I want to hear about yours."

I put my shoes on.

"But after that," I said. "After we're bored of hearing about each other's days. What about after that?"

He put some milk in my coffee.

"Can we just see?" he asked.

Sometimes I think that Tom and I are survivors of wars. Not so much the civil war, but wars we've fought with our hearts. Relationships. I think most of us are born knowing everything we need to know about love. When we're young and new to it, we know by instinct how to be with someone, how to merge, how to wrap ourselves around them and be wrapped. But with every breakup or falling-out, we unlearn what we were born knowing. We unlearn piece by piece, relationship by relationship. We doubt ourselves, mistrust our instincts, defend ourselves, prioritize the wrong things—by the time Tom and I met, we had barely any instinct left. We knew nothing.

But we were learning. Or, as Tamara on my app likes to say, we were open to the idea of being open.

✳

Question 44: What advice would you give to someone who wants to live a happy life?

MILDRED: *The poet Rilke says, "Just keep going. No feeling is final." He also says, "Give me your hand."*

✳

Mildred's breathing was labored and she had to pause between sentences to take in air. Her face and hands were swollen, and she couldn't smoke anymore.

She tried to tell me how sorry she was, about everything that had happened, but I stopped her.

"Mildred, can we please not?" I asked.

"Of course, dear," she said.

"Thank you," I said.

"I've got a wild hair to sit outside before Ruth gets here," she said.

It was a hundred degrees, but I agreed to it.

"We'll sit in the shade," she said.

"Perfect," I said.

"We don't want you getting skin cancer," she said.

I asked if I could brush her hair, and she seemed surprised but said that would be lovely. I ran to her room, found her hairbrush, and brought it outside. I told her that Tom had made me coffee and toast that morning, and she asked to see some photos.

"I don't have any photos of the toast," I said.

"You should take some," she said.

"Honestly, Mildred," I said.

"Pics or it didn't happen," she said.

As I brushed her hair, she told me how badly she felt about making everyone around her so glum. "So many long faces," she said. "They're everywhere now." She hated the look that washed across people's faces when they saw her.

"I don't like making people so sad," she said.

"Oh, come on, Mildred," I said. "Grief is such a small price to pay for your friendship."

She clasped her hand around my hand.

"That's it," she said. "There it is. That's your lede."

ACKNOWLEDGMENTS

Thank you to my agent, Naomi Eisenbeiss, and my editor, Jenna Johnson, for their steadfast support and dazzling insights, which have made this a better book.

Thank you to my best readers and brilliant writers, Betsy Boyd, Elisabeth Dahl, Jane Delury, Kathy Flann, Elizabeth Hazen, James Magruder, and Marion Winik. I'm so grateful for their critique, enthusiasm, and kind hearts.

Thank you to David DeJong, for far-flung writerly advice. Thank you to Chris Stevens, for being a great boss, even though he hates being called "boss." Thank you to Valerie Green, who knows me so well, and also knows the best cheeses.

Thank you to my parents and siblings, Barbara, Nick, Angela, Daniel, Anthony, and Nicholas, for decades of support and love.

Thank you to Lee Connah, for his love, care, and faith, and for always being game for one more civil war thought experiment.

And thank you to my children, Enzo Metsopoulos, Rita Metsopoulos, and Luca Metsopoulos, for inspiring me to care so deeply about so many things.

A Note About the Author

Christine Grillo is a writer and an editor whose short fiction has appeared in *StoryQuarterly*, *The Southern Review*, and *LIT.* Her nonfiction covers science, public health, food systems, agriculture, and climate change, and has been published in outlets such as *The New York Times*, *The Atlantic: CityLab*, *Audubon*, *NextTribe*, and *Real Simple*. Grillo earned degrees at Columbia University and The Writing Seminars at Johns Hopkins University. She lives in Baltimore, Maryland. *Hestia Strikes a Match* is her debut novel.